The Phoenix Lottery

The Phoenix Lottery

a novel

Allan Stratton

The Riverbank Press

Cover and text design: John Terauds
Cover image used by permission from the Musée d'Orsay

THE CANADA COUNCIL | LE CONSEIL DES ARTS
FOR THE ARTS | DU CANADA
SINCE 1957 | DEPUIS 1957

We acknowledge the support of The Canada Council for the Arts for our publishing program.

Canadian Cataloguing in Publication Data

Stratton, Allan
  The Phoenix lottery

ISBN 1-896332-16-1

I. Title.

PS8587.T723P43 2000   C813'.54   C00-931700-7
PR9199.3.S72P43 2000

This is a work of fiction, and other than historical figures mentioned, the characters are solely the creation of the author. Any resemblance to actual persons is purely coincidental. Certain events in the novel are based on historical events, but some liberties have been taken with details for the purposes of the fiction.

All quotes from the Bible are taken from the King James Version.

The account of the Franklin expedition on page 65 is quoted from an article in the October 23, 1854, edition of the *Toronto Globe*.

The Riverbank Press
P.O. Box 456, 31 Adelaide St. East, Toronto, Ontario, Canada M5C 2J5

Printed and bound in Canada by Transcontinental Printing

For Daniel, Victoria, Peter, and Louise

Contents

I

The Haunting
of
Junior Beamish

A Medical Emergency

"I've had a bad day. It'll be on TV tomorrow. I need more pills."

Dr. Billing peers through the screen at the supplicant on his front porch. He glances at his watch, sighs, opens the door and ushers Junior Beamish down the corridor to the well-upholstered russet wingback in his sunroom. The sunroom is Billing's favourite part of the house, a rambling Victorian curiosity in Toronto's Annex, which he shares with his mother and an assortment of stray cats. The wingback is where Junior has sat twice a week for as long as Billing can remember, though never at such an ungodly hour without appointment.

The good doctor slides into the chair opposite, taking care to crease neither his black silk pyjamas nor his red velour dressing gown. He wiggles his toes in his lambskin slippers, locates the snifter of brandy from which he had been distracted, checks that his pad and pencil are beside the bowl of pistachios at his right, and turns to observe his patient, who waits coiled in the wingback impatient to begin.

Junior is remarkably fit for a man in his mid-forties, but Billing knows that those muscled arms and torso are owed not to a commitment to physical well-being, but to untidy family relationships. Each morning and night, Junior executes four hundred push-ups to the rhythmic chant of "Screw—You— Screw—You," eyes fixed on a photograph of his father that is attached to the wall by a dart.

Tonight there are other signs of distress. Junior, never a clotheshorse, wears threadbare jeans, ratty Adidas, and a ripped T-shirt commemorating some street protest from his youth. Taken with the puffy eyes, bitten nails, peroxide hair and stubble, one would never guess that here is the heir-apparent to a fortune made in booze.

Junior, meantime, has thoughts of his own. He finds Billing's silence irritating on a good day. Tonight, he wants to scream. He reminds himself, however, that his confessor has a flair for pharmaceuticals, a talent which has levelled his depressions and kept his periodic hallucinations in check. If he's to get what he came for he'd best play dog and sit for master.

As Junior holds this tenuous grip on mind and armrests, Billing smiles down at the declawed tabby idly batting the tie of his robe. He takes a sip of brandy, swirls it round his mouth, closes his eyes, and nods for Junior to begin.

Junior takes a deep breath. "My father's dead."

The brandy snorts through Billing's nose; he jolts upright, a portrait of sympathy engaged. "I'm sorry."

"Naturally," Junior arches an eyebrow, "you weren't his son."

Billing recalibrates. "When did it happen?"

"Two nights ago sometime, just outside Port Elgin. The cops investigated yesterday. They called last night to see if someone could identify the body. Mom's off on her semi-annual detox. That left me. Me? I burst out laughing." Junior pauses. Dr. Billing's eyes have once more drifted shut. They appear in no hurry to reopen. "Is this boring you?"

"Heavens no!" The Keeper of the Pills blinks reassurance. He cracks his joints, refreshes his snifter, and props open his right eyelid with the soft rubber end of his pencil. "I'm all ears. Give me the works."

And Junior does.

Junior's Tale

Fine, here goes, and I swear it's all true—

I make the identification at the morgue, okay? Well it's not like in the movies. They flick on a switch and Dad's face comes up on a closed-circuit TV monitor. He looks like his photographs in *The Globe*, only with his eyes closed.

They say, despite the situation, it was just a heart attack, so they've been discreet, the press doesn't know, we can make up what we like. Fine, I think, we'll say he pulled over en route to the cottage on Sauble Beach. Next, they give me the woman's name and number so I can get his car back, it's still there, the old Accord he drove when he didn't want to attract attention.

I make funeral arrangements at Bigelow's, then call. Her name's Millie Gingrich. She says how sorry she is and gives me directions. I say I'll be up in the morning—this morning past. Before hitting the sack, it hits me I'll need company. If I'm driving Dad's car back, someone'll have to drive mine.

Naturally, I ring Emily. I feel bad about it. I mean, it's a long trip and she's getting on, but this is top secret and who else can I trust? Okay, I can trust *you*, Dr. B., but you can't get involved. Like, you're just supposed to sit there, check the clock, and scribble prescriptions, right? Besides, I figure Emily's tough, she was his secretary after all, she can button her lip, and she and the family go back to Havana. In fact, I figure I'm obliged to ask her: if she found out I didn't, she'd never forgive me. Or that's what I say to myself so I won't feel like a prick.

Anyway, I tell Emily that Dad's dead. I fill her in on the details, as carefully as I can. I thought she'd be shocked, especially since she's a Baptist, but she's not. It's like she already knew. Am I the only one who didn't? Write that down, Dr. B.: Is Junior the only one who didn't know about his father? That should give us someplace to start Monday.

So where was I? Oh, yes, Emily says of course she'll come, she'll be in her lobby at five A.M. I say, How about nine? I arrive at ten.

Emily's something. She looks as tidy as Mom's closet after the maid's been through. A little wren in a no-nonsense dress, plain white blouse, and sensible shoes. I feel kind of ashamed. I mean I'm in *this*.

Anyway, the drive starts great. We swap stories and jokes. But the talk sputters out when we hit The Bruce. By the time we turn on to the concession road Emily's just staring out the window, gripping her handkerchief.

I envy her. She's able to feel something. Not me. You know, once upon a time I wanted to make peace so I wouldn't feel guilty when they shut the box. Well, I didn't make peace and I don't feel guilty. I just feel detached, like my life is this very slow foreign film filled with significant pauses that are all supposed to mean something—only I haven't a clue what.

Bastard! I'm middle-aged and I have no emotions. No life. I'm just Junior. A stupid reaction to him. HIM! BASTARD!

Excuse me.

I hit the accelerator, spray gravel, swerve, and slam on the brakes. We've arrived.

Emily asks if I'm okay. She's understandably terrified.

Do I look okay? I scream. That doesn't help matters. But you'll be proud of what I do next. I close my eyes like you tell me to do and imagine I'm floating on clouds. When I open them, I'm calm, even though I'm looking at the place where Dad died.

An S&M brothel.

I take a few deep breaths and say, I'm sorry, I'm fine, let's go. Emily nods, daubs her eyes, tucks the hankie up her sleeve, and together we head for the front door.

From the outside, it doesn't look like a whips and chains funhouse at all. A couple of miles outside Port Elgin, it's just a plain brick bungalow on maybe fifty acres, with a big picture window and a front yard full of tulips and lawn ornaments, including some brightly painted cement gnomes and this metal bird with a weather vane for a tail. Out back there's an old children's swing set, a vegetable patch, and beyond that a barn. Oh, and how can I forget—by the front door, a wood plaque with folksy lettering: The Beaten Path Bed and Breakfast.

What am I doing here? I think. What was *he* doing here? Had he been here before? Often? Who was he? Who was my Dad?

The screen door opens and out comes this woman in a faded housecoat, hairnet, and fuzzy pink slippers, puffing a rollie. It's Millie Gingrich. Weird, I'd pictured someone a bit more, well, dominating. Emily smiles politely. The kind of polite that says, I know what you are, but I'm too ladylike to say so. We shake hands. I can tell Emily's itching to pull out a Sani-wipe.

Millie says it's a tragedy, not to mention a shock, she runs a quiet operation, perfectly legal, i.e. no penetration. Whether that's the truth or just a load to satisfy the cops and grieving relatives, I don't want to know. She pads in front of us to the kitchen. Yikes. Busy linoleum, pressboard cupboards, sunflower wallpaper, scorched counter, rubber dish rack buried in mugs, and a card table holding a big ashtray piled with butts.

I see Emily stiffen. Not from the kitchen decor, but the two people at the table: George and Chelsea, we discover. Chelsea's a chubby twenty-something with a sunny farm girl aura. I picture her milking cows. George is not so sunny; he's a big guy with a walleye. I try not to picture him at all.

We're offered cookies and tea. Emily asks could she have hers with lemon. Millie says they're out, but there's concentrate. Emily struggles to keep down breakfast. If you'd give the cup a rinse I'd be obliged, she chokes.

We sit opposite George and Chelsea as Millie brings over the teapot and pours. George says he's sorry about Dad, how he was a great guy, told funny jokes and whatnot.

Emily corrects him: Mr. Beamish was an accomplished after-dinner speaker.

No kidding, Chelsea pipes up. He'd tell stories and I'd laugh and laugh and then he'd try and pull my hair and I'd have to slap his wrist cuz that stuff's only for downstairs.

Well that sets George off, snorting away with this goofy hiccup, Yup, he was a really great guy, yuk yuk.

Then Millie launches into this eulogy, saying all sorts of nice stuff about Dad, ending with his last visit. Apparently it was all pretty ordinary. He had a little activity in the afternoon, then came up for supper: some chicken noodle soup, spaghetti, a Sara Lee brownie, vanilla ice cream, and a decaf. He had some indigestion, so he took an Eno, toddled back downstairs, watched the Blue Jays, went to bed in his room off the dungeon, and never got up. When ten o'clock rolled around and he hadn't surfaced, she knocked on his door. And there he was, peaceful as a lamb, just like he was sleeping.

Ah, memories. Millie stops talking and we sit in silence, but for the ticking of the owl-clock. Its eyes dart back and forth, counting the seconds. Everyone's still, too, except for George's left eye, which is making lazy figure eights in counterpoint to the clock.

It's all too strange. Not because this is where Dad came for kicks, but because they remember someone so different from the man I knew. When they think of him they see a happy, friendly guy—smart, sociable, and just plain folks. I'm so jealous I want to cry.

I guess Dad came here a lot? I ask, to break the silence and so they'll stop staring at me.

Millie nods. About once a month, she says, ever since they started advertising in Toronto. Pleased as punch, she hands me a newspaper ad from under the banana magnet on the fridge. It reads: The Beaten Path Bed and Breakfast. Catering to the liberated and adventurous! Enjoy a weekend of fun-filled activity in cottage country with our obedient and well-disciplined staff. For more information, fax Madame de Sade at . . . blah blah blah.

My shoulders heave. Millie pats my arm gently and tells me again how special Dad was and how I have every right to be proud. I nod, take a deep breath, and ask to see the dungeon. I want to see what he did. I need to see where he died.

Millie takes us down. I'm kind of disappointed. I mean, I'd pictured a dark, dank hole with spiders and mice. But it's a '70s rec room, which I guess is scary enough: fake wood panelling, fluorescent lights, TV, shag carpet, pool table, furnace in the corner, dustballs. Everything normal, in fact, except for two doors and a curtain, each marked with a skull and crossbones.

I catch a whiff of rot. Is it from the shag? The nap of the pool table? The magazines on the coffee table: *Spanking*, *Bound*, and *Leather Toys*? Or is it the final memory of Dad?

I don't want to think about it, so I ask what's behind the curtain.

Our Detention Room, Millie whoops. She throws the cloth back to reveal prison bars opening on a cell. The bars are authentic, from the old Middlesex County Jail, she whispers, reverentially stroking the keyhole. As for the leg irons, manacles, and stocks—they're all genuine replicas made in Owen Sound. She says there's a judge who shows up for detention each Friday night. They lock him in the stocks, feed him gruel, and let him scream till Sunday. Then they tickle him like crazy. Apparently you can do a lot with a feather duster and a little imagination.

Meantime, Emily's left the tour. Good Lord, she screams. She's opened the door to the Torture Chamber.

You can say that again, beams Millie. With the lights out it's pretty darn atmospheric.

In the centre of the room is what looks to be a Universal gym, except the stations all have hooks at various heights from which hang leather, rubber, and metal restraints. But that's nothing compared to the black concrete walls. They're high, windowless, and covered in leather and rubber fetish gear: hoods, jockstraps, and bras, all studded with clips, Velcro, and snaps—the possibilities are endless. And then there's the props: bits, crops, hooks, handcuffs, paddles, pokers, prods, candles, chains, knives—and to top it all off, an executioner's axe, this last bolted tight behind a block.

According to Millie, her dungeon's a labour of love. She adds to it each year, even got a St. John's Cross last spring.

A what? Emily smiles vacantly, on social autopilot.

Why, it's a rack, dear, Millie explains, for stretching. Sure beats the chiropractor. She keeps it back in the barn since it's way too big for the basement. That's a shame, she says, because the barn's not insulated, which means you can't use it in winter unless you wear a parka, and being on a rack in a parka kind of ruins the effect. She cracks her knuckles and tells us about this Pentecostal up last July to reenact the deaths of the apostles. According to her, when he saw that St. John's Cross, it was love at first sight. He hung from his feet, babbled in tongues, and grew two inches.

I don't understand, I blurt out, What are you doing here? I mean here in the country?

I like the lifestyle, she says, all matter-of-fact. I cross-country, skidoo—

But here! I shout. This . . . place! I picture righteous burghers storming the castle of Dr. Frankenstein.

Millie laughs, you think city folks are the only ones with "special interests"? Don't rub your business in people's noses and they'll see what they want to see. Correction, they'll see what they let themselves see.

Point taken. Who would have guessed about dear old Dad?

Millie hesitates, then asks if I'd like to see where he stayed.

I nod and she opens the final door, as if we're about to enter a chapel or something. It's a small room with a metal cot, pillow, mattress, and chenille bedspread, its threads pulled half-bare. Next to the cot, a white pressboard chest of drawers with a Bible and a china bedpan on top. A plain mirror. A five-year-old calendar with pictures of kittens. A cardboard wastebasket.

I sob and run back out to the main room. Emily starts to follow, but I wave her away. Millie makes a discreet exit upstairs. Emily stays in the bedroom.

I want to scream in Dad's face, Why? Why didn't you tell me? Why didn't I know? I smash my fist into the couch.

And then I hear a voice. So what do you think of your old man now?

Dad?

It's impossible. I identified the body. He's dead. Then I see it. There on the coffee table. On the cover of *Spanking* magazine, a dominatrix in fishnets, stilettos and corset is paddling the naked man across her lap. He faces the viewer.

It's Dad, laughing. I asked you a question, he roars. Cat got your tongue?

I rub my eyes. I look at the cover again. It's different. Now the dom's paddling a young guy. I stagger to the bedroom calling for Emily. But she doesn't hear me. She's sitting on the bed, staring into space, stroking the pillow.

We drive home, me in his car, she in mine. We meet for supper, eat quietly. I don't tell her what I've seen. I can't. I can't tell anyone. Dr. B., there's a press conference tomorrow. I have to hold it together. I have to keep up a front. Then up to The Grove to get Mom out of detox. Then next day, visitation. Then, next day, funeral. Then next day, next day, next day—

"—NEXT DAY, NEXT DAY, NEXT DAY—HELP ME—I WANT TO BE NORMAL—DON'T LET ME BE CRAZY—NOT AGAIN—PLEASE—I WON'T BE LOCKED UP—PLEASE—GIVE ME SOME PILLS!"

Billing waits until the fire consumes itself and Junior is whimpering, overwhelmed by misery. "You've seen a fearsome thing," he consoles. "And, yes, I believe you've seen it." Junior looks up, uncertain whether it's worse to be haunted or insane. "The death of a parent," Billing continues, "much less under the circumstances you describe, is capable of shaking the soundest constitution."

"So you think I'm hallucinating?" Junior brightens. "Does that mean a new round of Lithium? Chlorpromazine, maybe, like when I saw The Pillow Lady?"

It annoys Dr. Billing when the pharmaceutically precocious presume to self-prescribe. "This is no Pillow Lady," he lectures. "The Pillow Lady comes from psychosis; your father from mere fatigue."

"*Fatigue?*"

"Mental projections of the sort you describe are absolutely common in the recently bereaved," Billing assures, with an airy flick of the wrist. "To be sure, the deceased is generally perceived to be standing in a white robe, rather than naked on the cover of a pornographic magazine. That, however, appears a natural consequence of your circumstance. I'm going to up the Paxil to deal with your family obsessions. As for your exhaustion, a few sleeping pills should do the trick."

Billing writes the prescriptions, then raids his private stash of Lorazepam, slipping his patient sufficient to see him through the looming horrors. As Junior drives off into the night, Billing lists against a front porch pillar and waves. "Night night. Sleep tight. Don't let the bedbugs bite."

The Widow Beamish

One Lorazepam might have worked; two most certainly; three knock Junior out till noon. He awakes refreshed to a pleasant surprise: the media is feeding elsewhere. Despite his well-publicized family feud, nurtured in public over a lifetime, the few reporters who call accept his pro forma expression of grief and move on.

Naturally, this is neither for reasons of taste nor humanity. Rather, the vultures smell death at the corporate headquarters of Beamish Enterprises Inc., and circle accordingly. A sprawling hydra, BEI is, or rather was, Edgar's private company and personal fiefdom. Anchored by the formidable Maple Leaf Breweries, it includes: stakes in Ontario and B.C. lumber and mining concerns; Beamish Orchards, which controls a chunk of prime Niagara Escarpment real estate; and Kitty Trucks, a firm which transports BEI produce and resources to market and rail links at preferential rates. Edgar was a brilliant micromanager, planning for all contingencies save his death. Whither the behemoth now, in the absence of its visionary founder?

With no clear line of succession, Frank Kendal, Vice-President of Operations, stakes his claim to leadership. Shoulders back, belly out, he lumbers into the media's maw. Sadly, if nature abhors a vacuum, it absolutely abhors Frank Kendal. Grilled about BEI's future, Kendal melts under the camera lights and flees, humiliated, sweat flying from his jowls. The media glory at the rout, wallow in the apparent corporate shambles, and predict BEI's incipient implosion. Then, with the blood lust of medieval pundits elbows deep in entrails, they lick their lips and wait upon the reading of the will.

Junior, meantime, has more pressing concerns, namely the disposition of his mother, Catherine "Kitty" Beamish (née Danderville).

Kitty cuts a wide swath in society circles. Tall, wafer-thin, with high cheekbones and sensational wigs, she's known for sweeping through gallery openings in the latest Donna Karan, imperiously aloof from envious eyes. Elegant to a fault, she has a voice to match. It's a low purr, a husky velvet from her trademark Scotch and cigarillos, softened by a hint of Demerol. One can almost imagine an anorexic Peggy Lee, speech ever-so-subtly out of sync with her lips.

Junior picks her up at The Grove, a private clinic north of Toronto. With the visitation set for tomorrow, Junior had thought a good night's rest back home might be the ticket. But it's been a difficult ride. Kitty's in her second week of withdrawal and feeling rather cranky.

"So where did he die? A whorehouse?"

"At a Bed and Breakfast en route to Sauble Beach."

"Don't feed me that crap. I'm your mother."

Junior avoids comment. He turns on the CD player.

Kitty turns it off. She glares at him. "Who did you get to put out the word?"

"Emily."

"Ah yes, Miss Pristable. The Baptist creature who can't spell."

"And I made funeral arrangements with Bigelow's. They do a nice job."

"Thanks so much for consulting," the widow Beamish spits, arching her neck like an enraged swan.

"I'm sorry," Junior says, gripping the wheel, eyes on the road. "The doctors said we should save you stress."

"Did they now? After all, what do I know? I'm only the widow!"

"We can make a change if you'd like."

"No. The damage is done. We must all move forward, but I shall never forgive you." She draws on her cigarillo. "At least, I trust you got Archie B. to do the service. Or is there someone else the doctors would like to recommend?" she enquires sweetly as they pull into the drive.

"No, of course I got Archie."

Of course. The Reverend Canon Archibald Belltower, B.A., M.Div., Th.M., Th.D., D.D., is the priest guaranteed to give his father the most sympathetic sendoff into the great beyond. Dry as a prairie dust bowl, and twice as windy, Canon Belltower has served as Rector of Saint Jude the Obscure for the past thirty years. He has a halo of white hair, a Latin witticism for every occasion, and a keen appreciation of the spiritual needs of his Tory Rosedale clientele.

Not for him the yapping of those dreary United Church drones forever nattering about the Social Gospel. Tales of the widow's mite, or of some poor camel struggling to squeeze through the eye of a needle, are all well and good for the saintly poor who need something to feel good about. But the saintly poor don't go to St. Jude's. The saintly rich go to St. Jude's, and while prepared to accept Christ as their personal Lord and Saviour, they're quite adamant that God never intended his Son to be taken seriously as an economist. Canon Belltower is wise enough to know that any priest lunatic enough to suggest otherwise will quickly find himself embroiled in conversations with front-pew parishioners curious to know who, precisely, the church expects to pay for the renovation to the west wing.

Consequently, the Reverend Canon Archibald Belltower, B.A., M.Div., Th.M., Th.D., D.D., preaches the Gospel of family trusts and downsizing. "Reading from Matthew 25, verses 29, 30: For unto everyone that hath shall be given, and he shall have abundance: but from him that hath not shall be taken away even that which he hath. And cast ye the unprofitable servant into outer darkness: there shall be weeping and gnashing of teeth."

"Archie figures there'll be an overflow, so he's booked St. Paul's," says Junior, helping his mother into the house.

"You must get my mourning wig to Stephen."

"Done. The premier's coming. He'd like to sit with us in the front row."

"Ah, the Stick-Man. So we're in for a circus. I'd best get myself prepared."

That's what Junior's afraid of. So, he's taken care to sweep the master bedroom for booze and drugs. The silver flask of Scotch under the mattress is a well-known family secret. The Dewars in the armoire is another snap. But the mickey on the book shelf is a new wrinkle, as is the twenty-sixer in the ensuite toilet tank.

"Now get some sleep, mother. Tomorrow is going to be hell."

"Hell? You have no idea."

Junior closes the door of the master bedroom and locks his mother inside. Kitty hears the key turn, but she's too much the Danderville to acknowledge the humiliation. She makes her way to the armoire with elegant precision—only a true alcoholic would run—and reaches to the back left corner of the second drawer. Strange, she could have sworn she'd hidden a wee surprise.

She turns to the bookshelf with great control. A sharp intake of breath. "Somebody's been reading my Judith Krantz!" Most peculiar, but not to panic.

She drops to her knees and crawls on all fours to the bed. Her hands race like nervous hamsters between mattress and box spring. "Christ on a pogo stick!"

Throwing caution to the wind, she runs to the bathroom. The toilet tank is empty. Kitty sinks to the tiles, hot, bitter tears coursing down her cheeks. "I have been betrayed!"

And then it comes to her. A vision. Three years ago. She flies to the lamp on the right side of the bed. The base is an imitation Ming vase. She tears off the lampshade and removes the top. Inside—Yes!—inside is a plastic tube she filled with Courvoisier and hid long ago for just such a rainy day!

"Fools! You'll never outfox Kitty Danderville!" she crows in triumph. Tube in hand, she skips to the closet and retrieves the baggie of pills taped in the toe of her left Bruno Magli black stretch patent-leather bootie. Then, a diva unleashed, she vogues to the vanity table, places her spoils just so, and removes her wig.

Now I won't overdo it. Tomorrow is a busy day and I've got to look my best, she thinks, rubbing her hands in glee. She peers at the pills. Why, they look so lovely—like a tropical fruit salad—she hardly knows where to begin. She chooses a pink, washes it down with Couvoisier, and turns to the mirror. The skin is taut over the bones. The eyes hollow. The head shaved.

"My God, I'm ready for the catacombs!"

Another sip to steady her nerves, and then a pre-nightcap, and things don't look so bad after all. The laser surgery on her liver spots is almost healed—just some light pink watermarks and—damn if she isn't a goddess!

"Poor Edgar. I ought to feel sad for the bastard," she giggles, "but I am a supermodel!" She vamps up and down the bedroom. "I'm thin as Melba! Do you hear me Claudia? Lauren? Naomi? I can out-vomit the lot of you!"

Oh, oh. What if Junior's listening? He'll think she's drunk. She puts her finger to her lips. "Shhh." But no one's coming. No one's heard.

She smiles hugely and cackles, "What to wear, what to wear. . ."

Junior knocks on the door. "It's noon, Mom. We leave for the visitation in an hour." Silence. Junior unlocks the door. The light from the hall spills into the bedroom. The furniture appears to be rearranged. Sheets, shoes, clothes are draped, piled, thrown about. His mother is nowhere to be seen. He flicks the light switch. The room stays dark. Then he hears a low plaintive purr.

"I have removed the light bulbs."

The voice comes from under a tangle of Halston and Dior in the corner. And then a heart-wrenching sob. "Oh, my God, Junior, what am I going to do? What am I going to do?"

"It's okay, Mom. I know his death is a shock, but we'll get through it."

"What are you talking about?" Another sob. "I'm fat."

"Pardon?"

"I'm fat. And I'm too old to throw up."

"Have you been drinking?"

"How dare you use that tone with me?"

"For God's sake, Mom, you're in rehab."

"I'm in mourning. And I have nothing to wear!"

Three coffees and a cold shower later, Kitty agrees to a classic Ralph Lauren black button-front stretch skirt—"You're all trying to kill me!"—black baggy cashmere sweater over white cotton body suit, and black belt with simple pewter clasp. Fortunately, the occasion also allows for dark shades and a heavy veil.

"You're an angel, my angel. You're all I have left."

Paying Respects

Junior arranges for his mother to sit in a private room at Bigelow's undisturbed. "Not up to visitors. Overcome with grief," he whispers to Mr. K.C. Bigelow Sr., the presiding mortician.

Mr. Bigelow is much like his clients. Stiff as a board, he smiles little, speaks less, and smells of embalming fluid and talc. His job is to point the mourners to the receiving room, reminding them of envelopes to the Canadian Heart Foundation and Art Gallery of Ontario for those wishing to make a donation in lieu of flowers.

Junior is to wait near the coffin, the only family member to receive visitors. Granny Danderville's still ailing—almost forty years now—but will be down from Caledon tomorrow. His mother, well . . . And that's it for the immediate family. "I'm the proverbial end of the line," he grins, and at once feels a chill. Though not religious, he makes a quick prayer of contrition and enters the visiting suite.

Heavy oak baseboards and mouldings lend weight to both space and occasion. In counterpoint, the wallpaper, a pale yellow-beige with embossed off-white lilies, affords peace and serenity. Junior notes the casket at the end of the room. Only the profile of his father's face is visible from the door. Cascading floral tributes explode on both sides, including an arresting presentation of orchids from the duPonts, who will be represented by a senior lawyer and two sisters-in-law, that Cuba scandal having long since been forgotten.

He approaches the casket gingerly, knees wobbling, and looks inside.

Bigelow's has done a good job. In death, Edgar Beamish looks so much more at peace than in life. What a difference from Junior's memory of Grampa Danderville. Henry's lips, painted bright red, had stiffened into a grotesque leer. And there'd been nothing subtle about the mascara. For weeks, five-year-old Junior had nightmares that his grandfather was a cartoon monster jumping out of television sets and eating little children and their pet kittens. "There, there," Beamish had comforted, "Grampa never ate kittens."

His Dad looks to be sleeping. Miss Pristable chose the wardrobe. She always knew how to make him look his best. He sports his favourite blue-grey pinstripe with the silk maroon tie from Tangiers and his signature gold tie clip. A rose on a hint of baby's breath dresses the left lapel. The glasses are as in life. Even the hair looks real.

Junior remembers the last time he saw his father alive. Edgar had sat in his leather chair behind his large mahogany desk, slowly swivelling back and forth. He'd closed his eyes and let his glasses sag down his nose. "Junior . . . Junior . . . Junior," he'd said with infinite weariness, letting each word drop with the weight of a lifetime of disappointment, "You . . . could . . . have . . . done . . . anything . . . you . . . wanted."

If Junior had disapproved of his father, the disenchantment had been mutual. Junior was his father's single overwhelming failure. It was as if in every circumstance, and in every choice, his son rubbed sand in his eyes.

"Goddamnit, you live in a two-room apartment over a Laundromat. Where? On Dupont, God spare me," the old man had intoned, warming to the litany of complaint. "And this, this hole, is where you hold your press conferences whenever the Americans invade some two-bit-Third-World-tin-pot-excuse-for-a-country-that-ought-to-have-known-better. And the press come! Of course they come. Why? Because you're my son. My son! The son of Edgar Beamish, the guy they love to hate! The guy who whipped their asses in court! They know they can't take me on *mano a mano*, but they can sure as hell quote my own goddamn flesh and blood. What a joke! The only reason you get to piss on my carpet is because you're my son. Without me, you're a nobody! A nothing! A big fat zero!"

Junior had spun on his heel and marched to the office door.

"Not so fast. Where do you think you're going? I'm not through with you yet. Look at you in your blue jeans and T-shirt with that attitude stud in your nose. You're not a teenager anymore. You're forty—what? Two, three, four?"

"I'm forty-*something*."

"Who gives a shit? You're middle-aged! And you can't even get a job! Oh right, you work at a Food Bank! Well it must be nice up on that cross looking down on your old man, but down here in the dirt, in the real world, people have jobs. Real jobs. They don't waste their time packing cans of beans for lazy bums who hate their guts. And, yes, they hate your guts. To them you're just some rich kid slumming. Some tourist who can run back to Rosedale if things get tough. You think I use people? Well so do you. You use them to feel holier than the pope's ass!"

"I must say I'm terribly sorry," a voice intrudes. Junior jolts out of his reverie. Where is he? Oh yes, the funeral home. He realizes he's spent the last ten minutes shaking hands and mumbling "Thank you, so glad you could come" without hearing or seeing a thing. Now the room snaps into focus.

It's full of suits. There are suits from McCarthy & McCarthy, suits from Dominion Bond Rating Service, suits from Goodman and Associates. There are suits from the stock exchange and the arts councils, and an entire frat house of suits from the premier's office, dorky rich kids who get to play with the grownups, trading their teething rings for membership cards to the Albany Club.

Above all, there's the biggest suit in Toronto. Literally. "So terribly, *terribly* sorry," its voice warbles again, rich with the unction of God's chosen. It's the voice of Rudyard Gardenia, a man poured into his clothes by someone who forgot to say "When."

Gardenia, the well-placed art critic, has been paid a retainer by Beamish for inside information leading to the procurement of under-the-table masterpieces. A political barracuda, his influence with arts juries and tastemakers strikes fear in sculptors and painters young and old, while his gossip, vicious to a fault, puts him on society's *A* list.

Gardenia billows across the room. He's remarkably light on his feet for a man of such ballast. Well over four hundred pounds, he reminds Junior of a hippo ballerina from *Fantasia*. "It's such a shock."

"A terrible shock." This last from Bob, Gardenia's private secretary, a young man with wild plastic glasses and bad skin who follows downwind. Bob is known to police as a former regular of Hamburger Hill, the spot behind a Yonge Street Burger King where suburban husbands pick up street kids. But that was then. Now Bob lives with Gardenia and Gardenia's wife, Betty. It's a curious menage, best explained by Betty's distaste for sex, not to mention her large inheritance, which allows Gardenia to live in the style to which he presumes he deserves to be accustomed. Once asked if he thought Gardenia was in the closet, Junior had replied, "That ain't no closet, honey. It's a *pied-à-terre*."

Gardenia presses Junior into the mottled folds of his bosom. "Poor, poor boy." Junior suffocates in the humid expanse of stale sweat and cologne. He attempts to pull back only to find himself staring at bits of food wedged between back molars. Through thick, fleshy lips, Rudyard breathes fermenting lunch in his face; Junior detects Caesar Salad, warm brie, and Chianti. "Our dear Kitty must be beside herself."

"Well, you know Mom," Junior allows politely, breaking free of the damp caress. "How are things at the Inner Circle?"

"Fabulous. Fabulous," enthuses Gardenia, wiggling his pudgy digits.

"Really fabulous," Bob nods deeply. "Rudyard is brilliant."

The Inner Circle is a private club, admission to which is select and coveted. Select because Gardenia chooses the artists; coveted because his contacts buy art. Each week, Circle members bring their works-in-progress to be critiqued. Gardenia chooses an artist to disembowel. Group members, anxious to curry favour, follow his lead and heap their own invective on the hapless creature. Gardenia is rumoured to take bets on how long it'll take each victim to crack.

"Speaking of fabulous, doesn't your father look wonderful? They do a good job at Bigelow's."

Bob seconds with conviction. "He looks fabulous."

Gardenia inches closer and whispers conspiratorially, "The *Self-Portrait* is authentic. We got the call on the way over."

"What?" says Junior.

"The van Gogh. The Rémy. From which lucky beneficiary do I collect? Not that I'm in a rush at a time like this, poor lamb, good heavens. We can resolve this filthy money business next week sometime, when you're rested. Speaking of which, do give me a dingle if you come undone. I've a line on a fabulous grief counsellor." He gives Junior's arm a solicitous squeeze. "Be brave, *mon brave*." And with that, the Great Helmsman, Slayer of Philistines, and Keeper of the Inner Circle performs a delicate pirouette and vanishes with his protégé, propelled by a discreetly florid fart.

Dearly Beloved

Enemies of Edgar Beamish are delighted with his funeral. It's a fiasco. Spectators are divided on the most compelling image. For some, it's the sight of communion trays flying through the air, dropping wafers like manna on the assembled mourners. For others, it's the widow carried screaming from the church in her underwear. Or the priest with the black eye. Or the son collapsing on the altar, a hypodermic stuck in his backside. But whichever image spectators dine out on, all agree it's hard to ignore the star turn of the corpse.

Having failed to keep his mother sober for the visitation, Junior is determined she be presentable for the funeral. He takes no chances. Kitty's bedroom door is kept ajar, with servants posted in rotation through the night. Kitty is not a happy camper. Fortunately, her tirades the following morning are checked by a migraine of some consequence. Kitty is quite the study in pathos. If she so much as looks sideways, her brain throbs. It is too painful even to sob. In such dire straits, she sits immobile, or walks, when absolutely necessary, very slowly, carefully, as if competing for Posture Queen.

Kitty's migraine is not helped by the arrival of her mother, who has been deposited from Caledon in her gardening outfit. "She insisted," the nurse apologizes. Mrs. Danderville hasn't been the same since Henry's death. In fact, in recent years she has turned into someone else altogether.

It is for Kitty to dress her for the funeral. An eternity of buttons, zippers, and straps later, Kitty turns her mother to face the full-length mirror in the master bedroom. Seeing their reflections, Mrs. Danderville becomes positively shy.

"What lovely dresses everyone has on."

"Yes, mother. Lovely black dresses."

"Are they going to a party?"

"No, mother. *We* are going to a funeral."

"That's nice. Anyone we know?"

"Edgar."

"Edgar? We don't know any Edgar."

"Yes we do, mother. Edgar. My husband Edgar. The one you can't stand."

"Oh, but I can't stand Edgar."

"Then you'll enjoy his funeral."

"Will he be there?"

"God willing."

"What lovely dresses everyone has on."

Junior has taken pity on his mother and allowed her a Demerol to help her through the service. It's a move he will regret. Kitty may have been next to immobile, but she's been plotting revenge.

She begs Junior to take her to St. Paul's an hour and a half in advance: she needs more time with her belovèd. A quick glance at the open coffin on the chancel to make sure he's well and truly dead and she's overcome, retreating to the study commandeered for the occasion by the Reverend Canon Archibald B.

"Please, Archie," the widow Beamish daubs her eyes, "might I have a private moment with my son?"

Belltower, labouring on his eulogy—specifically, a tasteful allusion to St. Jude's west-wing renovation, so faithfully supported by the dear departed—readily accedes.

Kitty turns to face her quarry. "Junior, my pet, you have done so much for me these past few days, and I do appreciate it. But, between you and me, I am just a tiny bit thirsty, and I was wondering if you might arrange a wee Scotch and soda?"

"You shouldn't drink."

"I didn't ask for an opinion," Kitty purrs sweetly. "I asked for a drink."

"No."

Kitty sighs. Clearly the lad is simple. "Junior," she explains patiently, "I am having a drink, and you are fetching it for me. Otherwise, when everyone is seated, the premier, the archbishop, captains of industry, and the press, I will march to the front of the church, whip out the old bugger's pecker, and give him a goodbye kiss that will curl his toes till Doomsday."

Junior blanches.

"The Scotch is in the car under the spare tire. And I'd better not taste the soda."

Kitty gratefully accepts her tumbler of "tea" and retreats to the study's restroom, the better to compose herself. By the time the dignitaries begin arriving, Kitty is so composed she resembles a still life. A Zen philosopher in shades, she floats through the sea of mourners, an oasis of calm, murmuring, "*Qué sera sera.*" The last syllable is inaudible, but one gets the point.

Premier Divot holds her hand. "He was a loyal Tory and a great friend. I'm so sorry."

"*Qué sera se . . .*"

The premier extends his arm. Kitty melts into it and lets him waft her up the aisle. She is Grace Kelly. She is Audrey Hepburn. She is Blanche du Bois died and gone to Heaven. She waves in gracious slow motion to all those strange people she thinks she ought to recognize, "*Qué sera se . . . ,*" and blows a kiss in the general direction of Rudyard Gardenia.

Junior follows, escorting his Granny Danderville. "They say you're dead!" she hisses at him. He deposits his grandmother in the front row beside the premier and his mother and goes to bid his father a final goodbye.

The premier has never met a widow he didn't like, and he likes Kitty more than most. Indeed, he's barely managed to get them to the pew before anyone can notice how the tantalizing musk of her perfume has aroused his tender instincts. He puts a compassionate arm around her and whispers gently in her ear, "I must say you're holding up very well."

"Well," she purrs confidentially, "It's easy when the corpse is a shit. That bastard shtupped every skirt he could catch, including the pallbearers' wives." She winks, "He even shtupped your mistress."

The premier shrivels.

Meanwhile, at the coffin, Junior is overcome with a wave of emotion. When he looks at his father's face he sees a man more vulnerable than he remembers. "Dad, wherever you are, I want you to have this." Junior takes a photograph from his pocket.

In the picture, he's four, sitting with his father in the semi-enclosed rooftop bar of the duPont mansion in Varadero. They're sharing a Coke float through two straws, a panorama of Caribbean sky behind them. It's December of 1958. Within the month their lives will be turned upside down, but this photograph holds a moment of pure, irreplaceable joy. Junior remembers that day: the ride in the new DeSoto, head out the window, salt breeze in his hair; the hot dog at the beachfront grill he'll learn was once home to Al Capone; the shallows at Playa Corales where he saw his first boxfish; the piggyback ride on his Dad's shoulders up the narrow winding stairs to the bar for that Coke float.

Carefully, Junior places the photograph in the inside pocket of his father's suit jacket. A memento to travel with his father to the land of the dead. For a moment, Junior sees himself as an ancient Egyptian, a bereaved prince burying a talisman with his Pharaoh father. "There are so many things I wanted to say to you." He pauses, then kisses his father gently on the forehead. "Goodbye."

"Not so fast, you little shit."

Junior blinks. The corpse is staring at him.

"Dad?"

"Keep your voice down. Do you want people to think you're crazy?"

Junior is about to take a step back. The corpse grabs his hand. "I said not so fast. I'm not through with you yet."

Bewildered, Junior looks out at the congregation. His mother is nodding off. Mrs. Danderville is whispering in the premier's

ear, "When does the play begin?" The Reverend Canon Belltower
is studying the eulogy. The organist is playing the largo from
Handel's *Xerxes*, while members of the choir keep silent time
with their heads, or fan themselves with the Order of Service.
The archbishop, sundry incumbents, deacons, cabinet ministers, and reporters variously clear their throats or check their
watches. In the back row, Miss Pristable bites her lip. None of
them seem to notice anything unusual.

"Pay attention." The corpse squeezes his hand. Hard. "So
many things you wanted to say to me. Bullshit. You don't get off
that easy, sonny."

"Let go of me."

"It's that night in Varadero, isn't it? You've hated me ever
since."

"I haven't," Junior whispers hoarsely.

"Age ten you went around asking people to adopt you. Age
eighteen, you set up a picket on the front lawn."

"Dad, you're hurting me."

"Cry me a river. You picketed your own goddamn parents!"

"You hired scab labour."

"Your mother comes home from a facial and there you are
on the front verandah screaming into a megaphone, 'My Dad is
a Nazi Scumbag!' I'll always remember that news clip of your
poor mother scrambling through the bushes like a hunted
animal."

"I'm sorry."

"You're such a piss-ass weasel." The corpse lets go its grip.

Junior drops to his knees, massaging his knuckles. "I'm
sorry, I'm sorry!" he sobs.

A hush falls over the congregation. The Reverend Canon
Belltower glides over and puts his arm around Junior's shoulder. "It's all right." With a lifetime of professional compassion
at his fingertips, the Canon raises Junior to his feet. An audible
sigh from the congregation. Belltower acknowledges their relief
with an infinitely caring nod of the head. He gives Junior's
shoulder a fatherly squeeze. "I'm afraid it's time."

Junior stares blankly. "Time."

Belltower smiles awkwardly and repeats, "Time. It's . . . time. You know . . . *time* . . ."

"Time for what?"

Belltower casts tact to the wind. "We have to close the lid."

"But my father's not dead," Junior whispers.

"Of course not," Canon Belltower agrees. "He's alive in the arms of Jesus."

"I said, my father's alive! He talked to me just now!"

The congregation leans forward. Canon Belltower gives a vague priestly wave to calm the congregants, specifically the archbishop, who sees the fourth estate furtively pulling out their note pads. "It's all right, everyone."

"It's not all right! You're trying to bury my father!"

"We must be brave," says Canon Belltower.

"Get away from me."

"Let go and let God."

"Let go yourself." With that, Junior hauls off and punches The Reverend Canon Archibald Belltower, B.A., M.Div., Th.M., Th.D., D.D., smack on the nose. Belltower executes a perfect back flip off the chancel steps.

All hell breaks loose. Three deacons rise to subdue Junior, but he runs behind the coffin, grabs a large crucifix and holds it like a baseball bat. The deacons cower.

"MY FATHER'S ALIVE!"

"WHAT DO YOU MEAN HE'S ALIVE?" Kitty snaps bolt upright. "HOW DARE HE NOT BE DEAD!" She lurches to her feet. "IF THAT SONOVABITCH ISN'T DEAD, I'LL KILL HIM MYSELF!"

The premier grabs her shoulders to restrain her. Kitty swings her purse to break free. It hits Divot on the mouth, the catch snaps open, and the mickey of Scotch smashes to the floor, spraying shards of glass and booze.

Kitty charges forward. There's a huge rip and the premier finds himself holding the top half of the widow's dress.

"Bravo!" squeals Mrs. Danderville, clapping her hands with glee. "What lovely dresses!"

Seeing Junior distracted, the deacons go on the attack, but he recovers and swings wildly, hitting a home run with the communion trays. In the ensuing melée, BEI Vice-President of Operations, Frank Kendal, makes his move. A former high-school linebacker, he dives for Junior's knees.

It's a clean tackle. Junior buckles backwards against the coffin. It topples over, sending the body flying. The corpse loses its toupee as it bounces off the top chancel step. It loses its glasses as it ricochets off the second. It rolls another ten feet, then comes to an abrupt stop as its head whacks the front pew. The jaw cracks open. The dentures fly out.

"DIE, DAMMIT, DIE," the widow screams in her underwear, kicking the corpse in fury.

"Bravo!" squeals Mrs. Danderville.

Junior struggles gamely to his feet, but Dr. Billing has leapt from his pew and into position. He jabs Junior in the backside with a hypodermic of Chlorpromazine. The last thing Junior sees before collapsing on the altar is his father's corpse staring at him with a bug-eyed, gummy grin, while its teeth roll merrily down the centre aisle toward the waiting hearse.

Last Will and Testament

Junior is still under sedation at Homewood when the will is probated two weeks later. Miss Pristable has been named executor. She is also granted a permanent position at BEI at an annual salary of $150,000, a position which may only be terminated upon payment of one-million dollars in cash. That a secretary should be named both executor and a major beneficiary raises eyebrows, but there is no question that Edgar was in his right wits, and any suggestion of impropriety between himself and Miss Pristable is immediately dismissed owing to Miss Pristable's transparent Baptist rectitude, such rectitude being especially noteworthy coming from one employed by "Fast Eddy" Beamish. Gossip is further squelched as Edgar's generosity to his secretary is dwarfed by his largesse to his wife.

The Widow Beamish is given full title to the homes in Toronto and Palm Beach, the townhouse in London, and the condo in L.A. She also inherits all stocks, bonds, and cash assets. What is not generally known is that access to the money is conditional on Kitty kicking her addictions to booze and pills. Failure to pass weekly urine tests for two full years following probate will result in her inheritance being placed in a trust to be administered by Miss Pristable. On Kitty's death the trust would revert to the estate and thence to Junior.

This wrinkle tempts Kitty to litigate. She refrains, however, as Edgar has carefully included a "notwithstanding" clause stripping all inheritance from any who dare contest his will. The bastard, she fumes. Ah well, *Qué sera se* .... A little holiday from her hobbies, up at the Grove, will be good for the bod, and then she'll consult dear Rudyard; Gardenia can be trusted to craft a stratagem.

Of other interest, the Beamish Collection, containing some two hundred nineteenth-century Impressionist oils and drawings, is donated to the National Art Gallery of Canada. There are exceptions: the boardroom Monets will remain where they are, and a newly acquired van Gogh *Self-Portrait* will go to Edgar Beamish Junior.

So far so good. But jaws drop at the news that Junior has also inherited complete control of Beamish Enterprises Inc. The notion of the activist gadfly attempting to ride herd on the egos of men like VP Frank Kendal prompts chortles up and down Bay Street: surely Beamish the Lesser will more easily inter his inheritance than he did his father.

Junior hasn't time to worry about water cooler scuttlebutt. He's too busy fleshing out a new direction for the corporation, specifically a master plan hatched in his private room on the psychiatric ward. Junior intends nothing less than to create a major philanthropic foundation—to fulfill on a grand scale the altruistic impulse which had hitherto fuelled his endeavours in the local soup kitchen.

To this end, immediately upon his release from Homewood, he summons his brass to company headquarters. Needless to say, they're late. "They'd have been early for Dad, shining his shoes with a toothbrush," Junior fumes. Frank Kendal is particularly tardy. He calls to say he's tied up in traffic, though the background noise over the cellphone sounds suspiciously like daytime television.

Alone in his father's private office, Junior drums his fingers on the old mahogany desk, and finally, with nothing better to do, fishes from his inside jacket pocket the crumpled private letter which had accompanied the will.

Dear Junior:

I've a feeling I won't last the week. It's probably just conscience or gas. But in case, this note.

There are three things you need to know about Rémy, France.

1. It's the birthplace of Nostradamus.

2. It was home to Saint-Paul Hospital, a private nineteenth-century madhouse then known as The Asylum for the Alienated.

3. In that madhouse, Vincent van Gogh created a masterpiece that will change your life.

What the hell is the old man talking about? Here's the scoop.

A couple of months back, Rudyard Gardenia tours France with Betty and Bob. He says he and Betty are on a second honeymoon. Hah! He wants to give Bob some culture.

In Rémy, Rudyard gets wind of an estate sale near the asylum. A widow, one hundred and ten, has dropped dead leaving a century of garbage filling her home, barn, and outbuildings. So he pops by for a look-see, expecting some turn-of-the-century bric-a-brac and Art Deco kitsch. Only, instead of a giggle, he finds himself drawn to a pile of paintings stacked against an old washstand.

They're ripped and rain-damaged and some of the canvases are mildewed and you get the general idea. Still, flipping through, he spots a picture that gives him goose-bumps. It's covered in cow shit, but through the crap he sees fierce vermilion eyes against a wild blue background. It's a van Gogh—unmistakable. But at a lawn sale?

Well, the whole bundle's going for maybe twenty francs—it's all basically kindling. So he figures, what the heck, buys the lot, and leaves it on the property, except for the painting with the eyes.

Back at the hotel, he does a little investigating. It turns out the old widow's name was Marie Legault. But her maiden name was Poulet, and, as someone like Rudyard would know, Poulet was the name of the attendant whom van Gogh attacked during his stay at the asylum. No bullshit: Jean-Francois Poulet, twenty-seven, died two years later.

Rudyard gets so excited he cleans out the corner bakery. Since old Vince-a-rooney gave away paintings like there was no tomorrow, wouldn't it be natural for him to give one to Poulet by way of apology? And if he did, what would happen to it? During his lifetime the God-fearing middle-class thought his work was rubbish. He only sold one painting and those he gave away were usually lost or refused. Dr. Rey, for instance, used his to fix a hole in his chicken coop.

So Rudyard thinks, if an educated doctor can do that, what can you expect from an illiterate orderly? To him, the painting's probably a joke. A souvenir from a one-eared lunatic. Something ugly to scare his daughter when she's bad. And after he's dead and she's married off to Farmer Legault, something to keep out back to amuse the cows because, hey, she's a pack rat.

Okay, it's all speculation, but it's fun to dream, especially when you wipe the muck off the bottom right corner and see the word "Vincent" painted bright as day. To cut a long story short, Rudyard brings it to me. I take one look at the impasto and get shivers.

Naturally, I play it cool. I tell him it's a long shot, but, on the off-chance, I'll make him a deal. In exchange for the painting, I'll guarantee him a million dollars and put up the costs of restoration, authentication, and insurance; then, if it's genuine, I'll give him another ten.

Rudyard knows it could be worth forty or fifty million, but if he goes it alone and it's a fake, he won't have a pot to piss in, plus he'll be buggered by the costs up front. Rudyard's no gambler. The putz takes the sure thing, and I ship the painting to the Rijksmuseum for authentication.

Word's expected shortly, but I know already. It's the real McCoy.

Junior, I have a nose for things, and my nose tells me you were meant for this painting. Look in its eyes each day. They will haunt your imagination. They will change your life. And, sonny, you need to change. Since Varadero you've blamed me for your troubles. Well, it's all too damn easy. Take some responsibility!

That's why I've bequeathed my life's work to the kid who's likely as not to piss on my grave. Each day, as chief executive, you'll make decisions with stakes you can taste. You'll make less-bad choices from impossible options and forge your character with each choice you make. Who are you? What do you stand for?

In the end, you'll make yourself under the judgment of a wise madman with fierce red eyes staring at you from an indigo maelstrom. Trust me on this. My nose is never wrong.

Think smart, my son. Fight hard. Grow up. Good luck and much love.

As always,
Dad

PS. I'm watching you.

Junior recrumples the letter and stuffs it back in his jacket pocket. "Kid." "Sonny." No matter how many times he reads it, the words never change. (Dr. Billing hadn't been the least bit sympathetic. "What do you wish he'd written?")

Emily pokes her head in. "Frank Kendal's finally arrived. They're ready to begin."

"Is that a fact?" Junior snaps. "Well I'm not. Tell them to cool their heels. I'm busy."

Emily beams. "That's the spirit! You're just like your father!"

Junior intends a studied delay of perhaps ten minutes. But he's so excited to lay out his vision that Emily's barely out the door before he's running to catch up. Guess what, Dad, his mind jitterbugs, I don't need some damn painting to haunt me into action. I've got plans—PLANS! Free food for the hungry, homes for the homeless, shelters, day cares, clinics, hostels. Are you spinning in your grave, you bastard? I'm giving back every penny you ever stole!

Edgar is hurt and angry. But he is also philosophical. If death teaches nothing else it is that life never works out as planned; a good thing too, for if the living knew the future, they would never be able to survive the present. Edgar understands, therefore, that it is only happy ignorance that permits his Clown Prince to skip insouciantly to the BEI boardroom. For in a few short years, Junior's vision of a New Jerusalem will come undone, and that "damn painting" will ride him to hell and back. That painting—the van Gogh *Self-Portrait*—will brand Junior a madman, pin him at the centre of an international firestorm, and forever bind his fate to that of a cardinal hip-deep in Vatican intrigue and to a teen runaway who channels the spirits of the dead at Mount Pleasant Cemetery.

In short, it will inspire him to create The Phoenix Lottery.

II

The Life
and First
Death of
Lydia Spark

The Spark Papers (1)

One lazy afternoon, several years later, *enfant terrible* Lydia Spark is sprawled on her bed reading entries from her teen diaries.

Dear Pickles,

Life sucks. I'm suspended and I'm grounded and it's not my fault and it isn't fair!

I hate Kim. She is such a suckhole. Everybody thinks she is so cute because she has long blond hair and big blue eyes and instead of writing like any normal person she prints everything with these big fat letters and dots her "*i*"s with a little heart and I mean who does she think she's kidding? Mr. Jeffries, that's who. And Mr. Watson, that's who. And all the other stupid teachers at my stupid school and my parents who should know better.

"Kim is pretty. Kim is smart. Why can't you be like Kim?" Because I'm not a stupid suckhole, that's why. Because I'm just this ugly reject and I don't have any friends because they're all stupid anyway, that's why.

Kim—I'm not even going to call her Kim anymore. I'm just going to call her Suckhole from now on and see how she likes it.

~~Kim~~ Suckhole was my best friend in grade eight. And in grade seven. All the way back to grade two. I even liked her in Bible Camp when she had braces and everybody laughed at her. Only now I have braces and Suckhole won't even talk to me because last summer, right before starting high school, she got boobs and now she's going out with Dave "Studly" Ramsay, who's in grade eleven and on the football team and I'm just a grade nine reject who supposedly doesn't fit with her crowd.

I mean one day I'm her best friend and the next I'm this gearbox who embarrasses her. She said it's okay to talk on the phone but she can't hang out with me in the halls or anything. I figure maybe if I had a cool boyfriend she'd like me better. So I think of all the cool guys I'd like to go out with, and one night we're on the phone because Suckhole needs help with some math homework, and I tell her I think Ricky Saunders is really cute, which is true. But next day, everybody is whispering and pointing at me because it turns out Suckhole went and spread a rumour that I, like, wanted to sleep with Ricky, which is so not true (well only a little true, but I wouldn't).

So all of a sudden I'm supposed to be this big slut and now Suckhole won't even look at me because I have this "reputation." Only she's the reason I have the reputation. And it's so not fair because she was doing IT all summer with her cousin Danny when his family came to visit from Saskatoon. (I don't care what she says, blow jobs do too count!!!) But oh no, because she's Little Miss Teacher's Pet, Little Miss Kiss Ass she gets to act like this goody-goody virgin. And because I'm a reject, I get treated like this big slut. This big slut that everybody can treat like shit and it's all a big joke.

A big joke. Right. Well how would you like it if you came to school and had a bunch of condoms blown up like balloons taped to your locker and shaving cream sprayed all over and a Magic Marker cartoon drawing of yourself naked saying, "Hi. I'm a slut!"??? Yeah. A big joke. Very funny. Ha ha.

I want to cry but I don't. I see Suckhole looking at me looking at my locker. And she's laughing behind her hand. And I turn to her and I say, "Who did this?" And she gives me this smirk and she says, "Gee Lydia, I don't know." And I go, "Yeah, I'll bet you don't know, you stupid ho." And she goes, "Gee Lydia, I guess it takes one to know one."

And I go, "As if," and I push her against the lockers—
I mean hardly even a push, just a little tap—and she starts
screaming her head off like I'm this murderer or something. Mr. Jeffries comes running out of the science lab
yelling, "What's going on?" and Suckhole sobs, "Help!
Help! Make her stop!" All her friends, like Murray, who
does that gross thing with his tongue in math, they're all
crowding around and they're all pointing at me and
saying, "It's Lydia's fault. She just starting beating on her."
(And Murray does his gross tongue thing staring straight
at me when Mr. Jeffries isn't looking.)

Anyways, Mr. Jeffries, he just puts his arm around
Suckhole to comfort her—ever sick, eh, with his clip-on
bowtie and the underarm stains on his shirt and his breath
like scrambled eggs, like no wonder there's supposed to
be a No Touching policy—and he says, "Are you all
right?" Suckhole just whimpers like she's this battered
child or something and her voice goes all trembly and she
says, "She called me a h-h-h-ho," and melts into his
arm—she is such a cocktease—and Mr. Jeffries sends me
to see Vice-Principal Watson.

So I tell Mr. Watson what happened and Mr. Watson
asks Suckhole, "Is that what happened, Kim?" And Suckhole makes her eyes go like these big blue saucers and her
lips go all quivery and she says, "No, sir. She just started
punching me and kicking me and calling me a h-h-h-ho
and I was just trying to study for a French test." And Mr.
Watson hands her a Kleenex and says, "There now, don't
cry. Did you see who defaced Lydia's locker?" And Suckhole—God I hate her more than cramps—Suckhole
sniffles, "No sir. I don't know anyone who would do such
a thing."

I go, "You are such a fucking liar!"

"What did you say, young lady?" Mr. Watson huffs,
his neck all red and puffed up. And I go, "Nothing." But
Mr. Watson suspends me for three days anyway and

phones my parents. Which is so unfair because if he didn't hear me how can he suspend me? And if he did hear me and just pretended he didn't he's a hypocrite.

But even more unfair are my parents. My Mom says, "You hit Kim? She's such a nice girl." A nice girl. Right. Like Satan is nice.

I try telling them what happened and how Suckhole spread rumours and now everybody says I'm a slut and how it's such a big lie. But they don't believe me! My Dad just says, "Where there's smoke, there's fire," whatever that's supposed to mean, and grounds me for three months. Yeah. Three months. I go, "Three months for being called a slut? You don't even get three months for manslaughter." Dad says, "Three months for dragging our good family name through the mud." And Mom starts crying about how it's getting so she and Dad are too ashamed go to their Fellowship Meeting on Sunday afternoons. So I go, "Tell your stupid Fellowship Meeting God doesn't want them judging people." And Dad says, "How dare you take the Lord's name in vain!" So now I'm even blamed for quoting the Bible!!!

Talk about typical, eh? I mean I get blamed for everything. I have maybe one beer at a party and all of a sudden I'm this big alcoholic or something who's out to corrupt the whole school. "But you're only in grade eight!" "Yeah, well I just turned fourteen so get used to it."

Or like last summer, my Mom finds this joint hidden in my old Barbie's Dream House box—which wasn't even mine, I was just hiding it for Suckhole because she wanted to impress Danny and was too chickenshit to keep it at her place. Anyways, my Mom throws a fit and wants to know who my supplier is (ha ha). But I told her off good. I look her straight in the eye and I say, "So what were you doing in my Barbie Dream House box anyways? I mean, hello, there's this new invention, it's called 'Privacy,' you should try it some time." And she goes ballistic and hits me, slaps me right across the face and everything. I go, "You do that again and I'll charge you, bitch," and she starts to cry like I'm this Demon Seed or something. So I go, "What is this? Some kind of guilt trip? Well I could care less. I mean, you started it. Whatever happened to trust, eh?"

Anyways, ever since then they supposedly think they have the right to search my room whenever they like, like I'm this major dope fiend and they're the FBI. As if. "One thing leads to another," my Dad says. Yeah right, whatever.

The worst is, I think they even read you, Pickles. I'm right, aren't I, Mom? You're reading this right now. You want to know if I'm sleeping with Ricky, don't you? Well I'm not.

But keep reading because guess what? I hate you. You are just so stupid. You and your stupid Beauty Parlour set up in the living room and Dad and his stupid insurance office in the basement. I couldn't invite friends over even if I had any. One step inside the door and they'd be gagging with all the hair sprays, perfumes, and that Wildflower Air Freshener shit—I swear I'm gonna come down with brain cancer or something from the fumes. And all that fuchsia chiffon and sheers around the windows that's supposed to make the room look classy, but just make it look like a big whorehouse with hair dryers—I hate this house! I hate this town! I hate this life!

And you think you can solve everything with prayer and Ritalin. Well I guess prayer didn't work, and as for Ritalin—what a joke. I mean I'm suicidal and all you want to do is turn me into a vegetable because some psychologist said it saved families on this "My Baby is a Hell-Child" *Jerry Springer Show*. WELL YOU CAN ALL EAT SHIT AND DIE! SO JUST GET OUT OF MY DIARY NOW!!!

I think I'm going crazy, Pickles. Thank God I have you. You're the only one I can talk to. The only one I can tell my secrets. The only one who'll listen. The only one who loves me. Why did you have to die? I just want to hold you. I just want to pet you. It hasn't been the same since you died.

Mom caught me crying last Easter. She asked what was wrong. So I told her. I told her I missed you. And she just hugged me and said, "That's okay, honey. He's with Jesus. We'll get you another cat." And I just started screaming and throwing things.

I don't want another cat! I want you! I miss you so bad, Pickles. I miss the way you curled up next to me at night. I miss the way you purred in my ear until I fell asleep. I miss the way you licked my fingers to wake me up. I miss everything about you. And you're never coming back. And I'll never have another cat like you. Not ever.

I wish you were alive and everybody else was dead. I do. I really, really do.

Bohemia

"P2, I'm trying to read!" Pickles Two, or P2 for short, has snuck up Lydia's belly, negotiating the crawl space between diary and breasts. Now he crouches, purring, gently kneading the flesh below her throat with his front paws, extending his nose to touch her chin, tickling her neck with his whiskers, and generally demanding attention.

P2 lives to be petted. From his perspective, Lydia lives to pet. It's a happily symbiotic relationship. Mind you, symbiotic is hardly a word which would cross his mind were he blessed with a vocabulary, for P2 is remarkably simple, a roly-poly orange tabby with nary a brain in his head. Sometimes, sitting on Lydia's lap, it occurs to him that a tummy rub is in order, at which impulse he rolls over and off her lap into the air.

He's the only male presence in the house that Lydia shares with Trina, Trixie, and Tibet, three shaved-head retro-punk refugees from Mississauga. His bond with her was immediate. A dead ringer for Pickles One, she found him mewing under the verandah, a six-week-old abandoned kitten. Initially, the household thought he was female, but at nine months he started to spray. "That little fucker deceived us!" Tibet railed. "It's creeping patriarchy! Pissing in the corner! Men are all alike!" She insisted that P2 be dispatched, but Lydia rebelled. Tibet denounced her as a fifth columnist. Peace was eventually restored when Trina proposed they get a vet to fix him.

Lydia puts her diary aside, gives P2 a quick pet—"You are such a little love bunny, yez-u-are!"—and rubs her eyes. Her diaries are voluminous; even as a teenager she was prolific. Her parents complained she was simply wasting her time locked up in her room scribbling endlessly: "If you spent as much time on your homework, you might amount to something." Little did they know that these scribblings would foster a talent which would, in a few short years, turn the lonely teenager into a serious underground performance artist and author.

In fact, Lydia's currently on a roll. Her most recent collection, *Spiritual Descents, Volume Eight*, published in a limited edition chapbook by Featherstone Press, received favourable mention in last week's *Toronto Star*. As well, the gates of academe are opening: a York University undergrad has phoned to interview her for his upcoming paper "Lydia Spark and the Art of Profane Dissent: A Postmodern Deconstruction of Apocalyptic Narrative Discourse in *Spiritual Descents, Volume Four*." And her current venture, "The Making of *Bulimia Sandwich*," a meditation on the creation of her most notorious performance piece, is scheduled for a midnight reading at the Rivoli and publication in *This City*.

Bulimia Sandwich. It was her breakthrough. A work of guerrilla theatre/performance art, *Bulimia Sandwich* challenged the audience to contextualize regurgitation as a political act in response to the excesses of First World consumption. It was not for the faint of heart. Indeed, it cleared food courts in every suburban shopping mall it played. Its final performance, an impromptu affair at Barberian's Steak House, led to Lydia's arrest on charges of assault when the minister of agriculture was sprayed with flying chunks of semi-digested brisket.

The celebrity of Lydia's victim created a whirlwind of publicity. *Saturday Night* weighed in with a piece on artistic expression and social responsibility, singling out *Bulimia Sandwich* as "a witless piece of self-aggrandizement." On the other hand, a professor at the Ontario College of Art defended the work as "difficult, brave and conceptually raw," while *Newsworld*'s "On the Arts" described it as "the most amusing challenge to received authority since Jubal Brown upchucked at the Art Gallery of Ontario."

In the end, the trial was an anti-climax. The judge informed Lydia that neither Brechtian alienation technique nor Grotowskian theory could be considered defences under law. He sentenced her to three months probation. But Lydia didn't care.

The media circus had drawn attention to her work and resulted in a publishing contract with Featherstone Press, not to mention cachet on Queen West.

She smiles at the memory and reaches for a rollie. She gave up tobacco a year ago and now restricts her smoking to home-grown from the basement hydroponic. She strokes P2 and exhales slowly. Homegrown. Home: a rundown first-floor/basement duplex off Toronto's Queen Street West. It's as far from her parents' place in Mitchell as Oz from Kansas. Designed like a rail car, all the rooms open off the right side of a corridor that runs the length of the duplex to a back bathroom. From the front door in order: the living room, her room, Trina's room, and the kitchen next to the bathroom. Downstairs: a low-ceilinged unfinished basement, home to the furnace, a cold room, a rusty metal shower, a drum set, the hydroponic garden, and Trixie and Tibet.

Over time, the foundations of the house have shifted, causing the walls and floors to undulate, so that the once-straight corridor now resembles something out of *The Cabinet of Doctor Caligari*. "That's okay," Trina said when they moved in. "We'll paint the whole thing purple and no one'll notice. It'll be this secret cave. This sanctuary. This womb." So the duplex ended up purple, except for the kitchen, which is black.

If the corridor is a mess, the bathroom is a nightmare. There's a large hole between the claw-footed bathtub and the toilet, through which one can see Trixie and Tibet's futon. This isn't an issue for T 'n' T, at least with respect to privacy, as their sexual acrobatics tend to the exhibitionistic. But it does cause a problem whenever the toilet jams, which is regularly. The other difficulty with the bathroom is the disintegrated light socket. Light is provided by a bare hundred-watt bulb clipped to the toothpaste-encrusted mirror and connected to a socket in the kitchen by a twenty-foot orange extension cord.

Wiring is generally a problem. In winter, the walls are hot to the touch. This unnerves Lydia, as they're insulated with old, crumpled newspapers, a discovery the commune made one night at a party when Tibet took a golf club to the corridor screaming, "I'm suffocating! We gotta go open concept!"

As for the kitchen, it is a curiosity, its floors a complex design of bare boards and chipped linoleum. The taps provide cold water; hot is created in the Goodwill pot on the old gas stove. The fridge, a collector's item on overdrive, pounds like a jackhammer in the middle of the night and frequently freezes its contents: beer and dead pizza.

Beside the fridge stands a brown metal card table with matching folding chairs. Like the rest of the furnishings, these came courtesy of a midnight stroll through the Annex before garbage pickup. "People throw out perfectly good junk!" Trina observes. She's heavily involved in recycling and, as a hobby, makes art from old bicycle tires.

Next to the card table is a large green garbage pail in which Trina has made several unsuccessful attempts at indoor composting. The last attempt ended one night when P2 ran howling from the kitchen in terror. Investigating, Tibet came face to face with a large, appreciative rat. "Pay rent or get the hell out," she yelled, whipping an empty beer bottle at its head.

Finally, on a festive note, the kitchen is decorated with a half-dozen dried fly strips hanging randomly from the ceiling, a gift from tenants past. Nubbly with a multitude of dusty wings and desiccated thoraxes, these strips pay tribute to the biological diversity housed within the duplex. Such diversity is a special treat for P2 who sees large roaches, not to mention small mice, as a steady supply of toys. Though hardly swift, he's often lucky; Lydia has gotten used to discovering little presents deposited on her pillow.

For all its problems, Lydia's world has the singular advantage of punishing her parents. In a moment of stoned insanity, she phoned them a week ago, her first contact since she'd come home at 4 A.M. on her fifteenth birthday to find the doors locked. "Sorry, honey. Your Daddy and I have been praying and we've decided you need a little tough love." "I'll show you tough love," she'd screamed, and hitched a ride to Toronto, never to return.

Her parents were so shocked to hear from her they dropped the receiver. Lydia was afraid they'd gone into seizures, but
they were soon back on the line insisting on driving up to
Toronto for a visit. The following morning they pulled up stiff
as corpses in their Sunday best. In their mind's eye, Lydia was
still a wayward teenager. They imagined it their duty to rescue
her from the cesspool into which she'd sunk. Her phone call
was a cry for help, was it not?

Their plan was simple. They would read aloud, more in
sorrow than in anger, from those shameful diaries she'd left
behind. She would be struck with remorse, a prodigal daughter
fit for a Sunday sermon. They would forgive her, put her in the
back seat, and head home to Mitchell. There, having learned her
lesson in the big city, she would return to the straight and narrow, perhaps giving testimony to the delinquents panhandling
outside The Rose and Crown. Thus redeemed in the sight of
God and man, the family could once more hold its head high,
and there would be rejoicing in Heaven.

But it was not to be. Her father never made it past the curb.
One look at Trixie and Tibet making out on the front porch and
he locked himself in the car, chanting, "I have no daughter. My
daughter is dead. I have no daughter. My daughter is dead."

Her mother was not so easily deterred. A Souwesto Pentecostal, she was determined to greet her wayward daughter in a
spirit of true Christian charity. She made her way to the front
door, her smile as tight as her girdle, nodded primly at the
young women perverting God's plan in broad daylight, and
knocked.

Lydia was prepared. She swung the door open proudly and
stood before her mother in full Haute Goth regalia: black slit
Morticia skirt with black fishnet ruffletop over black satin
waffle bustier, black lace fingerless gloves, black fishnets, and
black patent stilettos. To accessorize, a black satin vampire
cape, black leather belt with silver spider clasp, Hellraiser
Pinhead broach, Black Widow lashes, four-inch green nails,
and a white pageboy wig by Poontang. Her makeup featured

desiccated-purple lipstick (Plague) and purple eye shadow (Asphyxia) by Urban Decay, and Blithe Spirit, a pale blue pancake from Malabar.

"Good afternoon. I'm looking for a Miss Lydia Spark."

"Mom!"

Her mother screamed and fled to the car.

Tibet was offended. "Goth makes her scream? Well polyester makes me puke." Trixie, who had taken a correspondence course in psychology, remained dispassionate. "Now she'll start bawling. Don't get suckered. Tears are a control mechanism."

But there was no time for tears. In seconds her parents had deposited twelve cardboard boxes of diaries on the sidewalk and sped away, babbling in tongues.

Lydia savours the memory. She takes a drag on her joint. The walls are shaking. Downstairs, Trixie and Tibet have been tripping on Ecstacy since Friday and, judging by the non-stop thumping, are going for a world's record. On the other side of the wall, Trina's speakers blast Hole full bore. The upstairs neighbour is banging at the front door and the kids next door are screaming.

Lydia gives P2 a little chin scratch, puts Enya on her headphones, and ploughs through the remaining boxes of diaries before turning to the musty Hilroy exercise books in which she chronicled her first years as a refugee from Mitchell.

The Spark Papers (2)

Pickles,

This is my one-week anniversary of running away and I am so excited and scared and up and down and over and under and inside out I could scream!

First off, I am writing this from my new home in the middle of downtown Toronto! Ryder says it's what the city calls a firetrap and it is so cool! It's called The Strathcona Court Apartments, right near Maple Leaf Gardens!!! There's all these chains and padlocks on the front doors and the windows are all boarded up and it looks totally abandoned, only there's this secret way in at the back.

Maybe twenty or thirty of us kids live here and a bunch more sleep over and nobody knows we're here except for the police and they don't care — Ryder says the city even likes it that we're in these so-called firetraps because tourists don't like seeing kids freezing on the streets. (Tourists! They're just parents on vacation!) Anyways, since kids off the pavement are good for business, Ryder says we probably won't get busted. It'll only happen if there's lots of complaints from the neighbours, but they're too busy worrying about crack houses, so if we keep it down we'll be okay.

There's no electricity or heat, but there's a lot of flashlights and candles, plus blankets and parkas to keep you warm. Also the toilets don't work because there's no water either, so you have to pee in a bucket or go before you get here.

This brings me to the one bad thing. It smells of shit in the hallway which Ryder says is because of this guy who used to live here and was a real pig but who won't be back for awhile because he's in jail. But about the smell, you can't have everything, and it's way better than Mitchell is all I can say.

Ryder—full name Ryder Knight, wicked, eh?—he's the guy who found me this place. He is my new best friend. His real name is Bob and he's from Barrie and he's eighteen and he has cool glasses and is so hot—even hotter than Ricky Saunders except for he has a few pockmarks. Also a nose stud and a nipple ring and a pierced cock—he is just perfect!

We met in this donut shop on Yonge Street the first day I got here. The manager said I had to buy a coffee or he was kicking me out, only I didn't have any money and there was this blizzard outside, and I was so scared I was crying and all of a sudden I hear this guy saying, "Here's a loonie, asshole. Leave her alone," and I look up and there's Ryder.

At first I'm scared. I mean, I think he's a pimp or something, but he just laughs and says no, he doesn't even like girls, he's gay. You heard me, Pickles. He actually says he's gay!!! Right out loud! Just like that! And nobody even looks up! Ever cool. That would never happen in Mitchell! I mean it would be almost worth it to go back home just so I could invite Ryder over for dinner. And I'd get him to shake my Dad's hand and then I'd say, "Hey Dad, guess what, you just got touched by a homosexual." Watch him have a heart attack or something.

So anyways, Ryder and me start to talk and he is, like, amazing. He knows everybody! He even knows this guy at Maple Leaf Gardens who gets him into games for free. Gold seats too—no kidding!!! I asked him if he ever gets lonely and he says no more than he ever was in Barrie. He got kicked out when his Mom found these magazines of guys under his bed. His Mom and my Mom should get together. But he says it all worked out for the best because now he can be himself. I nod and go, "Cool." He smiles and goes "You just hit town, didn't you?" And my cheeks turn all red and I go, "Says who?" He just laughs and asks if I need a place to stay and I start to cry again — which is really embarrassing 'cause I'm trying to impress him.

But he doesn't care — I am so in love — he brings me here, to the Strathcona Court Apartments, and finds me some blankets that aren't too dirty and this mattress nobody's using. It belonged to a Cheryl Somebody, only no one's seen her for a few days and there's this rumour maybe she got murdered because she stole crack off this guy who's all twisted. So, like, maybe I'm sleeping on this dead girl's mattress!!! Only I don't have nightmares or nothing, which I think I would have if she was dead because of I think I'm a bit psychic, you know? That's why I think maybe she's just split to Florida or someplace warm or something. I think that's a lot nicer than thinking I'm sleeping on a dead girl's mattress.

Anyways, I see Ryder every day now. He knows everything. Like where to get clothes and where to get food and where to get money. He gets money by doing it with old guys like my father (GROSS!) but I said I didn't want to do that so he showed me this place where they pay you to hand out flyers and also good places where you can beg and adults will give you money because they feel guilty (or scared, ha ha). I like the place outside Majestic Electronics because they have a million TVs in the window and you can watch them when you get bored.

So all in all I have a place to stay, part-time work, food and new friends! Lucky or what? I can't tell you how scared I was that first day that I'd have to go crawling back home and have my Dad rub my nose in it. I can just picture him all smug and gloaty with my Mom in the background looking serious: "So you're not as grownup as you thought you were, eh, young lady? I guess that means you'll be wanting to say you're sorry. You'll be wanting to show a little respect. You'll be wanting to sign this Rules Contract." (Yeah, and suck your turds while I'm at it! No way, José. I'd rather eat glass.) But Ha Ha Ha, now I don't have to. Because I showed them! One week out of Mitchell and I have it made!

There's just one thing makes me sad. Last night I'm cold and I snuggle up to Ryder to keep warm. It's so romantic and he smells so good and I think he's sleeping so I try to put my hands inside his jeans. And he stops me, real gentle and whispers, "Come on, Lydia, I told you I'm not interested." So I ask him, "How come all the cool guys are gay?' and he just laughs and says, "That's what girls always say."

All I know is, if he was straight I would want his baby.

Pickles,

Ryder is gone. I don't know what's happened to him. He may even be dead. I mean really dead. I'm scared.

Sometimes he gets beat up. But last night was the worst. He's minding his own business, just standing there waiting for tricks, when they jumped out of a van, six of them with chains and bats. They called him fag and AIDS-fucker and smashed his head on the sidewalk. And no-body did nothing. Nothing. Didn't even get a license plate number.

I'm down the street panhandling. By the time I get to him, he's slumped against this wall not seeing so good. I take him to emergency. He's bleeding all over. And every-one stares. And I say, "What are you looking at?" And they move way back all disgusted. And I hold him. And the nurses come over and they have these rubber gloves on like he's this disease, this piece of dog shit. And he is the nicest guy in the world.

At home, in bed, he just turns to the wall. He pre-tends he's sleeping. I whisper, "Ryder, it's okay. I'm here."

And he turns to me and his beautiful face is all swollen and I can't even see his eyes. But the worst part is he's crying. He's just crying and crying and he can't stop. And he says, "I can't take it anymore, Lydia. I can't."

And I rock him and rock him and finally he falls asleep. You know, I think Ryder is so strong, but when he's asleep he looks so fragile I think he'll break, just from me looking at him. He never sleeps peaceful. I mean, sometimes he just twitches all night. I think it's dreams, but I can't wake him.

Anyways, next time I open my eyes he's gone and there's a note. It says, "I love you Lydia. Be good. Ryder." No one's ever said they loved me before. Not and meant it.

That was this morning. And he hasn't come back. And it's been all day. And I don't know where he is. I mean sometimes he takes off, doesn't come back for a day or two, I know that. But this is different. I have this feeling. This psychic feeling that something is different this time.

I check the donut shop, The Steps, The Spa, Covenant House, S.O.S., Burger King—nothing. I call hospitals, the morgue—nothing. I call the cop shop—nothing. And I can't call his folks, so I don't know what to do. It's like he vanished.

The cops, they don't care. They won't even fill out a Missing Person report for forty-eight hours. Forty-eight hours! That's a lifetime! I'll call back then, but it won't matter. They won't do anything . No way. Not for a hustler. They'll just think he's off with some trick. What do they know?

Well I know. I know something's happened to him. I know I'll never see Ryder again.

I want to die.

Doppelgänger

Lydia wipes her eyes. It's been almost twelve years since she wrote that entry, but for a moment she's that lonely, scared kid of fifteen. She butts her joint and sits very still. P2 looks up at her solemnly, then nuzzles his head under her hand. She scratches his ear absently.

Ryder Knight. Her first true love. Her eyes wander to her bookshelf with its eight volumes of *Spiritual Descents*. They are his legacy, a testament to his influence on her life. Ryder's disappearance had been a catalyst, unleashing a torrent of literary creativity. The writing that initially emerged, though therapeutic, had been largely embarrassing. Morbid teen poetry about love doomed, unrequited and/or dead. But, in time, Lydia had drawn purpose from her endeavours, recognizing in them an opportunity to construct something memorable with her life. She discovered her calling: to be an artist.

Her creative process was simple. She'd wander through Mount Pleasant Cemetery until she found herself drawn to a particular tombstone. Having selected the plot—or having been selected by it—she would lie over the grave and meditate, allowing her mind to channel for the spirit of the departed who lay beneath. Whether the prose poems which resulted from this channelling were produced by psychic connection or pharmaceutical ingestion, they were invariably vivid. Lydia would subsequently recite these prose poems at the St. Lawrence Market, earning spare change from her performances and, on occasion, five dollars apiece for the original manuscripts that came complete with brass rubbings of the stones that inspired them. Eventually, the texts were collated and became the first of her *Spiritual Descents*.

It was in the course of one such performance that she met the Three Ts. Money was tight, audiences unappreciative, and in mid-recitation she had been confronted by a forty-something taxpayer. "Get a job," he spat and Lydia morphed into a madwoman.

"I have a job, you asshole! I'm an artist!" she raved. "I'm not some Scarberian fascist in plaid, some life-sucking, bottom-feeder bleeding the poor, some dildo up Lord Tubby's butt! I'm an artist! A human being! I have a heart! A brain!" She free-formed a full ten minutes, at which point she short-circuited into a mass of nerve ends twitching on the pavement.

A small crowd had formed, the Three Ts front and centre. "Great act!" said Tibet.

"That's no act! That's my life!"

They were instant soulmates. She'd moved in with them that night and never looked back.

As for Ryder, her intuition had been correct. She'd never seen him again. She had, however, seen his Doppelgänger.

She remembers the first sighting perfectly. It was early in the new millennium. Like most days, she was spending time in Mount Pleasant seeking inspiration. The tombstone of Sarah Jeanette McCutcheon, wife of Hamilton Ambrose McCutcheon, Gone But Not Forgotten, had called to her. If her voice from beyond was to be believed, Sara Jeanette McCutcheon was a Victorian bluestocking who lived a secret life of unbridled depravity.

Lydia had been startled from her reverie by an astonishing cavalcade. Police, both mounted and on motorcycle, countless limousines, crowds in Armani and Dior, faces she recognized from TV, including the premier, had descended on a plot not two hundred yards away. This was an interment fit for a king. The only thing missing was an immediate family. Lydia wandered over.

"Who died?" she asked one officer.

"Edgar Beamish."

"The booze guy?"

"That's the one."

"About time."

Upset that her artistic pursuits had been disrupted by a dead suit, she considered leaving, but decided that a social event of this magnitude was a must-see. She stood on the stone of the depraved dowager to observe the festivities. And then she saw him. Ryder. Or someone who looked like Ryder, only manicured, with close-cropped hair and wearing a navy Nehru jacket. She couldn't believe her eyes, but the pockmarks and wild plastic glasses were unmistakable.

"Ryder, Ryder," she cried, jumping up and down on the stone, waving, but the mourners had begun to disperse, she was too far away, there were too many people, and he didn't hear. She ran through the thinning crowd. Spotted his jacket. "Ryder! Ryder!" He kept walking. "Ryder Knight!" Surely he'd heard. "It's me! Lydia!" She reached him, grabbed his elbow. He turned. He knew her. She saw it in his eyes.

"Ryder! What are you doing here? What happened to you?"

"Bob, do you know this person?" Ryder's companions, a woman and a giant slug, advanced.

"I've never seen her before in my life."

"It's me! Lydia!"

"This young man is my personal assistant. I will thank you to leave us alone," bristled Rudyard Gardenia, puffed up like a blowfish.

"I thought you were dead," she cried, as Ryder averted his eyes.

"Come along, Bob." Rudyard raised a chin and security descended. Bob turned and quickly followed the couple. He didn't look back.

Lydia called after him: "Bob! Bob from Barrie Bob! Your mother found pictures! You worked the Hill! Don't you dare say you don't know me! I loved you, you sonovabitch! Don't you dare walk away! I'm going to be a star! A star! Just wait! And then we'll see who walks away, you bastard!"

Within weeks came *Bulimia Sandwich*, she was a recognized *enfant terrible*, and they had met again. She was in the window seat at the Queen Mother having pad Thai. He saw her from another table and came over, an awkward tangle of embarrassment and guilt.

"May I sit down?" he hesitated.

Pause. "Do I know you?"

"Come on, Lydia."

Lydia sucked on a shrimp. "Suit yourself . . . *Bob*."

For the next ten minutes, Lydia stared out the window with cold disinterest as Bob poured out his heart. Rudyard had been a regular. He'd offered him a position as private secretary with an income and room and board in exchange for exclusive rights. Bob had refused. And then that final attack. "I couldn't take it anymore. I didn't know what else to do."

"You could have at least said goodbye."

"I didn't want to be followed. I wanted it all to go away."

"I loved you."

"I'm sorry."

Lydia twirled a noodle. "So what's it like being the pigman's butt-boy?"

"That isn't fair."

"Oh?" Pause. "So I take it you love him?"

"I meet interesting people, I have a nice place to stay, I don't get beat up."

"So you're still a whore." Bob opened his mouth, but she cut him short. "No, that's okay, you don't have to defend yourself. I can respect a guy who's making a living. I just can't respect a guy who cuts out on his friends."

Bob stared at the floor. He said, quietly, "Lydia, I don't even have grade ten."

"Yeah, well who does?" Lydia rose. She looked at her empty plate. "Put it on Daddy's tab," she said and walked out.

Memories. They're flooding back, each leading to other memories, other emotions. It's like a recurring dream Lydia has of entering an endless series of rooms opening randomly from one to another. She moves through each, uncertain of what lies ahead, knowing only that she's being drawn inexorably, irresistibly forward.

Why this sudden urge to draw together her past? And why today? Is there something in the wind, the air, the stars, compelling her to take stock before moving on? Something heralding a new beginning? Or is it just the dope?

Enough. Lydia gets up, stretches, and makes her way to the front door. She checks the mailbox. Instead of bills, she finds a brown manila envelope. She grabs it, drops to her knees, rips it open, and reads as if her future depended on it. It does. She shrieks with joy. Her life is about to change forever.

But little does she know how much. The letter in her hand is about to set in motion a chain of events that will confront her with the deranged mother of an illegitimate cardinal, thrust her into an imbroglio between Junior Beamish and the pope, rock the history of Western art, and lead to her own death and resurrection.

The letter comes from the Canada Council.

One-Eye Jack

The Council has approved Lydia's grant proposal. As she wrote in her application: "My vision is a one-year voyage of discovery during which time I will apply my working method to graves across the country. In the course of this exploration, I will commune with Canada's saints, rogues, explorers, and curiosities. The result, *Spiritual Descents, Volume Nine*, will be a cross-cultural collection of prose poems, a portrait of our nation's soul as defined by the celebrations and laments of its leading dead."

Lydia is hurt by the initial reaction of the Three Ts. There are no congratulations. Instead, Trina's first question is whether Lydia intends to continue paying rent. Trixie makes it clear that if she's planning a sublet, they have a right of veto. Tibet sums up the group's response: "Grant-whore!" But if Lydia is hurt, she isn't surprised. She knows that to be an artist in Canada is to suffer death by a thousand cuts, not all of them governmental. "Being in the arts is like living in a blender." In such a world, it is incumbent on those guilty of good luck to be apologetic. They should not, like Lydia, jump up and down on their verandahs screaming, "Yahoo! I'm gettin' out of this hole!"

Still, Lydia can be excused. The knowledge that her twenties are slipping away fills her with panic. She has dreams in which she is trapped in the top half of an hourglass, but no matter how hard she struggles she runs out of time and slips down the vortex of sand, disappearing forever.

This might not bother her if, in her own mind, she had truly made it. Although she's been published, and enjoyed some academic interest, the cover of *NOW*, and a small circle of acolytes, she is far from fulfilling her secret revenge fantasy. In this fantasy, she returns to Mitchell as famous as Margaret Atwood—even the pastor at Gospel Tabernacle has heard of her—her folks beg her forgiveness, and everyone else eats shit.

She pictures it vividly. A big Mitchell District High School reunion with banners and bunting. The whole town has turned out. And after the goofs have had a few hours to talk over old times and Mr. Watson has told Murray how his car wash is "Aces!" and hasn't Murray come a long way since he used to get kicked out of class for doing that tongue thing, in she strides, a former grade nine dropout and the only one who's made a name for herself outside Perth County. There are suitably awed whispers; Lydia surveys the crowd, supremely confident and unimpressed.

Her gaze fixes upon the hapless Suckhole, now considerably puffed up after six—no, better yet eight—kids in fifteen sordid years of marriage to Dave Ramsay. They had to get married in Dave's graduating year because Suckhole always did have a hard time applying advanced math skills, such as counting—*as in counting up the days since your last period, you stupid bitch.* But we mustn't be petty because Dave is no longer Mr. Studly in grade eleven on the high-school football team. Instead, he's bald with a beer paunch, laid off from his job at Canadian Tire in Stratford, and the crack of his ass shows when he bends over.

Lydia imagines herself floating over to Suckhole, who doesn't know if she should cower or go all gooey now that Lydia is such a success. "Why Kim—is that you?" Lydia coos. "That weight looks so good on you. How's Danny?" Turning to Dave she says sweetly, "You've met Kim's cousin, Danny? You know I really admire you. It takes real love to raise another man's child." Seeing Mr. Jeffries, she calls out, "Why Patrick, so good to see you. I was afraid some former student would have had you locked up by now."

Lydia's fantasy may be small-minded, but it has helped her survive many a depression. Still, she knows that if she was to attend a high-school reunion tomorrow all she'd get would be Mr. Watson saying, "Why Lydia, are you the one who threw up on the minister of agriculture? I certainly hope you're not planning on throwing up on anyone today. Ha ha."

This grant, however, has the potential to change all that. It gives her the chance to do something memorable, to become the poet of the nation's soul! Of course it's a long shot. But every long shot is home to possibilities, and at this stage in her life, each possibility may be her last.

So Lydia puts her diaries in boxes and stores them in the basement; the Three Ts have kindly relented and agreed to keep them for the year. That done, she packs her pens, pencils, paper, and P2, and sets off on the writing adventure of a lifetime.

Lydia's first port of call is Masset, at the north end of the Queen Charlottes. Here, she communes with a seventeenth-century Inuit, OD'd hippies, and a drunken Scot who carved faces in the corks of local fishing nets before drowning mid-bender one tragic high tide. Then on to Victoria and a chat with dead maiden aunts, Canadian born and bred with English accents, who pined for Mother Country over high tea at the Empress. From there to Spuzum, Hope, and Vancouver, and off to Alberta, "Bible Bill" Aberhardt and a T-Rex.

In the Saskatchewan badlands, she falls in love with Edouard Beaupré, the sweet, doomed Willow Bunch giant. A turn-of-the-century French Catholic, Beaupré toured with Barnum and Bailey. On his death, the circus had him stuffed and put on public display. When his body no longer made money, it was unceremoniously dumped, ending up at l'Université de Montréal. It was not until 1991 that he was finally cremated and returned to his home to rest in peace. From Willow Bunch on to other towns whose names tell a tale: Old Wives Lake, Moose Jaw, White Bear, Matador, Rosetown, Outlook, and then to Prince Albert, where a terrifying encounter with John Diefenbaker gives her nightmares for weeks.

And on it goes, a six-month odyssey of cheap hotels with bad lighting, worse odours, and unspeakable food. She keeps beer cold in the back of the toilet, as trips to the downstairs bar/pool hall are an invitation to trouble for a female stranger in black fishnets and cape. It's a lonely period, but a productive one, charged with creativity: whenever she's down, it takes no more than a snort or a toke to make all things seem possible.

Lydia has just checked into The Hotel Fort Chimo at Ungava Bay in far northern Quebec. The hotel boasts a Laundromat, barber shop, restaurant, cigar store, and bar on the first floor. Its amenities, however, do not include gracious accommodation. Catering to rich American businessmen up for a week's hunting and fishing, the rooms are designed for city boys who like to think they're roughing it. Lydia finds hers frightening: a spare affair with dull lavender floral-print wallpaper and indoor-outdoor carpeting. The TV, which carries CNN, the Weather Network and a channel featuring twenty-four hour reruns of *The Red Peters Fishing Show*, is on the fritz. So is the pink ceramic lamp on her night table, with its dusty cardboard lampshade.

Lydia puts her six-pack in the toilet tank—which is orange with rust stains—sits on the edge of the bathtub, stares at the bleak pattern of black and white tiles, and weeps. No matter how far she travels, she might as well be back at her Queen West duplex. Suddenly claustrophobic, she's overwhelmed with the need to flee. In a flash she inhales a joint, grabs a duffle bag of dirty clothes plus the complimentary hotel magazine from the chest of drawers, and goes downstairs to do her laundry.

Lydia loves being stoned in Laundromats. There are so many weird people to watch, and the patterns of colours tumbling in rows of dryers are endlessly fascinating. What grabs her attention today is the hotel magazine. The front cover, a red masthead proclaiming *Fort Chimo, Gateway to the North* superimposed on a garish blue photograph of an iceberg in the bay, promises endless visual delights. Flipping through, she comes across a feature article on the Franklin expedition captioned: "They Feasted on the Dead." Lydia is rivetted. The section quotes the *Toronto Globe* of Monday, 23 October 1854: "From the Esquimaux, Rae's search party obtained certain information of the fate of Sir John Franklin's party, who had been starved to death after the loss of their ships which were crushed in the ice, and while making their way south to the Great Fish River, died, leaving accounts of their sufferings in the mutilated corpses of some who had evidently furnished food for their unfortunate companions."

Returning to the top of the article, Lydia reads how Franklin and a well-equipped crew of 129 seamen set out in search of the Northwest Passage. They sailed up the east coast of Baffin Island, then west through Lancaster Sound to tiny Beechey Island where, one by one, they began to die. Lead poisoning from solder in the tins of their canned meat provisions killed some, botulism others. Turning south along the west coast of the Boothia Peninsula, those that survived poisoning were trapped at King William Island when the yearly ice pack swept down McClintock Channel, crushing their boats, the *Erebus* and the *Terror*, leaving them stranded in the Arctic Circle. Here they succumbed to scurvy, cannibalism, madness, and death.

Lydia sits slack-jawed, her imagination firing. Suddenly possessed, she scribbles the note, "Artist seeks ride to trace the final voyage of the Franklin expedition with stopover at Beechey Island. Please contact Lydia Spark, care of the hotel desk by June 5," and tacks it to the community bulletin board. No sooner has she returned to her room than reception calls to say that a Mister Jack McBean, a.k.a. One-Eye Jack, is waiting for her in the hotel bar.

One-Eye is a wiry demon of five-foot-six and indeterminate age who lives on tequila, beer, and pretzels. His face is as wizened as a dried apple, and his five teeth as brown. A jagged white scar bisects his head on a diagonal. Depending on which rumour you choose to believe, the scar is the result of a tangle with a bear in a back alley or a beer bottle in a bar fight with Maude "Tomcat" McTavish. In either case, it crosses what would have been his right eye. The glass eye which replaces it is worn at a jaunty angle, generally peering up and out. He won the eye in a poker game, and it's not only the wrong colour, but slightly oversized as well. Consequently, his right eyebrow is permanently cocked, the eyelid permanently open. Who cares, it's an eye, and One-Eye spoils for a fight with anyone who stares.

One-Eye lives ten minutes from town by Ski-Doo at Right-Cold-By-Gar, a hamlet of eight families of cousins all descended from Hamish McBean, the deranged Newfoundland trapper who founded the settlement six generations past. The McBean clan are proud owners of a Twin Otter used to take tourists for a spin, transport hunters to remote lodges, and drop off supplies to isolated communities throughout the north. It's an ancient beast with a right-wing flap secured by what appear to be clothes hangers. Nonetheless, it flies, and at bargain rates.

The bartender points Lydia to One-Eye's table. As she approaches, she's overwhelmed by the stench of body odour and dried urine, but mostly she's transfixed by his eye, its blue pupil staring blankly at the ceiling.

"What are you staring at?" he growls.

"What are *you* staring at?" she counters.

A dangerous silence, then One-Eye lets out a peel of laughter. "Buy me a beer, girlie. You smell some nice."

Two hours later they're the best of friends. One-Eye even pulls the party trick he reserves for poker games. Excusing himself to go to the washroom—"Time out fer a leak"—he pops his eye and sets it in the spare ashtray facing Lydia. "Can't keep my eye off ya, girlie!" During poker games, the eye is set on his cards; One-Eye never has to worry about cheaters.

As it happens, One-Eye is planning a supply run in two days up to his sister's place at Mercy Inlet, on the north shore of Baffin Island. From there, Beechey's a hop, skip, and a jump. His sister runs The Mercy Inlet Diner. One-Eye lets it drop he's flying up extra provisions on account of she's expecting overflow crowds, what with the papal visit and all. Maybe the pope'll be worth a look-see? He's sure his sister'll put 'em up in sleeping bags on the floor.

Lydia, who's been stoned the past few weeks, hasn't a clue what he's talking about. One-Eye explodes. "You folks from outside, you think the pope only has time for Toronto? Jesus-Teakettle-Christ, girlie, get a life."

As One-Eye explains, the whole deal's as natural as a morning piss. The previous pope, John-Paul II visited remote outposts like Canada's Tuktoyaktuk. Now his successor, Innocent XIV, is picking up where he left off. Innocent's already plopped his butt down in Malaya and Madagascar, and now this here northern swing's takin' him to Baffin Island, Greenland, Iceland, and Scandinavia.

"There'll be thousands flyin' to Mercy Inlet from all over Nunavut, Québec, Labrador, even over the North Pole from Russia. 'Sides, the pope an' Mercy go together like Jack an' Jill or ham an' eggs. Wanna hear a true story? They call it Mercy Inlet on account of the poor buggers what got frozed over there one winter while out lookin' fer that Franklin fella. By the spring there was only one of 'em left alive. They found him crazy as a coot, chewin' on a dead mate's thighbone screamin', "Mercy! Mercy!" So now it's called Mercy Inlet. Fancy that, eh? If it'd bin me they found, why, today they'd be callin' it Pass-The-Salt Inlet." One-Eye lets loose a raucous cackle, an exertion that brings on a cough, dislodging a thick wad of brown phlegm which he horks into an empty draft glass.

"Wow, talk about a trip!" Lydia whoops. "Have I lucked out or what?" She jumps up and kisses the bush pilot on the forehead.

One-Eye promptly springs a woody and announces that Lydia can come for free; says he reckons she'll make good company, "specially bein' as how yer the first female from outside to come within ten feet a' me in a bear's age." What One-Eye would blush to admit is that a three-day outing with Lydia will count as the most romantic interlude in his life, excepting his twice yearly run-ins with Maude at the Kandy Kane.

And so, early morning two days later, Lydia prepares to take flight into the land of the midnight sun.

Over the Rainbow

Lydia brings a knapsack with a change of clothes, paper and pencils for channelling at Beechey Island, and the previous day's *USA Today* in case she gets bored. Naturally, P2 is along for the ride, his lined Kitty Carrying Case strapped securely to Lydia's seat in easy reach of an ear scratch. Over the course of the past seven months he's become an excellent traveller; all Lydia has to do is glance his way and he turns into a purr machine.

Lydia is still recovering from her night at the bar, but One-Eye is in fine fettle. "Hair of the dog that bit ya?" he asks, cheerily proffering a mickey of tequila. Lydia turns green.

They take off into thick fog, which doesn't appear to bother One-Eye, who assures her things'll be Jim Dandy in a dog's breath. Moments later, they've flown through the soup and Lydia relaxes. Seen from above, the fog is transformed into a massive white eiderdown. By the time they cross Cape Hope's Advance, at the mouth of the bay, the eiderdown disappears and Lydia is staggered by the crystalline beauty of the open water. Icebergs, from growlers to bergy bits, dot the speckled waves like delicate meringues. She stares from the plane, watching the shadow of the Otter, relaxing in the steady vibration of its engines.

One-Eye is smitten. Lydia in her black parka, black Gortex leggings, double black mittens, and Asphyxia eye shadow is a vision of loveliness, a vision which grows lovelier with each swig of tequila. A quick lunch and a refuel at Frobisher fan the flames of his new-found passion. A further five hours, by Kangeeak Peak, and One-Eye is blind, whether from love or tequila it's hard to tell. Past Ekalugad Fjord, he's a husky in heat. Time for some serious courting. Without warning, he pulls a double loop-the-loop.

"AAAAAAAAA!!!!!!!!!!"

"YEE-HAW!"

"JESUS CHRIST, ARE YOU TRYING TO KILL US?"

One-Eye mistakes Lydia's misgivings for flirtation. That filly there's mine fer the takin', by gar, he winks to himself. A couple mor'a them twisters 'n' more'n them Northern Lights'll be dancin', that's fer dam sure. He takes a deep swig of tequila, banks to the right, and cuts the engines. The plane slices out of the sky.

"YABBA-DABBA-DO!"

Lydia screams. One-Eye laughs, revs the engines, and makes a steep ascent. This'll be the mother of all loop-the-loops. Upside down, spinning over, hurtling towards earth and then — One-Eye pulls up sharply, rebalancing the plane.

"YA-HOO! MOUNTAIN DEW!" he yodels. And then a funny thing happens. A searing pain shoots up his arm and socks him smack in the chest. He grips the controls and jerks backwards, sending the Otter straight up.

"STOP IT!" Lydia cries. The Otter is vertical and rising fast. One-Eye's head jerks toward her, his face a bewildered grimace. His left eye bulges, but his right — it pops right out and plummets to the back of the plane. He doesn't react.

"Christ on a pogo stick," yelps Lydia. "The bugger's dead!"

She scrambles over the body — pries its locked fingers from the controls as the plane flips upside down. Gravity calls and One-Eye drops to the ceiling. The plane goes into free-fall. One-Eye flops to the rear, dislodging the barely secured cargo, then tumbles like a drunk, ass over teakettle, onto the passenger seat by Lydia's side.

The cargo — crates of Coke, Oreos, and canned ham — smashes about the craft, spraying contents like shrapnel. A double corkscrew. For a moment Lydia gains control, but a series of air pockets buffet the craft. It's a bareback bronco ride at two-thousand feet. One-Eye appears to dance the merengue.

Below to the left, a sheer-blue glacier juts through a low cloud, calving bergs to open water. Below to the right, three whales cavort, blow-holes spouting.

"Hold onto your tail, P2," she cries. "We're in for one hell-uva landing."

Luck is with them. They hit thin ice over water. It collapses beneath them, but not before lending a cushion and a bounce. A second bounce. A third. A fourth. A fifth. The engine cuts out. They roll to a stop. The front of the plane kisses the edge of the fjord, but the tail is suspended on broken ice. Smoke billows from the underbelly. Lydia fears an explosion, but the ice separates and the tail sinks slowly, extinguishing the flames. It comes to rest in six feet of water.

Lydia sits stunned. She checks P2's cage. He hisses but is otherwise okay. She tries to collect her thoughts. The radio. She needs to call out on the radio. It's dead. Flares. Where are the flares? Under debris in the submerged tail. Maps. What's the point? Where's there to walk to?

She is suddenly aware of the monumental silence, all the more awesome for the periodic crackle of white thunder as icebergs tear free of the distant glacial tongues. Lydia cries out. Her voice is a cannon, but the silence swallows it whole. A slice of wind whistles under the left propeller and vanishes into the void.

Lydia is too frightened to cry, terrified she has exchanged a sudden death for a slow one. She takes P2 and tucks him inside her parka, next to her heart. "This happens to other people. It's not supposed to happen to me. It's just a dream. If it isn't, I'll be rescued. I just have to hold on."

She decides to read, anything to distract her until help comes. Rolling One-Eye to one side, she reaches under her former seat, retrieves her knapsack, and pulls out *USA Today*. It's the first paper she's read in a month. She scans the headlines.

"Congress Gridlocked." Who cares?

"Pope En Route to Baffin Island." Old news.

"Canadian Sparks International Outrage." Pardon?

It turns out the provocateur is none other than Edgar Beamish Junior. Since taking over his father's company a few years back, E. B. Junior has gained attention as an eccentric philanthropist, but thus far not as a maniac. Now all bets are off.

Lydia reads that Junior has hatched something called The Phoenix Lottery, a scheme that offers its winner instant fame and fortune. Fame by taking a blowtorch to a prized van Gogh self-portrait at an event beamed live to stadiums and Pay-TV hookups around the globe. Fortune by selling the story to tabloids, TV, and Hollywood. Apparently, Junior intends to reap untold wealth peddling lottery tickets, auctioning international broadcast rights, and hawking commemorative jewellry, coin sets, plates, and other collectibles via the planet's dizzying array of Home Shopping channels. Secondary merchandise featuring images of the doomed work on such items as T-shirts, posters, placemats, and coffee mugs will be licensed and available from novelty boutiques and his new event website, phoenix.com. The latter will also market lottery tickets electronically, and feature an interactive for-pay chat room where subscribers will be kept abreast of all backstage developments leading up to the immolation. The paper quotes Junior thus: "If I sell this painting, I make sixty mill, max, but burn the sucker, the sky's the limit."

Lydia giggles. It must be a put-on. Still, her imagination is fired with thoughts of herself igniting the blaze. She'd be bigger than Atwood and then some.

Reading on, she learns that each entrant will receive an official receipt embossed on high quality vellum, suitable for framing. Why, that could come in handy, maybe cover one of those holes in her wall.

Lydia flips through the rest of the paper, a dance in the limelight lighting her dreams. She turns to the back. It's a full-page ad for the lottery, with a special cut-out entry form in the top left-hand corner. This is one major practical joke. She tears out the form, folds it and puts it in her pocket.

"I'll enter as soon as I get to a mailbox," she jokes to One-Eye. He leers back, glass eye gone, good eye glassy. Reality packs a wallop. Hope, merriment, and distraction are knocked from her head. Who is she kidding? There won't be a lottery. There won't be a mailbox. At least not for her. She's going to die.

"Damnit, it's not fair! I'm working on a Canada Council grant!" An hour later, her feet are numb. She is quite calm now. It occurs to her she should write a few goodbyes. She gets paper and a pencil from her duffel bag. She thinks a moment and makes the following last will and testament.

> To Whom It May Concern:
>
> My name is Lydia Spark. The rest of my belongings are at the Fort Chimo Hotel. In my duffle bag is a large manila envelope filled with notes, sketches, and prose poems. Please send these to my editor, Mr. Bruce Jamieson at Featherstone Press, Markham, Ontario.
>
> Bruce, please use any royalties to pay for my cremation at The Simple Alternative. I want to be incinerated with P2. Scatter our ashes in Mount Pleasant Cemetery. Do not return to Mitchell!!!
>
> It's getting too cold to write, so just a few personal notes.
>
> To Ryder Knight, a.k.a. Bob—I'm sorry I hurt you. You were my first love, you know.
>
> To Trina, Trixie and Tibet—I'll miss you guys. Please hold on to my diaries in case I ever get really famous.
>
> To Mom and Dad especially—Sorry things didn't work out. I really wish you could have been proud of me.
>
> I keep thinking of that song grampa used to sing: "We'll meet again, don't know where, don't know when, but I know we'll meet again some sunny day."
>
> > Till then,
> > Lydia

Lydia tucks the note in her parka pocket, next to the lottery form, where the doctor or the mortician will be sure to find it. She is wearing clean underwear: her mother will be relieved. All the angry speeches she has practised for the ultimate confrontation with her naysayers are gone. Her rage doesn't matter anymore; in its place she finds serenity. Why couldn't she have felt that before?

P2 is purring inside her parka. Poor P2. He won't understand what's about to happen. She wishes she could explain so he won't think she's abandoned him. She hopes he won't panic.

Her mind begins to drift like the snow. She idly observes the roots of rock gnarling out of the ice along the shore, stone fingers clawing free from their frozen tomb. She thinks she'd like a closer look and finds them effortlessly drawing toward her. Can rock move? Is it alive?

Puzzled, she turns in slow motion and finds herself observing the half-submerged Otter from a distance of twenty yards. She is outside. How did I get here? she wonders. Am I dreaming? Yes, that must be it, because I seem to be able to fly.

She floats back to the plane and peers in through the window. Inside there is a young woman in a black parka, very much like herself, who appears to be sleeping. The round head of an orange tabby, a carrot muffin with eyes, wriggles through the open neck of the parka. Gently, he kneads the flesh below the young woman's throat with his front paws, extends his nose to touch her chin, tickles her neck with his whiskers to wake her up for a wee pet. This has always worked in the past. But not today. Today the young woman is sleeping too soundly. The cat looks perplexed.

P2, it's okay. I'm just having an out-of-body experience. Don't worry. I'll be back inside in a sec. But P2 doesn't hear her. Instead, he burrows back into his warm cocoon inside the parka.

Lydia, bemused, realizes she can't seem to get back inside the Otter, but is not in the least concerned. The ability to float agrees with her and she decides to see what the Otter looks like from above. She floats ten, fifteen feet above the craft and hovers.

Behind the plane, stretching back several hundred yards, she notices five holes in the ice where the plane bounced on landing. The right wing is separated from the craft and rests in the crust of a large drift some distance from shore. It must have snapped off on the fourth bounce. Circular gouges in the ice immediately behind the plane suggest the Otter spun a few times before stopping. Strange, she doesn't remember that. Maybe she'd closed her eyes on impact. Ah well, it doesn't matter.

Lydia floats higher. My God, it's beautiful, she thinks. To the northwest, she sees a ridge of mountains, rugged beyond measure, a blinding glare firing from the sheer cliff walls. And to the southwest—it looks like two dog teams racing towards the plane. Miles in the distance, they are very tiny, like miniature curiosities in a Victorian flea circus. Those fleas are well-trained, she marvels. If only P2 could have had parasites like that! What fun we could have had. I'd have made little ballerina costumes and had them perform *Swan Lake*. Oh well, no matter.

What matters is the extraordinarily clear light forming around her. Little shimmers in the air that crystallize, twinkling the colours of the rainbow, pure light as seen by a pointillist. And now it liquefies, and she is breathing, drifting in its smooth currents. I'm in a funnel, she observes, as the light assumes a form. A funnel, and I'm being drawn up through miles of warm, shimmering Jell-O. She has a moment of stoned clarity: "I'm in a birth canal stretching up miles and miles and miles and . . .

In the distance, high above, she sees shapes waving at her in slow-motion, waving in waves of liquid light. Drawing near, she sees their forms, translucent, clear—the spirits that she wrote about, though not at all as she once imagined them. First is Edouard Beaupré, the Willow Bunch giant, with his large, gentle, lopsided face. He scoops her up in his big hands, high above his head. She floats there on a cushion of air, quite secure, as he slides the cushion from spirit to welcoming spirit. "I'm in an otherworldly mosh pit," she marvels.

She swims toward more smiling faces—she thinks she knows them too—ah yes, Betty Two-Shoes who died of smoke inhalation when the Strathcona burned down a year after she left, and Reggie who died of AIDS at age twenty, and Geordie from Mitchell who was killed in a motorbike accident after a drunken school dance and—oh my goodness—family too—

grandparents and other relatives who have passed before, recognizable from old family albums.

And then, through the crowd of hosts scampers—could it be?—Pickles, good old Pickles, her bestest friend in the world. He leaps into her arms, licks her fingers, and nuzzles her ear. "Pickles," she weeps. "I knew I'd see you again! I knew you'd be waiting for me when I crossed over!"

Thus it came to pass that Lydia Spark died for the first time.

III

The Cardinal
and
His Mother

Sic Transit Gloria Mundi

When The Phoenix Lottery was first announced at a hastily arranged press conference, word had it that Edgar Beamish Jr. was simply grandstanding. His few years at the helm of BEI had seen the company attending more to good works than bottom lines, and it was thought his scheme to torch a van Gogh was no more than a cheap publicity ploy designed either to distract attention from such mismanagement or to promote interest in his charitable hobbies.

However, when E.B. Junior began publishing lottery forms in the world's leading dailies, the laughter stopped. Surely this was taking the joke one step too far. Or were the rumours true—had Junior gone mad? The chattering classes went into overdrive when the cheeky philanthropist raised the ante with the launch of phoenix.com. Overnight, The Phoenix Lottery went from back-page human-interest filler to headline news, and phoenix.com became one of the most visited and talked about sites on the worldwide web. As it became clear that a significant number of people were actually responding, mailing in money orders or entering electronically using credit cards, Junior appeared to be neither kidding nor so crazy as first had been supposed.

Who *were* these people prepared to toast an icon of Western civilization? Were they making a serious grab at instant fame and fortune? Were they social rebels—the deference to authority which had crumbled in the latter part of the twentieth century now blown sky-high? Or were they simply responding as a lark—ownership of an official framed Phoenix Lottery receipt a post-millennal equivalent to the Pet Rock?

It didn't matter. All that mattered was that Junior had hit the *Zeitgeist*. People were paying to enter; and the more people that entered, the more the media paid attention; and the more the media paid attention, the more people entered. Feeding the frenzy, BEI's PR machinery ensured that the geometrically esca-lating number of entrants, together with other tidbits of infor-mation, was dished carefully and regularly into the media's maw.

Before anyone knew what had happened, The Phoenix Lottery had taken on a life of its own as millions, from Rio to Vladivostok to Los Angeles, shelled out their ten bucks, eager to be part of a certified piece of history. Now, no matter what Junior's initial intentions, the lottery was making so much money he'd have to be mad not to carry through.

Junior must be stopped. But how?

The world holds its breath and waits for Canada to act. But the Canadian government, which has raised bureaucratic inaction to the status of public policy, sees no reason to intervene. Good heavens, van Gogh isn't even a member of The Group of Seven. Action might be necessary if Junior was threatening to inciner-ate a picture of northern scrub brush, but he's only out to burn the image of some homely Dutchman.

Worse, intervention by the government would provide the balmy philanthropist with a podium from which to lambaste its treatment of social programs. Proceeds from the travesty will benefit The Angel Foundation, which fills a need for hostels, food banks, and other services made necessary by the country's sacrifice of its poor to the multinationals, a truth Beamish can be counted on to exploit. Bad optics.

Indeed, such rabble-rousing might dislodge the comfortable myth that Canada is a nation of kind and gentle do-gooders, morally superior to its American cousin. In Canada, this myth is an article of faith, maintenance of which is a sacred trust for the country's politicians, as it is the one thing on which Canadians can agree. It is, indeed, the basis of Canada's national identity. Mess with it and one can kiss the country goodbye. To ignore Junior, therefore, isn't just good politics: it's statesmanship. A question of national unity. Nay, survival.

Naturally, such considerations go unspoken in response to stiff diplomatic notes from the Dutch, who are out to preserve the work of their most famous countryman. Instead, the federal Heritage Ministry passes the buck, declaring culture a provincial responsibility, while the province of Ontario, through its Ministry of Culture, Sports, and Recreation, returns the favour by declaring international culture a matter for the feds.

In a fit of pique, the Dutch recall their ambassador for consultations and threaten Ottawa with the loss of its yearly gift of tulip bulbs. They also begin making backdoor representations to the Americans.

For Democratic President Hamilton "Stonewall" Richardson, the timing could not be worse. His recent support of health-care initiatives for inner-city preschoolers has allowed his critics to portray him as a wild-eyed radical. As well, his administration is hip-deep in a widening sex scandal involving Congressional pages from Iowa and an unlisted telephone number traced to the White House bedroom of his teenage son.

Why would he wish to add more controversy to his plate? And what is to be gained by taking on an issue over which he has no control? Failure to dissuade Beamish from his plan will only lead to more of those dreary "Whither America?" cover stories in *Newsweek* and *Time*, full of dark ruminations about a leadership vacuum in the Oval Office and jeremiads on the nation's declining global influence. Nor will successful intervention provide an upside. The van Gogh *Self-Portrait* is private property, after all. For a Democratic president already targeted as a liberal, monkeying with property rights would be disaster, bringing down the wrath of both Dixiecrats and Republicans, for whom art is suspect at the best of times.

The Dutch acknowledge the problem, but propose that Richardson apply pressure behind the scenes. Might he not threaten to drop the Canadian prime minister from the guest list for his fishing trips on the presidential yacht off Hyannis Port? Or nix a scheduled round of golf? After all, opportunities to pal around with the president are prized in the sleepy northern capital, as they give Canadians the illusion their leader actually matters. This notion causes giggles in the State Department; although, to be fair, American officials try to speak of the Canadian prime minister with respect, even when they can't remember his name.

Richardson agrees that withholding buddy privileges from the prime minister is an effective diplomatic gambit. Unfortunately, he has already played this card to gain benefits on cross-border trade in wheat, lumber, and salmon, as well as to secure changes to NAFTA. It is one thing to screw the Canadian prime minister for a nickel. It is quite another to expect him to provide the K–Y.

Then might the CIA address Junior directly, the Dutch enquire innocently. Richardson rebukes them. Assassination is a tactic best reserved for Latin American dictators who have forgotten to whom they owe their power. Besides, Richardson is galled at the way European governments allow his flag to be burned on their soil at the slightest flex of Yankee muscle, while accepting the benefits of said muscle when it suits them.

Rebuffed, the Dutch turn in desperation to the United Nations. They ask that Junior Beamish be tried in the World Court as an international terrorist perpetrating a crime against humanity. The court, however, has spent the last decade attempting to bring Serbian war criminals to justice. Given the international community's halting progress on the prosecution of genocide charges, it would appear unseemly to act against a raving lunatic whose only crime is to threaten an inanimate object. So the UN dances the diplomatic shuffle. It denies jurisdiction, adding that it would be absurd to try the brewery heir for a crime he has not yet committed. Once the van Gogh is in cinders, mind, the Dutch are free to call again.

Naturally, none of the players wishes to send the Dutch away empty-handed. It is politic for each to suggest a more appropriate intervener, the better to assuage their consciences. In search of a donkey, Ottawa, Washington, and the UN offer up Pope Innocent.

The Vatican is a neutral state. The world's largest art collector. The backbone of Western history and cultural tradition. Not to mention the self-styled voice of God. Got any better ideas?

Pope Innocent's phone begins ringing off the hook.

Vatican Players

Defusing The Phoenix Lottery is clearly an historic mission: that it should fall during the watch of Innocent XIV drives many clergy to prayer. It is fitting this pope has taken the name Innocent, the first such in over two hundred and fifty years. Well-meaning to be sure, Innocent is hopelessly naive. Many a papal nuncio, over tots of late-night sherry in the anterooms of the *Segretario di Stato*, openly mock him as "The Bumbling Bavarian."

A simple man with simple tastes, Innocent XIV resembles a hearty meal. His body is a dumpling, soft and expansive, contained by a girdle worn to ease back pain from a herniated disk. His face is a cross-section of sausage, a bumpy topography of colourful cysts garnished with a beet-red nose. His hair, a tangle of grey sauerkraut, grows in profusion on his head, hands, arms, shoulders, and backside. These features, a media consultant's nightmare, are mitigated by friendly eyes, protruding ears, and a loopy, thick-lipped grin which lend Innocent an air of endearing pathos. It would be cruel to dislike this pope.

Born Karl Helmut Wachser, he was a compromise candidate. The Italian Curialists, masterminded by the brilliant strategist Cardinal Giuseppe Agostino Montini Wichita, conspired to claim the papacy for one of their own. However, on the seventy-third day of deliberation, with no election in sight, and their fourth candidate, Cardinal Carlo Alberto d'Ovidio, clearly stalled, they threw their support to the dark-horse Wachser.

Cardinal Wachser had his attractions for the Italians. He'd spent the last twenty years toiling mindlessly in the Curia for the Congregation of the Council; if he favoured schnitzel and schnapps to risotto at Les Étoiles, he was at least a known quantity who could be controlled. Besides, with his family history of stroke, it was hoped and anticipated that a second opportunity to install a Roman in the throne of St. Peter would soon be forthcoming.

So up went the puff of white smoke, with Wachser to follow shortly, God willing.

The future pope had done well at the Curia by virtue of doing nothing. Paper had been dutifully shuffled. Pressing concerns had been referred to plenary committees for further study. Rare opposition had been bored, delayed, and frustrated into helpless submission. In all of this, Wachser's chief weapon was his in-tray, commonly referred to as the Black Hole of Bavaria. Orders, edicts, reports, missives, and memos were cheerfully received and piled one on top of the other. When the pile grew to a sufficiently impressive height, it was packed, unread, in a cardboard box and stored in the bowels of the Vatican archives by an uncomplicated prelate from Nice. With action reduced to a snail's pace, Wachser was invincible; trying to outmanoeuvre him was like trying to swim through porridge.

While such skills are useful in a bureaucracy to which change is a heresy in need of correction, they hardly provided Innocent with a vision. Soon a restive clergy in both the West and the Developing World began making rude noises that the College of Cardinals had elevated a pudding to Supreme Pontiff. Faced with a crisis of credibility, the Secretariat of State chose to disguise the papal drift with a whirlwind of activity.

Cardinal d'Ovidio was placed in charge of this public-relations project as consolation for having lost the main prize. Within the year he had organized Operation Explorer, which launched the fledgling pope off to the Malay Archipelago, Palau Island, Madagascar, and an extensive pilgrimage to Greenland, Baffin Island, and parts north. What these tours lacked in content, they made up in symbolism and sound bites, projecting to the faithful an image of vigour and pastoral concern. Some feared for the ailing pontiff's constitution, but as Cardinal d'Ovidio dutifully pointed out: "God's will be done."

In the interim, the tours bedevil Innocent's herniated disk. When not exploring *terra incognita*, he is usually found in the steam room of Castel Gandolfo, the papal summer residence in the Alban hills just east of Rome. It is here that he summons Cardinal Giuseppe Agostino Montini Wichita to enlist his considerable skills in defusing *l'affaire Beamish*.

Cardinal Wichita, a post-war waif of unknown parentage, has been a fixture in the Church from age ten. He was first spotted by Giovanni Battista Montini weeping before the statue of Michelangelo's *Pietà*. Montini had been doing some weeping of his own. In charge of the Vatican's Office of Ordinary Affairs at the Secretariat of State, he'd been demoted by Pius XII that very morning to archbishop of Milan for having made the error of sympathizing with indiscreet French theologians. Montini, for whom suffering came as easily as breathing, had repaired to the Holy Door of St. Peter's to commune with Michelangelo's masterwork. Transported by the ineffable sorrow of Our Lady gazing upon the lifeless body of her son, Montini had stood transfixed for several hours before becoming aware of a young boy sobbing at his feet.

On investigation, Montini discovered the boy was a street urchin who professed to have suffered horrific circumstances in the back alleys of Rome since losing his mother at the age of two. Whether she'd died or abandoned him was unclear. All the boy knew was that his name was Giuseppe Agostino Wichita and he was ten. This morning he'd woken from a dream in which an angel had told him to go to the Holy Door at St. Peter's. He'd arrived fifteen minutes earlier, drawn by a frightening power to the base of the statue. Looking into the eyes of the Blessèd Virgin, he'd seen the mother he'd barely known, and wept, glimpsing through his tears the angel of his dream sitting on Our Lady's right shoulder.

An intellectual, Montini was inclined to give short shrift to tales of supernatural manifestations, especially when they came from a liar. This lad was no Roman street youth. He was clearly a recent arrival from the south: thick black hair, rich brown skin, bright teeth, and electric eyes—one could almost smell the olives. His dialect, too, was southern: Apulian, from near the seaport of Bari, if Montini's ear could be trusted.

Gazing at the young orphan, he saw a vision of himself, lost, abandoned, suffering. This was no hustler-thief, no magpie like the devils who hung around the Trevi and the Coliseum. There was an innocence about this boy, a lad clearly alone and, judging by his tears and trembling shoulders, frightened for his life. That the child professed no parents indicated a clear desire to escape circumstances which had, regardless of their literal truth, been horrific, the bruise on his cheek bearing witness to at least one terrible beating.

Montini experienced a moment of personal epiphany, sublime and transcendent. There was a reason God had drawn them together this morning of all mornings. The boy was a lost soul in need of salvation. Filled with compassion, Montini wiped away the lad's tears and called for assistance from Vatican personnel. Young Wichita was to travel with him to Milan. He would join the household staff at the archbishop's residence. There he would be raised, educated, and trained under the watchful eye of a mentor who saw in him a future leader of Christ's flock on earth. "A child shall lead them."

A gifted con artist, young Wichita could flatter without apparent guile. Within the week, he asked if he might take the name Montini. His delighted patron acceded, convinced more than ever that the hand of God had brought them together. He recommitted himself to give the boy every advantage possible.

Young Wichita rewarded this decision, proving bright, able, and charming, though his sleight-of-hand with the archbishop's silverware was a talent in need of restraint. In 1963, when Montini returned to Rome in triumph as Pope Paul VI, Wichita topped his class at Catholic University of the Sacred Heart in Milan. Ordained the following year at age twenty, he wrote his doctoral thesis on satanic iconography of the fourteenth century, displaying a breathtaking insight into art, the function of symbol, and the rite of exorcism. That accomplished, he joined his mentor in Rome, entering the Accademia Pontificia, the school for Vatican diplomats. Armed with academic honours, six languages (Italian, German, French, Russian, English, and Polish, with a smattering of Japanese) and the discreet support of the Supreme Pontiff, he entered the diplomatic service of the Holy See before his twenty-eighth birthday.

Recognizing the danger of being both gifted and visible, Wichita nurtured a low profile, a feat remarkable given his wit, connections, and easy success. Such talents, invariably fatal to the unwary, have been managed happily, thanks to gifts honed on the street: a preternatural cunning, shrewdness, and ability to read the hearts of others. Wichita has thrived in the Curia, cultivating power and eliminating enemies without raising a ripple of suspicion. In all things he is as quiet and lethal as a moth on an overcoat.

It is natural, therefore, that his desk at the Secretariat of State on the third floor of the Apostolic Palace should have an especially fine view overlooking the courtyard of San Damasco. And it is likewise natural that John Paul II should have named him cardinal deacon, titular bishop of Tangier. Indeed, the only unnatural thing about Cardinal Wichita's *curriculum vitae* is that he has not yet been elected pope, although as a relatively young man just past sixty there is ample time to correct the oversight.

But what of his unknown parentage? What of his secret life as a street urchin? Secrets, like grenades, exist to explode. Wichita buries his carefully in the root cellar of his mind. The truth is known only to himself and the ghost of the mother for whose death he was responsible.

A Most Unusual Martyrdom

Spring, 1954.

"Madre Raffaella, I have an important message from Santa Maria. Antichrist has been born in Cuba."

Madre Raffaella sets aside her reading glasses, cracks her knuckles, and sighs. A spry seventy-five, she can handle the southern Italian winter damp that grips throbbing bones and the summer heat that cracks poor earth. She can even handle the endless medieval stairs here at the convent of The Pious Sisters of Our Lady of Perpetual Suffering in the parish of Nivoli, ten kilometres southeast of Bari. But she is finding it increasingly difficult to handle Maria Carlotta Castelli. "So Antichrist has been born in Cuba, has he? How much does he weigh?"

"Five kilograms, Madre Raffaella."

"My goodness. Robust. Well, you must thank Santa Maria for her confidence. And now, Maria Carlotta, you may return to the garden."

"The whore bore him in great agony, Madre. He ripped through her belly with his horns, spewing fire."

"Horns and fire. Then it will be difficult for him to hide. I am sure the local padre will track Antichrist down, sprinkle him with holy water and send him back to the pit where he belongs."

"Oh no, Madre. The padre will never find him. The whore has fashioned him a bonnet to hide His horns, booties to cover his hooves, and doused his fire with her milk. Madre Raffaella," her lip begins to tremble. "Madre Raffaella, I'm afraid."

"Yes, well, Antichrist is rather frightening, isn't he? You must ask Santa Maria to provide you with cheerier messages in future. A nice story about Zio Peppe on the right hand of God, perhaps. That will be all."

"But Madre Raffaella—"

Madre Raffaella gives her a sharp look and returns to her reading. A short silence. Maria Carlotta Castelli turns to go, turns back, turns to go, turns back, turns to go, turns back. She stands, staring at La Madre Superiora, twisting the handkerchief in her hand again and again and again.

Without looking up, Madre Raffaella says, "The answer is No."

"But La Vergine is very insistent."

"Maria Carlotta Castelli, this is the third time this month that Santa Maria has favoured you with a visitation, and each time it's the same. The Antichrist is born in Cuba, or witches have cast a spell on the Holy Father, or Our Lord is returning to bless the children of Turin next Sunday, and, oh by the way, please allow Maria Carlotta Castelli to become a nun. The answer is No!"

"But La Vergine will not take no for an answer."

"Is that so? Well you tell Santa Maria that if she wishes you to become a nun, she can take you to Heaven and make you a nun herself!" Maria Carlotta sinks to her knees and begins to cry. "Madre di Dio, forgive me," thinks Madre Raffaella, hastily crossing herself, "why must you vex me with this child?"

She gazes with pity upon the young woman. The lumpen creature crumpled before her is but twenty-six, yet resembles nothing so much as an upturned tub of unwashed laundry. Thick rivers of filthy hair stream excitedly from a tenuous bun tied with old elastic. Flesh swathed in black ebbs and flows in all directions. But it is the eyes—now covered by thick, calloused hands, nails caked with red dirt—it is the eyes that tell her story. The large white, unnaturally luminous eyeballs; the dilated pupils dancing to a wild tune.

It was not always like this. Madre Raffaella remembers Maria Carlotta's confirmation, one of the dearest memories of her life. It had taken place when the girl was a twinkle shy of thirteen, poor beyond measure, but fresh as the sea breeze, with ripe cheeks, clear eyes, and flowing black hair tied back with purple ribbons. Her breasts were restrained in a chaste white dress, her feet, delicate as berries, skipped in the first pair of new shoes she had ever owned. She was a picture of innocence and beauty, as clean and bright as *la città bianca* set against the brilliant Mediterranean sky.

Madre Raffaella's most vivid recollection is of the moment Maria Carlotta took her aside and announced in a solemn voice that she had been given a sacred calling. She had been in the olive grove with her father and brothers when she'd heard the voices of angels whispering in the grey-green leaves. The angels had told her to go on her saint's day to the Grotte di Castellana. In a fever of exhultation, she had implored her father to take her, and he had agreed, and they had gone, and while parents and siblings ate a lunch of goat cheese and dry bread dipped in wine, she had entered the Grotte, that cathedral of alabaster stalactites and stalagmites the colours of the rainbow. And there Santa Maria, La Madre di Dio, had visited her for the first time.

"Oh, Madre Raffaella," Maria Carlotta confided with the earnestness of the young, "La Vergine, Santa Maria, was all in blue with a crown of jewels, and she smiled at me. I fell to the ground. I hid my face. But La Vergine said unto me, 'Fear not Maria Carlotta Castelli. For today I have come to ask you to be my handmaiden. On the day of your confirmation, you are to speak to La Madre Superiora of The Order of the Pious Sisters of Our Lady of Perpetual Suffering, and tell her: 'Behold, Santa Maria, La Madre di Dio, has claimed me for her own. I am to be a sister within your household, within the bosom of Our Lord.' Oh, Madre Raffaella, those were her very words, I swear on the cradle of the baby Gésu."

Madre Raffaella smiled, for she too had been young once: what fantastical sights the innocent delight in. Yet Maria Carlotta spoke with such purity that she wished it could all be true. So Madre Raffaella took Maria Carlotta's hands, looked deep into those trusting eyes and said that it was a rare gift and blessing that La Vergine had bestowed, and she was sure it would all come to pass, for La Madre di Dio would never raise false hopes. All the same, Maria Carlotta must wait until her sixteenth birthday to see what other plans God might have in store for her.

Maria Carlotta assured her that Santa Maria's mind was quite made up. However, she would be dutiful and wait, helping around the convent in all ways possible. True to her word, she waited diligently, working in the garden, sweeping the chapel, and each week accompanying Suora Francesca in a mule-drawn cart to Bari to purchase housewares and sundries at the port.

Madre Raffaella was relieved that Suora Francesca was escorted by one so young and capable. The old dear treasured her trips to town; they made her feel useful as she waited out the dreary years for God to call her home. Sadly, her mind was a thing of the past, and Madre Raffaella had worried that Suora Francesca might go missing if the mules were ever to forget their way home. She had prayed devoutly on the matter, and clearly the Lord had sent Maria Carlotta by way of response.

Still, all was not well. Suora Francesca would often forget that she had left the convent with a companion, and return in the cart alone. Search parties invariably found Maria Carlotta skipping back along the dirt road singing, but Madre Raffaella grew increasingly apprehensive. Although the war was over, American detachments remained at Bari, presenting dangers for young girls unattended. So she was not completely surprised when Maria Carlotta, on the eve of her sixteenth birthday, asked to speak to her privately.

"Madre Raffaella. . ." the child began uncertainly, staring at the floor. "I have been to the Grotte di Castellana. La Vergine has come to me a second time."

At the mention of La Vergine, Madre Raffaella breathed a sigh of relief. Maria Carlotta simply wished to remind her that she was now of an age to enter the novitiate. "I know why you are here," the old woman beamed. "You are truly blessed."

Maria Carlotta looked up, startled. "Oh, Madre Raffaella," she cried and threw herself at the old woman's feet, "I was so afraid you wouldn't understand."

"There, there," said Madre Raffaella, as she sank to her knees and raised the girl up beside her. "Now whisper in my good ear what La Vergine said to you at the Grotte on this her second visitation."

"Well," said Maria Carlotta, hysteria darting through her eyes and voice, "La Vergine says it surely must be a miracle sent by God and that she knows how I must feel, because when God rewarded her faith in such a way, she too felt frightened."

At first, Madre Raffaella did not understand. What did this have to do with joining the order of the Pious Sisters? Then the dull horror of Maria Carlotta's words froze the beatific smile upon her face. She had feared the worst and yet, confronted with the truth, it could not be!

Maria Carlotta's lips continued to move, but the old woman heard nothing. This went on for some time until the girl felt a stiffening in the arms that cradled her and, looking up, found herself staring into a stone face as hard and unyielding as the coast. The words, which had flowed so freely, choked in her throat.

A terrible silence.

"What is the father's name?"

A heartbeat and Maria Carlotta burst into tears. His name was Wichita. At least, that is what he called himself. He was an American soldier stationed in Bari, encountered on one of her weekly errands. She'd left Suora Francesca in the cathedral praying to the sacred bones of San Sabino and gone to buy a kettle at the market. And there he was. The most beautiful young man she had ever seen. He knew little Italian. She knew little English. It didn't matter. She found a way to let him know that she came to the cathedral every week. They said goodbye.

The next week he was waiting with a picnic lunch. And so the weeks turned to months and the picnics to more private pleasures. When she told him she was pregnant, he seemed happy. He would be going home soon, back to America. They would marry and he would take her and the baby with him. But the next week, he wasn't at the cathedral. Maria Carlotta, frightened, went to the base. The sentry at the gate said he'd never heard of a Private Wichita. One of the boys had come from Kansas, though. Maybe it was him? He went Stateside three days ago. Left no message. She saw the sentry turn to another soldier, point at her, and say something in English. Before they had time to laugh, she was running away, hot tears burning her cheeks.

That was the end of her story. Now all she had was a photograph and a swelling belly. A long pause. Awkwardly, Maria Carlotta took her catechism from her sweater pocket. Repentance, Madre Raffaella thought.

Heaven, alas, was not on Maria Carlotta's mind. Tenderly, she pulled a photo of her young man from the catechism. She wanted to show La Madre Superiora how decent and beautiful he looked. It was as though she had faith that if Madre Raffaella would give her blessing, a miracle might happen and God might bring him back to her. Instead, the old woman tore the picture from Maria Carlotta's hands, ripped it in pieces and tossed them in the air.

"*Putana!* You dare to take the name of Santa Maria, Madre di Dio, in vain?" she screamed, as Maria Carlotta cried, scrambling to retrieve the pieces of her memory. "*Putana! Putana! Figlia di putana!* And you would be a holy sister? You—you bitch-in-heat! You'd have your men sniffing the convent walls! Scratching the doors! *Putana! Figlia di putana!*"

Madre Raffaella raised her hand to smite the girl, but hadn't the heart. "Forgive me, Madre di Dio. I should never have sent her out with Suora Francesca," she wept. "Men. Those devils are all the same. They see a virgin and Satan licks their privates. Dry your eyes. You are not the first to fall. You will not be the last."

Of course, it would be impossible for Maria Carlotta to become a nun, but it was not the end of the world. The south was littered with the offspring of conquering armies. Over the span of two thousand years, Greeks, Normans, Byzantines, Lombards, Moors, Spaniards, Hohenstaufens, Franks, and Saracens had all left their mark in the blood of its people. Now, with the war, German and American blood had joined the brew. "They are all God's children," thought Madre Raffaella, though she would never have ventured such in public.

So, no, Maria Carlotta Castelli would never join the order, but she could continue working the convent garden. Madre Raffaella also promised to use her influence with Padre Renato to ensure the girl would not be admonished from the parish pulpit. As for Maria Carlotta's father, she would have a word with Vito Castelli. She knew from Padre Renato that Vito's two-acre field was not the only thing he ploughed, and it would be a shame if she were forced to discuss his animal husbandry with his wife, Sofia, or his neighbour, the cuckold Gonzago—he of the ten large and brutal sons.

(Madre Raffaella had a taste for gossip and savoured the sinful details of all the parishioners' lives. These had been faithfully reported to her by Padre Renato ever since the day she'd caught the hapless priest drunk on communion wine with her newest novitiate. The sin of violating the sanctity of the confessional caused Madre Raffaella some small discomfort. Still, she chose to regard it as a technicality, since she was a fellow steward in the vineyard of the Lord.)

Madre Raffaella was true to her word. When Vito Castelli received the news he neither struck nor abused his errant child. For his part, Padre Renato reminded the parish of Christ's generosity toward the woman taken in adultery. Whatever people said behind closed doors, they were circumspect in public.

And so it came to pass that Giuseppe Agostino was born into the welcoming arms of the Castelli family. This was the south: family is family, blood is blood, and they loved their little Yankee, though Wichita was a name unspoken, save between mother and son.

A breeze through the open window brings Madre Raffaella out of her reverie. The young woman, grown quite mad these past ten years, remains prostrate and sobbing, in much the same posture of despair she held those many years ago. Eventually, La Madre Superiora will comfort her, as she always does. Though not too soon: it would only encourage her, and Maria Carlotta, even unencouraged, is apt to have a visitation at the drop of a Hail Mary.

Instead, Madre Raffaella looks through her window to the countryside beyond. She sees banks of poor farms, many no larger than Vito's two acres, on dry red earth, divided by loose-laid walls of rough, weathered grey stone. She see roots competing with rock for their place in the landscape. She sees the convent lands, until recently malarial marshes.

Could it simply be the fever that makes us rich in holy visions, she wonders. Or do we make up tales to give us hope from our despair. Hearing the devil snigger, she grabs the armour of her faith. You'd like to take me now, you devil, in my weakness. Well back to the pit with you. I praise God for suffering, for suffering blesses us with grace, and surely we are blessed above all others!

Theology gives La Madre Superiora headaches; she'd rather *do* than philosophize—it gets one in less trouble. And so she sinks down beside Maria Carlotta and begins to stroke her hair. Hesitantly, Maria Carlotta looks up, eyes wild and bewildered. It is then that Madre Raffaella sees the marks on her throat and for a moment forgets about God, the convent, and the south.

"Who has done this thing?"

Maria Carlotta wails, "He wants to kill my son."

Madre Raffaella grabs her by the hair. "Who wants to kill young Giuseppe?"

"Il Padrone, Don Camardo."

Now it is Madre Raffaella who shrieks. Not even God can save a soul marked by Il Padrone.

Maria Carlotta blurts her burden. A clever child, with a quick mind and quicker fingers, Giuseppe had come to the attention of Don Camardo, who was always on the lookout for a young magpie. The Don had honoured their home with a visit.

"Vito Castelli," he had said, clutching the marble egg on his polished walking stick. "You have been blessed with many sons. My own, alas, have died. I would be honoured if you would favour me with a godson. In return, should drought attend your farm, or disrespect be paid your name, know that you shall have a friend." It had seemed so perfect. Only now, he wishes the boy dead, claiming Giuseppe has stolen his goods and killed his *capo*. One of Camardo's men, Rinaldo Sabatini, has threatened her father, demanding that the boy be produced. Beside himself with terror, Vito has demanded the child's whereabouts, attempting to choke an answer from Maria Carlotta's unwilling throat. This, at least, is the gospel of Maria Carlotta.

Madre Raffaella frowns; the tale is a few beads short of a rosary. While objects have a habit of disappearing when Giuseppe is about, he is only a boy of ten. What could he have stolen to so enrage the Don? And how can Camardo think Giuseppe capable of murder? Indeed, of the murder of Benito Benelli, his trusted and foul-smelling capo?

Suddenly all becomes clear. "Santa Maria del Cielo has had so much to say to me today," Maria Carlotta whispers. "She has told me Satan has been born in Cuba. And she has told me I must die to save my son. But before I die, Santa Maria del Cielo asks that you grant her one wish. She asks that you make me a holy sister of your order."

"You think you can play me like a fiddle?" the old woman rages. "You think you can win by deceit what you have forfeited by dishonour? Out of my sight, putana!" With that she boxes Maria Carlotta about the ears and pitches her from the study.

That evening, La Madre Superiora will rend her garments. Her cries will be heard echoing through the olive groves as far as Bari. She will fall on her knees and pray to La Vergine for forgiveness and intercession at the throne of God. For after being thrown out of Madre Raffaella's study, Maria Carlotta Castelli did a very strange thing.

She went to her home, the home of Vito and Sofia Castelli, and retrieved the white dress she had made so many years ago in imitation of those worn by novitiates in The Order of the Pious Sisters. The dress no longer fit, but no matter; she let it out by slitting the back and roughly sewing in a measure of old blue bedsheet. Next, she festooned her loose, dishevelled hair with purple ribbons. "Santa Maria del Cielo has shown me the way," she sang, in a lilting child's voice. Then she skipped outside and rode off on young Giuseppe's bicycle.

She stopped at the estate of Don Camardo. "You want my precious boy?" she cackled through the gates. "I alone know where he is. Come catch me if you can." And away she sailed on a glorious game of tag, this ample bridesmaid of Christ on a child's two-wheeler, purple ribbons dancing gaily in the breeze.

By the time Don Camardo and his men caught up, she'd reached the Grotte di Castellana. "*Cornuto!*" she spat at Il Padrone. "May Giuseppe take your walking stick and shove it up your *culo!*" No time for regrets. Maria Carlotta Castelli tore into the Grotte, a palpitating Don Camardo in pursuit.

He was too late. The mad madonna had seen what she was looking for: a fine, thin stalagmite growing from the Grotte's floor. In the twinkling of an eye, she leapt from a small ledge and impaled herself upon the spike, the words, "Santa Maria, Madre di Dio, protect my boy" upon her lips.

There were too many witnesses to cast doubt on the miracle attending Maria Carlotta Castelli's death. As expected, blood oozed down the calcite from the wound in her side. But how to explain the thin red halo of pinpricks, the marks of a crown of thorns, that blossomed around the madwoman's forehead? Or the trickles of blood that flowed from the palms of her hands and from the soles of her feet? These wounds, unbidden and unexplained, were why the spectators dropped to their knees in prayer, and why the cult of Maria Carlotta Castelli delle Grotte di Castellana began to flourish.

Canonization

The movement to have Maria Carlotta Castelli delle Grotte di Castellana declared a saint faced two apparently insurmountable obstacles. First, Maria Carlotta was an unwed mother. Second, she was a suicide.

Yet Maria Carlotta was fortunate, as no accurate record of events existed. Further, the few in the parish of Nivoli who were privy to the dirt were silenced by the weight of reverential gossip which, endlessly repeated and embroidered as it passed from mouth to mouth, assumed the authority of holy writ. Such conviction attended the telling of these tales that even witnesses soon doubted their own experience. The community was also eased into accepting the authenticity of the legends by the unstated recognition of the economic benefits that would befall Nivoli were it to be the birthplace of a saint; even as things stood, tourists to Bari had begun making day trips to pray to the heart of Maria Carlotta Castelli, preserved in the Nivoli parish church.

Naysayers were finally silenced in 1984 by the deathbed deposition of Madre Raffaella, signed on the thirtieth anniversary of Maria Carlotta's death. La Madre Superiora was one hundred and five at the time, and there were those who questioned whether she was in any condition to make a deposition, or if the scratchy signature was even hers. But La Madre Superiora wasn't around to answer, having taken the great leap before she could put down the pen. A visibly angry Padre Renato, who had simultaneously administered the last rites while acting as witness, stoutly defended both La Madre's mental agility and the authenticity of her signature.

A few cynics noted that Padre Renato had a vested interest in the outcome of any investigation by the Sacred Congregation for the Causes of Saints. Since installing the preserved heart of

Maria Carlotta Castelli in the nave, Padre Renato had been doing a brisk business in votive candles. And the crutches and memorabilia of those healed while praying to the relic, with which he had begun to decorate the narthex, had each come with a generous donation. Happily, it is well known that miracles attract cynics as honey attracts flies, and given the overwhelming number of eyewitness reports to the life of Maria Carlotta Castelli, such churls were easily swatted.

Madre Raffaella's deposition addressed the two major obstacles to Maria Carlotta's beatification. There was, first of all, no mention of a Private Wichita. Rather, the poor girl had sacrificed herself to a gang of brigands in order to rescue a convoy of elderly nuns she was escorting home from the Feast of San Nicola in Bari. Apparently helpless before the rapacious desperadoes, the nuns were saved when the jawbone of an ass miraculously appeared at the side of the road. Maria Carlotta wielded it like an avenging angel, rendering five of the ruffians senseless before being overcome by the sixth. While she was thus engaged, the holy geriatrics ran to Nivoli to raise the alarm. Alas, they returned too late to salvage the virginity of their saviour, who had sacrificed her purity for their lives.

Despite the mitigating circumstances described by La Madre Superiora, the Sacred Congregation, fulfilling the function of the devil's advocate, pressed a predictably narrow reading of the requirement of chastity, to the great disgust of the laity. It withdrew its objections on this point, however, when Promoters of Maria Carlotta drew parallels with the tribulation of Santa Agate, A.D. 178–203, whose valiant struggle at the Catacombs of San Giovanni at Siracusa, A.D. 202, saved two hundred of the faithful. Violated by a dozen Roman guards, she later gave birth to San Tomasito, the child who avenged her dishonour during the Slaughter of the Centurions, A.D. 210.

Madre Raffaella's account further pointed out that, despite the horrific nature of her son's conception, Maria Carlotta had dutifully brought the child to term. The boy, she added, was a model lad, who ran errands both for her and Padre Renato. It was at this point in her text that La Madre Superiora chose to cudgel the notion that Maria Carlotta's death had been a suicide. It was, she claimed, a murder. Or rather, a martyrdom. According to La Madre Superiora, the local Mafia, knowing Giuseppe worked with the padre, tried to force the boy to eavesdrop on the confessions of certain parishioners in whom it had an interest. It threatened him with death if he refused. The boy replied, "My mother, the saintly Maria Carlotta Castelli, who bore me in great love and agony, says that anyone who tempts a man to break the sanctity of the confessional is a devil bound for hell." Padre Renato had taken malicious pleasure in creating this embellishment for the old bitch to sign.

The deposition stated that, like the mother of Moses, Maria Carlotta had hidden her son away, after which she and La Madre made a final pilgrimage to the Grotte di Castellana to pray for some practical tips on what to do next. It was here that Maria Carlotta was captured by the gangsters. When, after much torture, she still refused to reveal her son's whereabouts, the monsters threw her upon the instrument of her death, whereupon she was blessed by God with stigmata. (La Madre Superiora took pains to point out that she herself had been in no position to help out, having been tied up at the time. She had, however, busied herself with prayer, which no doubt had the happy consequence of speeding Maria Carlotta's entry into Heaven.)

Promoters of the cause of Maria Carlotta pored through an embarrassment of eyewitness confirmations, testaments which multiplied faster than the loaves and fishes. Apparently, everyone living within a twenty kilometre radius of the Grotte, had been present, tied up, and praying during Maria Carlotta's martyrdom.

Although it seemed unlikely that four thousand Apulians could have been squeezed into the tiny space surrounding the lethal stalagmite, much less trussed and gagged, Maria Carlotta's Promoters took the position that where there's smoke there's fire. From their overstuffed files, the Promoters selected three supplementary accounts of Maria Carlotta's death from witnesses who, like La Madre Superiora, had slipped this mortal coil and were safely beyond cross-examination.

The Promoters also presented the Sacred Congregation with documentation of a wide range of miracles attributed to Maria Carlotta. These fell broadly into two categories: healings and visitations. The healings happened at the Nivoli parish church, witness the numerous canes and crutches mounted on Padre Renato's trophy wall. The visitations came in response to those who prayed at the Grotte.

In this respect, the first reported sighting was an anomaly. According to Rinaldo Sabatini, a hit man in the employ of Don Camardo, young Giuseppe had been tracked to the Gargano Peninsula. Camardo himself was about to put a bullet in the boy's temple when Maria Carlotta suddenly appeared sitting on a cloud, bandages, bedsheet and all. She opened her arms, and in the words of Sabatini, "I saw the kid shoot up, bang like a bullet, straight into his mother's arms. Then I saw pigeons." Sabatini experienced a conversion as sudden and profound as Saul's on the road to Damascus. Screaming about Maria Carlotta and pigeons, he went into hiding and began cooperating with the Italian authorities. Of his conversion there was no doubt; it was only his sanity that was in question.

Needless to say, the Sabatini sighting was quickly buried. Obvious difficulties were attached to it, not the least of which was visualizing Maria Carlotta on a cloud. In addition, Italian authorities needed Sabatini's testimony in the notorious Grapelli dismemberment case. They felt that if this story received wide coverage, his credibility would blow up in their faces. As it turned out, Sabatini's credibility was not all that blew up. Pieces of the hoodlum, three police, and a prosecutor were scattered all over Milan when a bomb exploded inside the glove compartment of the limo taking him to the courthouse.

Unlike the report from the flaky Sabatini, the countless visitations cited by the Promoters of Maria Carlotta came, uniformly, from respectable, sober-sided mothers. They'd prayed for Maria Carlotta to have a word with their delinquent teens and she had obliged, dropping by when the wayward youths were next engaged in the commission of a sin. The shaken adolescents described the apparition as having bandaged hands and feet and wearing a blood-soaked novitiate's dress with a blue bedsheet insert. Spontaneous conversions invariably followed.

Reports of these visitations gained wide circulation after they were cited in *L'Osservatore Romano*, the semi-official Vatican newspaper. Known for its banality, *L'Osservatore* kicked up its skirts with a tale of one particularly traumatized young woman who, as she was about to lose her virginity in the back seat of a Volkswagen, looked up and saw Maria Carlotta's bloody face pressed against the windshield. The young woman screamed, and entered a convent. The newspaper added that she now works for the Curia in a secretarial function and no longer rides in automobiles.

As it turned out, all the depositions and probing, official and otherwise, were mere window dressing. The fix was in. Despite the fact that Italy was awash with saints and the Vatican wished to spread the spiritual wealth, senior interests in the Curia pressed hard on Maria Carlotta's behalf. Thus, at the dawn of the new millennium, she was canonized and was henceforth given the appellation, Santa Maria Carlotta Castelli delle Grotte di Castellana.

A Picnic Basket

It's not every boy who gets a chance to arrange the canonization of his mother. It's not every boy who'd want to. But Cardinal Wichita is no ordinary boy. With respect to his mother, he carries a weight of guilt remarkable even in a Catholic.

The truth is that as a child he'd hated her. She embarrassed him. Like all two-year-olds, he enjoyed imaginary playmates. So, in principle, it didn't seem odd that his mother should as well. All the same, his mother's imaginary playmate was the Virgin Mary. And whereas he outgrew "Peppe" by the age of four, his mother chattered away to Santa Maria until the day she died.

Naturally, most people feel guilt if they resent the mother who bore them in love and pain and unbearable agony. Those whose actions have led to her death labour under a special strain. They are generally disposed to a life of prayer or pills. Wichita has chosen both.

The destiny of the future Cardinal Giuseppe Agostino Montini Wichita was sealed on that ill-fated day he went to Bari with Benito Benelli, the foul-smelling capo of Il Padrone, Don Camardo. By late afternoon, the young boy would be found in a confessional with Benelli's dead body, and chased through Bari's medieval streets carrying a picnic basket containing the head and assorted extremities of Bruno Grapelli.

Ten-year-old Giuseppe embarks to Bari happy as a clam. These trips with Benelli are always an adventure, for he gets to be important, standing lookout at the Basilica di San Nicola while family business is conducted inside. Today's trip is more special than most as it is the Feast of San Nicola, the holy man best known as jolly old Saint Nick.

The remains of San Nicola were brought to Bari by local pirates who stole them from Myra, now Turkey, in the eleventh century. This saint was so revered throughout the medieval world that the Norman invaders who sacked the town in 1152 spared the basilica which bears his name and holds his crypt. His bones, preserved beneath the twelfth-century altar, continue to secrete a "holy manna" said to have miraculous properties, though its use is not for the faint of heart. The citizens of Bari hold a feast in the saint's honour each May, which, for sheer exuberance, rivals Naples at Easter. The statue of San Nicola is taken from the basilica and put on a ferry for a ride around the harbour. Horns toot, whistles blow, flags wave and the streets are alive with carnival.

Giuseppe, bursting with excitement, sits as always on the passenger side of the Alfa Romeo, feeling the soft leather and making sure to be seen by as many of the local children as possible. Since he began riding in Don Camardo's car, they have stopped teasing him about his mother.

As usual, there is a plain, covered picnic basket in the trunk, packed by Benelli. The gangster, who works in a small abattoir in a remote part of Don Camardo's estate, rarely changes his clothes, and there is about him the constant, pungent odour of decaying flesh. This no doubt explains why the Don insists he use the car with the plastic cover on the driver's seat. It is certainly the reason young Giuseppe likes to ride with his head out the window.

The contents of the picnic basket are a mystery. Once, Giuseppe asked what was inside. Benelli gave him a dry look and said, "Cold cuts," an odd explanation, because they never ate from it. Instead, Rodolfo the grocer, a friend of the Camardo family, who has a shop on the Via Venezia, always provided them with *fave e fogghi* and fresh *scaldatelli*.

Benelli parks the Alfa outside the old city. He takes the picnic basket from the trunk. Then he and the bug-eyed Giuseppe make their way through the narrow winding streets, toward the basilica. The route bristles with colours, sounds, smells, life. Skeins of newly dyed wool dry on long poles, their yellows, oranges, reds, and greens set off by brilliant sun and sky. Bright laundry hangs on lines across the narrow streets, while walls, in all directions, display the gaudiest of banners. Vendors hawk vividly painted statues of San Nicola, intricately carved rosaries, some with beads the size of walnuts, and grotesque rodent puppets made of rat hides baked in the sun and hooked to elastics and thimbles to create skittering toys to delight children and frighten wives. Local bands compete on every corner, brass, woodwinds, and guitars dancing mad, staccato rhythms in the air. Chickens and goats, pigs and sheep add squawks and bleats to the soundscape, while the air tumbles with smells of fresh basil, oregano, black pepper, and fine, plump, purple-veined garlic.

Tubs of anchovies, mussels, and hake tweak the nose. Baskets overflowing with Calabrian citrus tang the eyes. There are vats of oil, sacks of nuts, walls of wine, trolleys of produce and ornate glass jars crammed with pickles. Rough boards on trestles bend under the weight of massive rounds of cheese. Firm purple eggplants tumble from wheelbarrows, jostling with carts teeming with vine-ripe tomatoes, zucchini, and peppers in a wild profusion of colours. And pasta! Spaghettini, orecchiette, linguine, ravioli, troccoli, strascenate, maccheroni, manicotti, and more. It is the Feast of San Nicola and young Giuseppe wants to smell, taste, touch, see, and hear his fill.

By the time they near the basilica, Giuseppe's belly is stuffed with figs and nuts snatched from under the noses of wary grocers. His pockets, too, bulge with bills husked from dozens of wallets. The packed streets provide easy pickings for a boy with "the touch" and a pair of large, innocent eyes.

Were Benelli aware, he'd box Giuseppe's ears. Why risk police on trifles when the family's business involves such serious money and deadly stakes? They pass Rodolfo's shop. The grocer glances toward the basilica, signalling Benelli in such a way that a casual observer might think he was sizing up the attractive woman across the street.

"Good," notes Benelli. "The judge is inside with the money." He turns to Giuseppe, putting his free hand on the lad's shoulder. "Wait here and watch for friends. I'm off to make my confession. Then we can eat, nap, and catch the fireworks." He turns and carries the picnic basket into the church.

Giuseppe jumps for joy, then sits on the basilica's top step, the best place from which to scout, and pulls a fistful of walnuts from his right coat pocket. From his left, he fishes his precious brass corkscrew, its handle the head of a monkey. "A little monkey for my little monkey," Don Camardo had said when he presented it in reward for the boy's first errand. The boy loves the simian face, but, being ten, he has little use for a corkscrew. Initially he used it to skewer cockroaches, but Sabatini quickly put him straight: a gift from Don Camardo must be treated with respect. Since then he carries it with him for the sheer joy of rubbing its brass features when he's bored. Or for cracking the occasional walnut when no one is looking, which is what he is about to do now.

"Giuseppe."

Who has seen him disrespecting Don Camardo's gift? Terrified, Giuseppe looks up into the face of Padre Jacopo.

Padre Jacopo is completing his first year in charge of the basilica. Thin as a stick of spaghetti, and twice as brittle, he is overwhelmed by his duties. His face is gaunt, his skin pale, and the whites of his eyes quite yellow. Today, however, is different; his voice rings with a clarity of purpose, his skeletal frame advances with crisp intensity, and his pupils burn with an otherworldly light.

"Giuseppe," the padre says again.

How does the priest know his name?

"No need to be frightened, my son."

"I'm not," the boy replies, ears burning with shame.

"We are honoured to have Don Camardo's men pay a visit to our basilica on this the Feast of San Nicola."

Men. That includes me, thinks the boy. "The honour is ours," he beams.

"We wish to share a glass of wine with our friend Benito. But sadly," and here the good padre bows his head, "sadly our corkscrew is broken. Benito says we might borrow yours. He would ask you himself, but he cannot be disturbed." The padre gives Giuseppe a conspiratorial wink.

"It is my pleasure to provide you this favour," the boy intones gravely. He delivers his corkscrew to the priest as if passing the sacraments.

The priest takes it, tousles the boy's hair and gives him a candy. "Benito will return shortly, *mio Donito*," the priest confides drily.

Mio Donito. The boy is chuffed. He is not simply Giuseppe Castelli, bastard brat of a madwoman. He is *il Donito*! He has arrived.

Padre Jacopo turns and reenters the church, squeezing the corkscrew like a worry egg. He has no intention of sharing a glass of wine with Benelli. In the confessionals of the basilica all that separates priests from parishioners is a thin curtain, the hem of which touches a low wooden partition. In such intimate proximity, Padre Jacopo has heard the grisly fate of any number of Bari's citizens at the hands of Don Camardo's associates. He has learned, too, that the Camardo family is using the basilica as a front for its business arrangements.

An observant man, Padre Jacopo knows the drill. Benito Benelli comes to Bari with his lookout, Giuseppe. The grocer Rodolfo signals when the client is inside the basilica. The boy is posted guard and sits playing with a corkscrew while Benelli enters the church with a picnic basket. Benelli goes into the priest's side of an empty confessional. The client goes into the other. Once behind closed doors, they open the curtain separating them. The client sees a souvenir of the victim, proof his problem has been dealt with. He hands over payment and leaves. Benelli moves to a booth with a priest, gives his confession, and returns to Nivoli primed for Heaven.

Of immediate concern to Padre Jacopo is the fate of Bruno Grapelli, an oily playboy with a string of pick-up lines slicker than his hair. All of Bari congratulated seventy-year-old Judge Scarlatti when word got out that his young wife was pregnant. Unfortunately, Judge Scarlatti has been impotent for the past five years. Bruno Grapelli, clearly, is not—this information courtesy of a tearful Signora Scarlatti. Scarlatti has privately raged that his honour has been tarnished. He will end his days raising another man's child and wearing a pair of cuckold's horns to boot. The judge has met with Don Camardo, and Grapelli has disappeared. Now, on the Feast of San Nicola, Padre Jacopo has seen the judge enter the Basilica holding a thick manila envelope, with Benelli following shortly after.

Padre Jacopo has concerns beyond the fate of Bruno Grapelli. It is his responsibility to keep the basilica fit for Christ's flock, but under his stewardship the House of the Lord has turned into a den of iniquity. A notorious killer dismembers his parishioners, is paid off in a confessional, receives absolution, and waltzes off to kill again. Padre Jacopo has become ashamed of his own calling—and of his impotence. He cannot break the sanctity of the confessional by going to the authorities. Even if he could, officials are on the take and he would find himself strung up by his rosary beads before returning to his quarters. Yet, keeping silent while the family of Don Camardo commits blasphemies against God is a sin that haunts his conscience, driving him quietly insane.

That is, until last night, when the padre cried to God and heard the voice of the Almighty. Yea, the Lord had taken pity upon his poor servant and spake unto him thus: "Be not cast down, thou good and faithful servant. For have I not sent tongues of fire that my prophets might inflame all godly hearts to wield the sword of justice? Did I not guide the arm of Samson who slew the Philistine, and of David who felled the dread Goliath, and of my daughter Judith who smote the mighty Holofernes with a sword so that the blood of the Assyrian drenched the land of Israel? So I call upon you, my son, to smite the house of Don Camardo and drive his money-changers from my temple, yea, to drive them in a charnel wagon even unto the gates of hell itself!"

Padre Jacopo was quick to grasp the Lord's point: while murder is a mortal sin, to exterminate the ungodly is to sit at the right hand of God.

And so Padre Jacopo clenches the brass corkscrew. He sees Judge Scarlatti leave the confessional without the envelope. Moments later, he sees Benelli exit with the envelope and picnic basket, and enter a booth opposite. Jacopo relieves the priest about to hear Benelli's confession. Heart pounding, he hears Benelli speak.

"Forgive me, father, for I have sinned."

Pause. And then by rote: "How long has it been since your last confession, my son?"

"One week."

"And what sins have you committed since your last confession?"

"I took the name of the Lord in vain. I had impure thoughts. And I cut off the head of Bruno Grapelli."

Pause. Padre Jacopo bites his tongue. He must appear dispassionate. "Is that all?"

"I also cut off his fingers and toes. Oh, and some bits of a more personal nature."

"I meant have there been other sins."

"No, I think that about covers it. I've been pretty good."

Pause.

"Signor Benelli, I know it is you to whom I speak."

"Yeah, I know it's you too, Padre Jacopo. So how many Hail Marys?"

"Signor Benelli, Bruno Grapelli is the eighth parishioner of this Basilica whom you have dismembered this year."

"Sorry. We've been busy. How many Hail Marys? I got a kid waiting."

"Absolution is accompanied by the understanding that you will sin no more. At least that you will *try* to sin no more."

"I appreciate your concern, but I got a wife, kids. I need to make a living. This Grapelli was an adulterer. He dishonoured a fine old man. I rid your parish of a sinner."

"Signor Benelli," says Padre Jacopo, in no mood for irony, "your confession is a travesty."

"Look, Padre, I have a job to do. You got a job to do. I've done my job and come to confess. Now you do your job and give me absolution."

"There can be no absolution for you today, Benito Benelli."

"Think again, Padre Jacopo. My employer will take it as a sign of dishonour if you refuse me."

"Is that a threat?"

"Don Camardo is a man of respect."

"He is a lying, murdering spawn of Satan!" Jacopo snaps. "He pimps his sons, he sleeps with sheep, and his grandmother whores in ditches!"

Outraged, Benelli leaps to his feet and whips open the curtain separating them. Padre Jacopo is ready. " 'Vengeance is mine,' saith the Lord." God guides his aim. And yea, verily, as the hand of Judith drove a sword through the neck of Holofernes, so the hand of Padre Jacopo drives a corkscrew through the eye of Benito Benelli. It punctures his brain, killing him instantly. Benelli collapses back onto the seat.

"Thanks be to God," exults the padre. No muss, no fuss; barely even a trickle of blood; the corkscrew in Benelli's socket makes a fetching plug. Padre Jacopo giggles. What to do now? He takes the bulging envelope from Benelli's side, closes the curtain in order not to laugh at the comic expression on the gangster's face, and begins to count some serious cash.

Meanwhile, outside, Giuseppe worries about Benito's drink with the priest; once Benelli's into the sauce, he doesn't stop. The boy frets he'll be stuck sitting on the basilica's steps all day. Surely it wouldn't be a crime for him to go inside. If Benelli is knocking it back, the family business can't be all that serious. Who knows, if Benelli is in his cups, perhaps il Donito will be offered a glass of wine himself.

So Giuseppe enters the basilica in search of the cutthroat. It doesn't take long to find him. Walking up the row of confessionals, he picks up Benelli's scent. "How clever," the boy thinks. "They're getting drunk in a confessional."

Quick as a palm, he slips inside the booth and hops onto Benelli's knee. It strikes him as odd that Benelli doesn't respond to his arrival and that the curtain between priest and parishioner is drawn. He looks up at Benelli's face. The head of a brass monkey perches atop the gangster's left cheek.

In a flash, Giuseppe grasps the situation. Benelli has been killed with his corkscrew and he will be blamed. A normal boy might cry. But ice-water runs in Giuseppe's veins. He thinks, I must grab my monkey and escape. However, he discovers a complication. The groove of the corkscrew has gotten stuck behind a ridge of bone in the eye socket. Giuseppe will have to yank hard and hope for the best.

On the other side of the curtain, Padre Jacopo is so busy counting the wad of lire that he hasn't heard the boy enter. He is startled by a series of loud thumps, the sound of Benelli's head thwapping the back wall of the confessional as Giuseppe struggles to dislodge the corkscrew. The priest, however, is confused. "Madre di Dio, the bastard's alive!" he curses and throws open the curtain to finish the job. But instead of a live and kicking Benelli, he sees Giuseppe, one foot on Benito's chest, yanking at the monkey's head with both hands. Simultaneously, Giuseppe sees the priest.

"AAAAA!"

In a flash, Padre Jacopo throws open the confessional door "Murder!" he screams. "Benito Benelli has been murdered!"

There is no time to lose. Giuseppe abandons the corkscrew, grabs the picnic basket, and races from the church. From his shop, Rodolfo sees the boy disappear into the crowd as the priest and a terrified group of the faithful spill from the entrance.

That night, Rinaldo Sabatini will check out the rumours of his colleague's murder. He will hear from Padre Jacopo, Rodolfo the grocer, and others, then report to Don Camardo.

Immediately, Giuseppe will be marked for death, and within hours his mother, Maria Carlotta Castelli, will have martyred herself at the Grotte di Castellana.

Giuseppe is never seen in Bari again. Nor, more to the point, are the lire. Padre Jacopo, a man of God, has no time for such earthly concerns. Instead, he delights in the new moral tone of his Basilica. Over the next few months, he discovers a capacity for joy and a talent for smiling. "Blessèd are the meek," he sings, "for they shall inherit the earth." He pauses for a moment and admires the rich, powerful tones of the mighty new church bell, the bequest of an anonymous benefactor.

Visions

Whatever else Rinaldo Sabatini saw on the day he professed to have witnessed young Castelli shoot up to a cloud and into the waiting arms of his blessèd mother, Santa Maria Carlotta delle Grotte di Castellana, it wasn't Giuseppe.

Having run some distance from the Basilica, the boy enters a secluded alley to check the contents of Benelli's picnic basket, hoping to find the money Benito had come to Bari to collect. Instead, he comes face to face with the debonair head of Bruno Grapelli, tastefully arranged against a spray of fingers, toes and sweetmeats. It is a striking presentation.

A born strategist, Giuseppe realizes he is in a no-win situation. To run will invite suspicion that he killed Benelli and stole from Don Camardo. For either offense, he will die. On the other hand, if he goes home, he'll be arrested for murder. Il Padrone will hardly trust the silence of a ten-year-old; he'll be dead by dawn.

Of two lethal alternatives, running offers Giuseppe the sole possibility of survival. He races to the Bari transportation terminal down at the waterfront. He finds an unattended produce truck, slips under the burlap flap that hangs over the back frame, scales a wall of crates, and advances across their tops until he's hidden.

The driver returns shortly, ties down the flap and drives off with his cargo of almonds and olives. Giuseppe Agostino Castelli is bound for Rome.

It is night by the time the truck reaches the southern outskirts of the city and stops at a food terminal by the banks of the Tiber.

Giuseppe slips away before the driver discovers he's been carrying a stowaway. A thin rain is falling. He finds an abandoned
wagon and crawls underneath to sleep.

The following morning starts the long trek to the city centre.
The shock from the previous day's events is settling in, and occasionally Giuseppe stops, overcome by delirium. Surely that
explains the vivid midday image of his mother riding past on his
bicycle. But what of the sudden pain in his side an hour later?
And why the tickle ringing his forehead and the burning in the
palms of his hands and the soles of his feet?

By nightfall he has reached Trastavere, the major resi-
dential section of the city's core. He enters a small, walled park
and makes his way to the shrine of Santa Maria on the far side.
Within minutes, he falls asleep behind some bushes, the moonlit
statue of the Blessèd Virgin watching over him.

There follows a fantastic dream of waking in the middle of
the night, bathed in a cool, blue pool of light radiating from the
shrine. His jaw drops. There is no longer a painted statue of the
Virgin on the pedestal; it is his mother wearing a makeshift
white dress with a blue bedsheet insert. She has purple ribbons
in her hair, a gaping wound in her side, and stigmata on her
forehead, hands, and feet.

"Santa Maria tells me you've been a naughty boy, *mio
bambino*."

"Madre?"

"Yes, it is I, Maria Carlotta Castelli, the mother who bore
you in love and shame and unbearable agony. Your conception
destroyed my dreams, your youth destroyed my mind, and now
your sins have taken my life."

"You're not dead. You're alive with Nonno Vito and Nonna
Sofia."

"Not anymore. But don't be upset. Sons always break their
mothers' hearts, and mothers always forgive them. That's what
Santa Maria says, and she should know. 'My little Gesù was
quite the handful,' she tells me. 'I never knew what mischief he

was going to be up to next. Telling off his elders, changing water to wine, raising the dead—next to him, your little Giuseppe is a perfect angel!'

There follows the grating sound of stone on stone as the statue descends from its pedestal, "Besides, I'm quite happy to be dead. Madre Raffaella used to say, 'If Santa Maria wishes you to become a nun, she can take you to Heaven and make you a nun herself.' And that's exactly what she's done, so who's crazy now?"

"Why are you here?" Giuseppe asks in a small voice.

"You are my son. Where you are, there shall I be also."

The statue strokes his cheek with its cool, stone hand. The boy begins to cry.

"Hush now, no time for tears. The Antichrist has been born in Cuba and you have been chosen to deal with him. So don't let Don Camardo catch you or you'll be dead and God's plan will be all messed up."

The boy continues to weep. "I said hush!" She gives him what is intended as a gentle smack on the cheek, but being stone she doesn't realize her own strength and the boy crumples. He stops crying and looks up at her in terror.

"First, you must take the name of your father: Wichita. It is a name unknown to all but us and God. Second, you must make your way to the Holy Door at St. Peter's, there to stand before the statue of the Pietà. You will recognize it, for Nonno Vito and Nonna Sofia have a lovely carved miniature on their bedside table. Here you will be adopted by the new archbishop of Milan. He will raise you as a son and keep you safe."

With that, the statue climbs back on its pedestal and blows him a kiss. Giuseppe rubs his eyes furiously. This can't have happened. He looks at the statue again and is relieved. It isn't his mother after all. It is once again La Vergine.

Giuseppe bursts out laughing. He's had a strange dream, that's all. Only now he realizes his cheek hurts. And in the light of early dawn he notices something odd: around the statue's neck hangs a long purple ribbon.

The dome of St. Peter's dominates the sky to the northeast. Despite himself, Giuseppe is there within the hour. He enters by the Holy Door and goes to the Pietà, that ineffable monument to a mother's grief for her dead son. A man of the cloth stands beside him, but what of that? He doesn't look like an archbishop. And he certainly hasn't offered to take him in.

"What a fool I was," Giuseppe scoffs. "Afraid of dreams! Hah!" He is about to leave when his eye catches a strange movement on the right shoulder of La Vergine: it is a tiny apparition of his mother waving at him.

Giuseppe falls to his knees in terror and confusion. The man standing beside him turns, kneels, and comforts him. "Madre di Dio, that bruise upon your cheek!"

The prophecy is fulfilled.

Over the years, Cardinal Wichita has become inured to his mother's interferences. These were particularly frequent when he took the undergraduate course in exorcism at The Catholic University of the Sacred Heart in Milan. ("Why do you want to be rid of the mother who bore you in love and shame and unbearable agony?") On the whole, he has been grateful, as all his earthly triumphs are traced to her: a rare upbringing and a privileged seat at the table of the Lord. But therein lies the rub—the self-doubt and loneliness known to only children throughout time. What would he be without her ministrations? And how can he redeem her sacrifice, each honour deepening his obligation? Who *is* he, naked before eternity?

That is why as he doffs red robes to join Pope Innocent for a sauna at Castel Gandolfo he tingles with the thrill of possibility. According to the grapevine, Innocent plans to name him Vatican legate for The Phoenix Lottery. It is a gift from God: the chance to prove himself, to forge a personal legacy without the well-intentioned help of his mother.

Yet Wichita knows great risk attends. He will be acting on the world stage, a dangerous place for a bureaucrat used to working cloisters. The knives will be out: buzz at the Curia may consider his selection an act of divine inspiration, but jealous cynics whisper it's a reward for his role in the papal election.

Both views will alter shortly and sharply, for if Wichita's selection is divinely inspired, God's wit is satanic, and what today seems reward, will tomorrow seem payback. Gossip is as changeable as the wind, and reputations, like weather vanes, spin helplessly before it. Turbulence is about to beset the Holy See. Yet, as Wichita prepares to take steam with His Holiness, who but the Almighty could foresee that his involvement with Edgar "Junior" Beamish will thrust the Vatican into the tabloid press, linking a Prince of the Church to a Mafia hit, a basket of body parts, and an S&M bed and breakfast in rural Canada?

IV

Revolution
and
Witchcraft

The Pillow Lady

"Mom was hysterical. She thought they were going to chop off our heads. And what did Dad do? The son of a bitch took off in a golf cart! He left his four-year-old son to be murdered!"

Following the reading of the will, his father safely buried, Junior emerged from Homewood to take up his duties at BEI. To be sure, he had plans to turn the company inside out, but it never occurred to him that those plans might one day drive him loony enough to create The Phoenix Lottery. In fact, all that occurred to him was that his unfortunate performance at his father's funeral might signal a few unresolved issues.

With this in mind, he finds himself a frequent guest on the overstuffed wingback in his psychiatrist's sunroom. Dr. Billing is usually an ally, sitting quietly and writing prescriptions. Not so today. The revelation that his father once abandoned him to die has raised no hint of moral outrage in the man, much less commiseration. Dressed in a Lincoln green paisley silk smoking jacket, burgundy lounging pants, maroon ascot, and slippers, Billing sits surrounded by large bowls of nuts and shells, absorbed by an obstinate pistachio. A blue-point Siamese luxuriates between his feet.

"Aren't you going to say anything?"

"What would you like me to say?" Billing asks, holding the pistachio to the light.

"Something. Anything."

Billing peers quizzically at Junior. Unable to breathe, Junior says, "I want you to say you understand why I hate my Dad. I want you to say I don't have to feel guilty about it."

A long pause. Billing resumes his study of the nut. "Why do you need my approval to hate your father?"

"I don't! I—Look I don't come here to pour out my guts so you can stare at a goddamn pistachio."

"Then why do you come?"

"Fuck you."

Dr. Billing rolls the nut slowly between his fingers.

Junior is instantly contrite. "I'm sorry."

Billing puts the pistachio back in its bowl, folds his hands across his modest paunch and closes his eyes. "You said that when your mother phoned your father, she was afraid the locals were going to chop off your heads. Do you think your mother's judgment is reliable?"

"Okay. You've met my Mom. You know what she's like. One hand on a highball, the other down her throat. She's a mess. Fine. But she was at Lansky's Riviera when they took to the streets. She was an eyewitness."

"Do you think your mother's judgment is reliable?"

"Dad thought so. He took off in a golf cart."

"Do *you* think your mother's judgment is reliable?"

"Why are you taking his side?"

"Am I?"

Junior leaps to his feet. "Just give me the refill and let me out of here. You're all the same. You don't care if I live or die. I'm a nothing. A nobody. My life doesn't matter! I might as well not exist. I might as well be The Pillow Lady."

Ah yes, The Pillow Lady. Billing knows she's been a visitor since Junior's youth, though his patient has refused to speak of her in any detail. He stares at Junior like a frog on a lily pad. Junior feels increasingly uncomfortable. He wavers. He shifts his weight. Overcome with self-consciousness, he sits down again. Dr. Billing contains an all but imperceptible smile.

"So, would you like to talk about The Pillow Lady?"

In retrospect, Emily Pristable is convinced Junior began seeing The Pillow Lady when he was six months of age. At that time, Edgar Beamish Sr. was working in Havana for the duPonts, and Emily, who originally had gone to Cuba as a Baptist missionary, had just started as his private secretary.

Emily recalls Junior as an unusually cheery infant. He would lie in his crib pointing heavenward and gurgle with delight for no apparent reason. However, Junior's ability to respond to the unseen shortly took on an unsettling aspect. In the middle of a game of patty cakes, he would stop playing, flail the air, and burst into tears. Or, without notice, he would drop his favourite toy, press his little back to the bars of his crib, and shriek in horror.

These sudden mood swings became increasingly disconcerting. Kitty, terrified the child was simple, spent the better part of his first birthday in the bathroom weeping.

"He doesn't want to play with me. He just wants to cry."

"All babies do odd things," Edgar comforted from the other side of the locked door.

"My baby isn't odd. He's deranged."

Kitty found support for this view when Junior began talking. After "Mama" and "Papa," his first words were "Pi-woe Wehwee," which in due course developed into "Pillow Lady." There followed a series of alarming incidents in which Junior would point wildly, scream, "Pillow Lady Pillow Lady Pillow Lady," and run into his mother's skirt.

Junior called his unseen visitor The Pillow Lady because she looked like his favourite pillow: all puffed up, round, and covered in white with a stripe of blue down her back. She could come in all sizes, tiny as an egg, or filling the room like a big hot air balloon. He also described her as being very old which Kitty took personally. "It's me, damnit. It's always the mother. I've read my Freud. Old and fat. The little bastard!" Edgar tried to reassure her, to no avail, that when Junior said "old" he simply meant someone over the age of ten.

Initially, Junior remembered thinking The Pillow Lady was a clown because of the funny purple ribbons dangling from her head. But soon she began terrorizing him, hiding under his bed or in the shadows of his closet or, more spectacularly, materialising through walls and whizzing past his head.

As Junior's terrors increased, both in frequency and degree, Kitty developed a nervous condition. Her drinking turned into a vocation and it was concluded that she and Emily should fly Junior up to Toronto's Sick Children's Hospital for testing. Emily would stay in Toronto, attending to Junior, while Kitty would commit herself to The Grove for two weeks of uninterrupted rest.

The doctors at Sick Kids had good news and bad news. The good news was that Junior was perfectly healthy; the bad news was that there didn't appear to be a problem. "What do you mean there's no problem?" Kitty demanded. "What kind of an attitude is that?" The doctors replied that the Pillow Lady appeared to be no more than an imaginary playmate who would disappear in the fullness of time. Until then, they suggested she keep Junior out of the sun at midday and ensure he drink plenty of liquids. Kitty blamed the subsequent bedwetting for the worsening of her nervous condition.

Junior's bedwetting, incidentally was solved thanks to a fortuitous visit by an old school chum of Kitty's, Helena "Bunny" Bender, née Drummond. Helena was now married to Dr. Franklin K. Bender of Baltimore, a pediatrician with an enthusiasm for electricity. Dr. Bender had developed The Potty Alert, a grid of thin metal coils that was placed under the bed sheet and hooked to the nearest wall socket. At the hint of a tinkle, the bedwetter received a low-voltage wake-up call. The Potty Alert worked wonders on Junior. Indeed, it was so successful that Kitty, thinking ahead to the messy teen years to come, asked Dr. Bender if his contraption might also work for nocturnal emissions. Here Edgar drew the line.

The doctors at Sick Kids, however, were mistaken in the view that The Pillow Lady was an imaginary playmate of no consequence. Her intervention the night Fulgencio Batista fled Cuba was to change the world.

The Reunion

Varadero. December 15, 1958. Two weeks before the revolution triumphs.

Edgar and Kitty, along with four-year-old Junior and private secretary Emily Pristable, have arrived from Havana to celebrate Christmas and welcome in the New Year. But the main purpose of their visit is not relaxation. The couple hopes to use the holiday cheer to mend fences with Kitty's parents, Henry and Althea Danderville.

Edgar had once been the Dandervilles's darling. He'd met them at their Caledon estate, claiming to be a comrade of their late lamented son. They brought him to the drawing room where his three-hankie recollection of Joseph's heroic death in battle earned him both a sherry and a job. Bright and enterprising, Edgar rose quickly through the ranks. Then, betrayal! Elopement with their daughter Kitty! And her a Havergal debutante!

The Dandervilles sought to have the marriage annulled, but Kitty proudly announced herself pregnant. Swallowing hard, Althea contacted her second-cousin, Irénée duPont de Nemours, the French-born American industrialist. Within the week he had the young couple out-of-sight-out-of-mind in Cuba, where Edgar was put to work on family interests in Havana. Oh, the howls and recriminations when Kitty's pregnancy evaporated under the hot Cuban sun. Even the birth of grandson Junior, some years later, failed to melt the northern cold front.

This visit may change all that. Winter is increasingly hard on the Danderville bones, and for once the invitation to Christmas in Cuba has been accepted. Edgar is determined to heal the breach. Leaving nothing to chance, he has arranged for the family to stay at Xanadu, the private retreat of Irénée duPont himself.

The redoubtable duPont, now a fierce eighty-four, is vacationing in the south of France and is only too happy to give

Edgar the keys to his estate. Edgar has served with distinction for the past eight years; he's a young man with a future, a "comer," and drinking companion to boot. As for Althea, she and that Danderville fellow of hers raise damn fine horses on their Caledon estate. Definitely our sort.

When Irénée duPont arrived at Varadero in 1928, the little fishing village was an outlying section of Cárdenas, a city once renowned as "The Holland of the Americas." Created out of swamp by French, American, and British interests, Cárdenas was the first Cuban city to have electric lights and the second to be serviced by a railroad. While these amenities spoke to its power as a centre for sugar and coffee, its attractions were more than economic. The endless, unspoiled beauty of its Varadero beaches brought tourists by steamer and sailboat as early as 1872. In fact, Varadero was the first beach to see Europeans dressed in lightweight bathing attire. Unfortunately, Cárdenas unravelled when nationalists razed its plantations and destroyed its rail links at the close of the nineteenth century. From that point it had declined, its people mired in poverty, its magnificent architecture ravaged by neglect, and its tourism reduced to a faint sea breeze.

DuPont was a visionary who saw an opportunity to recapture the lost glory of the area, or at least of its beaches. A philanthropist of the old school, he financed a purification plant that delivered potable water to the area, underwrote the village school, which provided free education to the peninsula's children, and paid to rebuild the local church, the Iglesia Católica de Santa Elvira, when it was decimated by a cyclone in 1933. He also invested more than one and a half million dollars to create his spectacular Xanadu retreat.

Set on 512 hectares of land on the east end of the Varadero peninsula, Xanadu's features included an airstrip, a yacht harbour, a nine-hole golf course, and a stunning three-storey Spanish-colonial-style mansion. The mansion, perched atop the San

Bernadino butte, was designed with impossibly high ceilings, green tile roof set against white stucco walls, and a parade of elegant mahogany-framed windows and balconies. Surpassing these in magnificence, its *piece de resistance*, an expansive semi-enclosed rooftop bar with a breathtaking view of the powdery white sand beach along the peninsula's north coast.

DuPont's extravagance caught the attention of the world's politicians, entertainers, and mobsters. Varadero began to change. While duPont maintained his Xanadu mansion at a discreet remove from other habitation, he sold off snippets of land at its western border to members of America's social elite. Soon luxurious *pied-à-terres* of white stucco and terra cotta tile dotted the shoreline. Film stars like Cary Grant could be seen jogging along the brilliant sand, while gangsters like Al Capone grilled lobster on their marble beachfront patios. Offshore, Hemingway indulged his passion for deep-sea fishing, while regattas and a dizzying spin of lavish private parties provided endless recreation for the socially inclined.

Varadero never looked back. By 1958, its name alone conjures Latin rhythms, romance, and intrigue. It is heaven with a twist; paradise straight up. Small wonder, then, that Edgar and Kitty have chosen it as the fairy-tale backdrop for their planned reconciliation with the Dandervilles. But life, in the form of witchcraft and revolution, is about to provide the couple with something quite other than a fairy-tale ending.

The Dandervilles arrive fresh from a Miami stopover on a private plane arranged by Edgar. This is only their second trip to Cuba. It's also the first time they've seen their grandson since Kitty flew Junior up to Toronto's Sick Children's Hospital. The atmosphere is electric. Fortunately, the Dandervilles had a good flight.

"Kitty, Kitty, Kitty. My own, dear Kitty," says Althea, emerging from a formal embrace on the tarmac. "You ought to have told me the good news immediately, my dear."

"What good news?" Kitty enquires.

"That you're in the family way, my precious."

"I'm not!" Kitty splutters.

"Oh, you can't fool me with those pudgy cheeks and thick waist."

Kitty bursts into tears. "Mama, you know what the doctors said!"

"Oh, my angel, forgive me. However could I be so cruel? Why, then it must be the happy marriage that has you so nicely fleshed out. As for the problem down there, please don't cry. What do doctors know anyway? In the meantime, if I may be permitted a word of advice, mind the sweets. A mother worries."

With that, Althea sails off to the waiting convertible, her perfect hourglass form encased in a tasteful linen ensemble, her pale skin shaded from the sun by white gloves, an enormous soft-brimmed picture hat, and a large floral-print umbrella carried by her doting husband, Henry.

Junior is waiting for them on the front steps of the mansion. Emily has dressed him in a blue blazer, grey wool shorts, knee-high socks, and a polka dot bow tie. He is four, but confronted by Granny D. he quickly regresses.

"Aren't we the proper little man?" Althea enthuses with what she presumes to be grandmotherly affection. She turns to Kitty. "Why he's cute as a button." Extending her hand to Junior she says, "Would you like to shake Granny's hand?"

Junior shakes his head, thumb stuck firmly in mouth.

"It's your Granny Danderville," Kitty encourages. "You remember her, don't you?"

Junior shakes his head and hides behind Emily's skirts. His pants itch. He scratches his bum.

"He's just making strange," says Emily, placing a comforting hand on the boy's shoulder.

"Some things never change," Althea replies darkly. She remembers well the five-minute encounter with Junior that she and Henry endured at Sick Kids. The child not only refused to look at them, he kept his hands clamped over his eyes. They tried

coaxing a peek. No luck. Not to be denied by a tadpole, Althea
pried the screaming boy's hands from his face, finger by finger.
But the stubborn beast kept his eyes squinched shut. Not even
a bribe of chocolate could tempt the creature to open them.

"Not to worry," Althea brightens, "lots of peculiar children
grow up to be normal."

"Would you like to play horsy, Junior?" Henry asks, dropping to all fours.

"Henry, please! That's what servants are for."

The company passes through the foyer and enters the main
reception area. Tension is instantly relieved with a chorus of
appreciative oohs and ahhs; servants have decorated a sixteen-
foot pine tree flown in from New England for the occasion. The
boughs bend beneath the weight of crystal icicles, colourful
balls of eggshell porcelain, seasonal figurines, and large cones
gilded with gold leaf. Atop the tree is a large Christmas angel
with a glittering halo and a flowing robe of real ermine studded
with jewels.

Junior has been in awe of the angel since he first laid eyes
on her. He's so proud to show her off that he forgets he's shy.
"Look at the angel! Her hat is as wide as Granny's."

"It's called a halo, dear," Kitty intervenes with a nervous
laugh.

"I want a halo!"

The adults smile indulgently, but Junior is not to be patron-
ized. He has found his vocation. "When I grow up," he announces proudly, "I'm going to be a Christmas angel. And I'm going
to wear a beautiful dress and have a big halo and long, golden
hair, and fly around giving presents to poor people. Everybody
will want to kiss me." He begins to dance around as he imagines
the Christmas angel would dance, with his hands high in the air
and his long, imaginary hair flowing behind him.

"Yes, well," says Edgar brusquely, "Anyone for rum punch?"

It is at this point that Junior lets out a hair-raising shriek,
drops to the floor, and skitters backwards into a corner like a
crab. Terrified, he scrunches into a ball and points at the ceiling.

"The Pillow Lady's in the chandelier!" he screams. Emily runs to comfort him. "Pillow Lady! Pillow Lady!"

"He's still going on about the Pillow Lady?" Althea demands, her right eyebrow arching off her forehead. "I understood those Toronto head doctors had put an end to that." Her gaze swoops to the unfortunate Kitty who collapses sobbing at Edgar's feet. Edgar, in turn, implores Henry with the helpless look of a man who knows he ought to be doing something, but can't figure out exactly what.

No such indecision affects Sara Pérez, the head maid. She knows she must visit the high priest, the *babalawo*, immediately. There is witchcraft afoot.

Santería

Sara has been at Xanadu for ten years, employed by duPont on the recommendation of the local schoolmaster. She lives in the village with her mother, husband, and four children, in a three-room house built of wood and tin. Every morning before dawn she bicycles out to the mansion. Here, with other servants, she tends to the kitchen, does light housekeeping, and makes the beds of late-sleeping guests.

A striking, literate woman with a wry smile, Sara is a descendant of Yoruban slaves. Rulers of the once-powerful kingdom of Benin, these Africans, from what is now southwest Nigeria, were brought to Central and South America by Spanish, Portuguese, and French slave traders in the first half of the sixteenth century.

The Yoruba followed an animistic religion presided over by the deity Oloddumare. If Christians struggle with the concept of the Trinity, admire the Yoruba for handling a Pentad: Oloddumare is the nature of god eternal, Olorun is Oloddumare in action, Olofi is Oloddumare as creation itself, Eledáa is Oloddumare as the holy spirit in humanity, and Ori is Oloddumare as the power awakening us to the divine.

At the moment of creation, Oloddumare as Olofi grew until he became so big it was impossible for him to deal with the tiny problems of mere mortals. So he created the orishas, a group of over four hundred sub-gods, each with a specific area of expertise. It is to these orishas that believers pray rather than to a preoccupied Almighty. In this respect, the orishas function like Catholic saints, mediating between humankind and an all-powerful God. But unlike Catholic saints, the orishas were never living, breathing mortals. Ironically, once-human Catholic saints embody notions of spiritual perfection, whereas the wholly ethereal orishas, like the gods of ancient Greece, are given to all manner of human foibles. One such quirk is a lust for blood, particularly for that of chickens and goats. Animal sacrifice was, and is, one of the primary payments to the orisha for the casting of a successful spell, compensation being necessary as magic is ultimately a business transaction between a willing god and a needy supplicant.

Sixteenth-century slave traders carrying their Yoruban captives to the Caribbean were understandably unnerved to discover that their human cargo was practising witchcraft below deck. They sought to stamp out the heathen practices, but the Yoruba camouflaged their faith with the simple expedient of adopting the religious forms of their Catholic masters: they would hide dolls representing their orishas inside hollowed-out statues of Christian saints, and pray accordingly. The warrior god Changó was camouflaged by the name Santa Barbara; Babalú-Ayé, god of sickness and epidemic, was raised, appropriately enough, by calling upon Santo Lazaro; while the great god Oshún responded to prayers to Our Lady of Charity.

In Spanish-speaking colonies, such as Cuba and Puerto Rico, African witchcraft and Christianity syncretized into Santería; in the Portuguese colony of Brazil, the amalgam became recognized as Candomblé; most famously, in the French colony of Haiti, it developed into Voodoo. Santería is now so integrated into the culture that it numbers over one hundred million adherents throughout Latin America, with millions of other devotees belonging to its cousins Voodoo and Candomblé. Nor are these religions the preserve of the illiterate or outcast. Initiates include devout pillars of the community who attend Eucharist by day and animal sacrifice by night, a juxtaposition of rituals which should not surprise the Vatican; after all, the doctrine of transubstantiation, which claims communion bread and wine transform to the literal body and blood of Christ, turns Roman Catholics into cannibals.

At least that is Sara's view.

Destined to become a *santera*, a member of the Santerían priesthood, Sara has seen much that Western eyes would scarcely credit. To her, it is beyond question that Junior has seen the Pillow Lady hiding in the chandelier. Let Western materialists think what they may, she knows the household is in need of a spell. She forgoes lunch, pedalling to the home of her spiritual leader, the babalawo, at the corner of Avenida Tercera and Calle 48. She confers with him briefly, promising a chicken and a bottle of rum by week's end, and returns to Xanadu in time to serve pre-dinner cocktails.

Emily is upstairs with Junior, distracting the boy with rousing Baptist hymns, a triumphant progression of big fat chords belted out in no-nonsense four-four time. Kitty considers Emily's singalongs unspeakably déclassé, but there can be no denying their power to entertain the very young. What Baptists lack in subtlety, they make up in exuberance.

Meantime, Althea holds forth in the library with a dry martini. "Our Joseph, may his soul rest in peace, was a war hero. He didn't want to grow up to be a Christmas angel. He wanted to grow up to be a soldier!" Althea sets her glass down firmly, serving notice that cocktail hour is over. She and Henry navigate their way upstairs to dress for dinner, leaving Edgar and Kitty to knock back a pitcher of Mojitos.

Sara seizes the initiative. "Forgive me, but I hear the little one cry. I see his eyes. He is in some danger, yes, for he is haunted by an *espíritu intranquilo*. You call that, I think, a restless spirit. Please, do not worry. I have seen the babalawo. All will be well. You make for your son a *resguardo*—a talisman, yes? Sew a small, white bag. In it put garlic, yerbabuena, and perejil. Camphor also—evil spirits love camphor. Sew this bag shut and dip it in the holy water of seven churches. The espíritu intranquilo who frightens your boy will vanish."

There is a pause. Kitty smiles graciously. "Thanks ever so much, Sara, but that's not how we do things in Ontario."

Sara considers this. "You are right. I do not know the ways of Ontario." She clears the sideboard and exits. Edgar leaves Kitty with the Mojitos and follows Sara to the kitchen, picking up a pencil and notepad en route.

"Sara, I'd like to have a word with you."

"I am sorry if I interfere."

"Not at all. About that talisman . . . Where can I find some perejil?"

One Night

In the middle of the night, Junior wakes in time to spare himself the agony of The Potty Alert. Half-asleep, he gets up without disturbing Emily, who has set up a cot for herself beside his bed. "It's no never-you-mind," she'd said to Edgar and Kitty. "If he wakes with nightmares, I'll be there to see to him. You need to be fresh as daisies to entertain the Dandervilles." He makes his way down the corridor to the bathroom. The door is closed. There is a funny smell coming from the other side and the sound of someone crying.

When Junior pushes against the door, it opens. He sees his mother slumped on the floor beside the toilet in her nightgown. At first she doesn't notice him.

"Mommy? Are you okay?"

Kitty looks up, face drawn, eyes glassy. "Mommy's okay, sweet pea."

"What are you doing on the floor?"

"Oh, Mommy's just looking for something. Go to bed."

"I have to tinkle."

"Good boy." Kitty rises. She pulls the overhead chain and the toilet flushes. She walks unsteadily to the door, leaving the boy to attend to his business. At the last minute she turns and implores pitifully, "Junior, do you think Mommy's fat?"

"No Mommy."

"Would you love Mommy more if she was thinner?"

"No Mommy."

"You're an angel, my angel." With that, Kitty wafts down the corridor.

This incident is never referred to again, but Junior notices how after every meal his Mommy excuses herself to go and look for something in the bathroom. He often wonders what she's lost and why she can never seem to find it.

Mrs. Resguardo

Christmas morning arrives in less time than it takes to slide down a chimney. The brightly wrapped packages around the tree are ravaged in a trice, leaving the floor awash in ripped tissues, wrapping paper, ribbons, boxes, and bows. Everyone at Xanadu receives a gift prized above all others. For Kitty and Althea it is a set of silk scarves by Chanel; for Edgar and Henry, hand-rolled Cohiba Espléndidos in cedar boxes of twenty-five; for Emily, a new leather briefcase with gold embossed monogram; for the servants, a framed Kodak photograph of Irénée duPont signed with "Best Wishes, 1958."

Junior has a favourite present too. It is a dolly. And not just any dolly. This dolly is homemade, personally stitched by his father. The body is a small white sack. A hand-painted thimble is attached for a head and knotted pieces of cloth sewn to the sides and bottom of the sack serve as arms and legs. It looks terrible and smells worse. Initially, Junior isn't sure he likes the dolly.

"Is this some kind of joke?" Kitty asks. Junior wonders the same thing until he hears his father's reply.

"No joke at all. This is a magic doll that protects little girls and boys from The Pillow Lady." His father's back is to him so that he won't see the sly wink made to the grownups.

"It stinks," says Kitty, ignoring the signal.

"The smell comes from the secret ingredients. Those ingredients are what make the magic that keeps The Pillow Lady away."

"I'm not surprised. That stench would keep anyone away," says Althea, feigning an attack of the vapours.

"I wish you'd told me about this nonsense beforehand," Kitty says, with an eye to her mother's approval. "Sara, be a dear and put this in the garbage. We'll get you another dolly,

Junior. A proper dolly that talks when you pull her string. Won't that be nicer than this stinky old thing?"

"No!" cries Junior, clutching it to his bosom. "It's my dolly to keep me safe!"

"But Mommy keeps you safe," Kitty reassures, a forced smile on her face as she attempts to extract the offending present from her son's grip. Junior clutches his talisman as if salvation itself depends upon it. Which, of course, it does.

"Let. Go. Now."

"Leave the boy alone, Kitty! You'd rather he have fits about The Pillow Lady?"

"You're not helping matters," says Kitty, shooting daggers. "Junior, you're being naughty. And Mommy doesn't love naughty little boys!" Surreptitiously, she digs her fingernails into Junior's hands. He responds by biting her wrist. Kitty screams. Junior tears upstairs with his dolly and hides under his bed.

"Wait till I get my hands on you, you little bastard!" Kitty roars. "Don't think you can hide under your bed. I'll have Sara poke you out from under there with a mop!" Kitty, it must be said, is not herself this morning. She started her day with two rum eggnogs and a Mojito. "It's Christmas, for Christ's sake," she exclaimed when Edgar caught her sneaking a refill.

Edgar prevents Kitty from giving chase and, in a rare show of force, orders everyone to sit down. They do. "The doll stays," Edgar says. "It smells, but that's a small price to pay, don't you think?" His voice is so cold, ice cracks in Kitty's glass. He signals Emily to make sure Junior is safely out of earshot. "In four years nothing has managed to get rid of The Pillow Lady. Not discipline. Not doctors. Nothing. Junior believes in her. And as long as he does, he's going to throw fits. We need to fight fire with fire: attack imagination with imagination. Junior has faith in the power of this doll. That's all that matters. Never underestimate faith."

Edgar's audience ranges from hostile to dubious. In the absence of an effective counter-argument, however, opposition is reduced to low-level grumbling. Edgar assures the group that, in any case, the doll will soon be gone: if The Pillow Lady shows her face, it will be judged a failure and consigned to the trash; if she stays away, it will soon be discarded as Junior grows up.

In the end, only Althea remains obdurate, but she is known to be difficult on principle. As she and Henry go upstairs for a mid-morning nap, she mutters fiercely, "A dolly indeed! Our Joseph, may he rest in peace, never played with dollies. He played with dinky toys. I swear to God that boy will grow up to be artistic."

Kitty, who has been gobbling shortbreads to calm her nerves, excuses herself to go and look for something that seems suddenly to have gone missing. Sara, having exchanged a significant glance with Edgar, sets the servants to a quick tidy-up and retires to the kitchen to prepare roast duck with a plum-pear sauce, decorated with edible flowers. Emily, allowing her practical nature to override her aversion to hocus-pocus, gives Edgar's hand a quick squeeze, whispers, "Well done," then retires for an hour of Bible study and prayer. And Edgar?

Edgar goes for a long walk along the beach. He smiles recalling the reaction when Junior first pulled the talisman from its box. The family had been taken aback by its smell. What would the reaction have been were it known that two days prior he had dipped the doll in holy water at churches in Cárdenas, Coliseo, Matanzas, San Miguel de los Baños, and the Iglesia Católica de Santa Elvira de Varadero?

Why tempt fate? It was the same question he'd asked himself in wartime, rubbing his lucky rabbit's foot before skipping through a field of landmines. His buddies used to tease him, but he was the only one from his platoon who could still skip.

To Edgar, such behaviour isn't superstitious, it's simply an awareness that the universe is controlled by powers unimpressed by logic. "How can anyone who ever played a hunch mock second sight?" For this reason, he defers to religious rituals whatever their source. While they may be no more than spiritual bells and whistles, they may also be keys to the great beyond. In this he practices the self-interested calculation of atheists who, on the off-chance, reserve their final breath for a deathbed repentance.

Edgar is now some distance from the mansion. His shirt clings to his back. He removes it. Although December is winter in Cuba, it is still balmy for a Canadian, even one who has lived in the country for years. He lets the heavy salt breeze stream over him. Suddenly, he is overwhelmed by an emotional riptide.

He staggers to a nearby palm tree, collapses, digs his fingers into the sand and lets out an otherworldly wail. Tears course down his cheeks, an inarticulate cry of yearning and loss. He strips naked and hurls himself into the surf. "God! God! Where are you, God?" He lets his body be pummelled by the whitecaps, beaten until he can return to the mansion and carry on as if nothing has happened.

Today it is waves, but one day release will lead him to a bed and breakfast in Port Elgin.

God's Spy

Santa Maria Carlotta Castelli delle Grotte di Castellana had fibbed on at least one occasion about her conversations with La Vergine. If the truth be known, La Vergine never told her the Antichrist had been born in Cuba; Maria Carlotta had desperately wanted to grab Madre Raffaella's attention, and mentioning La Vergine and the Antichrist in the same sentence had seemed a likely ploy. Nor was it entirely a bare-faced lie, for La Vergine had implied very strongly that the boy born in Cuba would grow up to be the nemesis of her son, Giuseppe. Surely a loving mother is entitled to think of her child's nemesis as an Antichrist, if not *the* Antichrist. So from Maria Carlotta's point of view all she had done was to stretch the point.

Her intrusions into the life of Junior Beamish began harmlessly enough. She simply wanted to check up on the brat's development. Maria Carlotta didn't consider this nosy; it was basic research. What better way to protect Giuseppe in his confrontation-to-come than by getting to know his enemy?

Imagine her surprise, then, when the infant responded to her hovering figure with gurgles of delight. Surely her purple ribbons could not be tickling the munchkin's nose; she was a spirit for heaven's sake. But her discombobulation had only begun. Surprise turned to annoyance when she realized the child found her a source of hilarity, and annoyance turned to positive rage when the child began referring to her as The Pillow Lady. Her English might be rudimentary, but she knew all words relating to the bedroom, thanks to her interlude with Private Wichita, and the idea that a toddler would dare compare her to an overstuffed sack of chicken feathers drove her to distraction.

Maria Carlotta threw herself into revenge with an appetite befitting an opera diva. Leaping from behind furniture or dive-bombing through the ceiling, she soon was able to throw Junior into fits of hysteria at will. Most fun was when she'd curl up beside the boy in his crib. He'd roll over half-asleep and there she'd be, eyeball to eyeball.

Her delight in tormenting the lad grew as he began walking. She discovered she could induce the best reactions in the bathroom. She'd zoom out the spout when he brushed his teeth, appear in a bubble when he took a bath, or balloon out of the toilet when he lifted the lid to make potty. So skilful was she at tormenting the poor creature that Junior soon refused to go to the bathroom after dark. This, in turn, produced the bedwetting which, to Maria Carlotta's delight, threw the entire household into an uproar. One can only surmise her glee at the arrival of The Potty Alert. On a nightly basis Junior was forced to choose between supernatural visitation and low-level electrocution.

In short order, what had begun as spying rapidly developed into deliberate psychic aggression; Maria Carlotta's mission became nothing less than to drive Junior insane. There was ample motive beyond spite. If the boy was institutionalized, she reasoned, he would pose no threat to her Giuseppe. While unbecoming in a saint, a ruthless streak is to be encouraged in a mother, and expected in one who so recently sacrificed her life for her imperilled son.

With the arrival of Junior's Christmas dolly, however, Maria Carlotta opted for a change of tactics. Unlike evil spirits, she abhorred the smell of camphor. Consequently, she decided to lie low, biding her time until Junior's defences would drop. Thus Maria Carlotta added the principle of dynamic contrast to her arsenal of emotional sabotage. The next time she pounced she was determined to jar the child's psyche forever.

And she did.

Hypnosis

Junior, splayed on the russet wingback in Dr. Billing's sunroom, is in an hypnotic trance. Dr. Billing is an advocate of hypnotic trances. With his patient semi-conscious, he is free to catch up on his correspondence or to floss bits of pistachio from between his back molars. Today, however, the hypnosis is a critical part of his patient's therapy. Billing is not only listening but taking notes, for Junior is talking about The Pillow Lady, his father, and the night Castro drove Batista from Cuba.

Memory is a conundrum for Billing. It informs his patients' assumptions and therefore their behaviour. Yet the good doctor has noticed that his patients often reconstruct their past according to their current frame of mind. In Junior's case, this opens two possibilities. The first is that his childhood was as he has described it. The second is that he has fashioned his recollections to conform with his adult perceptions.

Billing recognizes that, either way, coming to terms with the father/son dynamic is necessary to Junior's healing. The question is whether Junior's memory of that night in Varadero is a red herring in this struggle, or whether it holds the key to the parent/child rupture that has so devastated his life.

Complicating Billing's thinking is the knowledge that Junior speaks of The Pillow Lady as if she is real. If Junior treats this boyhood fiction as fact, what stock can be placed in his other memories? Billing hopes that hypnosis will clear his patient's mind of subconscious filters. He listens to Junior with the attentiveness he usually reserves for his cats.

Granny and Grampa flew to Havana with Mom for the big New Year's Eve blowout at The Riviera. I was glad

Granny was gone. She smelled of dead flowers. I don't think she liked me. I certainly didn't like her. She's a lot nicer now that she's lost her mind.

Dad stayed behind. Emily stayed behind, too, to keep me out of Dad's hair. After tucking me into bed, she was going to spend the night with friends she'd bumped into at the Baptist Mission in town.

After supper, the servants left for home and Dad, Emily, and I went to the upstairs bar. They watched the sunset while I played with Mrs. Resguardo. That was the name I gave my doll. I think the name came from Sara. I loved Mrs. Resguardo. She'd been with me since Christmas morning, and thanks to her The Pillow Lady had stayed away.

I remember Emily gave me a brown-sugar sandwich, which was my favourite bedtime snack. Then I'm lying with my head in her lap, playing with Mrs. Resguardo's hair, and Emily's singing, "When Mothers of Salem," until I'm half asleep, and she carries me to my room, tucks me in and gives me a good night kiss. I hear her car drive off.

The next thing I remember is a dream. I'm in my bedroom and the Christmas Angel is at the foot of my bed and she's doing a little ballet to "Dance of the Sugar Plum Fairy." Well the dance is pretty amazing, because being an angel she can subdivide in time to the music, so that pretty soon I'm seeing a gazillion angels doing a Busby Berkeley number. This is very exciting, especially as I want to *be* the Christmas Angel.

The music stops and I start clapping and the Angel, who is back to being a single angel, curtsies. But when she curtsies, her halo wobbles and I realize it's just a wig. She rips off her face, like it was attached with Velcro, and I'm not looking at an angel anymore. I'm looking at The Pillow Lady. She opens her mouth and laughs, and her teeth are huge.

I holler and wake up.

I'm in my bedroom, covered in sweat. I reach out for Mrs. Resguardo, but she isn't there. I'm alone and it's dark and I'm afraid to call out because if I do I'll rouse The Pillow Lady and she'll come after me.

Down the hall, the telephone starts to ring. Daddy doesn't answer it. I wonder where he is. The ringing stops. I'm overcome with this fear that Daddy's gone. I tell myself, no, he's just down the hall, asleep. I just have to go to his room and crawl into bed next to him, and I'll be safe.

I get up very quietly and tiptoe down the hall. I stop at his room. I look inside. He isn't there. Where is he? I need protection. Where's Mrs. Resguardo? The last time I saw her, she was in the upstairs bar. To get there I have to climb the narrow winding staircase.

Suddenly, out of the silence, I hear drums. Drums coming out of the dark. And someone, something, is moving around in the bushes outside. I hear a swoosh of leaves, the crack of branches. Who is it? What is it? Where's Daddy? I race up the staircase, reach the top. The light of the moon throws shadows across the room. Shapes grow out of the furniture.

I run to the sofa where I played with Mrs. Resguardo and throw off the cushions. The telephone rings again. Somebody downstairs answers it. They're in the house, whoever was outside. And now they're crashing through the rooms below. I hear a plate smash. I hide behind the sofa. Where are you, Daddy? Why did you leave me?

They're coming up the stairs. They're in the bar. And then they're gone. I hear a motor in the driveway. I run to the open balcony. Down on the golf course, I see Daddy driving away on a cart.

"Don't leave me, Daddy! Please, Daddy! Wait!" He doesn't. He just speeds off, veers behind a stand of palms, and disappears into the night.

Outside, the drums are getting louder and I see torches dancing up the road from town. They're coming to the house! What will they do to me? I hear the laugh of a dead woman, turn, and see the Pillow Lady sitting on the bar.

I start to run. Down flights of stairs, through the entrance hall, out the door. I don't know where to go next, so I run after Daddy, the sound of drums filling my head. And everywhere, The Pillow Lady, behind bushes and trees, laughing at me. I fall in a sand trap. There's sand in my eyes, ears, mouth.

"Daddy!" The Pillow Lady's getting closer. I try to get up, but I can't. I keep slipping and she's closer and closer and closer.

A blinding light zooms toward me. Headlights. The car screeches to a halt and Emily jumps out. She cradles me, "Junior, it's okay. I'm here. You're safe."

I pass out.

Loose Lips

Junior remains unconscious with a raging fever for three days. He wakes up to find himself in his bed, safe and sound. Emily, sitting in a chair beside him, is holding his hand. She has been with him the whole time, sleeping in a cot next to his bed.

All the sound and fury of New Year's Eve has vanished. In its place, celebration and rejoicing: the dictator Batista has been put to flight, and even if he's managed to smuggle out a small fortune to Florida, this is a tiny wrinkle to the revolution's storybook ending.

It has been one of the most peaceful insurrections in world history. The worst Havana saw was a couple of broken windows and a few pigs and goats in the lobby of The Riviera. In the end, the hatred for Batista was so pervasive that government soldiers simply laid down their arms after a few minor skirmishes. Everywhere citizens dance in the streets to the rapturous beat of "*Mamá, Son de la Loma,*" a tribute to the guerrillas of the Sierra Maestra. Justice on the impoverished island appears to have arrived. The air is alive with possibility.

Even the orishas give their blessing, or so it seems. Months later, Cuban exiles will mutter that Castro owes his success to the black magic of the *mayomberos*. But for now the entire country is abuzz with the miracle of the dove. As Castro began his victory speech in Santiago de Cuba, white doves filled the skies, one of them descending from the heavens to perch upon his shoulder. Surely this was a blessing from Our Lady of Mercy, Obatalá, orisha of purity and peace. A political endorsement of the first order.

There is a slight cold front to the north. Washington has dispatched three naval destroyers to sit in Havana's harbour, a signal that Uncle Sam is not indifferent to events in his own backyard. This move is more symbolic than substantive, however, a reassuring gesture to those American nationals of faint heart. Indeed, until its business interests are confiscated following agrarian reforms in May 1959, America's attitude toward the *Fidelistas* is best described as one of forbearance. As a result, initial fears of radical upheaval within the country have quickly subsided.

Yet, if life at Xanadu has resumed its idyllic pace, the events of New Year's Eve have caused a tectonic upheaval in Junior's psyche. Like children everywhere, and more than a few adults, he sees himself at the centre of the universe. And so he emerges from his fever gripped with the conviction that he, four-year-old Junior Beamish, is the ultimate cause of the recent tumult. The Cuban revolution means nothing to him. All that matters is that his father abandoned him even as he cried out in the night.

Junior has idolized his father, a mysterious man who, following each absence on business, has delighted the boy with astonishing presents. Why would such a god abandon him? The unavoidable conclusion is that he is unworthy of love.

Irrefutable proof of his worthlessness can be found everywhere. Who, if not he, is to blame for his mother crying in the bathroom? Who, if not he, is to blame for his father spending so much time away? Who, if not he, is to blame for the rift between his parents and grandparents? Yes, he, Junior the Malignant, is clearly the supreme cause and architect of all his family's problems.

Any doubts on this score are put to rest by his granny on the day she and Henry take their leave and return to Canada. Junior always pretends to be asleep whenever his granny is in his room. It is the best strategy he can devise to avoid her. This day the ruse results in his overhearing a devastating conversation.

"That's what you get for marrying beneath you," his granny tells his mother, with a glance in his direction. "I mean for heaven's sake, we all make mistakes, but that's one mistake you could have avoided. Dr. Betts should have taken care of it; a little D. and C. and no one would have been the wiser. I even

made the arrangements. Oh no, you had to have him. Well now
it's too late. I hope you're satisfied. That boy is a curse on the
family."

His mother begins to cry. Althea watches, making no move
to comfort. It isn't that she is cold; she is embarrassed. She
glances at her watch, but Kitty isn't about to stop. Althea is
forced to relent. She crosses to her daughter and holds her
awkwardly. She has always held her daughter awkwardly, even
when Kitty was a baby. "Of course I want to hold her," she'd
pleaded. "But she's so . . . squishy. I'm afraid she'll break." The
truth is that Althea has always feared touch.

"There's no use crying over spilt milk," Althea says, stroking
Kitty's hair. "You must make the best of it." Now it is she who
bursts into tears. "Kitty, Kitty, my own dear Kitty, forgive your
mother for being harsh. It's just that I can't bear to see what's
become of you. You had such promise."

Junior doesn't catch all the words, but he knows what they
mean. He should never have been born.

Junior turns in on himself, refusing to eat or speak. He
throws away Mrs. Resguardo, who eventually had been found
under his covers exactly where Emily placed her. When Maria
Carlotta pops up next to inspect her handiwork he doesn't respond. He has shut down.

After a week, doctors are called. They try force-feeding. He
spits out everything they put in his mouth. Tubes are stuck in
his arms in an attempt to drip nourishment into him. He rips
them out. As a last resort they strap him down. Finally the in-
travenous does its job.

There follows another revelation that spins his head like a
top. It comes as the result of a volcanic fight in which his
parents each blame the other for his condition. "Why weren't
you watching him?" his mother yells. "Me? If it wasn't for your
cock-and-bull phone call from Havana, none of this would have
happened." "Don't you blame me, you sonovabitch," Kitty re-
joins, zeroing in for the kill: "Why did you leave on that golf
cart with Junior still in the house? You ran away! You aban-

doned him to die! If that secretary of yours hadn't found him, who knows what would have become of my boy?" The upshot of the ensuing battle over the phone call is to redirect Junior's self-hate toward the father who left him to die.

Revolution at the Riviera

The story of the phone call.

That fateful New Year's, Kitty and her parents arrive in Havana set for a spectacular evening at The Riviera, the famous hotel owned by the equally famous Meyer Lansky. Lansky, a one-man Mafioso brains trust with the face of an underfed bullfrog, has a way with a balance sheet. He's moved his operations to Cuba since the Feds shut him down stateside, opening the Montmartre Casino, The Riviera, and other Havana landmarks. Now, with a wink to the American Revenue and Justice Departments, he bills himself as The Riviera's lowly kitchen manager, but there's no doubt who calls the shots.

Goodfellas like Lansky are everywhere in Havana. They rule the joint with the help of Batista's police, goons bought off with a little moolah and skirt. Whether pedalling cards, flesh, or a night on the town, Lansky and Co. are pros who know their market: American businessmen with more money than taste. Showgirls at the Hilton and Tropicana make Carmen Miranda look dowdy, while those at the Casa Marina come equipped with features most people presume do not exist.

Of all the monuments to the nouveau riche, Lansky's Riviera is in a class by itself. Its sweep of windows provide a breathtaking panorama of the Malecón, the famed avenue of lovers that rims Havana's sea. Best of all, it features a rococo casino that glitters brighter than a Fabergé egg. The Riviera, in short, is a Fifties wet dream come true.

A pro like Lansky should twig that something big is going down on this last day of 1958. While American tourists gamble and sunbathe as usual, the Riviera's switchboard is flooded with calls cancelling reservations for the big New Year's blast. By showtime, the only guests are out-of-towners who've flown in on private planes, oblivious to the change in the political weather.

Kitty, flying high on Mojitos since lunch—"It's New Year's, for Christ's sake"—doesn't notice. Seeing double, she thinks the room looks pretty full. What Henry thinks is anybody's guess, but he seems to be enjoying his party horn. It is for Althea Danderville, Ontario doyenne extraordinaire, to pass judgment on Havana's finest hotel. "Very nice," she sniffs, "but it hasn't a patch on The King Eddy."

At one in the morning, the show is in full swing. Banks of statuesque Latin beauties dazzle down the neon staircase to the insistent beat of the orchestra's rumba. Breasts tremble at the lips of sparkling bikini cups that redefine "lift and separate." Buttocks sprout plumage in colours unknown to nature. Cascades of fruit and feathers explode from impossible hats. *Muy sabroso*!

Lansky interrupts, whispering in the conductor's ear. The conductor signals the orchestra to stop playing. It does, stranding the dancers in mid-beat.

"Ladies and gentlemen," Lansky hushes the crowd. "I apologize for the interruption. Fidel Castro has taken Santiago de Cuba. The government has fallen. Fulgencia Batista, President of Cuba, has fled the country with his family." A stunned silence. "Please keep calm. American naval destroyers are en route to Havana as we speak. I repeat: Keep calm. Stay inside. Guards have been placed at all the doors of the hotel to ensure your safety. Now back to the show. Happy New Year."

The conductor looks at his audience. They look back, a wall of frozen fish. He turns to the dancers. Their smiles haven't budged, but their eyes are pinned. He checks out the orchestra. The third trombone looks iffy, but the show must go on. He raises a nervous baton.

Before the first downbeat there is a low rumble. It seems to be coming from all directions. It grows deafening. Is it an earthquake? The running of the bulls? Dancers bolt the stage, musicians hug their instruments and, as one, the audience swarms The Riviera's windows for a panoramic view of the mayhem beyond.

They see the source of the noise for themselves: Cubans from the squalid slums which surround the Yankee palaces are taking to the streets. To the din of voices and feet are added whistles, horns, a tumult of drums, and the squawks, squeals, and brays of animals running wild. The Malecón is filling up — no, it is packed. Cars are trapped; celebrants coat deSotos and Fords.

How long before they storm the casinos? Castro promised the people he wouldn't just deport the Yankee gangsters, he'd shoot them. In his tux, Lansky looks cool as a cucumber, but he's shitting bricks.

He sees George Raft down the street. The Hollywood tough guy is standing on the steps of the casino of which he is part owner. Incredibly, Raft is daring the horde to take him on. Lansky grabs a megaphone and shouts out a window, "What the fuck are you doing, George? This isn't a goddamn movie set!"

Then his jaw drops. Up and down the Malecón, he sees Cubans lopping the heads off parking meters. Batista claimed money from these meters went to the poor, though everyone knew it fed his family's foreign accounts. "My God!" Lansky exclaims in solidarity with the meters, "They're chopping off their heads!" Unfortunately, he forgets he's speaking into a megaphone.

Panic ensues. Drunks, conjuring nightmares from *A Tale of Two Cities*, run wild in all directions. Before Lansky can restore order, Kitty has propelled herself to the mezzanine. If they're chopping off heads in Havana, she thinks, what must they be doing in Varadero? Her baby is in danger. Where's a phone?

Several swim into view, but each is surrounded by a crowd. In Kitty's case, two crowds. She looks over the mezzanine railing. The lobby is a tempest of sunburned bald spots and hysterical wives. Outside, a mob of celebrating Cubans presses its face to the plate-glass window, fists raised in a victory salute.

Suddenly security is breached. Kitty watches in horror as The Riviera's front doors give way to a flood of humanity and goats.

What is she to do? Salvation comes in the shape of a thirteen-year-old Italian bellhop lounging insouciantly against a mezzanine pillar. What's an Italian bellhop doing in Havana? If Kitty had time to ask, she'd have discovered that Lansky had shipped him over as a favour to friends after his father got iced in some church, stabbed in the eye with a corkscrew.

Kitty lurches over to him. "Get me a phone,"

The bellhop shrugs, nodding down at the press of crazed tourists, locals, and livestock.

"Look, you, I don't give a damn about those yahoos. I am Mrs. Catherine Beamish, née Danderville, a Caledon Danderville no less, and blood relation to Irénée duPont. So get your pimply ass in gear and find me a phone. A private phone. Now."

"No comprendo, señora," comes the smirky reply.

"I don't have time for your teenage bullshit!"

The bellhop holds up his right hand, rubs his fingers together and whistles. Kitty hands him a ten-dollar bill. "You're an extortionist!" He nods proudly and signals for her to follow him.

Going up a back stairwell, he leads her to the fourth floor. Amid the commotion in the hall he picks a lock. The door opens on a magnificent suite with a private phone.

"You've been very helpful," Kitty observes dryly. "Your parents must be proud."

"I don't have parents."

"Lucky you," says Kitty, and slams the door in his face.

She dials. The line is busy and busy and busy. Finally she gets the operator, but Edgar isn't picking up. "Terrific," she thinks, "I'm gone eight hours and already he's off whoring." Then a horrible thought. "Maybe I've phoned too late. Maybe he's dead." Kitty hangs up, shocked to find herself smiling. Then another horrible thought. If Edgar is dead, what about Junior? She dials frantically. Busy and busy. The operator finally answers and Kitty places her call. This time Edgar picks up.

"Edgar, the streets are a river of blood. They're chopping off heads. Take Junior and whatever will fit in a bag and go to the airstrip. We'll send the plane as soon as we can."

Edgar hears Kitty's door crash open, a few words of Spanish, and the bleat of a goat. The line goes dead.

Revenge

Piecing together fragments from his parents' fight, four-year-old Junior understands that his mother had been perfectly safe that night in Havana. She'd ended up toasting the revolution with the invading Cuban, a cheery sort with a bottle of rum scarfed from the hotel bar, who'd wanted to see for himself how Americans lived.

He also understands that his father's flight had nothing to do with ridding himself of a worthless son. It was worse: he wasn't even a blip on his dad's mental radar. His father had run because he was scared. Period.

Junior is too young to understand the world, but he is not too young to feel betrayed. He is stunned, then overwhelmed with blind rage. He has been deceived. His father, the man whom he has worshipped as a god, is a fraud. A gutless coward who didn't think twice about leaving his son to be murdered by strangers.

What other lies has he told? Why is he really away all those nights? Suddenly everything falls into place. Junior's life makes sense. His father is the enemy. The source of his pain. Yes, all the hurt and fear and confusion—it's all his father's fault.

Junior is determined to exact revenge. His father must be brought to justice. He must be punished. And his mother too, for good measure. Why hadn't she protected him from this sudden stranger? Junior broods: What form should their punishment take?

The four-year-old reflects that he's received the most attention from his parents when his behaviour has distressed them. These occasions have occurred, hitherto, as a result of attacks by The Pillow Lady, but Junior decides that from now on he will take a more proactive role in his family's distress. This will require a little imagination, but imagination is something Junior has in abundance. Honing his talent for self-destruction, he resolves never to speak again, except to Emily. They didn't care about him? He won't care about them. He will show them what it feels like not to be loved. If he felt pain, they will feel hell.

Junior's plan requires tenacity and will in the face of common sense and self-interest. In arming himself, he draws upon his birthright, the stubborn streak with which he avoided his granny at Sick Kids. Remarkably, the young warrior makes good on his decision. Six months and a dozen doctors later Junior has still not said a word.

Edgar and Kitty are at their wits' end. There are tears and recriminations. Kitty considers leaving Edgar, but the only thing worse than living with Edgar is living with her mother, and Kitty has nowhere else to go. Edgar considers leaving too, but that would ruin his career, and he saw how his father died.

One morning Edgar arrives home just before dawn. As he tiptoes down the hall he sees Junior sitting up in bed. Junior's eyes are wide open. He stares straight ahead. Tentatively, Edgar enters his son's room and sits at the edge of his bed. Junior says nothing, does nothing. Edgar gently tousles the boy's hair, but the lad doesn't react.

Silence.

"Junior," Edgar implores quietly, "when are you going to speak?"

The child, now five, looks at him with calm dispassion. "When I'm ready." Those are the first words Junior has spoken in six months. They are the last he will speak for another two years.

And then he won't shut up.

V

Northern Lights

Pope resurrects frozen vampire

This was the arresting headline splashed across the cover of *The National Eye*, a best-selling tabloid found at grocery checkouts throughout North America. The inside article, written in an appropriately lively prose style, was only slightly tamer.

It seems a Goth performance artist, one Lydia Spark, had been pulled from an Arctic plane wreck along with her pet cat by two Inuit hunters en route to the historic papal mass in Mercy Inlet. In a near-death coma, the young woman had been whisked by dogsled to the feet of the Holy Father, who was completing the benediction before repairing to a reception hosted by the Nunavut Territorial Government and The Inuit Tapirisat of Canada. While one of the hunters called out for medical assistance, good Pope Innocent prayed over the stricken performer. A trouper to the bone, she knew a good entrance when she saw one and responded on cue, miraculously re-entering the world of the living to a standing ovation.

Lydia's neat upstaging of the Supreme Pontiff also made headlines in the mainstream Canadian press. She was, after all, the second Canadian to make international news in a week—an event in itself—the first being BEI Chair Edgar Beamish Jr., who had scandalised the world with his controversial Phoenix Lottery.

Putting Lydia's five minutes of fame in its proper perspective, *The New York Times* buried the incident in a brief tag to an article on the northern chapter of Operation Explorer. "In a bizarre twist to an otherwise smooth stopover on Baffin Island, Mercy Inlet locals claimed the pope resurrected a young woman who had succumbed to the Arctic cold. Embarrassed papal spokespersons denied the claim, observing that the Land of the Midnight Sun is rich with superstition and folklore. The young woman has since recovered."

Lydia does more than recover. Summoned by destiny, she will make a grand jeté back into the international spotlight within two months. And when she does, the hapless *Times* reporter, Franklin K. Bender III, who had consigned her to a footnote, will scurry to find an interview he recorded the day following her "resurrection," a tape which, by the grace of God, he has not reused. This interview, which he first dismissed as stream-of-consciousness rubbish, will emerge as the centre-piece of a major profile on Lydia in the *Sunday Times* Arts and Leisure section.

So I'm dead, right? And I'm in the middle of this white light with a bunch of my deep-sixed ancestors and Pickles, who's snuggling up against me like I'm catnip or some-thing, and I'm feeling all teary and sentimental when, out of nowhere, this old guy comes flying by on a harpoon. No shit. He stops in mid-air, sitting side-saddle like a witch on a broomstick.

He's wearing sealskin boots and a beaded caribou-hide parka with fox-fur trim and handmade ivory buttons sewn on with dried sinew. He's got caribou mitts deco-rated with paint and ivory bits carved like tiny faces. The hood of his parka is pulled back and on his head is this bizarre hat made of ermine and topped off with the head of a loon. But what I really notice are the two parallel scars on the left side of his wizened face, deep scars, running from chin to cheekbone. I mean, this guy is way cool.

He says, "Hey, *kaðluna*, you ride with me to the land of the living. Owl says you got things to do."

Normally I'd be freaking out, but at this point I'm like, "Okay, sure." It's been one of those days, eh? So I look at Pickles and I say, "Sorry, honeybunch, Mommy loves you, but she's not ready to be dead yet. See you later." I give him a little chin scratch, yell, "Wait for me," to the old guy, hop on board his harpoon and off we go.

In less time than it takes to toke we've whistled down the funnel of light like we're in some supernatural luge event, and we're skipping over the clouds cleaner than a flat stone on a smooth pond. Needless to say, I'm holding on to the old guy for dear life, if you'll pardon the expression, cuz he's crazier than One-Eye, navigating his harpoon like a regular Captain Ahab.

Down below there's a glittering wash of ice, rock, snow, and water. The big fjords are open, chunks of ice and glacier bobbing to sea like kids racing from school on summer break. The smaller fjords, like the one where I crashed, are still covered with ice. It's a wonder the Otter didn't explode on impact.

Looking back over my shoulder, I see the plane wreck getting smaller and smaller. Looking ahead, I see the two dog teams that were racing towards it before I died. Only now they're racing away, up this steep range of hills, and we're flying like crazy trying to catch up. We're gaining fast, though. Soon I can see them in some detail. And—hold the Ecstasy—strapped on the back of one of the sleds I see someone who looks a lot like me. In fact, it *is* me, covered in hides, eyes closed, and looking like shit.

The old man turns to me. He shouts over the wind, "Them boys is Billy Muskloosie and Johnny Kadniq. Up ahead is Mattimitalik. You're some lucky kadluna. See you later."

"What?" I say, like some stunned tourist from the burbs.

"This is where you get off," he says, gives me a shove, and I'm in this out-of-body skydive. In the few breaths it takes me to reach the sleds, they've nipped over the crest of the long ridge of hill. I follow and what I see next gives me one helluva jolt.

Spread out ahead is a coastal town: rows and rows of prefabs standing on piles on the frozen muskeg. I see crosses on what must be churches, a weather station, a gazillion telephone poles, and big stuff too—an arena, hospital, hotels, and schools maybe? It's unreal. It's also blinding—the glare of sun off water and ice and aluminum siding. Off aircraft, too, and Ski-Doos! Miles of them to the west of town!

If that isn't gonzo enough, between the vehicles and the town is an enormous open-air stage on a battalion of oil drums, surrounded by a sea of parkas and dogs, and covered in nuns, a children's choir, and a bunch of old white guys in robes.

As God is my witness, I will never do drugs again!

The Papal Mass

It's hard thinking holy thoughts when you're having a bad day, and Pope Innocent has definitely had better. First that emergency call from the United Nations, just when his plane hit turbulence somewhere over the west coast of Greenland, begging the Vatican to intervene in the Beamish affair. Then the call from Washington, President Hamilton "Stonewall" Richardson seconding the motion. He'll pray. Fine. But what else can he do? What leverage can the Holy See possibly have over a Canadian madman?

The Beamish affair is surely one more merry prank of a bored Almighty, a tribulation sent to afflict him for divine sport. Either that or God's gone AWOL, operating on some sort of celestial autopilot, a possibility which, on reflection, might explain the goings-on of the past few thousand years. Oh well. He'll conference with Cardinal Wichita on his return from this latest papal tour. Wichita will know what to do. He always knows what to do.

Innocent snaps out of his reverie and attempts to focus, peering out from the improvised stage over the Mercy Inlet airfield, a tarmac packed with devout and curious Inuit from Canada and Arctic Russia, as well as Euro-Canadian interlopers, and an international press which, like him, is freezing its collective butt off. The mass has gone well so far, a blessed surprise given his chattering teeth, but now it's time for the Eucharist. He's surprised the wine hasn't frozen solid. He hopes his tongue won't stick to the metal chalice. "Oh Lord, take this cup from me."

Why, oh why, did he ever allow the Curia to launch Operation Explorer? He hates travel. Foreign food gives him gas. He is painfully shy in public. And his destinations! Malaya and Madagascar would have tried the patience of a saint. First the typhoon in Malaya, then the incident in the Presidential Suite at the Antananarivo Hilton in Madagascar, when his quiet contemplation in the loo was interrupted by the tarantula lurking under the toilet seat. Yet if these venues were an ordeal, this Arctic jaunt is unbearable.

Descending from the plane that morning, his muscles seized in the sudden cold. Consequently, when he knelt to kiss the ground– a papal tradition which he hates; it makes him look as though he's searching for a lost contact lens—he threw out his back. The spasms of eye-watering pain are now barely controlled by a corset, which holds him next to immobile, and an injection of morphine, which leaves him barely sensate.

There followed the ride to the town hall on a Ski-Doo driven by the local priest. Getting around on Ski-Doo had seemed a good photo op to the Curia brains trust. Memo To Self: Banish Cardinal d'Ovidio to the archbishopric in Phnom Phen. The lunch buffet of bannock, fried seal liver, and pickled Arctic char had his body rebelling from both ends. A capsule of Immodium has this problem currently in check, but Innocent is in terror that its effects may wear off, as the numerous stays, straps, domes, and buttons securing his vestments are of such complexity that he will be helpless if nature makes an unexpected call.

(It is the same problem encountered by the cardinals during such gruelling eight-hour rituals as a papal investiture. Elderly princes of the church, whose prostates have long since offered up their last Hail Mary, are reduced to securing catheters beneath their holy finery, giving new texture to the term "Vatican functions.")

As if this was not sufficient tribulation, the papal woollies are no match for the biting wind now whistling across Eclipse Sound and up his robes. Already he can feel a runny nose coming on. As Innocent peers out from the improvised stage at the thousands of faithful in their parkas and boots, he is less moved to marvel at the majesty of creation than to wonder what on earth the Almighty had been thinking when he visited such a desolate habitation upon his children.

"Oh God, my God, why hast thou forsaken me?" Never have those words held such resonance for Pope Innocent as today.

Had the Tununermiut peering back at the holy kadluna been able to read his mind, they would have been amused. One of the most northerly people of the Canadian Arctic, they have called Mattimitalik (Mercy Inlet to outsiders) home since the fourteenth century, and two previous waves of their Inuit ancestors hunted this land happily throughout the four hundred years prior to that.

Mattimitalik is unique. Whereas other Inuit peoples lived a nomadic existence before the arrival of European traders, the Tununermiut have been content from the very beginning to confine themselves along the north Baffin Island shore, such are its joys and possibilities.

Game is plentiful. Arctic goose, hare, and char. Ptarmigan and duck. Caribou and whale. And, above all, seals. Seals in abundance. For sheer beauty, too, Mattimitalik is impossible to beat. The rugged tundra and fjords. The clear, cold waters of Eclipse Sound. And across the Sound, a bare twenty miles, imposing Bylot Island with its glacial rivers and mountains, some soaring as high as six thousand feet.

Nor are the Tununermiut alone in their appreciation of Mattimitalik. For if Pope Innocent is the most recent outsider to visit their frozen paradise, he is far from the first. Europeans have been coming for the better part of one hundred and fifty years. First were the whalers, who found the area's inlets a safe haven in which to hole up for the winter.

Where there are sailors, can seagulls, whores, and missionaries be far behind? In the case of whores, yes, as it turns out, for such an icy climate has a tendency to shrink the clientele. Missionaries, on the other hand, were common as ptarmigan. In the Tununermiut, a succession of Catholic and Anglican priests found a plentiful supply of souls ripe for harvest; and had worst come to worst, the glacial peaks of the aforementioned Bylot Island provided an arresting backdrop for a picturesque martyrdom.

Soon Mattimitalik was littered with kadluna. There were the fur traders of The Hudson's Bay Company, who set up shop in 1921. There was also the Canadian government, establishing one of its series of fixed settlements throughout the Northwest Territories, a move designed to defend its claims to the area from the United States, which was inclined to stretch its elbows into Arctic waters.

The settlement, christened Mercy Inlet, was anchored by the RCMP, a one-man detachment charged with hoisting the flag and keeping peace, order, and good government. This must have seemed rather silly to the Tununermiut as the fledgling settlement consisted of only the Hudson's Bay trading post, the Catholic mission, the Anglican mission, and the RCMP outpost itself. But the Tununermiut were about to learn that there is nothing so anal-retentive as a bureaucrat with time on his hands. Clearly, laws were required in order to provide the RCMP with something to enforce. In the case of Mercy Inlet this meant such regulations as keeping sled-dogs tied up when visiting the trading post, the nuisance of unleashed dogs having plagued the careless Tununermiut for the past five hundred years. Well, now something was to be done about it, hear! hear!

If the settlement began as a curiosity to the Tununermiut, it rapidly became a magnet. Furs, fresh meat, and narwhal tusks were traded for such novelties as tea, molasses, biscuits, sugar, tobacco, matches, guns, ammunition, southern cooking utensils, and cloth. Like consumers the world over, the Tununermiut discovered that novelties soon become necessities, and found themselves working at jobs in the settlement in order to have more money to pay for their newly required sundries.

This transformation from a culture of hunting and fishing to one of capitalism was given a Canadian goose in the 1960s when the southern government established the Department of Northern Affairs and deposited an administrator, mechanic, and teachers in the community, to be followed in two flaps of a seal's tail by a small army of bureaucrats and biologists, not to mention the infrastructure necessary to support them.

All appeared lost for the traditional Tununermiut way of life. Dog-teams were replaced by Ski-Doos and traditional summer and winter camps were abandoned for Mercy Inlet prefabs. However, just when colonial hegemony made assimilation a sure bet, a resurgence of ethnic pride upended all logical calculations, and a pan-Inuit coalition achieved self-government in Nunavut, a territory carved from the Northwest Territories.

Now, as Pope Innocent peers from the stage in a blossomed millennium, he sees a community living in southern-style homes but slowly recovering ancestral traditions. Although Ski-Doos are as thick as ice packs, dog teams have made a resurgence. So has the hunt, many young men taking time from their day-jobs to participate. And while most are baptised Christians, almost all make the traditional prayers to the spirits of the beasts they kill, as well as to those alive in rock and wind and water.

Pope Innocent is concluding the benediction when he becomes aware of an offstage kerfuffle. Behind him, and to his right, Billy Muskloosie and Johnny Kadniq are gesticulating wildly to Father James Kadniq, Johnny's elder brother. Father James is the first ordained Catholic priest to hail from Mercy Inlet, and it was a matter of some pride when word came from Rome that he'd been chosen to transport Pope Innocent about Mercy Inlet. Personally, Father James thought the church's all-terrain vehicle, an '03 Jeep Grand Cherokee, would have been more appropriate than a Ski-Doo, but who was he to quarrel with head office?

Father James is more than a little ticked off at the moment. Younger brother Johnny, the loon of the family, has always found a way to upstage his triumphs. When James returned after graduation from the University of Manitoba, Johnny had disrupted his homecoming, bursting into the settlement, late as usual, with a wild story about being caught in a white-out whipped up by Qaminiak, the old shaman woman who lives like a hermit in the abandoned winter camp at Aullguak, ten miles from town.

Then there was the episode shortly after his ordination. He'd been summoned to Rome by the previous pope, John-Paul II, for a special mass in honour of the world's aboriginal priests. It was a major event, covered by CNN, and a source of great personal satisfaction. A celebration was planned for his return. Sure enough, the celebration had to be postponed: Johnny and his ne'er-do-well buddy Billy Muskloosie had gotten themselves trapped on an ice flow. James was the one who had done the community proud, but it was his brother Johnny who commanded the town's attention during the week it took for him to be rescued.

And now, today, the crowning achievement of his career — Pope Innocent is blessing Mercy Inlet with a mass; he is the pope's personal chauffeur for the event — and his brother goes missing, only to show up and disrupt the papal benediction and humiliate him before his community and the international press.

Father James has a special affinity for the parable of the prodigal son. Only, in his view, Christ missed the boat and then some. The spoiled brat should have been made to learn his lesson out with the pigs in the back forty. Otherwise, he'll disgrace his family over and over again.

True to form, Johnny has an excuse for his current shenanigans. Father James has to admit it is better than most.

"Listen, Jimmy, listen — we're racing to town full-tilt when we see this plane go down twenty, thirty miles off, eh? So me an' Billy go check it out, an' it's One-Eye, Isaac's Uncle Jack from outside, eh? An' he's dead, eh? See, here he is right here — an' this lady too, don't know if she's livin' or dead, an' this cat in the bargain, so what's a guy to do? Yeah, yeah, we did that, went to the hospital straight off — 'cept it's all closed up cuz everybody's here for the pope, eh? Don't be like that, Jimmy, don't be like that, don't you go talkin' that way, I wouldn't screw up yer big day, no way—Jesus Christ, Jimmy, we got Isaac's dead uncle here, stiff as a prick, an' maybe a dead woman too, an' you're worried about a goddamn benediction? Get a life, will ya? Fuck!"

With that, Johnny pushes his brother aside and, before security can think to stop him, takes to the stage just as the children's choir, under the musical direction of Sister Dolores Laframboise, launches into Bach's "Jesú, Joy of Man's Desiring," which Father James himself has personally translated into Inuktitut in honour of the occasion.

"Hey!" he yells into the mike downstage centre. Loud feedback. "Hey! Is there a doctor out there? We got a dead guy up here an' some lady froze up colder'n a witch's tit."

For a moment, the children stop singing. But not for long. Sister Dolores wields a mean baton. With a withering glance at the boy sopranos who burst into giggles at the word "tit," she claps her hands, and soon her wee charges are back on track.

What follows is pure theatre: a mimed miracle play with the iconic power and simplicity of a soapstone carving, accompanied by the music of angels. As if in slow-motion, Johnny backs off stage-right as his buddy, Billy Muskloosie, bears the limp body of Lydia Spark down centre. Billy sinks to his knees, cradling Lydia, whose left arm arranges itself decorously on the stage floor. Pope Innocent, in a morphine-induced daze that makes him look remarkably like a medieval rendering of transcendent grace, moves up behind the pair to get a better look.

As the children hit Bach's ineffable musical climax, Innocent makes the sign of the cross. Lydia's eyelids flutter. She stretches her arms like Sleeping Beauty waking from her dream. She rises from the dead. Applause! Lydia bestows a gracious smile upon her audience, waves graciously, curtsies deeply, and then suddenly registers the sea of parkas stretched before her.

"Holy shit!"

Lydia faints into the arms of Pope Innocent.

C-r-ah-ck

3 A.M. Lydia is being held overnight for observation at the Mercy Inlet Hospital. She wakes, vaguely aware of someone, or something, moving around beyond the foot of her bed. "P2?" she says in a fog. No, that can't be right. The local priest is taking care of her cat until she is fully recovered. Whatever was moving is now still, but Lydia can feel its presence. Since she is the only patient registered in the hospital, this gives her some alarm.

Lydia squints, trying to pierce the gloom. Northern Baffin Island is enjoying twenty-four hours of sun, so the windows are heavily shaded to make sleep possible. It's like looking through thick plum jelly.

"Who's there?"

No response. Whoever, or whatever, lies very still. Lydia knows she is being watched. She rolls over quickly and turns on the lamp on the left side of her bed. Her gaze darts around the room in search of the intruder, but everything appears to be in order.

Lydia hesitates, then turns off the light. She lies back, counts to ten, and immediately turns it on again. But there is no one there. She is definitely alone. She turns the light off once more and attempts to go back to sleep.

Ten minutes later, just as she begin to drift off, she hears it again. The rustling movement. Only this time there is a voice, deep and gutteral.

"C-r-ah-ck. C-r-ah-ck."

Lydia realizes why she hadn't seen him before. The voice is coming from under her bed.

She turns on the light and throws back the covers. "Gotcha, you goddamn pervert!" she cries, leaning over to look under the bed. But there's nothing on the bare linoleum floor save for a few dustballs and a mouse pellet.

Slowly Lydia lifts herself back up onto her side. Surely she could not have imagined it. And then she freezes in terror. She can feel the creature, whoever or whatever it is, pressing on the pillow behind her. Very slowly she rolls over.

Perched next to her head, staring her straight in the face, is a large plump raven. It must be two feet in length, with sharp eyes, a shaggy ruff at its throat, a thatch on its head to match, and a heavy bill that means business. Yet what is most unusual about the bird is that it appears to be dressed up for a night on the town. A hospital towel is draped over its body. The towel is white with a blue stripe running down its back. Accessorizing this curious robe is a necklace of purple ribbon, no doubt gift-wrapping ferreted from some former invalid's wastebasket.

The raven looks at her inquisitively. Lydia doesn't know whether to laugh or scream. Then she sees the crumpled piece of newspaper in the raven's left claw. It is the entry form to Junior Beamish's Phoenix Lottery that she'd clipped and put in the pocket of her parka before drifting into her coma.

"What the hell do you think you're doing? Gimmee that."

Lydia grabs for the paper, but the bird rears its neck and flares its wings. Black, lance-shaped feathers spear the air. It cracks open its beak. "Putana! Putana! Figlia di putana! Non parlare con mio figlio!" it cackles.

Lydia flies from the room, her feet barely touching the ground. She hollers for the night nurse. The woman appears instantly and inspects the room. She finds nothing.

The raven has vanished into thin air. And with it, the entry form.

More Visitors

The raven is not the only visitor to Lydia's sickbed.

Members of the press, bleary-eyed from a night of hard drinking at The Mercy Inlet Hotel—Hattie McBean has closed The Diner out of respect for her brother—show up in dribs and drabs for morning interviews with the alleged resurrectée. Indeed, some come directly from the bar, having found it impossible to toddle off to bed with the sun still shining. The head nurse tries to hold them back, but Lydia, never one to let the spotlight go to waste, sallies forth in her hospital johnny shirt to tell her tale to any who'll listen.

By the time Franklin K. Bender III of *The New York Times* rolls over with his tape recorder, she has her routine down pat. A little too pat for Bender's taste. Bender, a recent college grad on his first foreign assignment, fancies himself a serious investigative reporter wasted on what amounts to a Vatican dog-and-pony show. He lets it be known on board the press plane that he is above all this: he is a Yale man and grandson of Dr. Franklin K. Bender, the famed Baltimore pediatrician. Bender neglects to mention that he squeaked through Yale courtesy of essays cribbed off the Internet, and that his illustrious grandfather narrowly escaped jail in the late 1950s after his Potty Alert fried two orphans in the state of Maine.

Nevertheless it is hard to dislike the Baltimore heir this morning. Bender is in a bad way. His head aches, he can't see to press the tape recorder's *On* button, and that's not all. Last night, after he blacked out, his colleagues from *The Post* and *The L.A. Times* carried him across the street to Minnie's Tattoo Parlour, where the aging Needle Queen, somewhat tanked herself, whipped off one of her more scurrilous designs across his downy bottom. Now, even after a pot of black coffee, damned if he can remember why it hurts to sit down.

By eleven Lydia is talked out and Bender is off on a painfully bumpy flight to the pope's next stop on the east coast of Greenland. Life in Mercy Inlet has returned to normal, save for the cleanup and the small parcel of tourists who've stayed for a look-see of Beechey and the bird sanctuary on Bylot.

Lydia's about to take a snooze—God knows she didn't sleep much last night and the morning has been a non-stop performance piece—but is interrupted by Father James Kadniq who pops by for a pastoral visit along with brother Johnny and Billy Muskloosie. Johnny and Billy are pleased as punch, having spent the day prior feted as local heroes. They accept Lydia's thanks with bashful shuffles and indulge in a little low-level flirting. Father James, feeling a bit guilty about his lack of on-stage charity the other day, assures her that her kitty has made a full recovery and is enjoying a nice tin of tuna. P2, in fact, is holed up in his carrying case and hissing at anyone who dares come within ten feet.

The quartet are still amiably passing the time at noon, when One-Eye's sister, Hattie, shows up with her common-law husband, Namisaat. "Good heavens, look at the time," says Father James. He gives his condolences and heads out to prepare for a wedding at three. Johnny and Billy mumble a few words of their own, wave, and take off for an afternoon of ice-fishing, leaving Lydia with a pair of bereaved relatives fit for a picaresque.

Hattie McBean is a four-foot-six fireplug with a square, confident gait and a jaunty set to her chin. A rosy, pug nose and bright button eyes are sandwiched between an imposing red toque and a generous wool scarf that disappears inside her oversized, knee-length, red plaid duffle coat. Sealskin boots and gloves accessorize the rugged ensemble.

Hattie has seen a few sights in her time and what she's seen has made her no respecter of rank or title. Eager to escape Right-Cold-By-Gar, she moved to Mercy Inlet in 1985 to serve as secretary in the local office of the Department of Northern Affairs. Her summers as a teenager working in northern hunting lodges with wealthy American outdoorsmen came in handy, as she'd picked up Inuktitut both from the guides and the Inuit women with whom she shared kitchen duties. Her knowledge of Tununermiut language and customs made her indispensable to the new area administrator, as nothing he'd learned in Ottawa had prepared him for life in the Arctic Circle.

Shortly after assuming her duties, Hattie met Namisaat, a lumbering bear of a man five years her junior, whose broad, open face and quiet smile would melt a rock. It was love at first sight. They began living together within the month. Twenty years and three children later, they're happy as clams, though still unchurched, Hattie not seeing the point and Namisaat out of respect for his mother who is still unreconciled to her only son being fixed up with a kadluna.

Namisaat's relationship with Hattie has only deepened the wedge between his mother and himself. The gulf, a silent wound on both sides, began when he was ten. Canadian authorities insisted the boy be moved to Mercy Inlet from his home in the winter camp at Aullguak in order to receive an education. His mother, who lived alone, resisted, but to no avail.

Worse came when the boy displayed proficiency in maths and science. This, coupled with weak sight and a trick knee that sidelined him from the hunt, led Namisaat to gravitate towards things southern. There was a scholarship to Carleton University, followed by a stint at McGill's Faculty of Education. In the end, although he returned north, he chose to live in the town, teaching white man's chemistry and physics at the high school and hooking up with an outsider. Namisaat provides for his mother, who stays at the camp to this day; but to her mind, family and birthright carry greater obligations.

While Namisaat still teaches, Hattie has long since left her position at the Department. Her third boss in as many years had taken the term Northern Affairs at face value and wouldn't keep his paws to himself. After repeated warnings to the paunchy Lothario, Hatty speared his hand to his desk with a letter opener. She filed a sexual harassment suit; he charged her with assault. In an out-of-court settlement both suit and charge were dropped. The government, typically, chose to ship its problem south with a promotion. Hattie quit in disgust and opened The Mercy Inlet Diner. Next to teaming up with Namisaat, it is the best move she has ever made. Today, The Diner is a hub of community life. Hattie is a wizard on the grill, serving up pancakes, toast and eggs, a mean pot of tea, and the best butter tarts this side of Fort Chimo.

Hattie pulls off her toque, revealing a close-cropped shock of salt and pepper hair. She appraises Lydia as if sizing up a young husky. "Welcome to Mercy Inlet. I don't suppose you're really Jack's girlfriend."

"What?" says Lydia, who finds the idea more disconcerting than the raven.

"That's what he let on over the phone, but you look to have some sense. You were coming up to see the pope then, were you? You sure managed a ringside seat."

"Actually, I was coming up to visit the graves on Beechey Island."

"One of that Franklin crew a relative?"

"No. I'm a poet. I channel."

Hattie and Namisaat exchange a glance.

"Well," Hattie says, "We're having a visitation for Jack over at Freddy's tomorrow at two. You're welcome to drop by if you're up and able. I'm sure it would mean a lot to Jack to have someone show up who didn't have to."

"Sure," says Lydia, whose social calendar is rather empty.

"Oh, and feel free to channel, if you've a mind to. I'd be curious to know what the old bugger's thinking."

At the Parlour

The Frederick Russell Funeral Parlour is a plain three-room prefab with fluorescent lights, beige panelling, and dark brown indoor/outdoor carpeting—the better to hide the mud. The small anteroom is lined with folding chairs that are loaned to the high school for commencement exercises and the annual school play. There is also a table, on which sit a guest book, ballpoint pen, ashtray, and a box of Kleenex in a yellow plastic container. Over the table is a homoerotic print of Jesus ascending to Heaven in a loincloth. Freddy substitutes Moses descending Mount Sinai or a nice sunset, depending on the clientele, but almost everyone in Mercy Inlet is Anglican or Catholic.

Two doors lead off the anteroom. To the right is the door to the office where Freddy discusses business with grieving relations. This is a somewhat less ghoulish affair than down south where profit is racked up by inducing the bereaved to purchase caskets well beyond their means. Not for Freddy the high-pressure sales pitch that works such wonders on the hysterical. (Paroxysms of guilt can be induced with the little words, "I'm sure everyone will understand if you choose to settle for the pine," while years of nightmare and therapy await those who resist The Eternity, a top-of-the-line model that comes with a posturpedic mattress to ensure a gentle slumber, and is steel-reinforced "to keep out the vermin.")

At Freddy's, most folks are cremated, given that the yearly two-month thaw affords such a brief window of opportunity for interment. "If all my clients got buried," jokes Freddy over a whisky, "come July they'd be stacked up worse'n the planes at Mirabel." Still, Freddy keeps two coffins on display, one pine, one oak, on the off-chance.

Straight ahead is the door to the main showroom. Like the anteroom, the showroom is lined with folding chairs, here interspersed with pressboard end tables, home to more Kleenex, and large green china vases, the latter filled with elaborate floral bouquets of silk and polyester kept fresh courtesy of a monthly once-over with the Dustbuster. At the far end of the showroom, the guest of honour sits in a small urn on a pseudo-Roman plaster-of-Paris pedestal, or, if in a coffin, on a dais covered in black bunting.

On this occasion, there is a coffin, pine. As the only surviving McBean who can read, Hattie is One-Eye's executor. The old rascal wanted but two things for his send-off, the first of which was to buy the opening round at a wake in his honour, which he sincerely hoped would be organized by the girls of The Kandy Kane in the Fort Chimo Hotel's Ladies and Escorts Lounge. While Hattie doesn't stand on ceremony, she's sure Mom and Dad, may they rest in peace, would have wanted something a tad less embarrassing for their son than Maude "Tomcat" McTavish, drunk as a skunk and dripping mascara, belting out karaoke "hurtin' songs" over Jack's well-pickled remains. So, she's arranged a more sombre event, following which the body will be shipped south, care of the hotel bartender, in whose tender mercies Jack's will be done, out of sight being out of mind.

Lydia arrives at the funeral home at two-thirty. The place is packed. Although One-Eye was well-known to locals owing to his frequent supply runs, the turnout is as much a show of love and esteem for Hattie and Namisaat as for the deceased. Lydia says a few words to the couple and is introduced to their three children: Rachel, ten; Judith, fourteen; and Isaac, nineteen. Isaac is the spitting image of his father; one grin and Lydia starts thinking inappropriate thoughts.

About to move to the casket, Lydia finds herself surrounded by well-wishers eager to know how she's doing. Her spectacular entrance into the community the other day has turned her into something of a celebrity. The rumour that she was One-Eye's secret girlfriend makes her a figure of even greater curiosity. Still, there is no coarse gawking, just shy tentative nods and gentle pats on the hand. Lydia is moved by the sincerity and generosity of the townspeople, and observes that unlike others elsewhere they don't react to her get-up, although in the context of a visitation, wearing black isn't much of a fashion statement. All the same, the Mercy Inlet residents give Lydia the most respect and affection she has received since Ryder Knight bought her coffee that first morning in Toronto, and her eyes well with tears.

Eventually Lydia makes her way to One-Eye's casket. She would scarce have recognized him. Bathed and deloused, hair neatly combed, he looks as respectable as the owner of a small-town dry goods store. The faintly sweet smell of talcum powder is also an improvement, as is his wardrobe. Hattie has bought him a new plaid sports jacket from Hank's Menswear, as well as a bow tie, white shirt, and underwear.

In one significant detail, Hattie's sense of propriety has given way to Jack's second request for his farewell. His hands, folded neatly at the base of his rib cage, clasp his glass eye, its pale blue pupil facing straight up. He wanted it that way, he'd said, so he could see who showed up to say goodbye. The eye was recovered yesterday when the local RCMP constable, Ted Beavis, went out to make an official report on the crash. It's slightly cracked, but, as Hattie allows, so was One-Eye.

Death has a way of turning characters, so aggravating in life, into warmly beloved community favourites. One-Eye is no exception. A wild and woolly rapscallion, he will be missed, which, in the end, as Lydia muses, is more than can be said for most of the high and mighty.

"Goodbye One-Eye," she says. She half expects him to curse or fart, but he rests serene. Death agrees with him, and he is clearly happy to stay put wherever he is.

Lydia is aware of a presence by her side. Looking up she sees Isaac.

"He was my uncle. He always remembered my birthday."

They stand quietly together for some time, then Isaac asks if she'd like to step outside for a cigarette. Lydia says she doesn't smoke but will be happy to keep him company. She notices that her heart is suddenly beating rather fast and her voice is a few notes higher than normal. Stop it, she tells herself, transfixed by Isaac's star-white teeth and long black eyelashes.

They talk about many things, and then Lydia hears herself ask, "Do you have a problem with ravens in this town?"

Isaac says, "Sometimes, yeah, if we haven't been careful with the garbage."

Lydia tells him about the raven who visited her at the hospital. "It swore at me in Italian."

"You had a raven swear at you in Italian?"

"No kidding. It called me a slut and said don't talk to my son. I know, because those are the exact words Tony Patini's mother said to me when he introduced me to his folks. Club boy by night, momma's boy by day, what a wiener." Lydia can see that Isaac is looking at her strangely. She's so turned on she can barely think, and hopes she hasn't been babbling. "You don't believe me, do you?"

"Oh, I believe you." He pauses. "You need to meet my gramma. She talks to polar bears."

He's laughing at her, isn't he? Lydia feels embarrassed. But then she looks in his eyes. Isaac isn't kidding.

To Grandmother's House We Go

The next morning Lydia is in heaven. She's sitting behind Isaac, knees pressed against his thighs, arms wrapped around his abdomen. They're on a Ski-Doo, riding out to visit Isaac's grandmother, Qaminiak, who lives alone at the abandoned winter camp of Aullguak ten miles from town. Isaac is bringing her some cloth, tea, tobacco, rolling papers, canned goods, and a seal heart, liver, and chops.

"Have your gramma show Ms. Spark some of her tricks," Namisaat winks at Isaac before they take off. Namisaat doesn't think much of his mother's magic, *takorhauneq* as she calls it. It's nothing he can't manage with a few chemicals from the high-school lab and a little sleight-of-hand; nevertheless, he has to admit she's pretty skilful, her routines both a harmless way to while away the long winter nights and an entertaining diversion for the town's new visitor.

Namisaat's lack of faith in Qaminiak's powers, discreet but evident to anyone with an ear for irony, fills his mother with indignation. She was the shaman to the camp's members and, even though they have all long since followed her disloyal son to the prefab comforts of the town, she is the *angakoq* still.

"She never married," Isaac hollers over his shoulder, his voice barely audible above the Ski-Doo's revved engines. "She says Dad's father is the spirit of a narwhal, claims it rescued her from an ice flow. She climbed on its back and it swam her up over the clouds. When she came back to earth, she says, she was holding Dad in her arms. He believed her when he was little. Came to town, age ten, and tells that to the public health nurse. He got teased for years and then some."

"How come? It's no weirder than finding babies in the cabbage patch," Lydia yells in his ear.

"The what?" Isaac yells back.

In half an hour they reach a cairn of rocks and ice on the outskirts of the camp. "We'll cache the meat here and take the rest of the stuff to her house," says Isaac. Lydia stretches her legs and helps him stash the chops.

"Gramma claims she can do lots of weird stuff," Isaac continues, "like change her sex or turn herself into a wolf. Call her nuts if you want, but she sure as heck spooked Johnny Kadnik and Billy Muskloosie. You think those guys are wild now? A couple of years back, they were crazy as otters. One day, late spring, they take off half-looped to raise a little Cain at the camp, eh? Rattle my gramma some. Pretty mean, with her past eighty and all. Anyway, they drive 'round her house on their Ski-Doos whooping it up, yelling 'If you're such hot shit, show us your stuff, you old witch.' Garbage like that. Then they turn 'round and head out back to town, laughing their fool heads off. They're not laughing long.

"Gramma talks to her spirits, and they whip up a storm something fierce. Before you know it, the wind is howling and the snow is mean, ice crystals biting into their eyes and cheeks. Billy and Johnny, they ride fast, trying to hit town before things get worse. But soon it's a whiteout. They have no idea where they are. They can't see each other ten feet off—heck, they can't even see two inches in front of their nose, or hear their Ski-Doos over the rage of the wind.

"In a panic now, they keep going, afraid if they stop they'll freeze to death. They're driving blind, stupid-crazy with fear, separated, each alone in the storm. They cry out to their mothers to come and save them, tears freezing on their eyelashes. Then Johnny, he finds he's driven to the flow edge. The ice gives way under him, his Ski-Doo goes down, it's lost, and he's fighting to pull himself out of the frigid water. He's not going to make it. Drown or freeze, he's going to die out there. Kaloopalik will take him. He curses the day he was born and begs my gramma to save his life.

"And as soon as he does, the storm lifts as fast as it came and he finds himself face down in the snow, safe and sound, in front of my gramma's door. He looks up and there's Billy, face down beside him, still alive and shitting his pants. Their Ski-Doos are there, too. So is my gramma.

"They kiss her feet. Johnny says, 'Forgive us, Angakoq. Forgive us.'

"My gramma says nothing. She motions them inside her house. She gives them tea and boiled *muktuk*, blubber off a nar-whal skin—real oily, good when you're cold. They sit in silence, then they go home.

"They tell the town what happened. Everyone laughs at them, thinks they've been huffing, or making an excuse for mis-sing the big celebration for Father James. See, there hasn't been a storm. The sky's been clear as a baby's bum all afternoon.

"I wasn't there. I didn't see what happened. But what I do know is, while Billy and Johnny are still mighty spunky, they've traded Ski-Doos for dogsleds and haven't huffed or touched a drop since." Isaac pauses and looks Lydia straight in the eye. "If magic didn't happen that day out here, I don't know what did."

Lydia feels goosebumps. And they're not from the cold, nor from looking at Isaac. They finish caching the seal meat with-out a word. Then Isaac points to his gramma's house two hundred yards off. "Let's walk." Isaac carries the remaining groceries in a knapsack on his back. Strips of crusted snow alternate with bare muskeg, the muskeg just starting to give; even the twenty-four-hour June sun has to work to gain respect from the Arctic cold.

"What are those?" Lydia asks, pointing at a series of long curved tubes growing out of the tundra in irregular circles.

"Whale bones," Isaac replies. "The remains of Thule homes from hundreds of years back. They covered them with sod. Gramma's is the same, only you can't see the sod on account of it's covered with snow. That's another funny thing. Even in August the snow over gramma's home never melts. Dad says it's because the crust acts as insulation, or the white of the snow reflects light. Well, okay, but how come it melts everywhere else? Science doesn't know everything."

They pass what appears to be an old garbage dump, an area strewn with broken bottles, rusty cans, and a few roughly cut squares of translucent plastic. "Those plastic squares are used to cover the window over the front door of homes in the winter camps. They're cut out of the town honey bags."

"Honey bags?"

Isaac laughs. "Disposable toilet receptacles, if you wanna get technical. We use 'em instead of sewers, 'cause of the permafrost. Honey bags—good name, eh? Even Father James can say it without blushing. He's a good guy, even if he's a bit of a wank. Gramma, she doesn't go for plastic, though. It's the old ways for her. Covers her window with seal windpipe and dried intestines."

They're at the house. A small round entry hall made of blocks of packed snow connects to a larger room of snow-covered bone and sod. "Shouldn't we knock or something?" asks Lydia.

"Why? Gramma knows we're here. She's been watching us since we left town." Isaac sees Lydia look confused. "She talks to owls and polar bears," he whispers. "What more can I say?"

A Seance

They enter the angakoq's dwelling. The small entry hall is empty, save for a harpoon propped against the wall, which Lydia almost knocks over in the near dark. Isaac puts down the knapsack of sundries and they enter the space beyond. A wooden platform piled with caribou hides takes up the back half of the room. Low risers flank the sides. The air is ghostly still.

"Maybe she went out for a walk or something?" Lydia asks. She wonders why she's whispering.

A sharp gust of wind swirls around the room and vanishes. As suddenly, a flame flares up from a shallow bowl that materializes on the lip of the raised platform. At once, the air is tinged with the aroma of burning seal fat and filled with the growls and snuffling of wolves. Instinctively, Lydia grabs hold of Isaac. "Don't worry," he says, "Gramma's a great ventriloquist."

The pile of hides begins to vibrate and, in seconds, to levitate. It rises to the ceiling, revealing the squatting figure of the angakoq. She is covered in heavily beaded robes made of skins trimmed with fur and decorated with painted designs, although in the flickering light of the *kudlik* it is hard to make sense of the brilliant red, green, and yellow markings. It is also difficult to distinguish the angakoq's features, as her head is shrouded in a large shawl, tied at the neck and flowing down over her shoulders. The large hide-covered drum in her left hand is shaped like a tambourine, with a handle attached to its bone rim. In her right hand she holds a wooden stick.

"How does she do it?" Lydia asks in awe.

"Ask Dad," Isaac mouths.

The wolves stop growling. Lydia wants to clap.

Silence.

The angakoq speaks. "You still have no dog team. What will you do one cold day when you're starving?"

"Eat my Ski-Doo," says Isaac.

His grandmother chuckles; it is an old joke between them. She comes forward and steps down from the raised platform. The hides fall in a heap behind her. She faces Lydia. "You have come about the raven."

Isaac gives Lydia a shrug as if to say, "I told you, she talks to polar bears."

The next twenty minutes are conducted in total silence. Isaac's grandmother pours them cups of tea from a metal pot on the small Primus stove to the right of the door. The tea has steeped for days; it is a bitter syrup, the leaves pallid.

As Isaac and Lydia sip, the angakoq shuffles into the entrance hall, retrieves Isaac's knapsack, returns, and unpacks it carefully on the platform to the left. She grunts and nods her approval when she finds the tin of tobacco. Taking great care, she fishes out a small wad, rolls herself a cigarette, and sits, smoking in silence, content to observe them observing her observing them.

At length, she stubs the butt on the floor and then, methodically, takes up her drum and stick and makes her way to the centre of the room. She plants her feet, bends her knees, and begins to beat the inner rim of the drum as she swings it rhythmically back and forth. The vibration sets up a rich booming cadence, and the angakoq responds, rocking, swaying, stepping in time, and now dancing, swirling, spinning about the open space. Voice joins movement, a pulse of sound possessed. It pitches higher as the drum beats faster and the angakoq's feet dance nimble as a doe's.

Then, without warning, an animal shriek rips from the angakoq's throat, and she collapses unconscious. Lydia looks to Isaac in alarm, fearful the old woman has suffered a stroke. But Isaac is calm: he's seen it all before. Now, as if manipulated by invisible strings, the angakoq rises with the ease of a rag doll. She floats for a moment and then settles comfortably behind the kudlik, cross-legged on the floor, palms open on her knees. Her head is still shrouded by the shawl, but her eyes are clearly visible, alive in the flame from the low lamp which throws her shadow up the back wall. When she moves it's as if that shadow has the power of a giant.

The breath of the angakoq is laboured. So are her words. One, two at a time they come, dragged up through her body from the depths of the earth. Most are in Inuktitut, which Isaac translates, but others come from a language unknown to humankind.

"She sees a journey south," Isaac whispers. "Many are waiting. There is a large flame. A bonfire in your hand. Many wish you ill. You must do battle. There is an open razor. Beware the man in red. Attend the man with one ear. Do not trust the raven."

There follows much wailing and gibberish. The angakoq convulses backwards. Froth flies from her mouth. She writhes in apparent agony, stiffens, and is suddenly limp. A heartbeat, then she gets up, shakes herself out, shuffles to the tobacco tin, sits, rolls a cigarette, and smokes.

"Why is she staring at me?" Lydia whispers.

"She's right there. Ask her," says Isaac.

Lydia swallows hard. "Why are you staring at me? What did all that stuff mean?"

The angakoq takes her time considering these questions. And then a moment Lydia will never forget. The old woman throws back her shawl. On her left cheek, now fully visible, are two deep parallel scars that run from her chin to her cheekbone.

"You're the guy on the harpoon!" Lydia gasps. Isaac catches her from behind.

The angakoq's lips twitch with the hint of a smile. "Owl brings this back to you," she says, extending her cupped right hand. "Take it. You got things to do." Resting in the old woman's palm is the crumpled entry form to The Phoenix Lottery.

VI

The Angel

From the Mouths of Babes

Within months of ousting Batista, Castro confiscates American property in the name of land reform. Xanadu is no exception. "Preserve my home," duPont pleads with government occupiers. "Let history know I was here."

Flying away in his private plane, he sheds a tear. Xanadu is the only thing of value he has ever lost, save for those jewels and heirlooms looted by thieves the night his house guest fled in fear of revolutionary mobs. Ah well, he forgives Edgar's terror. Things can be replaced; lives, never. DuPont is much less sanguine, however, when said valuables begin appearing on the Canadian black market. Speculation has Edgar running off with more than pillow cases in his overnight bag. The RCMP investigates. The press goes wild.

Nothing is proved, but the incident inadvertently unmasks the Beamish war record. Responding to published reports on Edgar's connection to the Dandervilles and their deceased son, a Corporal Peters declares that he served in Joseph Danderville's company and that Edgar is a stranger. Caught in his lie, Edgar retorts, "Well, I would have been Joe's friend if I'd met him." Henry Danderville drops dead of a stroke.

Disgraced, Edgar is cut loose from the duPont empire with a healthy stock portfolio and the nickname "Fast Eddy." Everyone writes him off, but he bounces back, out to give them all the finger. Playing a hunch, he uses the portfolio and his wife's inheritance to wrest control of Canadian food chain, Chicken Little. Thus Beamish Enterprises Inc. is born: The Little Poor Boy Who Could is now The Big Rich Guy Who *Has*.

Alas, Edgar's sixth sense for business does not extend to public relations. In 1965, Chicken Little workers defy his wishes and vote to join the Canadian Labour Congress. Edgar retaliates by stripping their company pension fund and selling the enterprise to its chief rival. Ontario and B.C. outlets are promptly folded; workers are left destitute.

National outrage.

Edgar is advised to lie low. "Fuck 'em." He makes a point of appearing at public events, blowing kisses at booing crowds. "Always smile," he advises his son. "It drives them crazy."

And it does. Labour calls for a boycott of BEI, especially Maple Leaf Breweries, which was bought with the Chicken Little proceeds. In Ottawa, New Democratic Party leader Tommy Douglas demands the Pearson government hold a public enquiry. Beamish snorts that the NDP is "a pack of Communist stooges."

Bar talk favours public lynching.

In March, the Canadian Labour Congress hangs Beamish in effigy, parades the dummy up Bay Street, and burns it outside City Hall while Edgar is inside making a presentation. Hearing the disturbance, he grabs a police megaphone, strides to the top of the front steps, and yells to the crowd: "My dad drowned a penniless alcoholic. Did I say 'Boo hoo, give me a handout'? No. I yanked myself out of the mud by the strength of my guts, my sweat, and my blood. That's why I'm rich and you're not. It's why I'm a somebody and you're just a bunch of whiny losers!" Miraculously, he avoids being hit by a hail of rotten eggs. The next day, bomb threats. Things are getting out of hand.

It is in this context that ten-year-old Junior Beamish takes his private war against his father public. Destiny calls on April 13th. It is *Hockey Night in Canada* — game six of the Stanley Cup semi-finals between Montreal and Toronto.

Edgar, Kitty, and Junior, along with BEI public relations consultant Merv Hampstead, are at the Gardens. They have aisle seats in the golds. Montreal leads the series three games to two; the Leafs face elimination. Bower has been spectacular in the Toronto net, stopping pucks with what used to be his teeth. His teammates Kelly, Keon, and Ellis have given the Leafs three goals, but Lapierre, Ferguson, and Rousseau have replied for the Habs. And so, when the buzzer sounds to end the third period, the game is tied 3–3. Sudden death overtime!

The fans go wild. CBC producers scramble for intermission interview subjects. In what will be his last public relations event with the Beamishes, Merv Hampstead has a brainwave. "The kid! The kid!" he shouts at Edgar. "I'll get Cornell to interview the kid! We'll show the world you're not a total asshole. You're just a regular guy taking his kid to a hockey game!"

Without waiting for an okay, Hampstead hoists the startled boy over his shoulder and runs to the *Hockey Night in Canada* booth at ice level. As Althea once observed, with his big brown eyes and little blue blazer, Junior is cute as a button. The producers nod instantly. It's a natural. They whisk the boy into the booth to the waiting seat beside interviewer, Ward Cornell.

"Well, young man, and what's your name?" asks Cornell, the live television signal beaming coast to coast.

"Junior. I'm ten."

Cornell smiles indulgently. "Ten. My oh my. Enjoying the game?" The boy nods, his eyes enormous.

Cornell gives him a poster of the Leafs, autographed by the entire team. "Thank you, Mr. Cornell," the kid beams, a picture of wonder and innocence. Cornell winks at the TV audience, and prepares to wrap up. He turns to Junior and asks, in his best Art Linklater voice, "So tell me, Junior, as we head into overtime, what's your biggest wish in the whole wide world?"

A normal boy would say, "I want the Leafs to beat Montreal!" A normal boy would say, "I want Davy Keon to score the winner!" But Junior isn't a normal boy. Junior is a terror. He opens his eyes wide. He turns straight to the camera. He says, "My daddy is Edgar Beamish. I wish he'd stop hurting poor people. I want to give them my allowance. I want someone to adopt me."

Junior's way with a sound-bite makes him a media darling. By the time he hits twelve, reporters who fear Edgar's bent for litigation are quoting his broadsides regularly. Edgar could sue his own son for libel, but that would lead to greater humiliation.

When it comes to embarrassing headlines, however, it is hard to top those which flow after CBC's public affairs program *This Hour Has Seven Days* airs its feature on counter-culture youth. Naturally, Junior is the star interview. With Edgar and Kitty skiing in Zermatt, he takes Laurier Lapierre on a *cinema verité* tour of the family home while smoking what appears to be a joint.

"I do drugs because of my family," he says cheerfully, opening the bathroom medicine cabinet to reveal a cornucopia of barbiturates. He picks up a large container of Valium. "As you can imagine, Mom finds life with Dad a bit hairy. She needs to relax, you know? A fistful of these with a bottle of Scotch usually does the trick."

Edgar threatens to sue the CBC for trespass; Junior, underage, was in no position to provide legal entry. But an enterprising staffer who checked the labels on Kitty's bottles asks him why Kitty filed one particular prescription with six different pharmacies in the same week. The lawsuit is dropped.

Edgar's had it. Junior is shipped out to the first of three boarding schools. Even here he makes headlines, getting expelled from the most prestigious private schools in the country for bootlegging uppers and downers from the aforementioned medicine cabinet. "Dad has given me a healthy respect for capitalism," he obliges reporters happily.

And on it goes; one dishonour, infamy, and scandal after another.

The worst conflict occurs in the mid-seventies when employees at BEI's Maple Leaf Breweries stage an illegal strike. Edgar calls the police. A confrontation ensues in which three workers are trampled by mounted constables. Incensed by the violence, Junior leads a protest march on the family home, prompting Kitty's third breakdown and Edgar's first heart attack. "You're going to kill your father!" his mother cries as she's driven off for a rest cure.

All Junior can think to say is, "When?"

Growing Up Edgar

Much has been said of Junior's rage, but Edgar's ran equally deep. He was raised in a tarpaper shack on what would become Toronto's Eastern Avenue. His father, Harry, blamed him for his wife's death in childbirth. Harry would sit up late drinking the home remedies he pedalled door to door. Then, drunk as a skunk, he'd wake young Edgar in the middle of the night. "You killed your mother, you goddamn shit-for-brains."

The beatings were horrific. Neighbours did nothing. Nor did police, who knocked but once. "Just whipping some sense into my boy," bellowed Harry, reeling at the door.

"It's okay, mister. I'm gettin' what's comin' to me," young Edgar called out. He'd been trained not to trust the coppers. ("You squeal on your old man, they'll lock you up in an orphanage.")

"Just keep it down, okay?" the police said. "There's people trying to sleep."

"Sure thing."

They left.

The beatings stopped two years later when Edgar turned fourteen. He and his dad were camping out on the east beach during a summer heat wave. Just past midnight, Edgar was squatting on a small incline by the water's edge, looking up at the stars. Suddenly, his nose told him to turn around. There was his father towering over him drunkenly with a large rock raised heavenward. "You killed my Becky, you goddamn shit-for-brains!"

Edgar rolled to one side as his father heaved the rock down at him. Harry lost his balance, fell forward, cracked his head, and ended up unconscious, face down in four inches of water. By the time the body was found and identified, Edgar was long gone. He lied his way into the army and went to war. No one was going to stick him in no orphanage.

In battle, Edgar was a madman, leading charges through minefields. As he roared forward, blasting away, each and every enemy carried his father's face. It was the same madness when he slept, legs and arms flailing, screaming his father's name.

After the war, he kicked around Europe, still unable to shake the nightmares. Then one day he was roaming the streets of Paris when his nose told him to turn into the little park on his left. He did. Inside the park, he was drawn to a simple building — La Musée de l'Orangerie, the Monet shrine celebrating the artist's lily pond at Giverny.

Edgar had never been inside an art gallery before, but when he walked through the door, the play of light, water, and sky on the large dappled canvases buckled his knees. It was a moment of wonder and awe such as Marco Polo must have felt on first entering Peking. For a moment, the ugliness of his life disappeared and he began to weep, all his pain and hurt washed away in the cool, limpid waters of Monet's pond. It was his baptism into the world of art.

That night, when Edgar left the Musée, something within him had changed. He never again dreamt about his father. In fact, he couldn't even remember what he looked like.

For the rest of his life, Edgar remained a monument to self-sufficiency. He neither asked for help nor received it, but saved his own skin, exorcised his own demons, and made his own luck. A survivor, he was able to let his father die to escape a personal hell and to lie about his in-laws' dead son to gain access to their fortune.

That last was a sore point with Kitty, its revelation having led to her father's stroke. She never let Edgar forget that he was responsible for Henry's death. The knowledge sat between them at the silent breakfast table, at society engagements, and at those increasingly infrequent moments in between when their paths happened to cross in the rambling Rosedale mansion they called home.

Edgar rationalised the deception: "Face it, Kitty, if I hadn't lied about knowing the sainted Joseph Danderville, your parents would never have let me through the front door, and you'd never have looked twice at me." He was right about her parents, but wrong about her. Kitty'd known he was a bad boy from the moment she laid eyes on him. It had been his chief attraction— a way to escape Havergal and piss off her mother at the same time.

One night, Edgar stormed off for a walk. He ended up on the railway tracks, raging at God. "You say you love the poor. Bullshit! You fix the deck! Poor kids who play by your rules end up in tarpaper shacks on Eastern Avenue. Well not me, pal. I risked—I dared—and I beat you! Got that, you sonovabitch? I'm nobody's doormat. I'm Edgar Beamish! That's right—EDGAR BEAMISH!—and you and your choir of bleeding hearts can damn well kiss my ass!"

Changing of the Guard

Edgar's victory over God proves pyhrric. He forgets the obvious: you can play fast and loose with the Almighty, but in the end, the house dealer has the trump ace up his sleeve. In Edgar's case, it takes the form of a massive heart attack at Millie Gingrich's bed and breakfast.

Edgar is pissed. Humiliated by the venue of his appointed hour, his life savaged by a press beyond the reach of litigation, he can't even get respect at his own damn funeral. Bad enough that the congregation is splattered with wafers and wine! Bad enough that his son ends up on the altar, a hypodermic in his ass! Or that the premier puts the make on his widow, while she kicks his frigging corpse in her underwear! For Christ's sake, the world gets to laugh at the sight of Edgar Beamish without toupee and dentures!

Other less self-interested souls drop to their knees in prayer. Here at last is proof positive that God exists. Indeed, reports of Edgar's funeral create more miracles than a Benny Hinn special, as former Chicken Little employees in nursing homes across the country throw away their walkers and cavort like spring chickens.

Meanwhile, in the executive offices of BEI, aging jocks who have long chafed under the stewardship of "Fast Eddy" Beamish uncork the champagne. Edgar's leadership style had been decidedly top-down. Now, with the autocratic bastard dispatched to that great safety deposit box in the sky—or elsewhere, speculation on Edgar in Heaven running decidedly bearish—they can spread their wings, these eagles of commerce. After all, heir Junior Beamish is utterly lacking in business skills. A headline chaser, he's a certified flake, amusing only insofar as he had a knack for embarrassing the deceased asshole. He needs them, the Beamish management team, no question. So let him have the limo and whatever titles he likes. They'll run the show.

Two months after the funeral, fresh from the psychiatric ward, Junior meets with "The Boys." Emily has arranged a spread of cold cuts, cheeses, and a chocolate banana cake from Dufflets with "Welcome Home Junior" printed in bold, gold icing. Junior is awkward in the company of these men, whose contempt shines through their smiles and cheery good wishes. After ten minutes of unbearable small talk, he calls his first executive meeting to order. At the table, besides himself and Emily Pristable, are the Vice-Presidents of Marketing, Operations, Purchasing, Human Relations, Distribution and Sales, as well as the five regional sales directors

"Emily, gentlemen, I'd like to thank you for your expressions of support. And for the lovely cake. As you can imagine, it's been a difficult few months, but my doctors have found what appears to be an appropriate dosage, so I should be able to function almost normally." A self-deprecating laugh from Junior, sideways smirks from the boys. "Okay then, first of all, I'd like to foster a sense of corporate community around here, a sense that we're all in this thing together." An appropriate rhubarb of hear! hear! and well said! rolls around the table. Junior smiles and plunges ahead. "Let's begin with a rethink of salaries and perks."

Whoops. Corporate community is a nice concept, but the devil is in the details. The mood turns sullen when Junior makes clear he values his secretaries and janitors as much as his brass. From now on, no employee, from janitor to executive, is to earn more than four times the income of any other. Junior includes himself in this directive, announcing that, as a point of honour, he plans to continue living with the cockroaches in his two-room walk-up over that Dupont Street laundromat.

As Junior prattles on, Western Regional Sales Manager, James "Jimbo" Humphries, excuses himself to use the facilities, a move followed shortly by Vice-President of Operations, Frank Kendal.

"He won't get away with it, the putz," declares Kendal, pissing furiously at the executive urinal. He's standing next to the cubicle where Humphries is enjoying a leisurely dump. "We gotta put the little pecker in his place," he adds, giving his own an emphatic shake.

A loud fart. "That's for damn sure."

This private conversation is interrupted abruptly. One by one, the entire executive has excused itself from the boardroom to join its colleagues in the can. After observing social pleasantries, "Christ Almighty, Jimbo, what did you eat last night?" the boys form an ad hoc cabal. They'll stare the little fucker down. Having shown him who's boss on his first executive foray, he'll be putty in their hands henceforth.

They return to the boardroom and stand, arms crossed, in a solid phalanx behind Kendal. "About the salary and perks, *Junior*," Frank announces, "back off or we're out. En masse."

"Resignations accepted," Junior shrugs, tossing a Lithium in the air and snatching it in his mouth with the practised ease of a trained seal snarfling smelt.

The gang stare at each other incredulous. "I don't think you understand. You need us to run this place."

"Well, to be frank, *Frank*, I don't. Dad ran a one-man show. Anyone with balls or brains cashed out years ago. Emily, here, has more of both than the lot of you put together. We'll get along quite nicely on our own, thanks."

"Just tickety-boo," Emily chimes in.

"Actually," Junior picks up, the two a verbal tag-team, "I was afraid I'd have to fire your sorry asses and get bogged down with a mess of pricey buyouts. But with your resignations, hey, that's one hour of therapy I won't have to pay for."

"Don't pout, Frank," Emily sniffs. "Retirement will give you much more time to help your new wife with her homework."

So out goes the deadwood to be replaced with recent university graduates, bright-eyed and bushy-tailed, full of ideas, devoid of prospects. What they lack in experience, they make up in energy and enthusiasm. Most important, they owe their futures to Junior alone.

With new troops in place, Junior makes it his mission to undo all the wrongs his father wrought in a lifetime of corporate empire building. To this end, he invites worker representation in decision-making, establishes daycares in each Beamish operation, practices aggressive equity hiring, and comprehensively upgrades the company benefits and sick-leave package.

But of greatest significance, he establishes what he hopes will be his permanent legacy — The Angel Foundation. The name comes courtesy of an interview with Ted Hopper in the financial pages of *The Globe and Mail*, in which Junior sketched his plans to make a charitable foundation the new centrepiece of BEI. At the tail end of the interview, Junior let slip that as a child he wanted to be the Christmas Angel when he grew up and now, he supposed, he had his chance. Hopper, who knows a good hook when he sees one, turns this into his lead: "Yes, Virginia, there is a Santa Claus. There's also a Christmas Angel and his name is Junior Beamish."

The Angel Foundation

The premise of The Angel Foundation is simple. Edgar Beamish made his fortune by squeezing anyone who lacked the muscle to fight back. Junior will now return this money through food programs for the poor, and the disabled; shelters for women, the homeless, and street kids; inner-city recreation programs—all these and more. Disbursements will come from six percent of The Angel's capital, an amount exceeding requirements for charitable foundations, yet sufficiently sound to withstand a market decline in its investments.

Wishing to create maximum impact, Junior realizes The Angel needs to open its doors with deep pockets in place. To this end he streamlines operations, liquidating all BEI holdings, save for flagship Maple Leaf Breweries, which he rechristens Junior Brews. Monies from the sale of those secondary operations are immediately donated to the Foundation. This creates a major tax write-off for BEI, the return on which is used to finance the Foundation's start-up costs.

Furthermore, Junior pledges that all future profits from BEI will be pumped into The Angel. To assure cynics that BEI will not cannibalize those profits through creative book-keeping, he places an indefinite freeze both on BEI's allocations for infrastructure and new product development. With this influx of capital, The Angel Foundation shortly becomes the largest private charity operating in North America. Junior has thrown down the gauntlet of social responsibility both to the world's financial community and to neo-con governments who have starved social programs at the altar of fiscal probity.

"So far as I know," Hopper notes sardonically during *The Globe and Mail* interview, "the law of gravity hasn't been repealed. How do you expect to fly high while ignoring basic economic principles?"

Junior's pupils dilate and he quotes José Martí, the nine-teenth-century poet and patriot of the Cuban Wars of Independence. "I have lived in the belly of the beast. I know its entrails."

This is madness. Corporate vultures grind their beaks with the prospect of picking clean the bones of BEI.

If the naysayers once underestimated Edgar, they now underestimate his son. It's true that Junior's meltdown of es-tablished practice exacts a heavy cost on the operation; however, it positions the company in a unique market niche: from rebellious teens to guilty boomers, those who claim a social conscience start drinking Junior Brews on principle. Indeed, the label becomes to beer in the millennium what Benetton was to clothes in the nineties.

Junior quickly becomes as widely admired as his father was hated, in short order receiving the Order of Canada, a host of honorary doctorates, as well as citizen citations, and a biography by Thomas Symes that borders on hagiography.

Although trumpeted a hero, Junior is targeted with enough spitballs to remind him he lives in Canada. The grousing surfaces on occasional radio talk shows and in letters to the editor. Over shots of tequila at The Rabid Squirrel, The Three Ts trash Junior with the party line: his generosity is just a design on market share. "That's so true. Pass me the lemon." Besides, why should he be praised for returning what should never have belonged to him in the first place? This from Lydia Spark, who arrives at the bar fresh from channelling at Mount Pleasant, plans for her soon-to-be historic national tour but a twinkle in her imagination.

From the opposite side of the political fence, Junior is hit by a financial press offended that he's confounded their wis-dom. Ezekiel Hammersmith, a bony proselytizer of the right, pens a series of op-ed jeremiads in *The National Post* denouncing Junior and all his works. The gist of his text is that the wages of sin are death, and the sooner Junior tumbles to wrack and ruin the better for Western civilization.

But to everything there is a season. Hammersmith brightens visibly when, several years later, Junior's finances crash in the wake of a crippling transport strike that ruins an entire summer quarter. Gross losses are estimated at two hundred million dollars, creating a serious cash flow crunch for BEI. This crunch is complicated by the company's neglected infrastructure which is in need of repair and upgrade, and its faltering product lines, which are fast growing passé.

Junior goes to see his banker, Horace McDermott, Chairman of Citi-Royal International, to negotiate an extension on his line of credit.

McDermott is a big man with big knuckles, and one enormous bushy eyebrow that appears to have been applied across his forehead with a trowel. "To be blunt, Mr. Beamish, we can't take a risk on loose cannons. Unlike you, we have shareholders. We have an obligation to protect our assets."

"Look, I've got a short-term cash-flow problem. That's all. There's nothing wrong with my fundamentals."

McDermott's eyebrow rolls across his forehead like a stadium of football fans doing The Wave. "For the past few years you've had a freeze on infrastructure investment and product development. Unsustainable. New technology has already passed you by."

"I have strong market share."

"Depressed for the past two quarters. A trend in the offing?" He reviews the auditor's report before him. His eyebrow dances the cha-cha. "Citi-Royal might see its way clear to the loan if you were to guarantee the infusion of a further two hundred million dollars to redress your infrastructure problem."

"If I had an extra two hundred million lying around, do you think I'd be here?"

"Are you a humourist, Mr. Beamish?" McDermott pauses, then adds helpfully, "One obvious route to raise capital is to take BEI public."

"No way. Shareholders only care about profit. They'd starve The Angel in a nanosecond."

"Its assets are already significant."

"Who cares? It's got to get bigger, better. It's got to be the best!"

McDermott's eyebrow shakes like a big feather boa. "We're afraid your past has caught up with you, Mr. Beamish. You can no longer afford to do as you please."

"Screw you and fuck you and bite me and die! You don't give a rat's ass about the poor."

"I also don't a have two-hundred-million-dollar cash-flow crunch. Have a nice day."

Other banks follow Citi-Royal's lead. The hangman prepares. Across the country, neo-con ghouls relish the prospect of Junior's upcoming execution. But damned if the little bugger doesn't slip the noose. Remarkably, Junior "Houdini" Beamish, his father's son to the bone, finds sufficient resources in places unnamed to allow BEI to weather its short-term crisis, and make those long-overlooked investments in infrastructure and product development. Where has the money come from?

Ezekiel Hammersmith is apoplectic. He writes a nasty diatribe that comes perilously close to libel. "Publicly traded companies are kept honest thanks to their accountability to their shareholders. By contrast, private corporations such as upstart BEI operate like bugs under rocks, carrying out their furtive transactions far from the light of day. Those contemptuous of free-market forces as represented by the stock exchange hold up Junior Beamish as a model of corporate citizenship. But until this Canadian saint is prepared to expose his books to public scrutiny, we must question whether his shrine is built upon a foundation of rot."

Emily Investigates

Where had the money come from? Emily Pristable doesn't know, but she's bound and determined to find out, such is her life-long obsession with the Beamishes, father and son.

The fierce loyalty she demonstrated to the senior Beamish, it must be said, had caused much consternation at Calvary Baptist. How could a bona fide, rock-ribbed Baptist be employed by a sinner as gleefully unrepentant as Edgar? His shocking transactions, profanity, and lifestyle might pass unnoticed by Anglicans, but surely such behaviour was beyond the pale for a true believer washed in the blood of the Lamb.

Lily Pigeon, a dental assistant who sports big hair, faux pearls and an unmistakable fragrance from Wal-Mart, cornered her once at a church supper. "I don't mean to pass judgment," she demurred, "but the man deals in alcohol!"

"So?" Emily snapped, "People see the light when they've a mind to. In the meantime, please pass me a second helping of those mashed potatoes."

Lily obliged, but pressed her case, loudly, out to score points with the pastor: "Yes, but how can a Christian work for such a degenerate? And at such a place?"

"The Lord moves in mysterious ways," Emily smiled tightly. "Though none so mysterious as your recent frolic in Las Vegas."

"My sister and I were sightseeing!"

"Of course you were, dear." They left her alone after that.

Still, if fellow congregants found Emily's choice of company strange, the unchurched considered her religious affiliation bizarre. "What are you doing with those quacks?" Edgar used to ask.

"That's for me to know and you to find out," she always replied, deftly removing bits of lint from his lapel.

Emily lives alone in a modest St. George Street apartment, as she has ever since the Beamish family relocated to Toronto.

Her kin have all passed away, save for a first cousin in Wisconsin with whom she exchanges birthday and Christmas greetings. Marriage was not in the cards, but she seems to have no regrets. Her life is full.

Monday and Tuesday she reads to the children at Sick Kids, Wednesday she has Bible study over church supper, and Thursday she's at choir practice. Emily is one of the few sopranos who regularly manages to remain on key, no small feat as she stands next to Angus MacBride, who is not only tone-deaf but a tenor.

In addition, she enrolls each fall in at least one course offered by The Learning Annex. Crafts mostly. Those which involve welding have proved a vexation, but weaving is a treat, as are her master classes in needlepoint, tapestry, and quilting. Putting these latter skills together, Emily passes many happy hours constructing elaborate renderings of stories from the Old Testament. Her evocative portrayal of Daniel in the lion's den, which hangs in the church nursery, is a favourite with the Sunday School set. Another triumph is her eiderdown depicting Shadrak, Mishak, and Abendago in the fiery furnace.

This last item is now owned by Lily, who bid a spectacular three hundred dollars for it at the annual church picnic and raffle. The three hundred was sin money she'd won on a gambling spree to Niagara Falls. She rationalized that spending it on Emily's eiderdown absolved her, as proceeds from the raffle were being used to underwrite a trip to the Holy Land for retiring Pastor Kincaid, whose adventures had hitherto been limited to marshmallow roasts at church camp.

Suffice it to say that Emily's social calendar keeps her hopping, especially as work for the Beamishes, like Jonah's whale, can swallow one whole. This has been true more than ever in the years since she began assisting Junior. He relies on her for advice and as a buffer against an outside world, the practical workings of which frequently threaten his emotional moorings.

All the same, Emily isn't getting any younger and it's past time she moved on. She's frequently offered to retire. Much as she loves being with Junior, he needs someone younger to help

him cope with the pressures of his ever-expanding philanthropic enterprises. While BEI pretty much runs itself, The
Angel is an octopus of good intentions with tentacles in so
many ventures that the beast threatens to tie itself up in knots.

To date, Junior has resisted her offers to resign. He can't
bear not seeing her on a regular basis. Emily reassures him that
she has no intention of running off to the Australian outback,
or some such, and will remain as close at hand as the nearest
telephone. However, he always looks so lost and his eyes get so
big that after much soul-searching she relents, agreeing to stay
a mite longer. Last year, granted, was a very near thing. She'd
been having dizzy spells. Happily, Junior gave her four months
off with full pay following the summer transport strike and she
was able to recuperate with her cousin in Wisconsin.

Emily's love for Junior is uppermost in her mind as she approaches his Dupont Street walk-up. She last saw him three
days ago reading his morning mail. The next thing she knew,
he'd fled the building hollering "Damn you to hell, Rudyard!"
He hasn't been seen or heard from since.

She rings the outside buzzer. No answer. She lets herself in
with the house key Junior once gave her when he was away
and needed someone to feed his goldfish.

The stairwell is dark, the overhead bulb burned out. No
matter. She knows these stairs blindfolded. She ascends,
engulfed by a strong odour; the smell is familiar, but she can't
quite place it. Then she hears a voice. "Stop looking at me. Stop
staring. Stop it. Stop. Go away. Why are you doing this? What
have I done? What do you want?"

Emily knocks on the door at the top of the landing. Silence.

"Junior, it's me. Emily."

A pause. "Emily?" The voice is that of a lost boy.

"May I come in?"

"Emily? Emily, he won't take his eyes off me. Make him
take his eyes off me. Make him go away."

Emily opens the door to the apartment. The smell assaults
her. Now she has it: camphor. Camphor mixed with garlic,

perejil and yerbabuena. A smell to ward off the espíritu intranquilo. A *resguardo* against the restless spirit.

The room is dark, curtains drawn, bulbs burned out as in
the stairwell. The sole light comes from six candles arranged in
a hexagon on the floor around Junior's futon. Junior huddles
at the centre of the hexagon, wrapped in a dirty bedsheet. He
is haggard. Dark bags of puffy skin sag beneath his eyes, while
stubble accentuates the hollows of his sallow cheeks.

"Junior, what's happened to you?"

"Unclean. Unclean. I must be punished. No—" he says, as
she takes a step towards him. "Stay back. He'll stare at you, too."

"Junior, have you been taking your medication?"

A convulsive sob. "It doesn't do any good. Nothing does
any good. I need a new spell. Sara will know what to do. Sara!
I have to see Sara! Book me a ticket to Varadero."

"Junior, you're raving!"

"I'm not raving! He's staring at me."

"Listen to me, Junior," Emily says firmly. "Your father isn't
staring at you. Your father is dead."

"Not Dad," says Junior, pointing over Emily's shoulder.
"Him."

Emily turns sharply. She gasps. By a sliver of streetlight
that slips through a tear in the curtains, she sees eyes—fierce red-
green eyes that leap at her from a charged, blue background.
It's the van Gogh *Self-Portrait*, propped on the kitchen counter.

"Junior, it's just a painting." Emily soothes, "But if you
don't mind my saying so, this is no place for a van Gogh. Good
heavens, the danger of thieves or fire—I don't think the
insurance company would understand."

"I didn't bring it here."

"Then who did, I'd like to know?"

"I came home three days ago and it was waiting in my bedroom," Junior says, pointing to the other room. "I shut the
bedroom door. I went for a walk. I came back and went to the
bathroom. And there it was, propped up over the toilet. I closed

the bathroom door, dragged my futon in here and tried to sleep. When I got up, it had moved to the counter. He was staring at me. He's always staring at me. He won't leave me alone."

"Junior, paintings don't just move about."

"You don't understand."

"Don't I just. You're cursed with imagination. All your life you've seen ghosts and goblins under the bed, Pillow Ladies in the closet—you've simply got to get a grip." She gives the painting another look. "I don't know why on earth your father gave you that thing. Honestly, if I had a mug like that I certainly wouldn't be painting it up for all the world to see. No wonder you have the heebie-jeebies."

She turns the painting around to face the cupboards. "There now, isn't that better? That old geezer'd put anyone off his lunch. What you need in here is something cheery. A picture of the Rockies, maybe, or a nice bowl of fruit."

Junior will not be distracted. His eyes remain fixed on the back of the canvas. "He'll turn around when you're not looking."

"I want you to get in touch with Dr. Billing," Emily says. No ifs, ands, or buts. You get him to adjust your medication. This craziness has got to stop. I'm too old for it."

"I'm sorry."

"Would you like some tea?"

Junior nods and Emily makes a pot. Tea has always settled him, ever since he was little. When she cared for him during Kitty's various rest cures, she'd pop a tea bag in and out of a cup of hot milk and sugar: it was mostly for colour and made him feel very grown-up. Then they'd sit in the kitchen and he'd pour out his heart. "Sometimes I wish I wasn't me," he'd allow. "Then I wouldn't have so many pwobwems."

Junior has more than a four-year-old's problems today. He rummages through a stack of papers balanced on the edge of the futon and find the letter that sent him howling from the office. It is from Revenue Canada.

Dear Mr. Beamish:

Re: Fourth Quarter Audit of BEI

Please be advised that our audits of Beamish Enterprises Inc., and of The Angel Foundation, reveal serious irregularities as per sections 343, 372 and 415 of the Tax Act. We find taxes owed by Beamish Enterprises Inc. on unreported earnings of $412,356,278.91. We further find The Angel Foundation to be in serious breach of tax law with respect to Canadian regulations governing registered charitable foundations.

We will be at your corporate head office to review these findings with you on May 22nd at 10 A.M. In the interim, be advised that you and Beamish Enterprises Inc. may be subject to prosecution for tax evasion and fraud. Further, our lawyers recommend that proceedings be initiated to revoke the charitable status of The Angel Foundation.

Sincerely,
Mr. Harold Grimsby
Revenue Canada

"Obviously there's been some mistake," says Emily, bewildered.

"There's no mistake. I'm a crook. Like father, like son. But here's the joke," Junior laughs bitterly. "My father robbed his workers blind, and no one said 'Boo.' I give everything to the poor, and I'll end up in jail, ruined, my Angel destroyed."

"But what did you do?" Emily gropes for a chair.

"Ask Rudyard Gardenia."

Rudyard Gardenia

When Junior was rebuffed by Citi-Royal's Horace McDermott and the rest of the Bay Street boys, he was at his wits' end. He was not about to hand over BEI to a gang of profit-hungry shareholders who'd kill The Angel. But where was he to find two hundred million? He took a deep breath and went to see his mother.

Kitty was loaded, in more ways than one. Following Edgar's death, her inheritance of one hundred and fifty million quickly trebled thanks to aggressive investment in overheated equity markets. Junior found her under a large umbrella by the pool, her body covered with delicate slivers of tomato and cucumber, her latest attempt to keep her skin supple against the ravages of time, alcohol, and cigarillos.

"For heaven's sake, mother, you look like a tossed salad."

"I love you too, my pet. What do you want?"

Would she invest half her capital in BEI, to be repaid with interest within the year?

"Of course I would, my darling. But it's entirely out of my hands. You'll have to speak to Rudyard."

Rudyard. Rudyard Gardenia. Former curator, critic, and consultant, sovereign of The Inner Circle, and now, of all things, his mother's private investment counsellor. Damn.

Rudyard had blossomed since Edgar's death, transforming himself from a well-connected snob devouring his wife's inheritance to a wealthy intellectual terrorist. His life was proof that there is nothing one cannot achieve if propelled by self-hate, wit, and a talent for cruelty. In the words of Benny Debuque, one-time Inner Circle whipping boy, "Shit floats, and Rudyard is the biggest turd in the bowl."

Rudyard Gardenia, as the monied well know, was not his real name. His parents had emigrated from someplace in eastern Europe following the war, settling in a neighbourhood of working-class bungalows in south Etobicoke. They were honest, hard-working, salt-of-the-earth people who scrimped and saved to ensure that their son would have all the advantages that life had to offer. Rudyard was ashamed of them.

With the money his mother earned as a cleaning lady, he had been enrolled as a day-boy at Upper Canada College. Here he had seen what money and power were all about; and what they were all about most certainly wasn't driving a bus like his father or scrubbing other people's homes on one's hands and knees like his mother. Such occupations were an embarrassment, as Rudyard learned through the daily ridicule of his classmates. "Hey Rudyard, how much for your mother to stick her head in my toilet?"

These schoolboy taunts finally ended when Rudyard discovered that he, too, had a knack for invective. He quickly mastered the art of the put-down, humiliating any who stood in his way with words deliciously cruel, exquisitely heartless. He was hated, but he was also feared. Not bad for a new boy who was bad at sports and used public transit.

On graduation from UCC, Rudyard took a double major in Fine Arts and Classics at the University of Toronto, studies made possible by a succession of scholarships and a second mortgage his parents took out on the family home. It was here that he met his future meal ticket, Betty Remington, heiress to the Remington Furniture fortune.

The Remingtons lived on a hobby farm north of Guelph, and Betty was true to her rural roots. An only child, she was pleasant and plain, with a slight speech impediment brought on by her father, who had never ceased to publicly catalogue her deficiencies. He died when she was sixteen, but the damage had been done. Although absolutely capable, she entered university frightened of her own shadow. Here she met Rudyard, whose intelligence and private school polish swept her off her feet. He introduced her to his circle, a glitterati of young, sharp-edged sophisticates in whose presence she was utterly cowed. Grateful for inclusion in such a smart set, she accepted his proposal of marriage, as readily as he accepted her inheritance.

The day before the public announcement of the engagement, Rudyard phoned his parents to inform them that they would not be invited to the wedding. He also informed them that he had legally changed his name. "Betty's people are quality. Surely you don't expect me to humiliate them with a name like yours?" He never contacted them again, nor returned their calls.

Rudyard graduated at the top of his class. His gold medal in Fine Arts and an impressive array of social contacts helped him to nab an assistant curator's post at The Art Gallery of Ontario. It was at a gallery function that he charmed Kitty Beamish, and through her gained the ear of Edgar. Soon, he was on an under-the-table retainer to feed the tycoon privileged gallery information on Impressionist paintings broached for sale. Before this duplicity could be uncovered, he had parlayed his wit and knack for impolite gossip into a social network sufficiently vast that he was able to quit the AGO's employ and venture forth as an independent art consultant.

The discovery of the van Gogh *Self-Portrait* had been a watershed event in his life. The money it brought him from Edgar's estate made him financially independent. For a time he considered dispensing with Betty, whose now dwindling financial reserves were no longer necessary to maintain his lifestyle. However, he quickly came to his senses when he realized she was a vital component to his master plan, the object of which was nothing less than control of the astonishing assets of the widow Beamish. Though the painting had made Rudyard rich, Edgar had suckered him out of its true worth. He wanted revenge on the Beamish clan to soothe his wounded pride.

Rudyard's putsch was conceived after canny observation of Beamish family frailties and fault lines. These were in full bloom following the reading of Edgar's will. Despite a month of cold turkey at The Grove, Edgar's stipulation that Kitty's control of her inheritance rested on her ability to pass two years of weekly urine tests still had Kitty chewing the scenery. "I'm to be dependent on a goddamn Baptist secretary? Jesus Christ Almighty! Why, you'd think I was an alcoholic! Or a drug addict!" she seethed over a Perrier on the patio of Ghazario's, a noshery deep in the belly of Yorkville.

"Outrageous. Simply outrageous," Rudyard commiserated, nursing a double Scotch, a Glenfiddich, her favourite. "Honestly, to deprive you of a little refreshment, it's cruel."

Kitty raised a scented hankie to her face, as though near tears; actually, she was looking for a polite excuse to cover her nose. The simple act of arching an eyebrow caused Rudyard to break a sweat. Under the hot sun his pong had grown richer than the effluvium of a round of ripe brie.

"It's the absence of trust that hurts most."

Rudyard leaned forward to within kissing distance, "Well, I trust you, Kitty. And I hope you trust me."

"Like a son," she solemnly assured him, craning her neck toward his mouth. The smell of Glenfiddich on his breath was enough for her to endure the stink.

"I have a little notion which just might interest you."

Rudyard's notion, in a nutshell, placed him in charge of circumventing Edgar's will. He would become her escort, chaperon, and advisor—a consort to her queen. In this capacity, he would accompany her to the weekly testing, en route providing a vial of clean urine appropriate for substitution. He would likewise attend to her needs at social functions, spiking her drinks and navigating her through whatever awkward moments might ensue.

Finally, Rudyard added, as her closest confidante, he would act as her financial advisor, putting his considerable intelligence, and information drawn from sources at Nesbitt-Burns, toward the development of her portfolio. For these and sundry services, he would be paid a tidy commission on her investment profits, such arrangement to last fifteen years, in consideration of the long-term social and legal risks entailed.

Kitty leapt at the proposal, which she thought eminently fair. She would be free to conduct her life without restraint, or fear of control by that damned Baptist. She would have Rudyard, whose gossip she cherished next to life itself, as a social companion, placing her at the centre of the most amusing circles. Finally, she would have in him an advisor whose intellect was without question and whose attentions would be hers alone.

It remained for Rudyard to come up with the urine. He ruled himself out immediately, as he was not about to forgo the grape, nor an occasional indulgence in nose candy. Secretary Bob was likewise a poor prospect, his street history making him a risky bet for a project that stood to earn millions. There remained wife Betty, teetotaller Betty, she of the dwindling Remington Furniture fortune.

He solicited her assistance one morning, over scones and tea, with customary tact: "I need you to pee in a bottle."

Betty looked askance.

"Oh, come now. Surely that can't be too difficult for you."

Naturally, Rudyard got his way. He always got his way, whatever viciousness was required. The evisceration of his parents had been thorough. His destruction of young artists was legendary; former members of The Inner Circle, many driven to attempt suicide, had gone so far as to organize The Rudyard Gardenia Survivors Society. Nor had the great man spared his lover. On the one occasion Bob had flirted with independence, Rudyard had brought him quickly to heel: "You've done rather well for a grade ten dropout with acne scars, but don't push it. You're not getting any younger."

When it came to ugliness, however, his control of Betty was in a class by itself. In the course of their twenty-three year marriage, he had managed to grind out whatever self-esteem her father had left intact. It was a game in which he took delight. The process began shortly after their honeymoon, in the late '60s, when he began referring to her as "the baggage." Dinner parties proved a special venue for humiliation. Whenever Betty ventured an opinion, Rudyard would roll his eyes indulgently and say, "Where does the baggage pick up such twaddle?" or "Time for the baggage to busy itself in the kitchen, *n'est-ce pas*?" Most embarrassing was when he did this in front of her mother and her friends.

By the '70s, endearments like "the baggage" and "the little woman" no longer raised chuckles at polite dinner tables. Accordingly, Rudyard switched gears. Now, whenever Betty offered an opinion his eyes would open wide and he'd gaze at her with a look of stunned incredulity. Alternately, he'd smile, say, "Yes, well . . ." and change the topic. Betty was made to feel as if she'd just passed gas and Rudyard was doing her the favour of ignoring it.

"How can you let him treat you this way?" Mrs. Remington asked, in a rare private moment.

"He's just joking, mother," Betty pleaded. "He's not like this in private."

Betty was right. He was worse. He took to calling her mother "The Dowager Hick," and her old friends from Guelph "the hicklets." Made to feel unwelcome *chez* Gardenia, her family and friends soon drifted away. By the time her mother died, Betty was utterly alone, her social contacts limited to those allowed by Rudyard.

It is a sick tribute to his powers of control that, to this day, Betty never considers herself abused. Rather, she assumes it's her fault that she feels so miserable. I'm lucky to be with someone as clever as him, she thinks. He must be a saint to put up with a wife so simple and plain. Nevertheless, deep within her tortured soul there remains a glimmer of hope that finds release in a recurring dream. In the dream, Betty is pursued by a white grub the size of a house. She has yet to find a tool big enough to squash it, but continues her search, convinced a weapon of annihilation lies just around the corner.

It does.

One day, in real life, Betty will find the weapon, and when she does her vengeance will be sure and swift. It will explode unexpectedly, in the wake of Junior Beamish's still-to-be-created Phoenix Lottery. It will erupt like a volcano and devastate her tormentor with a justice so appropriate one would swear it could occur only in fiction. For if Rudyard's psychological abuse has decimated Betty as utterly as the mayomberos' black magic turns human beings into zombie slaves, it is fitting that Betty's eventual triumph, blazing and absolute, will be realized with supernatural assistance. Specifically, with the help of a Santerían priest and a lunatic Catholic saint wont to behave like an orisha.

The Trap

"**W**ell, naturally I sympathize. The Angel is a national treasure. On no account must it be devoured by barbarians. All the same," Rudyard continues, sucking on an orange jelly bean, "two hundred million is a tidy sum. It represents half your mother's holdings."

Referred by his mother, Junior has come to Rudyard Gardenia to beg. The lord of the manor relaxes on a bench in his garden, a fan in one hand, a bowl of assorted bonbons beside the other. He is resplendent in a silk House of Versace muumuu with pink flamingo print. Junior, by contrast, is a bundle of nerves, driven to wearing a suit and tie for the occasion.

"The entire loan can be repaid within the year. With a good rate of return."

"All the same . . ." Rudyard's voice trails off.

For the first time, Junior fears the worst and it scares the hell out of him. The Angel is more than a charity: it is the antithesis of his father, the measure of his own life.

When Junior was formulating his plans in Homewood's sick bay, Edgar had appeared on the window ledge to ridicule and attack him for undermining the integrity of the corporation. Doctors were alarmed to observe what they took to be Junior's one-sided conversations. They upped his medication and Edgar retreated to the sidelines. But what if his father had been right?

(In truth, Edgar never wished despair upon his son. On full moons, when Junior lay awake, troubled and lonely, Edgar wanted to comfort him. He knew from experience how difficult it was to strike off in a new direction, and how important it was that his son establish an identity separate from his own. As The Angel became first a reality and then a success, Edgar longed to admit he'd been wrong. But Junior's relentless public digs at Edgar's life choked the words in his throat, and instead of entering Junior's dreams to say, Well done. I'm proud of you, my boy, he found himself floating through his nightmares whispering, You'll find a way to fail.)

"All the same . . . all the same . . . all the same." Rudyard pauses. "You know, I think I have an idea." He brightens. "I think I see salvation staring us right in the face."

"What is it? What?" asks Junior, clutching at straws.

"All your profits from BEI have gone into The Angel over the past few years, plus monies hitherto earmarked for infrastructure and development. The Foundation must have, what . . . three hundred million? Four?"

"Closer to five."

"Then the solution is obvious. Have BEI borrow two hundred million of Angel assets to solve its cash flow problems. Take a further two hundred for new infrastructure and product development. If BEI repays The Angel at six percent interest, The Angel will be able to maintain all of its charitable obligations. Why, it's a win-win proposition. BEI avoids its current squeeze, which keeps you in control, free of stock-market predators. This preserves the integrity of The Angel and ensures its continued contribution to the poor—about whom we all care so deeply."

Rudyard's plan is brilliant. Tears of gratitude well in Junior's eyes. He mentally retracts all the nasty things he's said about the man over the years. "It's perfect! Thank you."

"Don't mention it," the Great Man obliges. "We are artists, the two of us. And artists must stick together."

Things which look too good to be true usually are. Rudyard's plan stops being perfect the afternoon an anonymous tipster sends a fax to Revenue Canada alleging financial hanky-panky between Beamish Enterprises Inc. and The Angel Foundation. The fax lands on the desk of Harold Grimsby.

Grimsby is a stooped and squinty thirty-six. Thin as gruel, and less exciting, he is already grey, the colour of his soul. He is also newly promoted and determined to prove himself as tough as his elders. In the Beamish file he sees an opportunity to make a name for himself. He sets a pack of juniors on the hunt and is overjoyed when they report malfeasance.

It matters not to Harold Grimsby that Junior's manoeuvres placed BEI on a secure financial footing, nor that The Angel continues to fulfill its charitable obligations, nor that the loan is being repaid with interest above prime, or even that BEI has maintained its practice of sharing its profits with the poor rather than the rich.

To Harold Grimsby, this is all well and good, but it doesn't satisfy the letter of the law. The only thing that matters in this instance is that The Angel's investment in BEI was not an arm's-length transaction. Over the years, BEI's charitable donations to The Angel have created massive tax deductions for the company. Having those monies returned to BEI, even as a loan, makes The Angel look suspiciously like a holding account, a dodge used to launder profit, the taxes on which are rightfully owed Revenue Canada.

The size of the monies on which corporate taxes are owing and unpaid are of especial concern: four hundred million dollars. As Harold Grimsby sees it, this constitutes massive corporate fraud and a violation of tax law, which clearly calls into question the right of The Angel to claim charitable tax status.

Reviewing the work of his subordinates, Harold is aflame: there's nothing like a good audit to put fire in a man's belly! He smells blood. And not only Junior's. The thrill of unearthing fraud has prompted a spontaneous nosebleed. (The delicacy of his nasal capillaries is a constant embarrassment to Harold, not only at work but during his infrequent romantic forays. Such forays, sadly, peter out the moment he begins discussing his work. As a sexual stimulant, chartered accounting is an acquired taste.)

Harold staunches the flow and, damp with excitement, dictates the letter that sent Junior screaming to his Dupont Street walk-up, where he now rocks obsessively in his dirty bedsheet, surrounded by candles and comforted by his private secretary.

"Why didn't you come to me for advice?" Emily asks help-lessly, letting the letter drop from her hand.

"You were stressed out in Wisconsin. Besides, it seemed perfect. Rudyard's behind this" he says darkly. "BEI is a private family corporation. If I go to jail, mother will be first in line to take over. And Rudyard will be there to lick up the profits, gobble them whole, wolf down his commission and spit out the poor."

"The bastard!" Emily exclaims. Hearing an expletive come out of Emily's mouth makes Junior laugh despite himself. "Well he just *is*," Emily spits. "Don't worry. When it comes time for that meeting with Mr. Grimsby, you'll think of something. You always do." She gives him an encouraging smile. The tears come later, when she is alone.

The Dream

It's night. It's warm. I hear surf, smell salt. I'm in Varadero. Why? I'm supposed to be meeting Harold Grimsby. And I'm on a golf cart. Double why? I don't play golf. A tiny voice calls, "Wait for me! Please wait!" I look up and see myself as a four-year-old in the rooftop bar at Xanadu. The motor revs and the cart pulls away. I look for the brakes. There aren't any.

"Wait for me! Wait!"

"I can't," I cry to the boy-me. The cart accelerates. I try to move the steering wheel, but it has a mind of its own. I careen through a clump of jungle, giant leaves, tendrils, and trees whizzing out of the night. Children too. They leap from the undergrowth, hold out their hands. "Help us, Junior! Please! Don't leave us!"

The cart smashes into one, then another, runs them down. But there are more and more, everywhere, other faces—hungry, homeless, workers, widows—arms outstretched. They're bowled over like tenpins. Some, bleeding, cling to the sides of the cart. "Don't leave us!" I kick at their hands, claw at their eyes to make them let go. But they don't.

The cart hits a sand trap. It accelerates. The wheels sink deep in white powder.

Suddenly , a spotlight. I hear cheers and clapping. I shield my eyes and see a reviewing stand full of execs decked out in bunting and ticker tape. There in the front is Harold Grimsby. And right behind, munching peanuts, popcorn, and candy apples are Rudyard Gardenia, Horace McDermott, Frank Kendal, Ezekiel Hammersmith, and my father. Dad hoists an enormous megaphone. "Let's all raise a cheer as my son goes down!" he bellows. "Come on, failure! Sink!" And Harold and the rest chant, "Sink! Sink! Sink!" The cart revs faster and the wheels spin deeper. I try to get out, but I'm trapped!

All the people I hit begin to arrive. They scrape their broken bodies around the trap, crawling over each other across the sand like a human bridge.

I'm sinking fast. The sand is up to my waist, up to my armpits, my neck. I hear my Dad laugh. I see him clap. The poor cry, "Help!" I scream, "I can't!" as the sand fills my ears, my eyes, my mouth, and I'm buried alive in the trap!

Brain Seizure

As Kierkegaard reminds us, life is lived forward and understood backward, insignificant actions assuming, in retrospect,
monumental importance in the life of individuals and nations.
Surely a lottery is not on Junior's troubled mind this fateful day
as he slumps in the BEI boardroom, prepared for a 10 A.M.
gutting by the redoubtable Harold Grimsby. Nor is a lottery on
the mind of Emily Pristable as she finishes her breakfast of
porridge, half grapefruit, coffee, and toast, praying for a miracle
to deliver the young man she helped raise. If only Edgar was
alive: he'd know what to do. (I'd know not to get into this mess,
thinks Edgar, discreetly out of sight, if never far from mind.)

And a lottery is most certainly not on the mind of Harold
Grimsby as he peruses several of the periodicals he hides at the
bottom of his underwear drawer. These periodicals, mailed in
plain wrappers, relieve the tension which precipitates his public
nosebleeds, for which purpose he consults them now. Might he
claim them as a business deduction? No. His colleagues wouldn't
understand, least of all his unrequited passion, the lovely and unavailable Monica DeWitt, who will be providing him with legal
advice this morning. He would do anything for Monica, especially if it involved Italian footwear.

At 9:30 A.M., Junior stares around the empty boardroom.
The surface decor remains as his father left it. The room is a
large square, rimmed with elegant oak mouldings, chair-rail, and
wainscotting, above which is a pale pink-and-grey herringbone
wallpaper complemented by deep, maroon wall-to-wall carpeting. However, as part of his plan to humanize the workplace,
Junior has replaced most of the furnishings. He has left the
Monets living on either side of the imposing double doors, and
the Impressionist oils lining the other walls, but the massive oak
"power table" and equally oppressive chairs with their padded

maroon leather seats and backs are gone. In their place is a substantial coffee table—a round glass top resting on a section of wooden keg—surrounded by two semicircular, backless couches upholstered with a rich yellow-cream damask. Low occasional tables, holding simple vases filled with fresh flowers, soften the corners, while artfully placed halogens provide lighting both clear and atmospheric.

The one odd note is the van Gogh *Self-Portrait*, now re-turned to its place of honour. Measuring two-and-a-half-feet wide and four-feet tall it imposes itself upon the room like a homeless party crasher wolfing down the buffet at a black-tie gala. The other pictures pretend not to notice, but it is clear this edgy ruffian is out of place amongst the idyllic scenes of water lilies, ponds, and picnics. The likeness has been painted with an unusually hyperactive brushstroke, an aggressive use of colour contrast, and an ecstatic tension between the background of deep swirling cobalt and indigo whirlpools and the stark force of the foreground face and upper torso.

Van Gogh stares out, exposing the wound on the right side of his face where he had recently severed a large section of ear with a straight razor. As the wound healed, the scar tissue folded in on itself, creating a stump like a half-eaten Brussels sprout. The naked pain is shattering, and was apparently too much even for its creator; nowhere else in his work is the artist willing to show us the fruits of his mutilation, a fact that has increased the value of the painting enormously.

As for the palette, van Gogh wears a light, cloudy-blue rum-pled shirt, buttoned to the neck, under a waistcoat and jacket of lapis lazuli charged with streaks of yellow and purple that skitter like ferrets across the fabric. His skin is composed of ner-vous squiggles of sickly greens, which make him look in need of sleep and a wash. Greasy ropes of clay-red hair, pulled severely back off the high forehead, underline the need for hygiene, as do the fierce beard and moustache, which disin-tegrate into coarse daubs of russet scattered across the lower cheek. However, what one notices most is the sharp nose, which points accusingly from the canvas, and the incisive eyes which frame it. The eyes—dilated black pupils leaping from chrome green irises lined with vermilion—the eyes pin the viewer as if to say, I am returned from hell to tell you all—to tell you all.

It is a portrait of the sort of men Junior has seen, on late-night walks near abandoned warehouses, warming their hands over fires in oil drums, or at the backs of churches, taking shelter from the rain. Sometimes he thinks it is his face, or what his face would have been if, like Vincent, he were dependent on the charity of a brother struggling with a growing family. It is a face to avoid when one is alone, or drunk, or afraid.

"Dad said you'd change my life," Junior snarls, sitting opposite the *Self-Portrait*. "So far all you've done is driven me crazy."

Lesser paintings might have faded, but van Gogh maintains his withering gaze. Dust motes flicker disconcertingly across the right eyebrow.

"I'm sorry!" Junior retreats, shielding his face with his arm. "Stop it! Please! Stop judging me."

Emily arrives not a moment too soon, interrupting what would have developed into an embarrassing conversation. She pats his shoulder and they huddle in silence. BEI's lawyer, Ernest Hoyt, shows up five minutes later. He resembles a good-natured Frankenstein in a Brooks Brothers suit, with a square heavy face, bone protrusions over the eyes, and a thatch of short, clipped hair on an otherwise shaved head; there are even large matching moles where neck plugs might go. Ernest plans to do what any other self-respecting lawyer does when the facts are against him: ignore them.

Ten o'clock passes. The Revenue Canada contingent has elected to let them sweat. And sweat. Finally, at eleven, Harold enters along with Ms. DeWitt and his reedy assistant, Irving Schloesser, who will take notes. Ms. DeWitt, a sober analyst confused by humour, is wearing a navy power suit and a pair of new Italian stilettos that are driving Harold wild.

Formal introductions, polite to a fault, provide a prim opening movement to the legal minuet that follows. Harold initiates discussion with a dry account of the findings of Revenue Canada. Monica DeWitt follows with a legal appraisal, its conclusions as devastating as they are irrefutable.

Ernest Hoyt replies on behalf of Junior. He begins by lauding Junior's good works funded by The Angel. "Such disbursements were not his to make," Ms DeWitt interjects with a thin smile. "Said monies were taken from corporate tax revenue, control of which is at the sole discretion of the duly elected government of Canada."

Switching gears, Ernest launches an impassioned defense of his employer's character. The gist of his argument is that Junior is a man incapable of committing fraud; however, notwithstanding that he could not have committed fraud, if he has committed fraud, then he has surely committed fraud without intent. Junior's heart sinks. If Ernest is feeling as desperate as he looks, surely he could have managed a stronger antiperspirant. Junior imagines himself in a fetching prison ensemble and leg irons.

Mercifully, Ernest stops speaking before embarrassing himself further. Pause. Harold, Monica, and Irving stare at him blankly. He looks at his shoes. There follows a terrible silence of the sort Junior endures in the sunroom of his psychiatrist. And then, what appears to be a miracle.

"Despite our reputation," Harold begins, "we at Revenue Canada are not Grinches out to destroy Christmas, especially not for Angels." He allows himself a small chuckle at what he supposes a clever turn of phrase. Everyone smiles politely, except for Monica, who scrunches her eyebrows, perplexed. "We recognize the service your foundation has provided to this country, Mr. Beamish, and are prepared to accept that you have acted without criminal intent. It is not our wish to destroy a man for being stupid. Therefore, we offer an olive branch. We will waive fraud charges, providing back taxes are paid within eight months, with penalty, naturally. Further, we will allow The Angel to maintain its charitable registration if its four hundred million investment in BEI is returned within the year."

If it is true that Harold Grimsby is not a Grinch, it is like-wise true that he is not Santa Claus. Naturally, elected officials would not wish to interfere with arm's-length government audits conducted by Revenue Canada. Nonetheless, it has come to Harold's attention through back-door channels that the Prime Minister's Office has hardly viewed his efforts on the Beamish file with unalloyed delight. Jailing a member of the Order of Canada is not high on the government's list of pri-orities, nor is shutting down one of the world's most successful private charitable foundations.

Shelters, hostels, food banks, job training, and community recreational programs are not without their supporters. There is the well-organized women's movement to consider, as well as the rapidly increasing seniors' lobby, both of which have healthy demo-graphics, hence the interest of the media and the political clout which follows. Nor can the government ignore the families of those who have benefited from Junior's altruism, nor the municipal politicians and community activists for whom The Angel's programs have provided cost-free civic enhance-ments. These "special interest groups," formerly known as citizens, have one thing in common. Votes. Lots and lots of votes. Thus, the government is less than happy with Grimsby's diligence in protecting the public purse. As the PMO's toady so delicately put it, as he leaned his belly over Harold's impossibly tidy desk, "Perhaps you might wish to submit this file to further review."

Most individuals confronted with a diplomatic dressing-down would be embarrassed, especially were it delivered with the office door wide open, in full view and earshot of subor-dinates. But Harold is a bureaucrat. He is inured to humili-ation. Indignity and injustice come as naturally to him as coffee breaks. Consequently, he takes it in his stride and attempts to undo the damage his hard work has occasioned. If his political masters wish to let Beamish off the hook, fine. He will manage it, and in such a way that he will appear a generous benefactor to the disadvantaged.

Initially his offer to waive charges appears to do the trick. Ernest Hoyt has the euphoric look of a man who has just snorted a line of exceptionally fine cocaine. Emily, too, looks happily bewildered, as if she has woken up to discover manna falling from the ceiling. All eyes turn to Junior. As always, he confounds expectation.

"Blow me."

"Junior," gasps Emily, clutching his hand, alarmed lest he cause Mr. Grimsby to change his mind. Junior shakes her off. This is no gift horse; it's a Trojan horse.

"Taxes, penalty, and interest come to a cool two hundred million. As for the four hundred million investment, it's spent — gone — two hundred on infrastructure, two hundred on development. Your offer has a six hundred million price tag. And where's the money to come from? Answer me that, you pathetic little ink drop!"

"I'm afraid that's really not my — "

"Enough. You're as bad as the banks. You'd take BEI public. A public offering under these circumstances will see it go for peanuts. Sold on the cheap, I'll be out, it'll be bled, and my baby, my Angel will be gutted. You offer me freedom — but the price is my soul!"

Talk of souls is foreign turf for the apparatchiks from Revenue Canada.

From high-decibel rage, Junior's voice swoops to an intense whisper: "What are you staring at? Stop judging me."

"I beg your pardon?"

"I told you to stop it! I didn't ask for you to be here!"

"That's as may be," Harold observes, "but — "

"My father's behind this, isn't he? Did he put you up to this?"

"Edgar is dead, Junior! He's dead!" Emily cries in alarm.

"Not dead enough! That man wants to destroy me! Well I'm going to destroy *him*!" he rages, "I'm going to burn that fucking smile off his fucking face!" With that, Junior leaps upon the coffee table separating him from Harold and Company. "You're dead meat!"

"Help!" shrieks Harold, blood jetting from his nose. But Junior isn't yelling at Harold. He's yelling at the *Self-Portrait*.

"I asked you a question! Did Dad put you up to this? Did he?" he cries. "Where's a blowtorch?"

"Junior, it's only a painting," screams Emily, arms around his waist, valiantly struggling to hold him back.

"It's not a painting! It's possessed! And I'm going to burn it!"

"You can't burn a van Gogh! It's priceless!" Monica blurts, her stilettos clutched in her hands as weapons of defense. The sight of Monica's bare arches is too much for Harold, whose second nostril begins to haemorrhage.

"Priceless? Give me six hundred million for it!" Junior cackles.

"The man's deranged!" Monica announces, her gift for understatement intact.

"Mr. Beamish! Please, Mr. Beamish—" Harold begs, hiding behind Irving. He has fished his ever-present plugs of cotton batting from his jacket pocket and is attempting to stuff them up his nose.

"YOU WANT TO SAVE THIS PAINTING, YOU PARASITE? THEN GIVE ME SIX HUNDRED MILLION!"

"Six hundred million?"

"AND NOT A PENNY LESS! NOW FLEE, YOU BASTARDS! FLEE WHILE YOU HAVE A CHANCE!"

The terrified trio runs from the room, down the stairs, and out the door, the madman's frenzied cries of, "Six hundred million!" ringing in their ears. Junior, overcome, falls to the ground, convulsed in hysteria. Emily cradles him in her arms and calls to Ernest to phone Dr. Billing. "And no one else. If word gets out, deny it. I couldn't take another scandal."

Then, as Ernest makes the call, she soothes away his fit— and Junior has an epiphany. A moment of suspended clarity. In a flash, The Phoenix Lottery erupts full-blown from his brain, like Athena from the brow of Zeus.

"It will be wonderful, Emily," he whispers.

"There now, shh, shh."

"No, no, but it will be wonderful," he continues softly. "BEI will be saved. The Angel will be saved. It's going to be all right." He smiles, closes his eyes, and, curled in the fetal position, sucking his thumb, lets Emily rock away his cares.

It *will* be wonderful, he thinks to himself, drifting into a sleep so profound it will take Billing, Ernest, and two others to smuggle him out of the building, wrapped in a blanket, and load his dead weight into a car for the trip to Homewood.

He sees a lottery. An international lottery. He'll call it The Phoenix Lottery, for it will see his foundation reborn from the ashes of certain destruction. The winner will torch that god-damn painting! Destroy an icon of Western art! They'll have Celebrity! Yes, and Wealth, selling their story to the world! It will be fabulous!

Especially for The Angel. There'll be a fortune made from the sale of lottery tickets, satellite feeds, stadium gates, and the licencing of the *Self-Portrait*'s image. Junior dreams a smorgasbord of Martha Stewart inspirations—van Gogh throw cushions, terry towels, wallpaper, oven mitts, and ceramic lamps—and of fast-food conglomerates luring kids with van Gogh colouring books, baseball caps, and action figures complete with plastic razors and detachable ears.

But above all else, he dreams of exorcising this last vestige of his father. This painting—this possessed piece of canvas— once this painting has been destroyed, his father will know who's boss. His father sent it to drive him mad. To ruin his plans. Yes, that must be it. His father's to blame. It's always his father.

Edgar has been watching his son since the early hours of the morning. He watches now as Junior is carried out. He waits behind with Emily, who sits frightened and alone in the empty boardroom. My son hates me that much, he thinks. It is unbearable. He will trouble Junior no more. He will make his way to a country bed and breakfast and take up his spiritual exile in a world where pain is pleasure, a world wherein he once had searched for peace.

Emily finishes her prayers and rises to leave. She is about to turn off the boardroom lights when she finds herself startled by the expression on the face of the *Self-Portrait*. As always, van Gogh's eyes are disconcerting. They make her feel quite naked and she instinctively covers her breasts with her left arm. But what strikes her as most peculiar is the sardonic smile playing upon the portrait's lips. Emily hasn't noticed that before. Strange.

It must be a trick of the light.

VII

The
Phoenix
Lottery

A Sauna With the Pope

Pope Innocent is splayed upon a slab of mottled grey marble in the subterranean steam room of Castel Gandolfo. Cardinal Giuseppe Agostino Montini Wichita, wrapped in a thick white terry towel, sits opposite.

Innocent is in a bad way. He has been practically in non-stop conference concerning The Phoenix Lottery since he took the first of many phone calls from the American president somewhere over Baffin Bay. Junior Beamish's plan to publicly torch a van Gogh masterwork has created a personal nightmare from which there is no escape.

Except in food. Over the past few weeks, the pressure has driven Innocent to consume vast quantities of the fat-rich comfort food dear to his over-taxed Bavarian heart. Tubs of deep-fried potatoes, dumplings, and onions, greased by vats of lard, have slid down the papal gullet to a tummy bloated with schnitzels and platters of coarsely ground sausages thick as fists. Following on these, deep-dish brownies, stuffed with walnuts and topped with a generous caramel-coconut crust, have vied with strudels drowned in a thick brown sugar-and-butter melt, together with broad wedges of Black Forest cake drenched in rum and fashioned of ripe brandied cherries, Swiss chocolate, and beaten cream so rich and firm the very thought of it risks stroke. To wash it down, dark German beers with dense pillows of head have alternated with aromatic coffees that arouse the senses with the smell, taste, and texture of sugar crystallized from flaming liqueurs.

This overindulgence has led to a vicious attack of gout, Innocent's blood awash in uric acid, his joints swollen past mercy. It has also contributed to a virulent outbreak of shingles, vast tracts of flesh from armpits to scrotum erupting in itchy red blisters.

Members of the Curia have been solicitous to a fault, none more so than the enterprising Cardinal d'Ovidio, who has already begun to spend his off-hours consulting the *Britannica World Atlas* in diligent pursuit of exciting new venues for the next round of papal adventures. South America is a likely prospect; perhaps Peru with its sheer cliffs and impenetrable jungles — a land where the air is thin, the parasites thick, and the geography alive with potential disaster. D'Ovidio fancies his elevation to pontiff a certainty at the next papal election. He falls into a delicious sleep dreaming of Innocent careening at breakneck speed down an Andes river on a white-water raft into some remote part of the rain forest inhabited by hitherto unknown tribes possessed of large stew pots.

Be that as it may, Innocent is in sore need of assistance, to which end he has summoned his old friend Cardinal Giuseppe Wichita to partake of a little steam. He has outlined the situation and offered Wichita the post of Vatican emissary with responsibility for derailing the lottery. In the heavy silence that surrounds them, both men pray for guidance.

Wichita has not always feared The Phoenix Lottery. When his mother first whispered that he was tapped for the file, his thoughts on the matter had been entirely selfish. Cardinal d'Ovidio might think himself in line for the papal succession, but in politics it is never wise to demonstrate ambition, and the motives driving d'Ovidio's zeal as Innocent's travel agent are only too apparent. D'Ovidio has painted a bull's-eye on his forehead, attracting potshots from every grouchy cardinal from Rome to Tierra del Fuego. His star is waning. Wichita understands that if he can demonstrate the royal jelly on an international plum such as the Beamish file, he will be well-placed to catapult over d'Ovidio's head and onto the throne of St. Peter. Then, finally, he will have redeemed his mother's sacrifice.

Nevertheless, the more he imagines the peace such triumph would afford, the greater his horror of the dragon to be slain. The rest of the world, preoccupied with preserving a van Gogh, has given no thought to the lottery's long-term implications.

Certainly not Innocent, dithering away on what he appears to believe is an issue of public relations. The implications, however, cannot be avoided. They are so appalling that they fill the normally sanguine cardinal with visions of The Beast.

An intellectual, Wichita has never considered The Fiend to be more than a theological construct, a fairy-tale character, twaddle best reserved for naughty children and Southern Baptists. Yet despite his attachment to reason, Wichita has come to see the hand of Antichrist at play in the Beamish affair.

How to broach this dread to his boss? This is the substance of Wichita's prayers. At the moment, however, the said prayers are distracted.

Innocent bathes every Saturday so as to be fresh for Sunday mass. Unfortunately today is Friday. His sweat is acrid, a robust amalgam of bacteria, bile, and uric acid. It trickles in rivulets through thickets of grey body hair matted to pallid flesh, drips from armpits, breasts, bellybutton, and crotch, drenches the towel in which he is wrapped, irritates his shingles and tickles his balls. The genital itch is excruciating. In mid-prayer, Innocent, overcome, rips off his towel and scratches away like a man possessed.

There are some things best left to the imagination, and Pope Innocent's body is one of them. Wichita finds it impossible not to stare. There is something disturbing about the sight of the nude pope. It compels the sort of morbid curiosity attending natural disasters or grisly discoveries in hillbilly country. Bile from the gout has distended his belly and puffed his joints until the knuckles resemble golf balls and the feet inflated hot water bottles. As Innocent claws at his testicles, swollen the size of large speckled peaches, worse horrors are revealed. Clearly, the acid has also played havoc with his intestinal lining, causing haemorrhoids to blossom like clusters of grapes so firm and profuse that they visibly separate the papal chuds.

"O what a piece of work is man." Shakespeare was obviously not thinking of Pope Innocent. Wichita shudders and attempts to fathom the divine purpose. What on earth could the Almighty

have been thinking when he invented bodily functions?
Wherefore further need to mortify the flesh?

Under the circumstances, any attempts at prayer would be
pointless, but they are rendered impossible by the sudden
arrival of Maria Carlotta. "Madre di Dio!" Wichita exhales, as
his mother materializes through the mist. She gives him a little
wave, points in mock horror at the papal peter and proceeds to
observe Innocent's digital mania with fascination.

Wichita is awed by his mother's lack of discretion. When it
comes to indecency, her timing is impeccable. Whether he's
disrobing or sitting on the john, he knows he can count on her
surprise visitations and her cheery observation that "It's nothing
that I haven't seen before." On the positive side, her refusal to
afford him privacy has helped him keep his priestly vow of
celibacy.

"Madre di Dio, indeed," Innocent echoes. "Sadly, Our Lady
has not seen fit to answer our prayers."

Maria Carlotta rolls her eyes. "The bugger's got wax in his
ears."

Wichita glares at her. She pretends not to notice. Insouciantly, she pulls a black feather from behind her left ear and
begins to give herself a manicure with its quill. Her son should
be grateful she's chosen to keep her presence hidden from his
hairy pal. He should thank Heaven for small mercies.

"We're stuck. Completely stuck," Innocent continues. "What
should we do? I'm starved for paprikash."

"Holy Father—"

"Ah, for the old days. Everything went to my in-tray and
sat there until it was forgotten. That was the way to handle
problems. But now—dear God, I'd like to tell them all to go to
hell." Innocent's eyes twinkle at the thought. He sighs and
begins idly twirling his index fingers on his belly, creating
meringues of matted grey hair.

Maria Carlotta is aghast. It is clear the pontiff has no idea
of the stakes at hand. "Peppe, get to the point! Sound Gabriel's
horn! Warn him about the Antichrist!"

Wichita takes a deep breath and prepares to jeopardize his reputation as a man of reason. He leans forward. He clears his throat. "Helmut," he begins, "Awake! This lottery is the tip of the iceberg. Antichrist stalks the earth! Apocalypse is at hand!"

"Giuseppe?"

Having raised the spectre of the beast, there is no turning back. "What happens, my friend, when art is worth more destroyed than preserved? Which touchstones of the spirit will remain if fortunes can be made by razing civilization? Oh, Helmut, I see the skies alive with fire! A world ablaze with all that makes us human!"

Innocent struggles to reply, but words fail him. Instead, his mouth bobs open and shut like that of a fish out of water—not that Wichita would brook interruption. His words pour forth, a mighty flood, the prophetic voice unleashed.

"Perhaps like The Phoenix Lottery, the carnage will be excused at first in the name of the suffering, destitute, and sick. But with lucre in the air, how long before the butchery is used to pay for private pleasures? Dilettantes and feckless heirs, the indolent rich who know the price of everything and the value of nothing, they will be the first to ship their treasures to the fire. The first, but hardly the last. How long before corporations torch art holdings to finance their latest acquisitions? Or to puff the dividends of shareholders? How long before they hunt down art to profit from its liquidation—a leveraged buyout of the soul? Yes, art investment will be perverted: works prized not for their power to rejuvenate, but for the riches to be fetched at their cremation. More horrible yet: the greater the artist—the more transcendent the art—the more profitable the destruction, the more likely the obliteration.

"The blood lust of animals is insatiable. Soon it will not be enough to destroy one masterwork. The public will demand ever greater atrocities in order to open its wallets. Entire collections will hit the bonfires as the barbarians clamour for even more terrible decimations. In this spiritual wasteland, who will take a stand for the collective good? What government will support that which the citizenry howls to see wiped from the face of the earth? Over time, who will be left to care, as a generation is trained that the life of the mind is worth nothing but as fuel for savagery?

"Perhaps, oh yes, perhaps some art will remain, some last vestige of grace. But what of it? It will have been devalued utterly. We will have a world, Helmut, in which it is the *destruction* of beauty that is prized! In which the annihilation of imagination is entertainment. In which humanity salivates to see its nobler self debased. Humanity? Did I say humanity? No! There will be no humanity! For without beauty, imagination— without art—we will have lost what makes us human. We will be no more than pigs rutting and dying in the mud.

"A millennium ago, Antichrist prowled Europe. Peasants turned tapestries to potato sacks and worse. It was a world of pestilence, plague. Of spiritual darkness. That is nothing to the fiery hell we will endure when we immolate the creative gift, our glimpse of God on earth! Extinguish this immortal light within—put out our very souls—and there is no depredation, no abomination of which we are incapable. When that terrible moment arrives, Satan may do with us what he will. For we shall be his creatures, dancing to his tune, primed for the pit.

"I say to you that Antichrist stalks the earth. I say to you we face Apocalypse. For we are fighting for the heart of that which makes us human. And so it is that I accept your challenge, friend, with courage and determination. I shall put on the full armour of our Lord Jehovah to battle with the powers of darkness! It is one minute to midnight on the Doomsday clock. We must not fail our God!"

Wichita is swept away by his own rhetoric. He is glad the sweat and banks of mist conceal his tears. Once, he had fancied this posting as a means to self-promotion. Now he accepts it with a sense of destiny, charged with the terrible awareness of what shall pass should he fail.

As for Innocent, the pope has a short attention span. While initially devastated by Wichita's exhortation, a gastrointestinal cramp has yanked him back from consideration of the abyss. Now he stares at his friend with the incomprehension of a pithed frog. Has Wichita been drinking? Or reading the Book of Revelation before bedtime? Whatever. Wichita clearly will give himself body and soul to the lottery's derailment. He's on-side and Innocent has found himself a papal emissary. Good. That's one headache he can check off his list of burdens. Time for some seltzer and paprikash.

Maria Carlotta, by contrast, is exalted, for she smells vindication. Fifty years ago, Madre Raffaella had laughed when told that the Antichrist had been born in Cuba. Well let her laugh. She, Maria Carlotta—she who was martyred that very afternoon at the Grotte di Castellana—has observed the growth of the Beamish spawn. And she was right! He *is* the Antichrist, exactly as La Vergine had implied. Now it is up to her son, her only begotten Giuseppe Agostino, to best the serpent.

Maria Carlotta catches herself. She mustn't gloat or be unfair to Madre Raffaella. "After all, Satan is one cunning culo," she thinks. "Who'd have guessed that the Antichrist would turn out to be a Canadian?"

Separation Anxiety

Wichita strategizes privately for the first time since he fled Bari's basilica with the head of Bruno Grapelli. It is no easy task. His instincts are dull, having lain too long in Maria Carlotta's embrace. Nonetheless, he soon determines a line of attack and clears it with Innocent.

Maria Carlotta is not impressed. "You went behind my back? The back of a mother who martyred herself for her child?"

"I wanted to surprise you."

"You have."

"I thought you'd be pleased."

Her lip trembles. "What do you care what I think?" She bites her knuckle and floats around the room, an airborne dustball holding back tears.

"Mia madre," he follows after her, "you will be so proud. There's to be a special mass in St. Peter's Square. The pope is to publicly consecrate my mission. Me, your Giuseppe, I am to be a star in the Curial firmament."

"No, Peppe," she whirls in horror, "you must tiptoe. Blessèd are the meek, for they shall inherit the earth."

"Beatitudes are fine for Gésu, madre, but this is the real world."

"That is sin talking. Pride, the deadliest of the deadly."

"You think I do this for my glory?" Wichita adopts a pose fit for a stained-glass window. "As long as Mother Church is silent she gives consent. When she trumpets her condemnation, the world will boycott this anathema."

"Peppe," Maria Carlotta insists with as much patience as her temper will allow, "when was the last time anyone listened to the pope?"

"Well it's done. Decided!" Wichita snaps back.

"Mio figlio!" she cries, her anger morphing into tears.

"I'm not your little boy! I'm almost sixty!"

"You will *always* be my little boy!" She beats her breast and launches into a tirade of operatic proportion. "Madre di Dio, I give my life for you, but go ahead! Break my heart! Break the heart of the mother who bore you in love and shame and unbearable agony."

He tries to block her out, covering his ears and humming Gregorian chants. She rails the more. He puts on a CD of Handel's *Messiah* and closes his eyes. She projects herself on the inside of his eyelids. Four doubles and a Valium later she's still there, though muted around the edges.

Of course Maria Carlotta proves right. Far from creating a boycott, the publicity attracted by Wichita's consecration causes lottery sales to skyrocket; Vatican opposition to the lottery becomes a hot new selling point, a chance to assert individual freedom in the face of institutional orthodoxy.

Maria Carlotta is delighted, not because her son is in deeper water, but that he may now return to her counsel. Alas, when she appears, prepared to comfort and forgive, he carries on without apology or regret. "I've only just begun," he announces.

"If this is where you've begun, heaven knows where you'll finish."

Wichita counts to ten. "You have done so much for me, madre. Everything I owe to you."

"You owe me nothing," she interrupts, with shushing hands. "I am your mother. It is my duty to serve. Yes, and my joy!"

He bites his tongue. "God has given me a task, madre. Right or wrong, I must accomplish it myself. Please understand."

"How can I understand a boy who spites his mother's heart? A mother who—"

Wichita cranks up the Handel.

Having failed to damage ticket sales, Wichita next attempts bribery. He seeks to acquire the painting with funds pooled by a consortium of governments, only to have President Richardson veto the scheme. As Richardson points out, to pay Junior what would amount to a ransom would be to retroactively transform the lottery into an artistic hostage taking. International practice is clear in such matters: the world must never give in to terrorists lest it entice others to follow in their footsteps.

If, for instance, Junior is paid a billion to cover his potential earnings, what might future governments have to pay to protect a two-bit Titian? And how might this destabilize the multi-billion-dollar-a-year art market? Might it trigger a ripple effect in wider financial circles? They would be entering uncharted territory, and there is nothing politicians and investors hate more than uncertainty. Wichita grits his teeth. The president pawns his global obligations off on Europe while presuming to determine the rules of engagement. How typically American.

In the absence of a buyout, the cardinal's only hope lies in playing on Junior's professed good intentions, though having named him the Antichrist in St. Peter's Square has rather poisoned the well. This is especially unfortunate as increased media interest has raised the stakes. But in for a penny, in for a pound. Wichita has no option but to hold talks with Junior, no matter how dire his prospects for success.

So it is that Wichita takes the papal Concorde to Toronto and heads to BEI in the lead vehicle of a flotilla of black stretch limos. Maria Carlotta is not in the entourage. Her Peppe is in hot water of his own making. Good. Let him stew. Once he is penitent, begging forgiveness from his private hell, then perhaps she may return. Meantime, she's off to dish with her old friend La Vergine, whose ear is sympathetic on the subject of wilful sons.

Wichita finds his mother's absence exhilarating: performing a high-wire act without a net has a way of focussing the mind. He glances at the crowds lining the pavement as thick as spring crocuses. What are they doing? he asks himself. Then it hits him—they're here for me!

Indeed they are. They've seen him on TV; he's a celebrity,

and a handsome one at that. Lean and lithe, with his shock of black hair, white at the temples, perfect set of teeth, and tan, he appears to have arrived direct from Central Casting. They cheer.

Wichita thrills. Suddenly nothing is impossible. He waves back with the exuberance of a born showman, saving an especially dazzling smile for the clutches of paparazzi along the route and the scores of camera crews jostling for position outside the iron gates leading to the corporate head office. Yes, he remembers, this is what it was like to tour the streets of Nivoli in Don Camardo's car.

Then the crowds are gone, cordoned behind barricades at the heavy iron gates that lead to BEI's head office. Weighty and grim, these gates were designed by a Presbyterian at play. They have as their inspiration the entrance to a Victorian workhouse or some Dickensian bedlam. The cardinal thinks of Dante: "Abandon hope all ye who enter here."

Chez Antichrist

Once inside BEI's front gates and imposing bronze double doors, Wichita's smile vanishes. He and his entourage find themselves surrounded by an army of the earnest smelling of earth and sporting Doc Martens, piercings, jeans, and large hairy sweaters from Honduras.

"Greetings," they say as one.

Saints preserve us, thinks Wichita. It's a cult!

The sea of do-gooders parts and from its midst emerges a curious old bird quite unlike the others. Around seventy, she wears a navy suit, plain white blouse, and sensible shoes. "I'm Emily Pristable," the creature says. "Antichrist's private secretary." She shakes Wichita's hand. "I'm afraid Antichrist isn't here," she continues brightly. "He's out desecrating a convent. Till he gets back, might I interest you in a private look-see at the Dutchman?"

Wichita nods. His assistants are left to cool their heels in the lobby, where they're served raspberry tea and biscuits by Junior's zombie horde, while Emily leads him to the boardroom. "This is what all the hoopla's about," she says, turning on the light. "I hope you're not too disappointed. When I first saw it, I wouldn't have given it two pins, but it grows on you. I'm especially taken with the eyes. They change expression depending on the light."

"It is the soul of Vincent," whispers Wichita.

"Absolutely," she agrees. "He did a very nice job with that sky, don't you think? All those little blue curlicues. It must have taken forever."

"Curlicues?" Wichita retorts. "He deals in mountains and precipices. His mind erupts lava, a terrible mad brilliance: sublime, grotesque, pathological. He is the genius of the damned."

"Well, I never said he was nice."

The cardinal returns his gaze to the portrait with a ferocity designed to forestall further chit-chat. "Ah Vincent," he thinks, "you are God's warning to us all. A living sacrifice." He is distracted by Miss Pristable, who is staring at him with a passion equal to his own. "Yes?"

"Speaking as a Baptist, I found it a hoot you referring to Mr. Beamish as the Antichrist. A bit of the pot calling the kettle black, don't you think, you coming from Rome and all?" A hint of mischief plays across her lips. "As a girl, I played bagpipes in the Orange Day Parade. Those were the days. We'd march up Main Street singing songs about popery and eat fried chicken at the Town Hall. No offense, mind. No matter what they say about the pope, I think he has a nice smile."

"His Holiness loves all God's children," Wichita observes tightly.

"Right. It's just their mothers he has trouble with." Wichita's eyes flash, but before he can get a word out, Emily cuts him dead. "I appreciate that your mission requires you to be tough, Cardinal, but I was a special friend of Mr. Beamish's father and I won't sit by and see him abused. You may think you're the bee's knees, but to me you're just some big shot in a red dress. Got that, honeybun?"

Wichita is about to explode when Junior Beamish suddenly appears. Emily makes the introductions, tickled pink; she knows she's lodged under the cardinal's skin. She is troubled, however, when Junior remarks he'd like to speak to the cardinal in private. Is he up to the strain? She leaves to water the plants.

"Emily's been with the family for years," Junior opens wanly. "She's a second mother to me." His green eyes are lined with red, a russet stubble flecks his pale cheeks, emotions skitter unchecked across his face.

Wichita notes the twitching eyelid. He pauses, staring at Junior with a bearing as cold and impassive as Michaelangelo's Isaiah. At last, his voice rumbles: "This joke of yours has gone too far."

"It's, uh, it's no joke."

A frightening silence which Junior feels compelled to fill. "I wish there was some other way," he babbles, "but, well, I have commitments, yes, to the poor and, well, I'm afraid I haven't a choice. 'Give all that you have to the poor,' as Christ said to the rich young ruler."

"We are familiar with the text," Wichita observes acidly. "We are aware Christ also said, 'The poor you will have with you always.' But this painting, once destroyed, will be lost forever."

"There are lots of others," Junior ventures.

"Each work of art is precious. Unique."

"So is each human being I feed and clothe through The Angel. Did anyone offer you tea and biscuits?"

"We are neither hungry nor thirsty." Wichita prepares to hook the worm. He turns to the painting for inspiration. Van Gogh stares back, a hint of mockery on his lips. Wichita is shaken at what appears to be its change of expression. His gaze returns to Junior. "Satan is clever," he says. "He uses our best instincts against us. In your case, the desire to do good."

"Doing good is a sin?"

"People will stop at nothing to do good. They will lie, cheat, blackmail, and steal. They have even dropped nuclear bombs. Satan has taken your passion for good works and perverted it with the sin of pride. The world can survive without your generosity, Mr. Beamish. Mother Church, for one, collects hundreds of millions for the poor."

The tone triggers memories of Junior's father. "So I'm competition? Is that it?"

"The Holy See gives the glory to God. You steal God's thunder for yourself."

"No, you sonovabitch. I give to the poor. You use them. You milk good works like a cash cow. It's your calling card into people's wallets. A come-on to rake in dough for the Church."

"Our donations go to the needy," Wichita thunders.

"Bullshit. They go to cathedrals, robes, and real estate. Are the poor still hungry? There's a nickel left over, have a cracker, say your prayers, and wait for Heaven!"

"Blasphemy!"

"When I give, I give. I don't use food as bait."

"Sacrilege!"

"Is there anything else you'd like to discuss?"

Wichita towers over the philanthropist. "World powers will not have a cultural icon immolated by a pipsqueak."

"I'm afraid they have no choice."

"The World Court has given private assurances that, should this painting be destroyed, you will be tried for a crime against humanity!"

"Big deal. If it's not destroyed, my foundation will fail, and with it my reason to live. I'm not kidding, Cardinal Wichita. Why should I fear the World Court when I'm not afraid to die?"

The joint press release which follows speaks of the full and frank nature of the discussion between BEI and the Vatican, and announces that additional meetings have been scheduled. Wishful thinkers speculate that progress is being made. Nothing of the sort. Talks are scheduled solely because they serve the interests of both parties. From Junior's perspective, they generate more coverage, which generates more lottery sales. As for Wichita, he knows he has as much chance of dissuading Junior as stopping a suicide bomber. At least the announcement avoids the spectacle of a one-day rout.

However, Wichita runs out of spin. With four days to go before the draw, he falls to his knees and prays, not to his Father who has abandoned him, but to his mother, the blessèd Santa Maria Carlotta Castelli del Grotte di Castellana.

"Forgive me, madre, for I have sinned most grievously against you who bore me in love and shame and unbearable agony. Forgive my pride. Forgive my disobedience. Forgive the shame and disgrace into which I have fallen through my sin and my sin alone. You who have always comforted me, you who have always protected me, you who martyred yourself that I might live—comfort and guide me in my hour of need."

Maria Carlotta is touched. If only her son could be so nice when he didn't want something. All the same, she musn't actively intervene. As La Vergine has pointed out, her guidance has made his life too easy; she has become a crutch on which he depends, and which he resents for that dependence. But, oh, he looks so forlorn it breaks her heart. Surely it wouldn't hurt to drop him a few pointers. So she sends her belovèd Giuseppe a dream.

Wichita finds himself alone on a country road. He has lost his way. It is night. Wild beasts lurk in the ditch at the side of the road. He knows that their names are Pride and Envy and Despair. He begins to run and they give chase. Their red eyes light the air; their hot breath burns his heels.

"Madre, help me! Guide me!" Suddenly there is a wind. It flies up under his red robes. The robes balloon around him and the wind whistles him up above the trees, out of reach of the beasts. He finds himself parasailing across a countryside illuminated by the brilliant sky of van Gogh's Starry Night.

His mother floats by. "Where are we?" he asks simply.

"Off the beaten path," she replies and points to the farmhouse which has just materialized below. It is a plain one-storey red-brick rectangle with a collection of ornamental gnomes in front and a vegetable patch and barn out back. In the middle of the vegetable patch he sees a scarecrow. It is grinning. A woman in curlers and pompoms is whipping it with a cat-o'-nine-tails.

"Hello there," she calls out cheerily. "Madame de Sade at your service. I'm just beating some sense into this old scarecrow."

"Yippee-kai-yay-kai-yo!" squeals the scarecrow. "No man cometh unto the Son but through the Father."

"That's not the way it goes," thinks Wichita, "That scarecrow had better study his Scripture if he expects to graduate from seminary." He finds himself descending down the chimney, emerging into what looks to be a basement dungeon. The walls are covered in restraints, whips, and rubber undergarments. In the centre of the room is a chesterfield, chair, and a coffee table covered with magazines. On the cover of one of the magazines is a man being spanked with a paddle.

"My name is Edgar Beamish," the man says. "I suppose you've come about my son."

Cardinal Wichita wakes up. It is three in the morning. There is no way he'll be able to get back to sleep. He turns on the lamp on his night table and picks up the newspaper he left there. He is about to check the TV listings when something catches his eye. The newspaper, a *Globe and Mail*, is folded to a page headed "National Personals." Wichita reads:

THE BEATEN PATH
BED AND BREAKFAST
Catering to the liberated and adventurous! Enjoy a fun-filled weekend in cottage country with our obedient and well-disciplined staff. Fax Madame de Sade at 519-432-2003

The next day, Cardinal Wichita drops out of sight. History is in the making.

And the winner is . . .

Everyone remembers where they were the night Junior Beamish drew the winning entry to The Phoenix Lottery. They were in front of a TV.

This is hardly surprising given the hype surrounding the event. In the two months following the lottery's announcement, tabloids have enjoyed a field day. Each week, headlines trumpet either a poltergeist infestation at the offices of BEI, or the demonic possession of Junior Beamish, or revelations that the lottery had been prophesied by Nostradamus, the Dead Sea Scrolls, and Mrs. Eugene Smith following her abduction by extraterrestrials.

More serious print media, from *The Guardian* to *Der Spiegel* to *Paris Match*, have scolded their sleazy cousins for sensationalism, while repeating the wild tales they apparently deplore. "It's our moral duty," huffs Franklin K. Bender III, one of eight reporters *The New York Times* attached to the story. "By reporting the tabloids' crap, we expose their lack of integrity."

These authoritative organs of information and opinion, as well as their counterparts in television and radio, have added other stories to the mix. According to Reuters, UPI, and CNN, psychiatric hospitals worldwide have reported a rash of patients claiming to be van Gogh. And, according to *Salon*, at the last full moon a distressing number of ears apparently went missing.

The orgy of hype, speculation, and conspiracy theories has been exacerbated by misinformation and half-truths spread by endlessly proliferating chat lines and sites on the World Wide Web. It is like *The Sorcerer's Apprentice*, the world awash with a media feeding frenzy on a story made all the more electric by the fact that the public, through its ever-escalating purchase of entry forms, holds a vested interest in the outcome.

Consequently, tensions run high as Junior Beamish pulls the winning entry from a drum filled with entries pulled from other drums filled with entries pulled from other drums filled with entries pulled from other drums.

"And the winner is . . ."

Around the world, workers cease their toils and sleepers rouse themselves from bed. Humanity, whether engaged or appalled, amused or apoplectic, leans towards television sets for the next instalment of a saga that has tapped the international *Zeitgeist*.

The folks in Mercy Inlet are no different, packing both the hotel Sports Bar and The Diner. The hotel has the advantage of a twenty-foot TV screen that takes up the entire wall to the right of the door to the Ladies and Gents. But if The Diner only has an old twenty-four-inch Zenith over the cash register, it boasts Hattie McBean's butter tarts and that popular new waitress from outside.

Popular in most places, that is. Georgina Russell, who never speaks ill of the dead, owing to her position as wife of the town mortician, nonetheless manages a word or two about most of the living. "I've heard tell she prays to the devil, and I wouldn't be the least bit s'prised considering how she dresses. Anyone with eyes in their head can see the spell she's put on the men 'round here—their heads turn so fierce when she's about you'd think they'd spin right off their shoulders. Why, I'd be afraid to guess the half of what they're thinking. Hattie Mc-Bean better keep an eye after that son of hers, that's all I can say, what with the little flibbertigibbet sleeping under her roof, and him shy of twenty. Though I must say, Miss McBean's bin none too quick gettin' to church herself, if you catch my drift, and that Namisaat of hers a high-school teacher, as if our young folk don't get enough bad examples at home."

Lydia was stunned when she'd overheard Georgina carrying on at the Laundromat within a week of her decision to stay in Mercy Inlet for the summer. Georgina, back to the door, hadn't caught the discreet signals of her audience and warbled on for a good five minutes while everyone else pretended to sort socks and underwear.

"Don't mind Georgina Russell; nobody else does. She's nothing but a snipe," Hattie comforted back at The Diner. "Jealousy, that's all she's about. She has it in her head that every woman in town has eyes for her Freddy. Truth be told, if poor old Freddy stays out nights it's not because he's off tom-catting. It's because he's passed out at the funeral parlour. And who can blame him? Better that than go home to crawl into bed with a pickle."

Lydia laughed. On consideration, she realized she'd encountered tougher critics when reciting her prose poems at The St. Lawrence Market. Best to stick to her plan of accepting Hattie's offer to waitress at The Diner in exchange for room and board. Never good with money, Lydia had all but spent her Council grant and there were no prospects back in Toronto save for a hot muggy summer stuck with the Three Ts in their Queen West firetrap.

A summer on Baffin Island, now ablaze with wildflowers, would be a spiritual retreat. It would give her the chance to catch her breath after her turbulent cross-Canada tour, as well as the opportunity to hone her psychic skills through visits to Isaac's grandmother. These skills would be especially important once she won The Phoenix Lottery.

Of that eventuality she had no doubt. The omens were all in place: the Canada Council grant that had brought her death and resurrection among the spirits of north Baffin; the theft of her entry form by a raven curiously fluent in Italian; the return of the form following the shamanistic seance; and word from the angakoq herself that she, Lydia Spark, "had things to do."

That is why, as everyone else in The Mercy Inlet Diner cranes for a better view of the Zenith, Lydia sits remarkably detached. In fact, as Junior pulls the winning entry form from the drum, she has completely turned away from the screen and is staring out the window at a terrifying scene transpiring under the full light of the midnight sun.

"And the winner is . . . Lydia Spark. Care of The Mercy Inlet Diner, Baffin Island."

The Diner crowd sits frozen in disbelief. The silence is broken by Lydia: "Hit the deck!"

Outside, the hospital raven, costumed in its towel and ribbons, is flying hell-bent-for-leather toward the window. Lydia hears its voice shrieking inside her head, "Putana! Putana! Figlia di putana!!"

"Hit the deck! Hit the deck!"

She drops to the floor as an Arctic owl swoops out of nowhere, dive-bombs the raven, and sends it off-course. In the split second it takes for the crowd to turn its attention from TV to window, both birds vanish and the Mercy Inlet residents are left with the sight of their Goth waitress cowering in a ball next to the jukebox.

"Are you okay?" asks Isaac, instantly at her side

"It's after me," says Lydia. "It's out to get me."

"Nothing's after you. Nothing's out to get you. You're safe. You're with friends." He helps her to her feet.

"I think Isaac and I better get her back home," Namisaat says to the room. "I'll be back in a flash," he adds to Hattie, knowing they're leaving her to handle things alone.

As Lydia is helped out the door, Billy Muskloosie shyly offers, "Congratulations." Similar murmurs are heard from all corners, except from Father Kadniq, who is seated on a bar stool at the far end of the counter. It's understood he has to toe the official line from Rome. "We'll be praying for you," he says diplomatically.

With Lydia gone, Hattie breaks the sombre mood. "Butter tarts are on the house." But before the first tart hits a plate, the phone rings. "Hattie here . . . No, I'm afraid she just left . . . Who might I ask is calling? . . . Hong Kong? . . . Okey-dokey." She takes the message, hangs up.

The phone rings. "Hattie here . . . Lydia's off for the night. . . . Albuquerque? . . . Okey-dokey." She takes a message, hangs up.

The phone rings. "Buenos Aires? . . . Okey-dokey."

And again and again and again.

"Lisbon? Okey-dokey."

"Los Angeles? Okey-dokey."

"Nepal? Okey-dokey."

And on it goes—calls from around the globe until Hattie's had enough. She stuffs the phone in the crisper, slams the fridge door and calls out, "Billy, make yourself useful. Put some Barenaked Ladies on the jukebox and get Johnny there to give me a hand with these tarts."

Georgina Russell gives a knowing look to those seated at her booth. "Something's squiffy," she whispers. "That girl resurrects, wins a lottery, and falls to bits? It's her guilty conscience, on account of that devil worship, that has her carrying on. Yessir, afraid to meet her Maker, dollars to donuts, and I'm not the least bit s'prised. Whoever heard of black lipstick? The devil's answered her prayers, you mark my words, and Lord knows what else besides."

"Georgina," Freddy says, "stuff a sock in it."

That midnight, back in Toronto, Tibet gets a phone call.

"Tibet, it's me. Lydia."

"Who?"

"Don't be a douche bag. Lydia. Your roommate Lydia."

"Just a sec." Lydia hears Tibet call out: "Hey Trina! Trixie! It's the grant whore!" Assorted rude noises; they've just got back from The Rabid Squirrel. "All together now. One, two, three—"

"Hello, Grant Whore!"

Tibet speaks solo. "So are you dead or alive or what?"

"I'm in Mercy Inlet. I won The Phoenix Lottery."

"We heard. You want us to suck your butt?"

"Tibet, I need your help."

"Why don't you ask your friends in Mercy Inlet?"

"Because they're nice. I don't need nice. I need an agent. And you're the loudest, most obnoxious person I can think of."

"No shit, Sherlock."

"I need someone I can trust. To sell my story. To make deals. But mainly, to help me plan the big night. I don't want to just torch a painting. I want to create a work of art. The wickedest performance piece the world has ever seen. And I want you guys to be a part of it. 'Lydia Spark and The Three Ts.' We'll show those turds who called us losers. We're going down in world history! Whadeya say?"

"FUCKIN' A!"

In the Dungeon

In the lead-up to the draw, speculation was rife over Cardinal Wichita's sudden disappearance. The pope announced that he'd been recalled to Rome for top secret debriefing. Much more fun were Internet rumours of a kidnapping by Jesuits, a bender on communion wine, and/or assassination by a doomsday cult. Fortunately for Mother Church, the cardinal resurfaced the morning following the draw, at which point, the spotlight now on Lydia, reporters deemed chasing down his prior whereabouts to be about as exciting as sour breath.

If they only knew.

The cardinal's decision to follow his dream to an S&M bordello is accompanied by prudence. He tells no one of his itinerary, not even the Holy Father, from whom he secures an alibi; he has the Toronto Archdiocese arrange a nondescript Hertz Rent-a-Car, ostensibly for a Bishop Gunz off on a holiday in the Laurentians; and he travels at night in disguise—a Sears leisure suit, wig, sunglasses, moustache, and mole.

Arriving at The Beaten Path, he finds a '70s bungalow matching the establishment in his dream. He parks near the house and checks himself in the rear-view mirror. The wig is definitely Harpo Marx and the mole somewhat dicey, but Wichita figures that's naught but a wink in a house devoted to fantasy. He makes his way past the cement gnomes and knocks on the front door. Having called ahead from a pay phone, he's expected. Millie shakes his hand. "Mr. Benelli, I presume?"

Benito Benelli is the alias adopted by Wichita when travelling incognito. After all, it's safe: Benelli's a nobody from another world, dead the last half-century. Just as important, Wichita finds that speaking the name in public is therapeutic: to this day he can smell the bits of rotting flesh on Benelli's dirty work clothes, can see the brass monkey grinning from its nest in Benelli's eye socket, can hear Benelli's head thwhapping against the confessional wall. He longs to unburden his secrets, yet career interests deny him the confessional's release, much less that of the couch; the secrets of both may be a sacred trust, but the world is full of Padre Renatos.

Wichita grunts pleasantries and signs the register with his left hand, a precaution against handwriting analysts. He books the entire B&B for a week, paying cash in advance, double for the reservations in the guest book, which he bribes Millie to cancel. Business complete, he asks to be left alone, and retires downstairs to sleep in the dungeon.

It looks exactly as it did the day Edgar Beamish died, except that the collection of fetish paraphernalia has expanded beyond the Torture Chamber and now lines the rec room walls as well. Wichita's heart is beating fast. Clearly the dream indicated he should communicate with the spirit of the dead tycoon. But how? And to what end?

He thinks back to his class in exorcism at The Catholic University of the Sacred Heart in Milan. Monsignor Praxi had taken a no-nonsense approach to the supernatural. Students were instructed to use strict discipline with spirits, as if demons and the like were pit bulls at obedience school. They were to bark imperatives such as "Depart, impious one," or "Attend thou unclean spirit, thou spectre from Hell." These orders don't seem to strike the right tone for the situation at hand, but who is Wichita to question his professor?

Two hours later, hoarse from Latin imprecations, Wichita opts for a change of tactics. "Edgar Beamish? Please, I'd like to talk to you." Silence. By this point, Edgar is far too offended to materialize at the first gesture of civility from this holy prick.

Wichita checks his watch. It's two in the morning. He'll try again tomorrow. Back in the bedroom, he lies on the metal cot and reads the dusty Gideon's Bible he finds on the chest-of-drawers. "The Lord is my shepherd, I shall not want." Usually

Wichita takes comfort from the Psalms. Not tonight. Instead, he thinks only of the lumps in his mattress and of the dank basement air heavy with the scent of the untended septic tank.

Hell is not a place of fire and brimstone; it is a place of cold and shadow. This is the lesson Wichita learns during the four days leading up to the draw. Hour upon hour, he calls upon the spirit of the deceased booze baron to no avail. Could he have been mistaken about the dream? Might Satan have led him on a wild goose chase to a sin spa?

By the time his nemesis pulls Lydia Spark's entry from The Phoenix Lottery drum, the Vatican wretch is beyond despair. Alone in his dungeon room, staring at the old calendar photograph of calico kittens tangling a ball of wool, his own fingers absently nagging a loose thread on the chenille bedspread, he is tempted to suicide.

Touched by the depth of Wichita's torment, Edgar relents with an otherworldly courtesy call. "Cardinal Wichita, I presume?"

Wichita blinks. Sitting on the chest-of-drawers is the translucent figure of a man in his late sixties wearing glasses and toupee, a natty blue-grey pinstripe with a rose in the left lapel, white shirt, maroon tie, gold tie clip, and black Oxfords. "Mr. Beamish?"

"At your service."

Instantly rejuvenated, Wichita leaps up and crosses himself. "Mr. Beamish, I come to you under the guidance and protection of the belovèd Santa Maria Carlotta Castelli del Grotte di Castellana."

"Never heard of her."

"She has sent me a prophetic dream. You have been given a mission: to stop the burning of your son's van Gogh."

"Flattered, I'm sure. But you're scaring up the wrong ghost."

"Your boy is in thrall to the powers of darkness."

"Like father, like son," Edgar winks. "I'm an old sinner, Wichita. You don't need the likes of me to deal with evil. You need the services of a saint."

"You're wrong!" declares Wichita, determined to hold the spectre. "God didn't create saints to deal with evil. He created evil to inspire saints!"

"Pardon?"

"Without poverty, degradation, and death, human beings would be happy. And happy people having nothing from which to be saved, would have no need for a merciful God."

Beamish is stunned. "You're saying that God created evil in order to be loved?"

"It's one of our less popular theories," the cardinal allows.

"Your God is a monster," Beamish laughs.

"A father," smiles Wichita, casting the bait.

"What sort of father abuses his son?"

"Look in the mirror."

Beamish levitates, but Wichita has him hooked.

"Fathers and sons," the cardinal reels him in, "it's the relationship that defines Christianity. 'You are my only begotten son. I want to nail you to a cross.'"

"With theology like that, how did you become a cardinal?"

"We all have little secrets we keep from the world," Wichita observes with a wave to the torture chamber. "Never confuse what people think with what they say, or what they say with what they do."

"But you're a man of God."

Wichita's eyes flicker. "Those who would feast at the trattoria of our Lord had best not look in the kitchen."

"A realist. Good. Well, as one realist to another, you've been amusing, but time is up. And now, if you'll excuse me," Beamish adds wryly, "I have a pressing engagement with the Iron Maiden."

"Mr. Beamish," the cardinal pleads, "you hold the key to the painting, to your son's future. Santa Maria Carlotta would not have sent for you otherwise."

"Oh yeah? Well guess what—I'm the reason Junior's burning it in the first place."

"Then all the more need for you to save him from himself."

"Been there. Tried that. Never again. My son is dead to me of his own choice. Unlike God, I'm powerless to raise him. Now good day."

"No. I won't leave here without you!"

"Fine. Then stay and rot." Edgar begins to vaporise.

His last hope disappearing, Wichita goes for broke. "About your secrets, Mr. Beamish, your 'special interests.' I'd hate to see them exposed."

"You dare to blackmail me?"

Wichita grips his crucifix. "Human beings will stop at nothing to do good!" he cries. "And I am nothing if not human!"

"You're a bastard!"

"Yes, that too."

"Well, sadly for you," the ghost bellows, "I am beyond humiliation."

"And the public humiliation of your loved ones?"

"I don't have any loved ones!"

"None?" A cold wind whips through the room. A tornado of dustballs and bedsheets. Yes, he has him. Wichita holds fast the standard of his faith and roars to a peel of thunder: "AS GOD IS MY WITNESS, I NEED YOUR HELP AND I SHALL HAVE IT!"

In the Vault

Following the draw for The Phoenix Lottery, Junior goes for a long walk. At two in the morning, a BEI security guard finds him huddled by the front gates talking to himself. The guard brings him in at once and attempts to give him a coffee, but Junior shakes free and stumbles to the boardroom muttering about forgiveness.

Locking himself inside, he falls before the painting. "Vincent, Vincent, what have I done?" Junior weeps. "I've crossed the Rubicon. There's no turning back. Forgive me." Then he passes out.

Later, Junior will tell Dr. Billing about the dream that follows. But not what he sees when he wakes up.

It's that night in Varadero. My recurring nightmare. I'm in the golf cart. It's flying across the grounds of Xanadu, zigzagging around pockets of jungle, over the greens. As always, the poor are jumping in front of me, getting whacked like crazy. Only this time something is different. All the poor—the men, the women, even the babies—they all have the face of van Gogh.

The cart hits the sand trap. It starts to sink—sand rising over my legs, torso, neck. The van Goghs with the broken limbs crawl to the lip of the sand trap to get to me. "Thank God," I think, because I know we're getting to the part of the dream where I wake up.

But something's wrong. This time I'm not waking up. I look over at the reviewing stand. Usually Dad, Rudyard, Hammersmith, and the rest of those sons of bitches are cheering as I drown. But they're not there. And I've stopped sinking. Some kind of crane is lifting the cart out of the trap.

I try to get a better look at what's happening, but I can't. Why can't I move? Why am I frozen in my seat?

Suddenly, I understand. The cart and I are part of a painting. We're on a canvas. It's our frame that's being hoisted out of the trap.

The van Goghs are very excited. They start babbling away in Dutch and French, and I can't understand a word. I don't have to. I can see what they're doing. They're taking a long pole with a rag on one end — they're dipping it in kerosene — they're setting it on fire — they're lifting it to the edge of my canvas — they're setting me aflame — I'm burning!

Junior wakes in a cold sweat. He stares at the van Gogh *Self-Portrait* in relief. It's been a dream. Everything is all right. And then something happens that freezes Junior's blood.

The face of the van Gogh glowers. It opens its mouth. It rumbles: "You will not burn this painting. I will not let you do this to Theo!"

VIII

Artists,
Saints,
and
Madmen

Reunions

Three days after winning The Phoenix Lottery, Lydia flies into Toronto unannounced. She phones her roommates from the airport and is alarmed to hear the following message on the answering machine. "You've reached 3Ts Management Inc. We represent grant whore Lydia Spark. Double your offer and fuck off."

Horrified, she leaps in a cab and races home. Trina is in the living room constructing a mobile of inner tubes and wire hangers. The squeals of Pigjam, a local grunge-rock band of juvenile delinquents, blare over the house speakers. "Where's Tibet?" Lydia yells over the racket.

"Oh, hi."

"Where's Tibet?"

Trina, suffering short-term memory loss, scratches her head, then brightens. "Gardening," she says and skips down the corridor to the bathroom, hollering through the hole in the floor by the toilet: "What's-her-name's back!"

Lydia is already flying down the basement stairs. "Are you trying to ruin me?"

Tibet, who's been pruning the hydroponic marijuana plants, adopts a kung fu pose with the pinking shears. "Back off."

"I asked you a question. What's with the message on the goddamn answering machine?"

"You asked for obnoxious. I gave you obnoxious."

"You gave me insane."

Trixie plays peacemaker. "It's all part of being an agent," she explains, clipping a leaf the size of her palm and placing it neatly in the metal pan by her feet. "People expect you to be rude. They want it. It makes them feel like they're talking to someone important. If you're nice they just think you're desperate."

"What planet are you on?"

Trixie is offended. "I'll have you know, I happen to have a degree in psychology."

"What you have is a correspondence course you got off a matchbook."

"Well for your information, wuss, our strategy's worked," Tibet lectures. "The tape's been filling up twice a day."

"So who's called? What are the offers?"

"How should we know? We erased them," Trixie replies cheerfully.

"You what?"

"Get a grip," Tibet snorts. "You expect us to listen to hours of suits pitching shit? If they're serious they call back." Lydia is so apoplectic she's unable to form words. "Chill babe," Tibet continues. "Come upstairs, toast a few leaves, and get some per-spective. We're not total dorks. We've actually got leads for a coupla wicked gigs."

After putting the pan of grass in the oven, Tibet plays the most recent message tape, on which increasingly manic repre-sentatives of American tabloid TV and print, whose previous calls have clearly gone unanswered, promise ludicrous five- and low six-figure payouts for exclusive post-burning interviews. As well, there's a personal greeting from Junior Beamish, an SOS from her publisher, Bruce Jamieson, and two calls from someone claiming to be Cardinal Giuseppe Wichita, but who Tibet figures is really just Ernie, the Rabid Squirrel's bartender, having a lark. There appears to be method to Tibet's madness. Lydia gives the Ts a big hug.

"Welcome home, sister."

That night the Ts host a BYOB in Lydia's honour, attended by an army of Queen West vagrants attracted by rumours of an all-night booze can. When beer runs out, things turn weird. Luckily, by the time the police arrive, Lydia, P2, and the Three Ts have fled the premises with a bag of homegrown and taken refuge by the jungle gym in Grange Park.

Lying out under the stars, stoned with her best buds, Lydia grasps that she'll soon be rich. Her future is secure. So why does she feel uneasy? Why does she feel alone? And why does the word "home" suddenly feel so strange?

Lydia and the Ts return at noon the following day. Their place is trashed: what else is new? Tibet grunts and slouches off to bed with Trixie. Trina scratches her head and nips out to have her cards read. As for Lydia, she lies on the living-room floor and plays a game of Fearless Hunter with P2, while listening to the six new messages on the answering machine. There's a second SOS from her publisher, a sponsorship offer from Bic lighters, and three more nuisance calls from Ernie the Bartender pretending to be that Cardinal Wichita guy. What a butthead.

The sixth and final message comes from: "Miss Emily Pristable, calling for Ms. Lydia Spark. I'm private secretary to Junior Beamish. All of us here at BEI would like to welcome you back to Toronto and invite you for sandwiches and tea. Would this coming Tuesday be okay, say two o'clock? We can show you the painting and discuss arrangements for your big event which, to confirm, will be at Skydome one month from today."

Lydia, head throbbing, replays the messages, taking notes. She must get back to Bruce, and, yes, Tuesday to see the painting will be great. But before doing anything, she has to sleep. Lydia gets up off the floor and begins to wander down the hall to her room when the phone rings. Plans to ignore it go out the window when she recognises the familiar voice.

"Hello Lydia? I'm calling from The Diner. Anyways, if you get this, it's Isaac."

Lydia dives for the receiver. "Isaac!" she screams into it. The answering machine feeds back. Lydia turns it off. "Isaac, how are you?"

"Fine, yeah." There's a delay in the signal, causing them to talk over each other. "Geez, this connection sucks, eh? How's things down south? Any more raven trouble?"

"No, thank God," Lydia laughs. "It's great to hear your voice."

"Yeah. You too. Anyways, sorry to bug you like this, but Father James needs a favour. He's right by me. I'll put him on and he can ask you himself. Great talking to you."

"Lydia. It's Father James. I've been getting these calls from Rome. Cardinal Wichita would like to meet you at the Toronto Archdiocese. Says he can't get through."

So those Wichita messages were legit. "Look Father James, I'd like to help you and all, but I can't afford any bad vibes."

"Who's talking about bad vibes? Just meet him. Please? For me? The pope's putting on the screws."

Lydia bites her tongue. "Okay. I'll talk to him. But some-place neutral. Tell you what—have him meet me next Tuesday at three at BEI. Take it or leave it. And tell him if he messes with my karma I'll sic security on him."

"Thanks a million. Hey everybody, say hi to Lydia."

Lydia hears a chorus of well-wishers. Namisaat, Hattie, Isaac, Billy, Johnny, Freddy Russell, and the rest. "Hi Lydia! Hi! Hi! Hi! We miss you! We love you! When you comin' back?"

She wants to give them all a big hug. "Hi everybody. I love you too!"

"Lydia says she loves you too," Father James relays.

"Tell her to get back up here real soon," Hattie calls out.

"Tell Hattie I will if she sends me some butter tarts."

"She will if you send her some butter tarts."

"Oh, go on. Tell her I'll send her some tarts anyway!"

"She'll send you some tarts anyway."

"Thanks. Anything happen up there since I've been gone?"

"Not really. And with you?"

"Not much."

"Oh." Pause. "Well, bye for now then."

"Bye for now."

A chorus of voices in the background. "Bye. Bye Lydia. Be good. Bye. We love you. Bye. Bye."

Click.

Silence. Lydia sits very still. Tears well. P2 looks up at her solemnly. He jumps in her lap, nuzzles her chin and purrs. She gives him a pet.

"You're such a love bundle. What would I do without you?"

Two days later, Saturday, Lydia shows up for a book signing at Chapters. This gig is in response to Bruce Jamieson's SOS. Jamieson is a fifty-something elf, balding with a bushy salt-and-pepper beard, wire-rimmed glasses, pipe, plaid shirt, work-boots, and jeans. An alumnus of Rochdale College, he started Featherstone Press in the early seventies, publishing slim volumes of poetry armed with only a dream, a stapler, and a second-hand mimeograph machine bought with the proceeds of a summer panhandling outside The Riverboat Coffee House. Twenty years later, just when the company had developed into a respected literary press, government cutbacks savaged its operating grants. Featherstone, like Blanche du Bois, has since depended upon the kindness of strangers — with about as much success. All that stands between the press and financial collapse is a twice-yearly benefit at which Jamieson's authors and friends read poetry, pass the hat, and belly up to the cash bar. Writers may starve, but they always have money for booze. Jaimeson takes what is raised to the Woodbine racetrack. His luck with the horses brings a modest-to-healthy return that dictates the number of titles on his next season's list.

When Lydia's encounter with the pope hit the tabloids, Jamieson had the mad inspiration that Featherstone could cash in on the publicity by collecting all eight volumes of *Spiritual Descents* into a new deluxe edition. He rolled the dice and crapped out. Lydia's resurrection was a one-day wonder and Jamieson was left with a warehouse of books destined for the remainder bin. Featherstone looked out for the count.

That changed overnight when Lydia won The Phoenix Lottery. Suddenly, Jamieson went from being a fiscally irres-ponsible ex-hippie to a publishing genius. A few phone calls and Chapters agreed to buy up his entire Spark inventory, contingent on Lydia's presence at a book signing to launch its new outlet at Harbourfront. Hence the frantic phone calls.

Loyal to a fault, Lydia agreed to be there with bells on.

So now she sits behind a table signing books for a line of gawkers that snakes out onto the street. As always, Lydia is a vision. She sports a black bustier, crinoline, fishnets, and plat-forms. Her lips and eyelashes are likewise black, as is her hair, gelled in spikes and adorned with large metallic spiders. All this black stands in stark contrast to her face, which is coated in a thick albino pancake, save for a purple beauty mark in the shape of a cockroach perched on her right cheek.

Chapters has gone all out. Behind her is a reproduction of the van Gogh *Self-Portrait* mounted on a bank of ten-foot-high sheets of pressboard covered in crinkled tinfoil and cut in the shape of flames. The effect is enhanced by waves of red, yellow, and orange shimmering across the tinfoil courtesy of a floodlight illuminating the display through a rotating colour wheel. Advancing toward the Goth celebrity, book lovers can browse a wall of shelves on their left featuring *Spiritual Descents* and two-for-one offerings from Featherstone's extensive backlist. On their right, a wall of van Gogh coffee-table books invite the budget-minded with attractive discounts.

Jamieson is fairly bouncing for joy, a human flubber ball. He'll be able to put out his fall list after all. He claps his hands, skips about, and shakes hands with strangers until security ventures over for a chat. Meantime, the Three Ts sit in the in-house Starbucks, where they sneer at the shoppers and frighten their children.

"So you've really made it."

Lydia, massaging her cramped writing hand, looks into the face of a neatly-dressed man in his early thirties. "Ryder!" She leaps from behind the desk and throws herself into his arms. "I'm sorry I was so mean. It's good to see you. Oh, Ryder. Bob. I'm crying. There goes my pancake." She laughs, wipes her eyes, and takes a step back the better to see him.

"I'd like you to meet Betty Gardenia."

The pale middle-aged woman beside Bob smiles nervously. "Hello," she says, nodding her head. "Bob's told me all about you. I'm so pleased to meet his friends."

Lydia shakes her hand. "Hi," she says. She glances back and forth between the two. They look like companions. Or mother and son. Whatever it is, there's a bond.

"Look, you're really busy," Bob says awkwardly.

"But I want to talk to you. I really do."

"Why don't you come over to the house?" Betty asks, eager to help out. "You're an artist after all. There's a meeting of the Inner Circle Wednesday at seven o'clock. Come as my guest." Bob looks horrified. "No really," Betty says. "I'm sure Rudyard won't mind. He discovered the *Self-Portrait*, you know. This Phoenix Lottery business has put him in the news. He's tickled pink about it, despite what he says. And the kids would love to meet you. It would give them a chance to talk about something exciting for a change."

"Sure. Great," says Lydia, taking a card from Bob.

"Well we mustn't keep you," Betty says. "Sorry," she apologises to the people in the line behind. She turns back. "Before we go, could you please sign this?" She shyly thrusts forward a copy of *Spiritual Descents*. "Just write: 'To Rudyard, Best Wishes.'"

Lydia obliges, though within the week best wishes are the last thing she will wish on that pompous toad.

Poltergeist

Lydia adores Emily Pristable. When she returned Emily's call, she'd expected voice mail. Instead, she got a cheery, "Why hello there. Good to hear your voice. I saw your picture on TV with the pope up on Baffin Island. You've got yourself all thawed out again then, have you? Good. So how's Tuesday at two?"

"Sounds great. Oh, and I have a favour to ask. Cardinal Wichita has been bugging me to see him. I said he could meet me at BEI. I know I should have asked first, but is that okay?"

"Suit yourself, but take care. That fella's up to mischief, you mark my word. If he gives you any malarkey, you let me know and I'll take care of him."

When greeted at the BEI gates, Lydia finds Miss Pristable equally unpretentious in person. "Pleased to meet you. Come right this way, don't mind the gargoyles. But then, my heavens, what with that get-up, I'll bet they're right up your alley. Oh, to be young again. Why don't we go right up to the boardroom, shall we? By the way, Mr. Beamish sends his apologies. He's been taken away on business."

Emily uses the term "business" lightly. She'd arrived at work the day before to find the following message crumpled on her desk.

> Dear Emily,
>   I've had another incident with the painting. Gone south to Varadero for a new resguardo. See you soon.
>   Love,
>   Junior
> PS. Don't worry.

Emily is old enough to know that when someone says "don't worry" it's a signal that one should be worried sick. She is.

"There's the painting. How be you make yourself comfy, and I'll go get the sandwiches. We've tuna, chicken, and egg salad. And what would you like to drink?"

Lydia asks for a Diet Coke and Emily disappears. "She treats me like a human being," Lydia marvels, " and she's from Toronto."

She approaches the *Self-Portrait*. When Edgar first looked at it, he'd seen the fierce eyes of a wise madman blazing from an indigo background—eyes destined to stir his son to independence. Junior, ever contrary, had seen instead a torment from his father sent to drive him mad. To Cardinal Wichita, it was a living sacrifice from the genius of the damned. To Emily, a curiosity she didn't much fancy, save for the curlicues. And Lydia? She sees something else again: her future.

The idea of immolating a painting on the world stage was exciting in the abstract. Faced with the work itself, the reality is terrifying. Lydia finds herself overcome with waves of self-doubt. This is more than stage fright. It is raw, bowel-emptying panic: the knowledge that her name will forever be attached to this act, and the terror that she may live to regret it.

She sits on the couch and faces the painting, breathing deeply. This is a van Gogh, for God's sake, she tells herself. A van Gogh! And she's planning to burn it? What on earth could she be thinking? Look at the colours! The textures! The energy! Oh God, if only she were able to create art like that.

Then a little voice itches inside her brain—the same little voice that drove her wild in high school. So what if she created art like that? What would the world say if the painting was by Lydia Spark instead of Vincent van Gogh? Would her parents care? No one else in Mitchell would, that's for sure. Suckhole would take one look at it, smile and say, "Gee, that's so original, Lydia," then turn and make a face like somebody cut cheese. Dave Ramsay would look all soulful and say, "You're way sensitive, Lyd," as if that'd get him into her pants. Mr. Jeffries would make a stupid joke like, "I think you should stick to throwing up, ha ha ha," and Murray would do that gross thing with his tongue.

No, Lydia knows that if she painted that very same painting the world wouldn't be at her feet. It would treat her the way it treated van Gogh when he was alive. Her work, like his, would be used to line chicken coops. What a joke, she thinks. It's not the value of the work that matters. It's the value of the name. And the name only matters when the suits figure they can make a buck off it.

So now, instead of a piece of crap, she's supposedly looking at a "masterpiece." The kind of masterpiece that sucks money into the bank accounts of dealers and collectors while living artists starve.

Lydia casts a freshly critical eye on the work, and the more critical her eye becomes, the more the painting seems to change. Take away the name "van Gogh" and it's the work of an amateur. Those colours aren't vivid, they're garish. As for the textures? Anybody could do that if they could afford the paint. Just slop it on with a trowel, Vincent. After all, you never had to pay for your supplies. You had a brother to bankroll you, you lucky sonovabitch.

The subject is nothing to write home about either. Like, what's the deal with the ear stump? Were you trying to make Theo feel guilty, so he'd send you more cash? God, this isn't a painting—it's a guilt trip! A manipulative wank! And those curlicues in the background are a joke. Like, kitsch or what? When you come right down to it, not only is this no *Sunflowers*, this is a piece of shit.

Lydia is ablaze with anger and triumph and surprise. Her confidence has returned. She's not burning a painting; she's striking a blow for unknown artists everywhere, forcing the world to confront the arbitrariness of art hierarchies, establishing a dialectic about cultural assumptions, received opinion, and blandly assumed aesthetics. What the hell, she's creating a revolution! A revolution to which the world will pay attention. Before The Phoenix Lottery her name was a big fat zero, destined to remain a big fat zero no matter what she produced. Not any more. The lottery win is pole-vaulting her into the media stratosphere. She's enjoying hype beyond even the likes of Christo. She's making a grand jeté into art history, damnit. She has the suits by the gonads and boy is she ready to squeeze.

Just as Lydia's excitement hits full stride, Emily wheels in the tea service. It holds a colourful teapot shaped like a rooster, a tabby cat sugar bowl, a cow creamer, and cups and saucers with a Scottish thistle design. These are separated from a glass tray of sandwiches and petits fours by plain white serviettes anchored by utilitarian cutlery. Lydia looks past Emily to the man following closely on her heels.

"You'll never guess what the cat dragged in," Emily announces. "May I introduce Cardinal Wichita."

Cardinal Wichita ignores the dig. The impudence of the secretary had thrown him off his game in the meeting with Junior Beamish. That's not going to happen this time. He will maintain his dignity and best this bug with his authority and charm, or if all else fails, with his secret weapon, Edgar B., now hovering in the wings.

Wichita flashes a matinee idol smile and extends his manicured hand. Lydia's eyes pop. She rises, mesmerised, and finds herself curtsying for the first time in her life. The crimson vestments, the gold trim, the elaborate rings—it's quite the look.

"A pleasure to meet you," Wichita nods courteously.

"You too," she gasps. Before she can get a grip, Wichita throws her for a second loop. In his left hand is a copy of the *Spiritual Descents* omnibus. "I've been reading your work. Impressive. Might you favour me with a signed edition?"

Lydia knows a bullshitter when she sees one, but has to admit that flattery has its attractions. She takes the book, sits, and writes in a careful script: *All the best from a spiritual "descenter," Yours, Lydia Spark.*

Wichita notes the eagerness with which the innocent accepted his compliment. She'll be putty in his hands. He gives Emily a patronizing glance. "You may shut the door on your way out."

"Naturally," Emily sniffs. "I'm not the sort to pry."

Wichita waits until the door is closed. Then he lowers his voice and leans forward to take the prey into his confidence. "You've met Junior Beamish?"

"Not yet."

Wichita taps his temple with his index finger. "It's very sad."

"He's crazy?"

"A shame, really. In many ways he's a visionary. That's why I was pleased to hear that an artist had won The Phoenix Lottery. Together we can save Mr. Beamish from himself."

"I don't understand."

"When Junior Beamish comes to his senses and realizes what he's done—that he's obliterated an icon of the Western imagination—the knowledge will unhinge the poor soul forever. An artist of your stature, naturally, would never think of fulfilling such a desecration, no matter what the benefit. You are a fifth columnist for God. Mother Church gives thanks and more. For your refusal to burn this painting, she will reward you with an honorarium of no small consequence."

"Thanks, but I don't care about the money. I care about the art."

The Lord be praised, thinks Wichita. If the sweet child disdains cash there'll be rejoicing in Rome no less than in Heaven. "Art, yes," he nods sagely. "How true. My sentiments exactly."

"See, I'm not gonna just torch the sucker; I'm going to do it as an artistic event."

"I beg your pardon?"

"It's gonna be an international performance piece with poetry, music, dance, video, and rollerblades. I'm calling it *Inferno*."

"Inferno?"

Lydia's eyes burn with excitement. "It'll be all about the exorcising of icons, and the establishment of new forms. Death and rebirth. It's art for the masses, shown live around the world in stadiums, on TV, and over the internet. Not art for the few. Art for all. And it can play on video forever!"

The effrontery takes Wichita's breath away. He takes a moment to consider his options and decides to play uncle to Lydia's wayward niece. "That would make a most amusing party piece," he chuckles in honeyed tones. "But surely you don't consider it worth the destruction of a van Gogh?"

"I'm not destroying anything. This is the age of reproduction. After the burning, this picture'll live on in posters, postcards, and coffee-table books. They'll make it into holograms. Plus check out the Web—it'll be a more famous than ever as a virtual painting."

"But the work itself will be lost!"

"It might as well be lost right now. In case you hadn't noticed, The Work Itself is in a private collection. I don't see busloads of art lovers trekking through here."

"As long as it lives, so do its possibilities."

"Whoop-de-doo." Notions of grace and redemption play well with the faithful, but are lost on this urban terrorist. "Say it's hanging in the Louvre. How many people can afford to hop a plane for a look-see? I mean you're not talking about a loss to humanity. You're talking about a loss to tourists."

"You dismiss the Louvre?"

"Hey, if the Louvre got nuked it'd be just one less must-see in the Michelin Guide. Frantic sightseers trying to do Paris in a day might even be grateful."

Wichita's face turns as cold as the countenance of God on the Day of Judgment. "You, my dear, are an empty-headed poseur," he purrs, his voice the more chilling for its dispassion. "How dare you call yourself an artist?"

"How dare you lecture me?" Lydia snaps back. "I gave up security, my parents, and any chance for a normal life to be an artist. I've kicked around the country and *been* kicked around the country for a chance to do art. I've lived in a flophouse, an abandoned building, cheap hotels, parks, and old cars. I mean, where do you get off dumping on me? What have you ever given up besides sex—if that? All you have to do is wake up and they give you a meal ticket, free costumes and let you live in a tourist attraction."

"We're to feel guilty because you threw your life away?"

"I didn't. I stayed true to my vision and it's paid off. I've grabbed the brass ring. My future's in my hands. I have a chance."

"To make a fool of yourself? To lead a life of ignominy?"

"You sound like my father."

Wichita's flying blind. Diplomacy is easy in the Curia. It's a boy's club and he is near the top of the food chain. Even his nominal superior, the Holy Father, bows to his judgment. How galling, then, to be confounded by a child. Nonetheless, it is impossible to bully the wilful and Wichita realizes he must change course if he's to subdue Antichrist's handmaiden. Humility is the tactic most likely to bring success. Unexpected, it may disarm the demon. He shudders. Humility is to Wichita what speed-reading is to the dyslexic.

"When you speak of your father, your voice fills with pain. I share that pain," he says, eyes soulful as those in paintings of Christ at Gethsemane. "I, too, had a father who forsook me, who left his babe in a spiritual wilderness to suffer the torments of the damned."

Wichita knows he's gone a tad rococo, but he has her attention. "You see before you a man of position," he continues. "It was not always thus. In truth, I was a child of the streets. A boy who did such things as made the angels weep. Yea, a lad poised for a life of prostitution and petty crime. But God showed mercy to his suffering child and sent a miracle unto him. Under the dome of St. Peter's, wretched and downcast, I looked up to see the Pietà. And verily, as I gazed into the sorrowing eyes of the blessèd Virgin weeping for the lifeless son across her lap, I heard, as 'twere, a choir of the heavenly host singing 'Hosanna, glory to God in the highest.' And the angel of the Lord came down upon me and I was sore afraid."

So much for humility: Pride has his tongue and flaps it with abandon. "And the angel of the Lord said unto me, 'Fear not, for behold I bring you tidings of great joy. For unto you, Giuseppe Wichita, is given this day the miracle of grace. Forsake the road of sin on which you have embarked, give o'er your life

to God and see salvation in this world and the next.' And so I
did, and so I have, and so I shall. This is the same miracle I offer
to you today, Lydia Spark. The miracle of grace. Forsake the
evil tempting your soul, turn your back upon the pit, look up to
God, and live a life eternal!"

Wichita wipes his brow. In another life he will surely be a
Baptist.

"Are you done?" Lydia checks her watch. "Cause if you are,
I have to pick up a two-four for my roommates."

Wichita is aghast. But he's not about to give up now. He
prepares to call upon his secret weapon. "Know, Lydia Spark,
you tempt the powers of hell," he thunders. "Continue on your
current journey and face perdition, bereft of mercy forever-
more. Hear me, oh ministers of God. Send unto this child a
token of the wrath to come."

In presuming to order about the heavenly host as if they
were so many busboys, Wichita knows he skirts the hem of
blasphemy. "Forgive me, Lord," he prays silently, "but desperate times call for desperate measures." He strikes a pose more
fearful than Elijah, and Edgar Beamish takes his cue.

Submitting to the cardinal's blackmail, Edgar is a poltergeist for hire, an avenging fury in a staged apocalyptic nightmare. He makes a grand entrance, grabbing the cutlery and
tossing it in the air. It bounces off the ceiling and clatters to the
floor. Edgar is rather pleased with his startling opener. But
instead of horror, it provokes applause. "Wow!" exclaims Lydia,
with the wide-eyed excitement of a child at the circus.

Beamish is cross. How dare she mock his haunting? He
dives for the china, but can't bring himself to smash Emily's
keepsakes. Flustered, he confines his mayhem to waving the
cups in front of her nose.

Lydia squeals with laughter. "More! More!"

The little bitch. He'll give her more all right. Beamish squats
and hoists her end of the couch off the floor.

But Lydia is impervious to terror. "Whee," she cries. "Higher!
Higher! Faster! Faster!"

"Hell isn't a ride on the midway!" Wichita thunders.

"Maybe not, but it sure isn't Edgar Beamish either."

Edgar lets the couch drop to the floor. "You can see me?" he asks, incredulous.

"And hear you, too," Lydia says. "Frankly, I thought you were one helluva lot scarier when you were alive."

"Know ye that my powers have increased beyond the grave!" Beamish thunders, striking a theatrical pose worthy of Sir Donald Woolfit on a bender in the provinces.

"Yeah, right. Why should I be scared of ghosts anyway? I've been dead myself once."

Before the two men can recover their equilibrium, Emily throws open the door. "What's going on in here?" she demands, seeing the cutlery scattered about and the couch out of whack. "Has that man been threatening you with the tableware?"

"Actually we're in the middle of a haunting," says Lydia.

"Don't give me that nonsense."

"No, really. Edgar Beamish. He's floating right over there. Cardinal Wichita called up his spirit. They're working together."

"It's cruel to tease an old woman."

"I'm not. See, I'm an expert on the spirit world," Lydia tries to explain. "I started my artistic career as a channeller and I just finished a kind of post-grad course with this angakoq up on Baffin."

"I don't care what you think you know," Emily says with conviction, "but you certainly don't know Edgar Beamish. If Mr. Beamish, God rest his soul, were to pay us a visit, there's no way on God's green earth he'd arrive in the company of this humbug." She fixes Wichita with a look. "Did you put her up to this? Well, I'm a God-fearing woman, so you can take your necromancy and hightail it right out of here. Do you hear?"

Emily sees them to the front gates, Lydia apologising for the upset, Wichita waving to the paparazzi. She returns to pick up the fallen cutlery, weary and out of sorts. Her back isn't up to bending over and she sinks to her knees to complete the task, mist clouding her eyes.

Has Junior been telling the truth these past ten years? Is Edgar really in the air? Can he see me? Hear me? Might I reach him? No, she shakes her head sadly. That would take a miracle beyond the power of prayer. She has her dreams, but knows her life is not designed for happy endings.

Back at the archdiocesan guest house, Wichita finishes packing. In an hour he will return to Rome, his mission a failure. "Your secret life is safe with me," he tells Edgar, as he folds his underwear and matches his socks. "You did all that you could do to frighten the girl senseless. The cutlery. The cups. It was a fine display. And making the painting twirl around while you lifted up that couch was the work of a master." He sighs, "Who would have guessed the little devil had the gift? *Inferno!* Inferno indeed."

Edgar nods and takes his leave, relieved to be free of the cardinal. So relieved, he decides not to question Wichita's remarks.

But what on earth was he talking about? Edgar wonders. I never touched the painting.

Down South

The night Lydia Spark attends Rudyard Gardenia's Inner Circle is a night that will become the stuff of legend. It is the last night The Great Himself will ever inflict humiliation on another, or enjoy a moment's peace in this life or the next. For on this night a chain of events is set in motion that will seal his doom.

Members of The Rudyard Gardenia Survivors Society recognize in Rudyard's torment a revenge more delicious than that afforded by mere probability. Some see the workings of Divine Providence, others speak of harmonic convergence, but all gleefully recite the list of objects which played a role in Rudyard's demolition: the Puccini CD, the gumdrop, and the Jacuzzi. What but supernatural high spirits could have arranged these so as to rob Gardenia's fall of whatever pity it might otherwise have evoked?

Junior Beamish agrees that Rudyard's fall from grace was accomplished with the aid of forces otherworldly. However, he dates the decline of the beast not from the fateful evening on which The Inner Circle imploded, but from that day earlier in the week when he disappeared south to Varadero.

Junior checks into the Melia Las Americas, one of a dozen tourist hotels on what used to be the duPont estate. Without bothering to unpack, he wanders the few hundred yards to the mansion where his father once abandoned him. It's now a museum and restaurant.

He pays two dollars to the attendant and enters, his stomach alive with butterflies. He feels like Alice in Wonderland: everything is and is not as he remembers it. The major pieces of furniture and the decor remain as Irenée duPont had left them, but they seem to have shrunk. He remembers scooting under tables and hiding under chairs, but can't imagine how he used to fit. And what are tourists doing here? They seem to be operating in a different dimension. When they rub their hands across the carved mahogany sideboard and green ceramic tiles, they are touching "a piece of history"; he is reexperiencing his past. A version of it anyway.

That's the spot where we put up the Christmas tree and I saw the angel for the first time, Junior marvels, looking to the northeast corner of the Grand Room, past the pipe organ and the archway to the library. He goes upstairs and into the master bedroom. "This is where Mrs. duPont used to sleep," a guide says. "Mr. duPont enjoyed his whiskey. She made him sleep in the adjoining room so his snoring wouldn't bother her." How does the guide know that? Junior can't remember anything of the sort, though he'd barely met the old man. To him, Mr. duPont was this big person you didn't bother and he'd give you a candy.

He makes his way up to the semi-enclosed rooftop bar. How had he managed to race up the steps in this cramped passageway without bouncing off the walls? What could he have been thinking, getting underfoot of Sara and the other servants as they tried to carry trays of glasses up and down those tight circular stairs? No wonder they'd been upset.

And now he is in the bar. Like the first-floor library, the bar is full of small tables. Downstairs the tables are covered in white linen, and waiters serve tourists gourmet meals prepared with fresh cream and other ingredients unavailable to their own families. Upstairs the tables are for casual use, crowds of tourists coming for the two-for-one happy hour and the same exquisite sunsets he once enjoyed with his father.

Junior looks at the bar in the corner. That's where The Pillow Lady terrified him nigh unto death. He goes to the small walkout on the south side and looks over the golf course where he saw his father race off in the cart. He remembers the golf course stretching into an infinite nightmare of sand traps and jungle. Now, seeing it under the midday sun as an adult, it is hard to imagine how it might ever have seemed fearful.

If it is true that the world shapes us through the experiences it provides, Junior thinks, it's equally true that we shape those experiences through our perceptions. What a terrifying thought. Whether because of age, position, time, or background, what we see of events is necessarily limited; and yet we act on the basis of our impaired vision, bringing consequences upon ourselves that can never be erased.

Junior leaves unsettled and wanders back to the hotel for a nap, wondering what he will see when he visits Sara.

At seven-thirty, Junior takes a cab to Sara's home at the corner of Calle 42 and Avenida 1. His visit is a surprise: she has no phone and there wasn't time to write, the decision to come having been made the previous night. All the same, the letter he'd recently received indicated that her door was always open.

The cab pulls up to a simple home of cement blocks with a corrugated tin roof. Wood shutters and door are open to let in the evening breeze. Next to the door, Sara and her daughter Elena sit on an improvised couch of orange crates and old car seats.

Sara hasn't changed much. Her hair is almost as black, her skin almost as supple, and her eyes absolutely as bright as in the days she managed the household staff at Xanadu. To Junior, however, she is another person altogether. This Sara is rather short. The four-year-old remembers a giant. On the other hand, she is now almost as old as the child had once imagined.

What a life those years have seen. After the revolution she continued at the estate, helping the government take inventory of the duPont belongings, then cleaning the house once it became a restaurant. Retired for ten years, she remains active thanks to Santería. She is *santera mayore*, called upon by neighbours to recommend love potions, spells to ward off spirits, and herbal remedies to alleviate the sick. As she likes to say, "If you have friends, you don't need a sugar plantation."

Nevertheless, life has been difficult, particularly in the wake of the Soviet Union's collapse, and her husband's death from cancer. One of her sons died in a fishing accident and the second, jailed for offenses relating to the black market, left the country when Castro opened the prisons for the 1980 "freedom flotilla." Today he lives off Calle Ocho in Miami's Little Havana, where he works as a short-order cook at Versailles. He sends her letters, but the money inside usually disappears in transit. Her two daughters remain in Cuba. The eldest lives with her husband in nearby Coliseo, where she is an economist at the local sugar factory. The baby of the family, Elena, works as a housekeeper at the Hotel Paradiso, earning far more in tips than she ever did as a teacher.

It was Elena who helped reestablish contact between her mother and Junior, passing Sara's letter to a friendly tourist to mail when back in Canada.

> Calle 42 y Avenida 1
> Varadero, Matanzas
> Cuba

My dear little Edgar,

It is your old friend from Xanadu, Sara Pérez. This week I read about your lottery in *Granma*. It had a very nice picture of you. You have not changed. The boy is in the man.

Do you remember Señora Resguardo? She used to keep you so safe from the espíritu intranquilo who gave you many problems here. I do not mean to trouble you, but the night I see your picture in the newspaper, I have a dream. You are lost and crying for help. I cast the shells. I fear you may need a stronger resguardo than when you were a boy, for I see three espíritu intranquilos surrounding you. And more troubles beside from those living.

Forgive me if I interfere, but your father was so kind to me and you were such a sunshine. I do not forget. If you ever have need of me, my door is always open.

> With much love,
> Sara Maria Pérez Pérez

"So you have come, my little Edgar." Sara introduces him to Elena. At Xanadu, he never knew that Sara had children. In fact, he never knew that Sara had a life.

He offers the women a bag filled with aspirins, cough syrup, chocolate, jam, and other hard-to-come-by goods he'd picked up at the duty-free shop at the airport. Sara takes the bag and, in return, offers him a plate of Moors and Christians. Junior accepts, though having stuffed himself at the hotel buffet the thought of black beans and rice makes him queasy. With a smile and a nod, Elena offers him her seat and goes inside to prepare his plate. The moment she has gone, Sara says, "My little Edgar, the dream was correct? Yes? Or have you come to Varadero for a tan?"

"Please help me."

Sara nods and holds his hands in her own. She rubs them; they are so cold. They sit in silence for a time, as the sun drops quickly and the night air fills with fireflies and the sounds of waves and neighbours. Then Sara says, "Your father — he is still living?"

A discreet pause. "In a manner of speaking."

Sara understands. "He was always a restless spirit."

Junior begins to cry.

"He loved you very much." Junior laughs, but Sara holds her ground. "It was in his eyes when he asked for your *resguardo.*" A pause. "And your mother? She is alive?"

Junior laughs again. "Oh yes."

"Come." She leads him inside where Elena has made his place at the table. As Junior eats by the light of seven candles, Sara tells him how frightened she had been when she cast his shells. Her fear carries weight, since Sara is blessed as an *italera.* For this gift she gives the glory to her birth orisha, Babalú-Ayé, and to Elegguá, upon whom she calls for guidance in divining future action.

Once Junior has wiped his plate with his last crust of bread, Sara claps her hands. "To work." She takes one of three neck-laces hanging from a nail in the door frame. "You must wear this in Elegguá's honour," she says, putting the string of red and black beads around his neck. "Now take off your clothes."

Junior strips to his underwear as Sara draws a circle on the floor. She takes a dozen rusty spikes and places them around the perimeter, points thrusting outward, the rays of Changó. "Stand at the centre." Junior does as he is told, and the old woman stands before him, her eyes closed, concentrating on the beat of unheard drums. Her head rolls and her body sways as she chants prayers to Elegguá and Babalú-Ayé, while whipping herself rhythmically with a red cord tied to the blunt kitchen knife in her hand.

The candles on the table flicker. The three on either side extinguish, while the seventh at the centre glows more brightly than before. And now Sara begins to moan, the moans transforming to animal howls as her body is inhabited by something other. In a trance, she takes his right hand, sniffing it like a wild beast, gumming it until it drips saliva. In like manner she snuffles up his arm, across his chest, and down to the tips of his left fingers.

A throaty laugh, and suddenly she begins to speak in tongues, a rich mix of medieval Spanish, French, and Yoruban. Elena translates. "The ability of the three espíritu intranquilos to cause you pain is increased by the actions of an evil man. He is a snake in the grass who holds sway over your mother."

Junior gasps. "How could she know about Rudyard Gardenia?"

"She has sacrificed to Elegguá," Elena whispers. "He is a trickster who punishes those who do wrong, and is eager to take up your case."

Whoever, or whatever, is inside Sara has overheard. Excited grunts and gestures. Elena lights a cheap cigar and puts it in her mother's hand. Sara puffs it with the lit end glowing inside her mouth. More grunts. Smoke billows through the room, licking Junior's pores. The cigar is replaced with a glass of rum. Sara downs half in a gulp. The other half she rolls round her mouth, then sprays across Junior's face and chest.

More tongues and more translation. "Elegguá will act as guide as you rid yourself of this devil Gardenia. And rid your-self you must to find peace from these restless spirits who haunt you."

"But how can I touch him?"

Elena listens very hard, then says, "You must write his name with snake venom on a piece of paper. Glue the paper to snakeskin and cut to fit the inside of your shoes. Then walk, hard, on his name. As you do, the snake will be ground into the dirt."

"Ground into the dirt," Junior repeats slowly, relishing each syllable.

The creature inside Sara leaps with glee, then crouches, spitting its dictation hard and fast.

"Next, you must rid your mother of the snake's influence," Elena rattles, barely keeping pace. "To do this, take two seven-hour black candles. Carve in the shape of a man and a woman. At midnight, set one inch apart and burn for an hour. On the second midnight, two inches apart and burn for an hour. On the third midnight, three, and so forth until the week is over and the candles spent as that devil's spell."

The creature shrieks, collapsing on the floor. Instantly, the six dead candles burst back to life and all is as it was before.

Sara shakes herself back into her body and gets up. She smiles at Junior. "Elegguá has helped?" she asks, wiping the dried spittle and rum from his body with a handful of fragrant leaves plucked from a basin of cool water drawn by Elena. Junior nods.

"Good." Sara goes to a low box in the corner on which a black doll dressed in white sits behind a bowl filled with burnt coconut and cotton. The front of the box is open; within are an arrangement of seashells filled with a variety of herbs. Junior realizes the box must be some sort of shrine. He watches as Sara takes a small neatly folded plastic bag from a stack to the right of the box, bags which were retrieved by Elena from the rooms of departed guests at The Paradiso.

"Seven herbs for seven *despojos*," Sara says. "Bitter and sweet: escoba amarga, guairo, altamiso, canutillo blanco, cimmarrona, abrajo, and yerbabuena—your old favourite." She drops a pinch of each into the bag. "One thimble in each bath will keep you safe from spirits. And keep a flavour of this in your clothes," she winks at him, pressing a loose quantity of dried espartillo in his palm.

Elena interrupts to excuse herself. She's expected at work at six in the morning and must get to sleep. Junior thanks her for the food and translation. Then he and Sara move to the front porch and talk about old times into the middle of the night.

When they say farewell, Sara gives him a hug. "It's been too long since I have seen my little Edgar. You will come again?"

"Yes."

Sara pauses. "I may speak freely?" Junior nods. "They had problems, your mother and father, I think." Junior nods again. "There is something you should know. Your father was not perfect, but he was a good man. He loved your mother very much. He asked the babalawo for a spell to bring back her love."

"I guess spells don't always work."

"No," Sara says with a sad heart. "Sometimes the orishas are displeased."

Puccini, a Gumdrop, and a Jacuzzi

Lydia is an hour late for the meeting of the Inner Circle. She is greeted in the foyer by Bob. They hug—"Good to see you." "Sorry I'm late."—and he takes her down the hall to the living room.

"Quite the digs," says Lydia, admiring the lithographs, etchings, and paintings that line the corridor. She spots a Matisse, a Modigliani, and an Emily Carr that the McMichael Gallery has been after for years. "Are they fake?" she asks. Bob is horrified at the thought, but before he can answer they've arrived at the place appointed. "Wow!"

The living room is enormous. On the left is a mahogany writing table, its drawers carved with an intricate design of leaves and vines, and further along, a corner table with a Scandinavian smoked-glass vase, a purse, and some car keys. To the immediate right, a massive entertainment unit holding a television, CD player, bar and, most curiously, a wide shelf displaying an elaborate wig atop a marble bust of some long-dead dignitary. The right wall hosts a fieldstone fireplace, while the left is lined with books; Lydia wonders if the tomes were bought for their content or their attractive leather bindings, which play well with the hardwood floors and Persian rugs. Two tobacco-toned leather chesterfields, a glass-and-bronze coffee table, as well as sundry chairs, occasional tables, and antique lamps complete the decor; these have been arranged to form a large semicircle opening to the end of the room.

What lies there, however, is blocked by members of The Inner Circle, all present and accounted for, who have placed their works-in-progress hither and yon and are currently knocking back the wine in order to anaesthetize themselves for the ritual slaughter to come. Who is to be the Victim of the Week, they wonder, glancing nervously at each other's work.

These artists aren't at all like the gang of rowdies Lydia hangs out with at the Rabid Squirrel. These are middle-class kids with table manners and names like Trevor, Ashley, Melissa, and Bernard. The sort who've been to all the right schools and whose parents paid their shot at the Ontario College of Art, praying the while that their little rebels would come to their senses and at least become dentists, anything, so that they would no longer have to be embarrassed at the club when comparing notes with friends on the progress of their heirs apparent.

That is why, if Lydia stops to think about it, the crew before her is such ripe fodder for Captain Gardenia. Her crowd would happily tell him to take a flying fuck, but these gentrified babes, while they might affect the withering attitude of their mentor, are scared little bunnies. Gardenia can make their careers, such is his influence with galleries and arts bureaucrats. Equally important, his is a name their parents understand. They know him from the CBC, where his plummy tones are heard on innumerable arts programs discussing visual artists as if they're so many treats on his personal pastry tray. Morsels worthy of his palate are judged "delectable . . . to die for . . . a revelation." The rest are dismissed as offal to sate the appetites of dim grunters with low brows and lower tastes.

Truth be told, Rudyard's pronouncements have less to do with art than where the artists fit within his social cosmos. This doesn't matter to his audience. Listeners find in his patronizing air and studied Oxbridge accent the trademarks of a bona fide cultural maven to whom attention must be paid.

To be an artist in Rudyard's Inner Circle, therefore, is a sign to the general public — read parents and former classmates — that one has arrived, or is at least a young Turk rattling the gates. It means one can look them in the eye and avoid defending one's life at the family cottage or answering questions like "So when are you going to settle down and get a job?"

Lydia hears a voice etched in her memory not only from CBC but from that horrible day in Mount Pleasant Cemetery when she'd rediscovered Ryder Knight. "So," The Voice intones, dripping irony, "our guest of honour has arrived? The creator of *Inferno* has deigned to grace our company?"

The crowd parts, revealing The Great Himself, Rudyard Gardenia, lounging on an oversized leather beanbag chair at the far end of the room. The chair is perfectly positioned for the occupant to graze from the restored harvest table on his right, which labours under a weight of cheeses, devilled eggs, cold cuts, fruit, pastries, breads, hors d'oeuvres, and a startling variety of condiments, or to tickle the ivories on the candelabraed grand piano to his left.

Rudyard is an imposing figure, draped in an orange chiffon muumuu, a yellow turban, and matching yellow mink slippers. He makes no move to rise but simply extends his hand. Am I supposed to kiss his ring? Lydia wonders. She chooses to ignore the hand and waves instead. "Hi everybody. Thanks for having me."

"The pleasure is ours, I'm sure," comes the unctuous reply, "for we are in your debt. Artists of the Inner Circle occasionally question the value of obscurity. Your success puts such concerns to rest."

Lydia notices a few smirks and exchanged glances. "You're welcome, I guess," she says with an uncertain smile.

"Betty, fetch our guest a drink and we'll get down to business."

Inner Circle members arrange themselves throughout the room. Rudyard observes them. He is not amused. His artists may have tittered at his jibe, but they are awed by Lydia's stardom. They are puritans lusting in their hearts, these artists who profess disdain for fame and fortune; he may command their fear, but she commands their dreams. And she's upstaging him in his own home! Well, he will be revenged: the creature who brought this interloper to his party will pay. He waits until Betty has handed Lydia her wine. "Whenever you're ready," he purrs.

"Sorry." Betty reddens and scurries to the hall entrance, taking a seat on a chair by the writing table.

All eyes turn nervously to Rudyard. "We have a special treat this evening, ladies and gentlemen," he announces breathlessly. "New work from a new artist who has long wished to join the Circle." Rudyard savours the curiosity on the gathered faces, then rises and pirouettes to the grand piano. He plays the opening chords to Beethoven's Fifth, and plucks a manila envelope from behind the sheet music on the rack with the assurance of a magician conjuring a rabbit from a hat.

At the sight of the envelope, Betty gasps. "No, Rudyard! No!"

"My pet, whatever is the matter?" The Great Himself enquires, with a wink to his audience.

Betty's face drains of colour and expression. She knows what is in that envelope. It is her secret.

For some time, Betty has been under the care of Dr. Billing. She got his name from Kitty. "He lives in the Annex with his mother and cats. A little neurotic if you ask me, but he writes so many prescriptions you'd think he was on commission. If that isn't a recommendation, I don't know what is."

One morning over breakfast, Betty said she'd like to talk to Dr. Billing about her depression. Rudyard wasn't supportive. "You don't need a psychiatrist, my pet. You're constantly surrounded by people of heightened sensibility. No wonder you feel dull and unimaginative."

Despite the discouragement, Betty made an appointment and soon discovered the joys of Zoloft. Dr. Billing did more than provide pharmaceuticals, however; he attempted treatment.

Over the years, Betty's poor self-esteem had blossomed into pathological self-hate. Indeed, her nude reflection filled her with such nausea that she showered in the dark in order to avoid having to look at herself in the bathroom mirror. She'd even taken to wearing veils at all hours, indoors and out, until Rudyard ventured, "It's better to be thought ugly than peculiar."

Dr. Billing took an unusual approach to Betty's treatment. Unorthodox at first blush, it was essentially an analogue to established practice in the treatment of phobics, in which patients are forced to confront their fear in order to overcome it. Billing, an amateur shutterbug, loaned Betty one of his Minoltas with an adjustable timer. He instructed her to take portraits of herself in a variety of poses. The following week, they studied these photographs and compared them with a variety of candid poses in Billing's collection. By discussing her image in terms of photographic art, Billing helped Betty establish a clinical aesthetic in reference to her body, building an objective base for what became increasingly positive self-assessments.

As Betty became comfortable with the camera, she was instructed to pose wearing fewer clothes. First to go were her shoes. Then her nylons. Then her blouse. Then her skirt. Then her slip. Then her bra. Finally her panties. The nude studies which followed were of surprising delicacy and beauty. There was a vulnerability and sweetness about them which made her proud. It wasn't that they were great art, but plainly Betty had begun to develop a sense of composition, harmony, and balance. Her photographs were not incompetent. Nor was she grotesque. Betty had faced her fear and survived.

Rudyard noticed the change. His wife no longer cowered at gallery openings, nor fell over apologising for herself when serving drinks and hors d'oeuvres to The Inner Circle. "What's come over you?" he asked with a frown one morning when he caught her humming nonsense from some Viennese operetta.

"I'm not ugly," she sang and waltzed to the writing table, unlocked the lower left drawer, and pulled out the manila envelope containing her latest photographs.

"Who took these?" he asked, stunned to see his wife nude for the first time in years.

"I did. No need to be jealous."

"Don't flatter yourself."

Betty returned the photographs to the envelope, and put it in the drawer. "Be as stinky as you like. I'm happy. And I'm meeting Bob downtown for lunch." With that, she collected her coat and sailed out the door, humming those marzipan melodies.

But now Rudyard has taken her photographs and is preparing to show them around the room to the Inner Circle. They are to be a source of hilarity. They are to make her an object of fun. She has been selected as Rudyard's Victim of the Week.

"Those who think my Betty is nothing but a *Hausfrau* have another think coming," Rudyard winks to the crowd. "She's a revelation. Another Yousuf Karsh."

"No, Rudyard! Don't!"

"No need to be modest, my dear. We artists bare our souls. We stand naked before the world."

"Please don't."

"She said 'Don't'," Bob interjects.

"Oh piss off. Who made you Sir Lancelot?" Rudyard jeers. The Inner Circle snickers. "Betty's taken to portraiture. Her own," he continues. "Only now she's embarrassed, labouring under the misconception that art must deal with beauty." He covers his mouth and makes his eyes bulge, like a child caught blurting something naughty. Chuckles from The Inner Circle.

"You're one sick puppy, mister," Lydia shakes her head.

"Well, if it isn't Attila the Hen back from a hard day pillaging civilization. I thought you had an interest in self-portraits. Or do you only fancy self-portraits you can burn?"

Betty remains focused on the photographs in Rudyard's hands. "Rudyard . . . Everyone . . . I beg you . . . Don't . . . Don't."

Rudyard smiles at her, his eyes cold, as he hands the pictures to the artist on his right. "Of course you want us to look at them. Why else would you have taken them?" The photographs are passed in handfuls, devoured by the jackals who begin to whoop, laugh, and comment.

"Please," Betty says, too devastated to grab for them. "Please." But no one listens. She stands immobile, and silently repeats the mantra, "This too shall pass."

"Come on, Betty, it's all in good fun," comes a voice from the crowd. "We're laughing with you, not at you," shouts another.

"Real artists thrive on criticism," cries a third. These words of excuse from Circle members eviscerated within the past month. Misery loves company.

"Besides," Rudyard chortles merrily above the hubbub, "We want to admire your compositions, not your body. One of van Gogh's most famous nudes was Sien Hoornik, the pockmarked whore. If those tired old dugs can stand the light of day, surely yours can too."

"Fucking assholes," Lydia yells. "Bob, let's get out of here."

"Bob isn't going anywhere," says Rudyard with a malicious smile. "Is he?" he adds with a threatening glance at Bob.

"Hey Betty, these aren't bad," one member calls out.

"Not bad at all," Rudyard winks with heavy irony, "if you see art as a function of therapy."

"You betrayed her, you shit!" Bob shouts at Rudyard. "You've all betrayed her." A moment of shocked silence. One doesn't attack Rudyard Gardenia. At least not to his face.

Rudyard is not about to let this aging dropout upstage his show. Without missing a beat, he throws his head back, wrist to forehead, and exclaims, "Alone, lost and abandoned! *Sola, perduta e abbandonata!*"

The Inner Circle knows the cue. They stomp their feet and chant, "Montserrat! Montserrat! Montserrat!" The Great Showman bows with a flourish, pops a gumdrop in his mouth, and heads to the CD player.

This is the capper to Inner Circle festivities, a ritual comic turn relished by those with a taste for blood. If the Victim of the Week is unable to withstand Rudyard's psychic onslaught, The Great Himself favours the assembly with an entertainment: he lip-synchs an aria by one of his favourite opera divas, an aria of woe and tribulation designed to tease the victim back into good humour. The hazing is cathartic, releasing squeals of pity and terror from those lucky enough to have escaped the session intact. Even the victims seem to enjoy it, hyperventilating hysterically, their dilated pupils darting about the faces of the mocking hyenas.

Of course, some victims, like the unfortunate Benny De-buque, lack a sense of humour and run from the premises in search of the nearest razor blade. These were never true artists, however, Rudyard points out. "True artists prefer truth to praise. If I am a hard taskmaster, it is only because I have a passion for excellence, a gift I share with you. If certain former Inner Circle members have been unable to face their inadequacies so be it. Better that they abandon art than sully it." Rudyard calls it culling the herd.

Adrenalin is running high as the Inner Circle prepares for sport. Rudyard presses *Play* and group members wet their lips. The aria selected for their delectation, "*Sola, perduta e abbandonata*," is from *Manon Lescault*. It is one of Rudyard's favourites, as it allows him to impersonate Montserrat Caballé, the goddess of song to whom he bears a passing resemblance.

Lydia is horrified, and moves as one with Bob to Betty's side. The music begins. Bob wraps a protective arm around Betty. Lydia takes her hand. Betty stands rigid, staring straight ahead. She will not crack. She will not give the bastard that satisfaction.

Rudyard takes full benefit of the orchestral introduction. With sweeping gestures, he removes his turban, takes the wig from the bust beside the CD player, and places it like a crown upon his head. Anticipatory giggles, which Rudyard acknowledges with pursed lips and batting eyelids. The prima donna cups her hands, elbows out, and raises them beneath her chins—a winsome effect. And now the diva sings. The right arm extends forward to the heavens, the left sweeps back behind, and the crowd goes wild.

Fanning the excitement is Rudyard's singular animation. Usually when playing Caballé, he stands and delivers at the centre of the room, fulfilling the drama with gesture alone. Tonight, though, his eyes bug and his arms flail as he sends up the diva's passion. The Inner Circle falls about in laughter. He is on his knees, extending his pudgy fingers towards them. As he advances, they back off, egging him on with hoots and hollers.

He rotates in a circle, crawling from one to the next, face ruddy with exertion, tears streaming down his cheeks. This is too wonderful for words.

And now the climax: with one grand movement, Rudyard throws up his arms, as if playing to the rafters, and collapses backwards on the floor. Alone, lost and abandoned indeed! It is a performance for the record books. The Inner Circle erupts with cheers. "Bravo! Bravo! Bravissimo!"

But this was no performance. Rudyard had been enjoying himself thoroughly, exacting an exquisite revenge on his little baggage. Everything was going brilliantly until the first high note. When Rudyard tossed his gaze heavenward, he saw a vision lounging in his chandelier. It wore a billowing white robe with a blue bedsheet insert, had purple ribbons dangling from its hair, and was scratching its head in wonder.

It was, of course, none other than Maria Carlotta. While maintaining her distance from her wilful son, she couldn't resist checking up on the young woman who vexed him. What she saw confused her. Antichrist's vampire appeared to be giving comfort to a woman ridiculed by a man in a wig singing Puccini.

The vision made Rudyard gasp. The swift intake of air dislodged the gumdrop tucked between his right molars and cheek and sent it scuttling down his throat where a muscle spasm wedged it tight. Unable to breathe, he dropped to his knees, extending his arms for help from his protégés, but wherever he turned, all he saw were laughing faces mimicking his wild expressions. He crawled, he flopped across the floor like a walrus, but nowhere could he find relief. He was going to choke to death, damnit, with leering spectators cheering his demise.

It is Lydia who first realizes something is wrong. "The bastard's choking!" she cries as Rudyard prepares to twitch his last. Lydia's not the sort to let someone die, even if it's Rudyard Gardenia. She leaps in the air, yells, "Geronimo!" and lands knees first on his belly, bouncing up and down as if on a trampoline. On the first bounce, the gumdrop shoots from Rudyard's mouth and ricochets off the ceiling.

The room is hushed. Rudyard gets to his feet, shaken. With his wig askew and his muumuu bunched above his waist, revealing hairless Botticelli thighs, it's hard for the room to keep a straight face. "I could have died!" he gasps accusingly. Everyone bites their tongue and tries to think serious thoughts. "I could have died and you did nothing! You stood there and laughed!"

"We didn't know," comes the sheepish reply from assorted artists. "We thought you were kidding."

"KIDDING? DID I LOOK LIKE I WAS KIDDING?" Ringlets bounce indignantly in front of Rudyard's nose, provoking gales of laughter from the corner. "OUT OF MY HOUSE! ALL OF YOU!" he explodes. "YOU'RE NOTHING BUT A PACK OF TALENTLESS HACKS! BE OFF! BEGONE! LET ME NEVER SEE YOUR SORRY FACES AGAIN!" The Inner Circle flees to the safety of the streets and disappears guffawing into the night.

"AND AS FOR YOU," Rudyard screams, wheeling on Bob, "GET OUT! GO BACK TO HAMBURGER HILL WHERE I FOUND YOU! SEE WHO'LL TAKE YOU NOW, YOU TWO-BIT PIMPLY WHORE!"

"Don't worry, Bob." Lydia squeezes his arm. "You're coming home with me."

"Wait till I get my purse," says Betty.

"What do you think you're doing?" Rudyard sneers at her.

"I'm leaving you," Betty says simply. "It's something I should have done years ago. I'll take a hotel for the night and come for my things when I'm settled."

Rudyard is thunderstruck. There is silence as Betty collects her purse and makes her way with Bob and Lydia down the hallway. Rudyard is not about to let her have the last word. "Good riddance," he spits.

Betty stops in her tracks. She turns slowly. Rudyard is amazed to see that she is smiling. He feels a sudden chill as she says, "You know, my pet, tonight is not the end of your humiliation. It is only the end of the beginning. As God is my witness, you will endure such things—what they are I know not—but they shall be the terrors of the earth. When you weep for mercy, there shall be none, and the angels shall dance for joy. By the way, for supper tomorrow, you'll find a meat pie in the freezer." And with that, Betty makes her exit.

"I shall be revenged upon the whole pack of you!" Rudyard sputters to the empty room. Puffing up his chest, he takes a bottle of wine and what's left of the platter of cold cuts and heads upstairs. A nice Jacuzzi and he'll feel better.

Across town, Junior writes Rudyard's name with snake venom on two pieces of paper. He glues snakeskin to the papers, cuts them to the size of his feet, puts them inside his shoes, and heads off for a long evening walk.

A few days later, Betty returns to pack a few suitcases and make a list for the movers. When she opens the front door, she is astonished to find the room as she'd left it. Plastic goblets half-filled with wine dot the floor, bookshelves, piano, and other available surfaces. Next to these, paper plates sit abandoned with their crumpled serviettes and half-eaten hors d'oeuvres. The cold cuts are missing from the table, but the rest of the edibles remain untouched.

She is also aware of an odour, the air heavy with sweating cheeses and devilled eggs gone bad. She opens the sliding door to the garden to let in some air. The lights are on. So is the CD player, still playing the Puccini. She turns it off. What's the story? Did Rudyard just pack up and leave?

A tiny voice whimpers from upstairs. "Hello? Who's there?"

"Rudyard?"

"Betty? Is that you?" comes the pathetic reply. "Help me. Help me." The high squeaky voice reminds her of Vincent Price in *The Fly*.

She heads up the stairs. The voice leads her to the bathroom. She enters and can hardly believe her eyes. Or nose. A bottle of wine and a tray of rotting cold cuts sit untouched at the side of the Jacuzzi. As for Rudyard, he's *in* the Jacuzzi, naked as a jay bird, stuck like a cork in a bottle. His back and butt are glued to the tub by suction; his fleshy arms and thighs, too squashed for leverage. He has obviously been trapped here for the past three days, up to his chins in water.

Would that it were only water. Nature has taken its course, and Rudyard has soiled himself. Wee turds the size of rabbit pellets float beside his ears, cheeks, and belly like little boats docked along the shoreline.

Sensing rescue is at hand, Rudyard stops whining. "Give me a hand," he barks. But Betty just stands there, savouring the image. "Are you deaf, woman?" he shouts.

"Why no, dear," she smiles. "But I'm afraid I'm rather busy at the moment. See you later."

"You can't just leave me here!" he says, his bluster tinged with fear.

"Oh, but I can," Betty says sweetly. "By the time they find you, I imagine you'll be quite the sight. Think of the obituary: 'Canadian Art Critic Found Dead In a Tub Of Excrement.'"

"No! Please, Betty!" Rudyard pleads.

"Don't worry, I won't leave you to die," Betty sings out as she slips down the stairs. Before Rudyard has time to relax she adds, "I'm not that nice."

He hears the front door slam.

Night falls and Betty has not yet returned. Rudyard drifts into a nightmare in which he is trussed up like Saint Sebastian with all the artists he has ever abused shooting paintbrushes into his side. He wakes suddenly to a worse nightmare.

"Surprise!"

Packing the bathroom are the dozen members of The Rudyard Gardenia Survivors Society, as well as Betty, Bob, and Bob's new roommates, Lydia and the Three Ts.

"What the hell do you think you're doing here?" Rudyard demands imperiously. "Get out!" He tries to cover himself but his arms won't move.

"No need to be modest, my dear," Betty chirps. "We artists bare our souls. We stand naked before the world."

"I suppose you're doing this for my benefit?" he spits.

Betty considers. "I wouldn't say benefit."

"So does it have a penis?" asks Tibet.

"That's an excellent question. I never got a real look; it's very good at hiding," says Betty. "In fact, I used to confuse it for a navel. What's your opinion, Bob?"

"Hmm. I always thought it was more like the little nubbin left over when you tie off a balloon."

"Enough," cries Rudyard, outraged.

"Come now, we're not laughing *at* you. We're laughing *with* you," Betty assures him.

"I won't forget this," he glares.

"Well I should certainly hope not," Betty replies. "But just in case, I thought you might like a keepsake. I know I would." She raises her Minolta. "I've a roll of thirty-six. Who'd like a souvenir?"

"No! No photographs!" Rudyard screams in terror.

"But darling, we're not interested in your body. We're interested in photographic compositions. By the by, I recall you asked the Inner Circle if art was the same as therapy. In my view, absolutely. Say cheese!"

Click click

Of course, all the photographs hit the Internet and are eagerly e-mailed and faxed across the continent. The one that ends up on the cover of *Frank Magazine*, and is subsequently printed in the tabloids, features Rudyard with a toilet plunger stuck on top of his head like a dunce cap. The image is a little over the top, but everyone agrees that Betty has earned the right to be excessive.

Still, if Rudyard hopes this horror is the end of his humiliation, he is mistaken. Across town, Junior removes the snakeskin paper from his shoes and, at midnight, places two black candles carved in the shape of a man and a woman one inch from each other and lights them. Instantly, Edgar Beamish is overtaken with a strange compulsion to make a visit he has long avoided.

Coda: Just Desserts

Kitty is hysterical. One week after the fire department removed Rudyard from his Jacuzzi, she is bouncing off the walls of Junior's walk-up. "The dead have risen! It's Emily's doing! I know it! That damned Baptist has sicced God on me! I'm being punished for my sins! I wronged her! I wronged you! Oh, Junior, call the police! Have them take me away! Have them lock me up and throw away the key! Anything to make the visits stop! I beseech you!" She drops to her knees, a supplicant to her son, as if the younger Beamish has influence with the dead, the Almighty, or both.

"Mother, for heaven's sake," says Junior, as Kitty begins to kiss his feet.

"I was sure the sonovabitch would rot in hell. But he's back! And he's making house calls to Caledon!"

"Would you like some pills? I have a few Lithium."

"No! No pills! Never again! Not even Aspirin!"

This is serious. When the weekly drug tests ended, two years after the probate of Edgar's will, Kitty had given up all pretense to being off the pharmaceuticals and sauce. "I'd rather be a good liver than have one," she'd remark to all and sundry, a witticism she remembers hearing in some Acapulco bar. How she got to Mexico in the first place is beyond her, not to mention how she ended up with that man with the three gold teeth who romanced her the night before she woke up without her purse and passport.

Suffice to say, Junior knows that if Kitty refuses drugs he ought to pay attention. He sits on the floor beside her. He holds her trembling hands and listens to her tale.

It happened first about a week ago. She was sitting in the Great Room of her mother's Caledon estate enjoying a few sips of Glenfiddich—"All right, polishing off a mickey, if you must know!" Althea was sitting in the chair opposite, clipping an

imaginary hedge with her imaginary clippers. (Real clippers
had been removed from Althea's range after she'd terrified the
ladies of the local chapter of The Royal Horticultural Society
by attempting to clip a bouquet from the floral patterns on The
Society's upholstered furniture. The screams had intensified
when she'd turned her attentions from the chesterfield to the roses
on Mrs. James Monteith's rather busy spring frock.)

So there was Kitty engrossed in her mother's gardening
wizardry, when all of a sudden the Danderville matriarch delivered herself of the following: "You ought to divorce that man."

"What man?"

"*That* man. The one I can't stand."

"Edgar is dead, mother."

"Dead? Then what's he doing in those rhododendrons?"
Althea tossed her chin toward the wet bar. Kitty rolled her eyes
and looked over her shoulder. There was Edgar, large as life,
hovering over the liquor bottles. Kitty screamed and the ghost
disappeared.

He's returned every day since to haunt her. "It's because of
the will! I cheated his will! Me and Rudyard Gardenia! My
God, Junior, Rudyard Gardenia is my Rasputin!"

So the story comes out. Junior always had doubts about his
mother's weekly drug tests—it didn't make sense that she was
never mobile until four in the afternoon. Now she's confessed,
revealing it was Rudyard who masterminded the clean results.
By helping her cheat the will, Rudyard gained control of Edgar's
fortune, Junior's birthright. He's guilty of fraud against the
Beamish estate to the tune of hundreds of millions of dollars.

Junior consoles his mother, who is now fantasizing a future
in some prison melodrama. "I'll be a jailbird! They'll call me Ma
Beamish. I shall be forced to play poker for cigarettes! To talk
out of the side of my mouth! Oh, and worse! They'll make me
wear that uniform—Dear God, I look so fat in horizontal
stripes!" She pitches herself to the ground. "I swear to you my
precious, I shall throw myself upon the electric fence before I
let the warden have his way with me!"

"Mother, nothing's going to happen to you."

And nothing does. The Crown Attorney wants Gardenia—nothing more, nothing less—and once Kitty and Betty agree to testify in exchange for immunity, the case is a slam-dunk. Following two years of appeals, Rudyard is stripped of the fortune he earned by fraud and takes up residence in the new correctional facility in Guelph, where his warders are the "hicklets" he once had disparaged.

His cellmate is a neanderthal movie buff named Claude who has ripe feet and an aversion to soap. Claude loves cinema, and soon Gardenia is re-enacting the hillbilly scene from *Deliverance* at all hours of the day and night. "Squeal like a pig!" Actually, squealing is the one thing Rudyard doesn't do. He decides to keep his mouth shut, so to speak, when Claude lets drop that his second favourite movie is *The Silence of the Lambs*.

Four years later, Rudyard is released. He heads to the States and drops into obscurity, save for a "Where Are They Now?" feature in the *Toronto Star*, which resurrects his notoriety and reveals in passing that he is now "engaged in the American entertainment industry." The manufacturers of the revised Trivial Pursuit are not constrained by the limits imposed on a family newspaper. At parties across the continent, players cheerfully learn to answer the following question: "What Canadian art critic ended his career wiping down the stalls of a Baltimore peep show?"

The rest is silence.

IX

Inferno

Preparations

Plans for the immolation of the *Self-Portrait* had begun well before Lydia returned to Toronto. In fact, Junior commenced preparations before placing the first advertisement for the lottery and launching its website. Hyperactive to a fault, he poured his energies into the organization necessary to make the event a success, devoting as much attention to its details as a terrier lavishes on the textures of a new bone. Company insiders marvelled at the rapid recovery of their boss who, but a few days prior, had been hospitalized for having a screaming match with the doomed painting.

As always, Junior was assisted by his legal team, led by the intrepid Ernest Hoyt, who had barely recovered from the mauling at the hands of Revenue Canada. Together they phoned, faxed, and e-mailed international promoters in an attempt to sell the rights to showcase the burning. Initial contacts went unreturned, but as ticket sales to the lottery exploded into the stratosphere, the money boys began jumping over themselves to cash in on what promised to be a sleeper bonanza of singular dimension. Soon, competing consortiums bid up the various national rights beyond Junior's wildest imagination.

The basic deal is as follows: Junior contracts to provide live satellite feeds of the event to major arenas and stadiums around the world in exchange for eighty percent of the gate, against a guarantee based on sales at seventy percent capacity; local promoters cover the costs for advertising, security, sales staff, and rental fees, and pocket the remaining profits. A handsome fee is arranged for the merchandising of each product associated with the event.

Junior and his new partners find that the media provide them with more free publicity than they can handle: within two weeks, *Inferno* is sold out at all participating venues.

Commentary grows increasingly vitriolic, hence newsworthy; moreover it unleashes unpredictable, seismic splits across the political, artistic, and social spectra.

Brash young neo-cons realize the worst fears of Cardinal Wichita. They hail The Phoenix Lottery as a brave prototype of ventures to come, urging governments to cut arts funding and pass the savings back to taxpayers, since galleries can raise funds by sponsoring similar torchings. These can be stocked by culling holdings in storage, they enthuse, which will spare the general public any loss to its viewing pleasure. When it is pointed out that only a work of some cachet will create the kind of event for which consumers will be willing to pay, the corporate Visigoths suggest galleries offer up controversial works whose acquisition has raised the public's ire: *Voice of Fire* and other such pricey minimalist works come to mind. "Basically anything that can be created in ten minutes with a roller," writes the acerbic Ezekiel Hammersmith.

Old money, on the other hand, values conservatism's traditional concern with preservation of the status quo. Unlike the young neo-cons, many of these Tories actually have some life experience and prize their educations as more than an investment in networking. They see themselves in the role of latter-day Carnegies and Rockefellers, for whom personal wealth presumes social obligation. To them, the van Gogh's destruction is anathema, as the cultural accoutrements of civilization—galleries, libraries and concert halls—are temples named in their honour. To attack works of art is, therefore, to undermine the social status and public approbation their wealth has bought, not to mention their toehold on immortality.

The left is likewise split. The radical young mock the social pretensions of conservative arts benefactors, seeing their munificence as a PR smokescreen fronting activities that hurt the common weal. To them, the torching kicks ass; it's a stand for the common people over the elites.

The traditional left—educators, librarians, and such types as head up arts organizations—counter with statistics purporting to show that official culture is by no means the preserve of the rich. What galls these arts advocates most is that once again the social argument is being framed so as to pit artists against the poor. "Why are we always asked to choose between funds for the arts and funds for the destitute?" they demand. "Why not ask society to choose between financing tax breaks for the rich and financing the social safety net?" As these are good questions, the media quite naturally ignores them.

Even the arts community cannot be counted on to sing from the same songbook. Installation and conceptual artists, fringe collectives, and recent graduates of art schools across the continent trash the very notion of art preservation. To these hotshots, the notion of "art" and "the eternal" are mutually exclusive, a romantic ideal, passé at best. Art is immediate, not some embodiment of universal timelessness, the latter notion being espoused by critics who presume to dictate what is universal in order to elevate their frequently brainless scribbling to the authority of holy writ. Even official art can't cheat death, they ridicule, noting the disintegrating egg tempera in de Vinci's *Last Supper*. Contemporary art is even more insecure. Six- and seven-figure twentieth-century works made from house paint, mucilage, plastics, string, human waste, and meat by-products are busily decomposing at galleries around the world, unlikely to survive the decade, much less the new millennium.

Other interest groups join the fray. The Anti-Smokers Alliance challenges arts groups to defend their lobbying for renewed cigarette sponsorships in light of their attack on The Phoenix Lottery. "Those bastards won't sacrifice a single painting to save lives, but they'll let human beings die for tobacco blood money," former smoker and ASA poster boy Grant Winslowe wheezes through a tube in his throat.

The collective wimmin 4 wimmin scores a minor press coup. It puts out a press release applauding Junior for sticking it to the systemic forces of patriarchy: "We celebrate the womyn artist who, in solidarity with her sisters, will put the match to yet another deservedly dead white male." However, radical dissidents within the group put out a second press release attacking the first. "By deciding to immolate the work of a dead white male, Junior Beamish is a stooge of the oppressor, blindly accepting van Gogh's place within the racist/sexist/classist/capitalist canon used by the patriarchy to crush diss/cent. A real feminist would have burned a Georgia O'Keeffe."

As time presses relentlessly toward *Inferno*, the media are also full of human interest stories. Case in point: the attempted suicide of Professor Timothy Blakey. In the early 1970s, Blakey was a young man who dreamed of becoming a professional artist. To this end, he emigrated from Idaho to Manhattan, where he found a rent-stabilized closet in Greenwich Village. Manhattan shortly ate his savings, but no matter; Blakey was hired to teach at the New Jersey College of Art, outside Newark, a position that came with a studio and an income with which to support himself until his artistic career took off.

Sadly for Blakey, the market for pictures of table settings featuring bowls of potatoes and other produce had largely disappeared with the seventeenth-century Dutch bourgeoisie. Worse, he found no time to paint as his teaching duties took up all his time, save for his nights which were consumed by depression. Even the city conspired against him: the light which had flooded his walk-up replaced by heavy gloom when the parking lot behind his building made way for a wall of upscale condos. Alone in his dark hole, Blakey rocked back and forth, peering through an old pair of binoculars at the glittering soirées of his new neighbours: the dealers, artists, and taste mavens in whose company he ached to be numbered.

He knew it was not to be. Fame would forever pass him by. He was doomed to live and die a teacher, the one occupation for which he was singularly ill-equipped owing to his tendency to sweat, stammer, and squint in public, the amusement provoked by these ticks being, sadly, the only reason students took his courses. In this unhappy state, rendered worse by the absence of any self-delusion whatsoever, Blakey decided to do himself in. The Phoenix Lottery was the catalyst: he believed he would achieve personal glory if his death was a public protest against the torching of the *Self-Portrait*. He, Timothy Blakey, would die in the defense of art. Yes, his life had been without point, but his death would at least be a footnote in history.

So it was that one week before the immolation, Professor Blakey rode a bus to Toronto, consumed a hearty breakfast, and made his way to the top of the CN Tower, a banner proclaiming, I DIE FOR ART, rolled under his left arm. He waited calmly, reading *The Times*, until the window washers showed up for work. Then he pulled a plastic gun and hijacked their trolley, which was hooked to the rim of the observation deck. As horrified tourists stared through the glass, he wheeled the trolley around until it was high above the new west side miniputt, then turned, unfurled his banner over the trolley's edge, and experienced an overwhelming case of vertigo.

He stood there frozen, gripping the trolley railing as a large crowd materialized out of nowhere and exhorted the good professor to "Go for a hole-in-one!" But all that hurled itself off the top of the tower was Professor Blakey's breakfast. It hit the first tee with a splatter technique worthy of Jackson Pollock, and gave Professor Blakey a new lease on life.

His story earned him international press and profiles on both *Sixty Minutes* and the *PBS Newshour*. Better yet, a series of photographs of the upchuck under the collective title of Blakey's banner, *i die for art*, was exhibited at The Museum of Modern Art, where it received rave reviews and led to a scholarly article in *art///tra* under the title "Intertextual discourse in regurgitation texts: political narrative in Lydia Spark's *Bulimia Sandwich*, Jubal Brown's *Primary Colours*, and Timothy Blakey's *i die for art*." Professor Blakey had been discovered at last and was thereafter happy to squint, stammer, and sweat to the delight of his students until the day he died.

If everyone peripheral to the event is caught up in the media feeding frenzy, the same cannot be said of Lydia Spark. Along with Junior Beamish and company, she remains the calm eye at the centre of the tornado. She has a show to get on, damnit, and has little time to waste on spin doctors and the rest.

Her team is in place. Tibet is negotiating product endorsements and rights to the story, her abrasiveness having already proven itself well-suited to the task. Trixie is juggling requests for interviews, for although the concept of datebooks terrifies her, she can at least be counted on not to scream. Trina is using her flair for recycling and crafts to create the *Inferno* set. And Bob is her liaison with Junior Beamish, putting to use the ease with suits he acquired in his days serving drinks to Rudyard's friends. (Since that awful night at the Inner Circle, he has settled into the Queen West commune and now shares Lydia's mattress, sleeping spoons with her as he did in those faraway days when they were street kids on Carleton.)

Bob has already done Lydia good service. He has negotiated with Junior to change the title of the event from *Inferno* to *Lydia Spark's Inferno!* At first, Lydia had pulled a Canadian, pretending to be embarrassed. She let herself be overruled when Bob pointed out that her future position in the art world would be more secure if people could remember her name: "People are famous for being famous. And who gets famous? Some genius nobody or a no-talent star? Be a star and be talented, there's no stopping you." And about that exclamation mark in the title? "Think *Oklahoma!*" Bob has a genetic weakness for show tunes.

Bob has convinced Junior that Trina's set design is of such complexity and scale as to require an IATSE crew and the rental of The Canadian Opera Company's scenic workshop. It is a set fit for a rock show, and Junior quickly understands why Trina's attempt to build it in the impossibly cramped duplex had members of the commune in fear for their lives.

Trina's design features a stage one-hundred-feet wide by sixty-feet deep dominated by a spiderweb motif. This spiderweb is composed of an intricate backdrop of knotted black rope and twisted garbage bags fifty-feet high and eighty-feet wide, and by a series of oversized rotating flats on either side of the stage. These flats, covered in scrim with a spiderweb design on their upstage side, have three main functions. Lit from behind, the webs are visible, creating, in combo with the spiderweb backdrop, an effect of 3D entrapment. Lit from the front, the webs disappear and the flats become screens for projections of tribal sacrifices through the ages. Finally, when rotating, they create wild shadows, enhancing the otherworldly effect of the lasers, flash pots, light show, and fireworks finale, all of which are to go off at the cathartic moment when the *Self-Portrait* finally bursts into flame.

As for the *Self-Portrait* itself, "the symbol of a culture ensnared by a past which must be destroyed in order for it to rise phoenix-like from the ashes," according to the helpful notes in the souvenir program, it sits on an elevated neon altar immediately upstage of centre. In front of it is a pit from which Lydia will emerge on a hydraulic lift surrounded by a cloud of dry ice.

Both the pit and the painting are surrounded by two wide circular tracks. The inner track is on a revolve; on one section of the revolve, Pigjam, the infamous grunge-rock band, will open the show with a warm-up-cum-overture from their recent CD *Live at the Slaughterhouse*. The outer track is stationary. Steeply raked, it's designed to support The Four Horsemen of the Apocalypse, a.k.a. Trina, Trixie, Tibet, and Bob, in chaps and body paint, as they careen around the stage on rollerblades.

The last element of Trina's set is a large jagged screen composed of shards of mirror. This hangs high above the stage, and will descend in front of the *Self-Portrait* following the warm-up, as Pigjam rotates offstage and Lydia rises on the hydraulic lift. The screen is Bob's contribution, his association with Rudyard having done nothing to dim his fascination with glitter balls. Lydia also appreciates the payoff of having the screen remove the *Self-Portrait* from view during the middle stages of her production. At the climax, when the screen ascends back above the stage, the sudden reappearance of the van Gogh will provide an enormous theatrical charge.

Lydia has overseen the construction of Trina's design, and has adapted her text to maximize the set's scenic possibilities. This text, a New Age hybrid, incorporates a prayer to Isis, a dance for the protection and wisdom of Owl, and channelled prose poems to accompany the aforementioned images projected on the scrims.

Although she has remained calm throughout the production process, Lydia's concentration has been distracted by issues closer to home. Since her return from Mercy Inlet, she's felt a need for family. It must be possible to feel the kind of warmth enjoyed by her friends up north. It can't be too late to go back home, to see her parents, to patch things up. The past is prologue. Bring on the future.

"Well, you may wanna see your folks, but do you think they even care if you're alive?" Tibet asks, fearful and envious lest Lydia answer yes. Her own parents died when Tibet was thirteen, whereupon she had been sent to live with an aunt who kicked her out the day she came home with a shaved head, pierced labia, and a tattoo of dogs humping on her shoulder.

Lydia is afraid of the answer to Tibet's question. "All I know is, when I get up on that stage, I want to feel them with me."

Edgar's Chair

Lydia is not the only one longing for a reunion. From the moment she knelt on the floor picking up cutlery following Lydia's meeting with Cardinal Wichita, Emily Pristable has been in turmoil. It seems that everyone is getting a visit from Edgar except her. Junior, of course, well that's to be expected. But a visit to Kitty? That woman who never gave him a moment's peace—not that he was a saint mind you—and to Althea Danderville? Why it's gotten so total strangers enjoy a haunting over tea, even the Spark girl and that Wichita rascal. It's plain unfair.

So it is that three nights before *Lydia Spark's Inferno!*, Emily Pristable makes her way to Junior's office—Edgar's office, once upon a time. Everyone else has long since gone home. She'll be undisturbed. She pauses at the door. "Edgar? Are you there?" She tries not to breathe. "Edgar?" She enters the office, gently closing the door behind her. "Edgar?" she whispers again. "If you're there, please give me a sign? I want to see you. I need to see you. Please?" Emily listens so hard she can almost hear the dust floating in the air.

"You're still angry with me," she says. "Why did you have to die angry with me? Why? You didn't let me explain. I was wrapping the silk tie I'd bought you to say I was sorry when Junior phoned and said you were dead. Dead. I wouldn't be able to see you anymore. I wouldn't be able to say I was sorry."

Emily finds herself yelling, "I hate you for leaving me like that. Dear God, Edgar, my last memory is of you sitting there with that hurt look in your eyes and me slamming the door. It isn't fair. It just isn't fair. I loved you!"

She catches herself. Has anyone heard? People will think she's crazy. They'll say she's been boozing. Well, she's only had a tiny nip. And it was medicinal.

"You used to tease me. You called me Priss, the Baptist prude," she whispers, making her way to the old leather chair in the corner. It's the one Edgar used to swivel in when he was thinking. That's why Junior never sits in it. No one ever sits in it. Surely she can. Just this once.

"A Baptist prude," she murmurs again, sinking into its embrace. "Well, maybe I don't wear dresses that leave nothing to the imagination. All the same, I don't know too many Baptist prudes who check into the Park Plaza with a married man. All those years I lived in terror I'd bump into somebody from church or the bridge club. I'd go up the elevators and walk through the halls pretending to read, hiding my face with a wide-open *Globe and Mail* two inches in front of my nose."

She strokes the cracked leather armrests. "You thought it was funny. I didn't. It went against everything I believed. But inside those rooms . . . Those were the happiest days of my life."

She breathes deeply. The leather still carries his scent.

"I was always trying to put my foot down. Even after all those years, and at such an age. 'I'm a Baptist,' I'd say. 'I'm not going to die a two-bit whore. It's her or me.' That last time, when you finally said you wouldn't be leaving her ever, not ever, it tore me apart."

Emily grips the armrests. A long silence. She begins to swivel slowly in the chair.

"You always hurt the ones you love," she sings softly. "Shakespeare has nothing on the Mills Brothers." She closes her eyes. The chair rocks her gently. "I'll never understand. After all those years, everything you said, all the times you promised. I stormed out of this office with you looking like a deer caught in the headlights."

Kitty was in rehab, plays a voice in her head. *It would have pushed her over the edge.*

"Kitty had you wrapped around her little finger. All those pills, clinics, and doctors. I never had a chance. All I had was God. Well I love my God, but the Bible doesn't keep you warm at night." Emily catches herself. "I'm sorry, God. I'm sorry—

No, I am not sorry! I am in pain and it isn't fair! He's dead! You killed him and it isn't fair!"

Emily convulses, sobbing. Then, with a force of will, she collects herself, counting the gasps methodically until she's constricted them, organized them into neat little units. A long slow breath. She tucks her feet up under her and closes her eyes. The room begins to spin very gently.

"I went to the funeral. You know that. I sat in the back with the other employees. No one suspected. Nobody knew. Except her. Kitty. '*Qué sera sera*,' she said, like I was a nobody. I wanted to smack her. I wanted to shout, 'Who do you think reminded the big lug about your anniversaries, you stupid drunk? Who do you think bought your Christmas gifts? I wanted to be cruel and ugly and horrible. I wanted her to feel the pain I felt. But mostly I wanted to hold you. I wanted to kiss you goodbye. I couldn't. We were never alone. All I could do was straighten your tie when no one was looking. You were so fussy about your ties. And it was so crooked. I bet Kitty did it for spite."

The chair cradles her, waltzes her gently around the room.

"I miss you so much. I've tried to take care of Junior and keep him safe. He's a good boy. He loves you."

The chair comes to a sudden halt. *Bullshit.*

Emily opens her eyes. What's that? She listens hard, but all she can hear is the ticking of her wristwatch. She smiles nervously. "I can just picture you, looking down at me from some cloud saying 'Bullshit.' You and your language. I'll bet you make Jesus blush."

My son hates me.

"He loves you, Edgar," Emily whispers. "I see him staring at your picture when he thinks no one's watching."

You don't know Junior.

"You don't know Junior," she murmurs, as if from a dream. "You can't like yourself until you know who you are. And how can you know who you are when your father is someone like you. He's just trying to break free, Edgar. That's all. He doesn't mean to hurt you."

Emily realizes the room has started to swim again. She's twirling. She puts her feet firmly on the ground to stop the spinning. "Good Lord, whiskey is a terrible thing." She regains her bearings. "Look at me. I'm babbling away and there's nobody there."

I'm here.

"I'm alone. Still, I'm not complaining. I have a good life."

I miss you, Emily.

She rises from the chair, a little unsteady. "I wish . . . I wish . . . Dear God, you've given me so much, but the one thing I want is the one thing I can't have. I want him. I want him." Emily sinks to her knees and weeps.

But I'm here.

"I want to feel him holding me."

I'm here. I'm here.

"I want him not to be hurt," she weeps. "I want him not to be angry. But I want him to know I'm a human being. I want him to know I feel and hurt and rage and hate and love. I miss him so desperately. Please, God, wherever you are, *if* you are, please let him know that I love him."

I'm here. I know.

"Please let him know."

I love you too. The floorboards creak.

"I'm a proper fool," Emily says wearily, rising to her feet. "I've lived my life for daydreams." She straightens herself, and briskly brushes the tears from her face as if smoothing a difficult eiderdown. "Just an old boozer, that's all I am. As if anyone cares for a Baptist prude."

I care!

But Emily has wandered from the room. Edgar tries to consume the air, to take in her scent, a scent he once took for granted. How to reach her? How to let her know what she meant to him, what she continues to mean?

It hits him clear as day. He must see Wichita.

Home is Where the Heart Is

Obsessed by the idea of reuniting with her parents, Lydia has taken steps to make her dream a reality. Two days before her big night, she's in Mitchell with the Three Ts, fidgeting at a booth in The Kosy Kettle. When Lydia lived here, The Kosy Kettle was the last place on earth she'd have been caught dead in. That's why she's here now. She doesn't want to run into any old friends — "not that I ever had any" — as she settles her nerves before taking the terrifying walk to her parents' home on St. Andrews Street.

The Kosy Kettle is "Where Friends Come to Meet, Greet and Treat," according to the matchbook covers in the Elvis bowl next to the candy kisses by the cash register. Mid-morning it's home to a seniors' coffee klatch, while mid-afternoon it hosts homemakers who've left their little ones napping in the care of older daughters back from school. At suppertime it serves an older crowd the Daily Special: tossed salad with Thousand Island dressing, chicken noodle soup with crackers, a pork chop with Jolly Green Giant peas, corn, mashed potatoes, and a stale bun softened in the microwave. After that, dessert — either rice pudding or the cherry pie that Mayor Herb Francis and The Missus insist on ordering "à la mode," which is about all the French they can handle.

Most celebrities have to put on a disguise in order not to be recognized. Lydia, however, has needed to remove hers. She wears no makeup, her hair is in a bun, and she's dressed in a plain blouse and pleated skirt that Trixie shoplifted from Zellers.

The Ts are also trying to blend in. Acrylic bouffant wigs cover their shaved heads, punk gear is replaced by polka-dot polyester dresses, and, above and beyond the call of duty, they're all in pantyhose — though the hair on Tibet's legs is a bit too thick for her to really carry it off.

Bob, staying behind to deal with last-minute complications, had howled with laughter, watching them struggle with the hose. "My God, Tibet, you're twice the man I'll ever be." She'd whipped a workboot at his head: "Bitch!" "How do you get these things above your knees?" asked Trina, falling about. "Don't ask," Trixie replied, "Mine's scrunched up my crack." The Ts had ended up on the floor in despair. "We look like Burt Bacharach's warm-up act!"

Thus, intentions to the contrary, the Ts are the focus of Kosy Kettle curiosity, as locals sneak peeks at Tibet clicking her tongue piercing, Trixie tapping her toes like Thumper, and Trina sculpting a relief map of Africa with her mashed potatoes. They should never have dropped that acid.

"Jeez, Lyd," Trixie whispers in panic, "This place is so *white*. I mean it's whiter than white. Not just some of it. All of it. I mean, I've never seen so many white people in one place in my whole life."

"Except for the hair," Trina marvels, adding a bit of corn to the Sahara Dessert. "Their hair is so blue! They're like some sort of lost prehistoric tribe out of a *National Geographic* special. The Land of the Blue-Haired White People."

Trixie nods seriously. "Yeah. Like, I thought everybody this old was dead."

"Maybe they are," says Trina.

Trixie attempts to hide behind her Coke Float, terrified that she's surrounded by a convention of rural zombies.

Lydia gets to her feet. "Guys, I need some air. I need to be alone. It's time to see my folks." No sooner said than she is out the door and down Ontario Road, turning at the Sears outlet and walking up St. Andrews Street to the door that had been locked and bolted against her so many years ago.

As she walks, Lydia remembers being little, playing Noah's Ark in the bathtub with a Styrofoam boat and tiny plastic animals that came in special boxes of Cheerios; while she made them swim or saved them from drowning, her mother would sit next to the faucet singing, "Jesus Loves the Little Children," and tickle her back with a scrub brush. At the time, it didn't feel weird, it felt like love.

Love—like on that best of all possible Christmases, when she ran downstairs to find a nativity scene under the tree with an abandoned ball of fluff asleep in the manger. "Can I keep it?" she'd asked wide-eyed, and when her parents snapped the Kodak, she'd held it to her cheek. "Pickles! Pickles!" she squealed, as the waking kitten twitched its nose the way she did whenever she smelled fresh dills.

Lydia smiles. If she later considered her parents freaks, how must they have seen her? She can't have been easy. But that's in the past. Now that she's making a name for herself, her folks can be proud. They can make a fresh start.

With this thought in mind, Lydia arrives at her parents' vinyl-sidinged two-storey home, a tidy affair with a neatly edged cement walkway flanked by beds of petunias. Yews line the front of the house, while the yard is dotted with big-eyed plastic critters from White Rose.

A few other items set the place apart. The fuchsia chiffon curtains and sheers in the living-room window are as frightening as she remembers. So are the large rainbow-coloured wooden butterflies framing the front door. Most striking of all are the two six-by-eight-foot illuminated lawn signs on either side of the walkway. To the left, a bold challenge:

PERCY SPARK INSURANCE CO.
ARE YOU PREPARED TO MEET YOUR MAKER?
ENTER BY THE SIDE DOOR

To the right, a flowery purple script on pink invites one to enter:

!BONNIE'S HOUSE OF HAIR!
!!!DO WE HAVE A 'DO FOR YOU!!!

Needless to say, her parents are not the most popular couple on the block.

Lydia walks up to the house she used to call home, smooths her skirt, takes a deep breath, and knocks on the front door, unaware that back at The Kosy Kettle Constable Brice Hammond has called in reinforcements.

It had started innocently enough. Tibet was getting unbearably hot and itchy in her pantyhose, so she'd wriggled the suckers off under the table. No big deal, she figured. She hadn't counted on Mayor Herb Francis and his Missus. Finishing the Daily Special, Mitchell's First Family was shocked. The Missus knew she had to do something; as the Mayor's wife it was her civic duty. "Well, I must say, Shirl," she observed to the waitress, "some people certainly do like to make a spectacle of themselves."

Tibet took one look at the old snot in the flowered hat and leapt to her feet brandishing a spoon "Bite my trashy ass, granny," she brayed. "We're on our way to The Stratford Festival to get some fuckin' culture, do you mind?"

"AAA!" The Missus screamed. "Do something Herb! She's got cutlery!" Pandemonium.

That's when Constable Hammond sprang into action. Seated in a booth by the front door, he knew this incident was bound to make headlines in *The Stratford Beacon Herald* and he didn't want to mess up. "Emergency situation in The Kosy Kettle," he shouted into his walkie-talkie, bits of half-chewed date square spewing from his mouth.

"Get a grip, pig" Tibet taunted. "Do you know who we are? We're 3Ts Management Inc., entourage of world famous Lydia Spark, who's putting this tight-assed little backwater of yours on the map!"

A community gasp. "Holy Toledo! The Spark girl's in town?"

"You got it, Bub. The bitch is back. So wipe that drool off your face and show some respect!"

Tibet was crowing to an empty room. At word of Lydia's return, Kosy Kettlers had made a beeline to the door for a quick constitutional up St. Andrews Street to see for themselves if their hometown girl really looked the way she did in the papers.

Bonnie Spark is sitting in the living-room rocking chair, feet up on the coffee table, looking over a back issue of *Ladies Home Journal*, while hubby Percy lies on the chesterfield, trouser buttons undone and fly at half-mast, letting his dinner digest. The article that has Bonnie's attention is "The Secret He Doesn't Want You To Know About." She's read it dozens of times and it never ceases to appall her. Apparently over ninety percent of men masturbate—and continue to do so even after marriage! That means nine out of ten elders at Calvary Pentecostal! She tries to imagine which ones fall to temptation, but the images are just too disgusting. A delicious tingle of horror. What about the pastor? Or her Percy?

There is a knock on the door. Percy opens his eyes, and Bonnie quickly turns to a feature on muffins. Percy sighs. "Well aren't you going to answer it?"

"It's Saturday, sweetie. I've been on my feet all day. Could you be a lamb?" Saturday is Bonnie's busiest day. Her salon is full of Baptists and Pentecostals wanting to look their best next morning in church. This is especially true if there's to be a baby dedication, the first step toward a full-dunk baptism. Tomorrow's services feature a dozen such dedications, and Bonnie's been up to her ears in curlers, not to mention high as a kite on hair spray. Now she's crashed. Her shoulders are slumped, her corns are raw, and her lacquered beehive, a wonder of creation that makes her look like a British Beefeater, is listing starboard.

(Bonnie's had her beehive since the late-fifties. She credits it with saving her life. Percy, then her high-school sweetheart, had skidded the Chevy into a ditch one night after a school dance. She wasn't wearing a seat belt and would have gone through the windshield if her beehive hadn't cushioned the impact. "Praise God for my 'do," she rejoiced, and has kept it ever since as a testament to the Lord's mercy.)

A second knock.

With a put-upon grunt, Percy gets to his feet, hoists his trousers, tucks in his shirt, zips, buttons, belches, and pads his way to the front door.

"You're a regular Christian martyr, sweetie." Bonnie calls out with all the good humour she can muster.

"You remember that next time I forget to put the lid down," Percy says. She isn't the only one who's tired, he thinks.

Percy has owned and operated The Percy Spark Insurance Company out of their basement for the past forty-five years. Born and bred in Mitchell, he figured his hometown was a good place to set up shop as he knew the territory and had established personal relationships with many potential clients. Besides, rural Ontario offers ripe pickings for insurance salesmen, what with flash storms that destroy a year's crop, and accidents that kill a man faster than you can spit.

The country also provides opportunities for a God-fearing man like Percy who once hankered to be a preacher. For Percy doesn't just sell for Allstate. After he's signed up a client for life insurance, he follows with a pitch for *after*life insurance. "It doesn't cost a dime and it comes with a written guarantee. That guarantee is called the Holy Bible and it promises life eternal for all who confess Jesus Christ as their personal Lord and Saviour. But wait! There's more! Here in John 14, verse 2, it says, 'In my Father's house are many mansions. I go to prepare a place for you.' You hear that? Jesus is preparing one of them mansions for *you*, Reg. So open your heart! You're in good hands with Allstate, but you're in God's hands with Christ."

This generally plays well along the concession roads of Perth County, where evangelical Protestants urge him to keep up the good work. But while the county has precious few of the Jewish persuasion, and barely a Muslim to shake a stick at, it does have a few Catholics, and on their doorsteps the Word falls on stonier ground.

"Don't heed me. Heed God," Percy cries to doors slammed in his face. "'Thou shalt not make unto thee any graven image.'

Exodus 20, verse 5. Well what do you call them statues? God have mercy on your souls. Amen." And with that, Percy turns on his heel. They can go to hell in a handbasket, he fumes, though he does shed a tear for their innocent babes doomed to roast forever. Ah well, no one can say Percy Spark didn't do his damnedest to make them a crib in Heaven.

Catholics are not Percy's only spiritual trial. The most difficult has been his daughter, Lydia, a tribulation such as would have cracked the faith of Job. She is a walking rebuke to the godly, a fist in the eye of God. How can he hope to convert the heathen when his own seed mocks his claims of joy abounding for those in the arms of the Lord?

"Well, I'll bet you're mighty proud of yourself, young lady," he'd said the night they found her drunk and naked in the garage with Ricky Saunders. "You've broken every one of the Ten Commandments except murder, and you're already hard at work on that one, killing your mother and me."

"Judge not, that ye be not judged," she'd taunted, the only Bible verse she knew by heart and could be counted on to throw in his face every time he attempted to bring her back to the straight and narrow.

"The devil can quote Scripture to suit his purposes."

"So now I'm the devil. Great. You know, you're nuts, the both of you. Everyone at school says so."

"'Blessed are ye when men shall revile you and persecute you and shall say all manner of evil against you falsely for my sake.' Matthew 5, verse 11."

"Oh yeah? Well eat shit and die. Lydia 5, verse 2."

He'd smacked her good and hard for that. Spare the rod and spoil the child. Well, he'd never spared the rod. Leastwise not till she took to calling up the Children's Aid Society, and those damned secular humanists showed up on the doorstep, as if a bunch of government bureaucrats knew two pins about God's will for child rearing.

He and Bonnie had grieved when Lydia ran away, taking comfort as always from the Good Book. "The Lord giveth and the Lord taketh away." For years, they prayed for her safe return. When she finally phoned, they thought it was a blessing from God. Instead, it was another act of spite from a child born to make them suffer. The humiliation of driving up to Toronto only to be confronted by those two abominations fornicating on the front porch, and her tarted up like the Whore of Babylon had torn them apart. But that was nothing compared to this summer. First she's a vampire prancing with the pope on the front page of *The National Eye*. Next, she wins a lottery and taunts God with a mock inferno.

Last week folks caught him crying at Home Depot. He'd gone in to get a new Phillips screwdriver and started blubbering away out of nowhere. Everyone turned away embarrassed. He's closed up shop and stayed inside ever since. No one forgives weakness in a man. Leastwise not around here.

Percy opens the door.

Lydia isn't sure what she expected, but the sight of her father takes her breath away. He's sixty-five but looks eighty, long strands of white hair slicked across his bald scalp. Then there's the paunch, the pants hiked to mid-belly, the cloudy eyes, the liver spots, the turkey neck. Lydia wants to throw herself into his arms, but the screen door stands between them.

"What do you want?"

"It's me!" Lydia says. "Don't you recognize me?"

A pause. "I know who you are."

"Who is it?" her mother calls from the living room.

"Nobody."

"Mom! It's me! Lydia!" she cries out.

A silence. And then—is that the sound of someone weeping?

"You'd best be moving along now," her father says quietly,

"Dad. Mom. I've changed. I've grown up. I'm sorry for all that stuff back then. I want another chance."

"I'm sure you do."

"I'm your daughter!"

"Our daughter is dead. She died many years ago."

The front door is shut in her face.

Lydia stands there, alone, numb, staring at the screen. She can't breathe. Her hands, face, chest tingle. Her knees wobble. "Okay. Fine. Be like that. You think I care? Well I don't. I didn't even want to come here. I just came because . . . because . . ." and the next thing she knows she's in a ball on the stoop, her hands on the cement in front of her. Dry heaves convulse her body; the taste of bile is in her mouth. She has to get out of here. Now. Her eyes are swimming. She wipes her face, smearing tears across the side of her head, and feels the sting on her hands, scraped raw by the cement when she fell. Like a drunk, she staggers to her feet and totters down the walkway.

And then she sees them. Lining both sides of St. Andrews Street. It's as if the entire town of Mitchell has come to see her shamed. They've been waiting for this my whole life, she thinks. Well I won't give them the satisfaction. She pretends she's back in high school with attitude to burn, brazens her way to the centre of the street, and begins to walk the gauntlet back to Ontario Road.

The exercise betrays her. She feels like she really *is* in high school—walking across the cafeteria with everyone staring at her, judging her, trying to zap her on the back of the head with a paper clip. Only this time no one fires anything. It's even worse. They just stand there in silent clumps, staring at her like she's some kind of example.

They're all here, too, the jocks, the cheerleaders, the brainers, the nerds, all of them now turning into what used to be her parents' generation—twenty/thirty something retailers, clerks, plumbers, handymen, secretaries, nurses, and, oh God, there's Suckhole. She's standing with some goof, is it Murray? Is he her husband, and are those her kids? She's lost her figure, but not that smirk, that goddamn smirk, the goddamn bitch.

Suddenly, Lydia breaks into a run. Tears pouring down her cheeks, sobs bursting from her gut, she races back to The Kosy Kettle where the Ts are waiting for her in the car, the interior barely visible through the smoke of a half-dozen joints. She jumps inside and screams, "Drive—DRIVE," and, oh God, she hates this town, this life. If she had a flamethrower she'd raze Mitchell to the ground.

She'll show them. Yes. She'll show them all. She'll torch that goddamn painting, incinerate it good, and then they'll see what she thinks of them. Then they'll be sorry. They'll all be sorry.

That night, Bob gets in late from his meeting with Junior Beamish. The Ts tell him what happened. Tibet blames herself for setting the town on a celebrity hunt. Bob knows she's devastated because for the first time in memory she doesn't swear once.

He goes to Lydia's room, their room. She's facing the wall. He snuggles in behind her. She's pretending to sleep, but the shudders give the game away. Gently, he strokes her hair.

All she can say is, "Why? . . . Why?"

"It's okay," he whispers, kissing the back of her ear. "You're home now."

A Phone Call

Emily has been up for two hours. She's had breakfast, but is still in her housecoat, looking over the Sunday paper before getting ready for church. With one day to go before *Lydia Spark's Inferno!* the paper is full of stories about the lottery and art. The phone rings.

"Who on earth could that be at 7 A.M. on a Sunday," she thinks, a worry popping into her head. "Hello?"

"Ah, Miss Pristable. I hope I didn't get you up."

"I'm afraid that's none of your business." How did Cardinal Wichita get her home number? "The line is a bit funny. Are you calling from Rome?"

"No. From a Concorde. I'll be in Toronto by ten. We need to talk."

"We've nothing to talk about."

"Oh, but we do. I've been speaking to a friend of yours. I know about that night in Varadero."

Lydia Spark's Inferno!

Ten. Nine. Eight. Seven. Six. Five. Four. Three. Two. One.
INFERNO!

Time is a mystery. We anticipate an event for what appears an eternity, then suddenly it's here, and just as suddenly it's history.

So it will be with *Lydia Spark's Inferno!* Or so it will *appear* to be when Lydia stands on the Skydome stage before an overflow crowd of sixty-eight thousand screaming spectators, her blowtorch flaming. The Four Horsemen of the Apocalypse will careen around the stage as Pigjam shatters the speakers, pinwheels whiz sparks, and Lydia turns to face the *Self-Portrait*.

But what we expect is not always what we get!

To date, the biggest shows at Skydome have been the capacity crowds for Billy Graham's Very Last Farewell Crusade and the millennium instalment of Wrestlemania. But *Lydia Spark's Inferno!* puts even these to shame. Indeed, there is nothing to compare it to in the history of stadium events and Pay-TV Mega-Specials.

Hordes of revellers and protesters have built steadily around The Skydome throughout the week leading to The Big Night —The Night To End All Nights. The area from Front Street south to the Lakeshore and from Spadina Avenue to the CN Tower is a virtual tent city, with counterculture groupies dominating the territory to the north and van Gogh loyalists the territory to the south.

Eager to preserve Toronto's reputation as a safe, clean, "world-class city" that works, civic officials have bent over backwards to prevent confrontation between these forces, especially given that their conflict is being played out against the

glare of the international press. Barricades on either side of
Blue Jay Way, as well as the presence of mounted police, have
helped to separate celebrants and protesters, while keeping the
road clear for police cars and/or tanks should the situation
deteriorate.

Swelling the ranks of the city-within-the-city, and providing additional complications for law enforcement, are the
small army of panhandlers and pickpockets who have descended on the area in a practical demonstration of the market
economy at its finest. These have been joined by a proliferation
of street vendors, in addition to a multitude of advocates for the
protection of animals, children, and old growth forests, who
circulate petitions and harangue the crowd over battery-
powered megaphones. Meanwhile, social service agencies are
on hand distributing coffee and condoms, aging Guardian Angels
march about looking important, and a lonely Marxist/Leninist
begs passersby to take a pamphlet.

Naturally, in such an atmosphere, rumours spread like
wildfire: the real Junior Beamish/Cardinal Wichita/Lydia Spark
(pick one) has been kidnapped/has been murdered/died five
years ago in a mysterious car crash (pick one) and is currently
a vegetable/buried alive in Wyoming/about to appear on Oprah
(pick two or more). Other rumours are of more personal
interest, such as: the bald street vendor/the Marxist/Leninist/
the girl in the pink tank-top/that weird guy over there (pick all
four) are CIA agents monitoring this conversation with high-
powered listening devices. Of course, some rumours turn out to
be true: the pickpockets really are selling addresses from stolen
wallets to thieves who are showing up with moving vans at the
homes of people camping out at the tent city.

By Monday evening, as the gates to Skydome open and
ticket holders prepare to flood into their seats, there is a surreal
exhilaration and terror in the air, such as one might expect to
find at the Day of Judgment. Children are being abandoned by
parents who drop them off while they go look for a parking
spot never to return; couples who met at the all-night conga line

are getting married by out-patients from The Clarke Institute impersonating priests; while suburbanites drop acid and run naked in the streets.

The hysteria is so pervasive that no one thinks twice about the navy van with the tinted windows idling a block away from the periphery of the crowd.

Inside Skydome, Lydia, Bob, and the Three Ts have spent the afternoon of the big day on stage, doing dry-runs for the cameras, all too aware that this performance piece can have no second takes. Periodically, the painting has caught their attention. Surveying their rehearsal from its position at centre stage, it is hard to miss; its eyes are incisive and a sardonic twist plays on its lips. This disposition has grown over the course of the day, the *Self-Portrait's* colours appearing ever more vibrant, kinetic, alive even, no doubt a function either of the glare from the lights, the stress of the event, or the performers' intense concentration.

Such concentration is a unique experience for all save Lydia and Bob. It is especially unnerving to the members of Pigjam, whose musical accompaniment will culminate in their new grunge-rock interpretation of *Thus Spake Zarathustra*. Yet despite the focussed tone of the rehearsal, the mood has been far from dour. In fact, it has been bright, festive even, thanks to the antics of the Pigjam drummer, who has performed an infinitely amusing impersonation of a walrus by putting his drumsticks up his nose.

Junior Beamish approaches the stage in his shy, tentative manner and says a few short words which change the emotional dynamic utterly. "We're, uh, opening the house."

They hear an otherworldly roar and turn to see a sweaty mob storming the field in search of their seats. Bob and the Ts are instantly overcome by stage fright, the void in Tibet's stomach worse than the time she bungee jumped off the Bloor Street Viaduct. Nothing has prepared them for the adrenalin rush—not even the sight earlier in the day of their close-ups on the three-by-nine storey Jumbotron above the stage. For a split-second they freeze, then, as one, race for the wings.

Except, that is, for Lydia Spark. She turns for a moment to commune with the *Self-Portrait* which sits on the altar eyeing the arriving audience with cool disdain. Our destinies are one, Lydia thinks, a thought shared by Junior Beamish, who stands beside her. What the *Self-Portrait* thinks by way of reply is anybody's guess. Once coldly amused, it now appears as inscrutable as the Sphinx.

"Break a leg," Junior says to his star.

Lydia smiles seraphically, and floats off, a vision of serenity.

How odd she thinks. I thought I'd be a basket case, but I'm simply numb. If Lydia asked Junior to explain this odd sensation, he'd tell her that, in his experience, she's just having a breakdown, but not to worry because he happens to have a container of Lithium in his pants pocket and tomorrow he'll be happy to introduce her to his psychiatrist, who may be a quack, but can nevertheless write one helluva great prescription.

Junior is in need of one now. All day he's had the feeling that he's being spied on, and not simply by the ushers, technicians, security personnel, and staff. No, this watcher—this presence—is sharp, stealthy, and dangerous. It rustles too. Rustles like the creature he used to hear when he was a little boy alone in his mother's room, certain there was something breathing behind the last rack of silk and velvet dresses in her walk-in closet.

It's nerves, he tells himself, just nerves, as he makes his way to the upper corridor ringing the stadium. At his request, the private viewing rooms off this hall are locked and empty. He knows himself well, and has chosen to watch the spectacle alone with Emily in case he should suffer a spell.

A posted guard provides entry. The door closes behind him. He takes a deep breath, and walks down the corridor towards his room. Suddenly, behind him, the rustling. He stops moving. Whatever is following him stops, too. Slowly Junior turns. The door to one of the rooms he's passed is open; inside, the lights are off.

"Who's there?"

Silence.

Junior has watched a lot of horror movies. Consequently, unlike babysitters who investigate creaky attics only to end up on the wrong end of a chainsaw, he turns and runs like hell.

"What's going on?" asks Emily, looking up from her needle-point as Junior dives into the room and locks the door.

"Something's out there."

"You don't say. Now take a seat, the show's about to start."

"I heard rustling. Like feathers."

Emily rolls her eyes. "Probably some poor seagull that got trapped when they closed the roof to the Dome. Would you like me to investigate?"

"No," says Junior.

At that very moment, the room shakes with an unearthly roar. The crowd rips its lungs out as Pigjam takes to the stage amid lasers and fireworks. The band thrusts its guitars like phallic extensions, wriggles its butts, and launches into its warm-up number, the title track from *Live at the Slaughterhouse*:

> *Live at the slaughterhouse!*
> *Live at the slaughterhouse!*
> *AAAA! AAAA! AAAA! AAAA!*
> *Live at the slaughterhouse!*
> *Live at the slaughterhouse!*
> *AAAA! AAAA! AAAA! AAAA!*

And so forth.

"I believe this is what Mr. Hammerstein used to call an overture," Emily observes over the din, as fans scream the Pigjam lyrics. "Why they appear to know the words by heart, the clever dears." A screech of feedback. Emily grimaces, "Excuse me, but I'm a little too old for this. I'm just going to stretch my legs before Miss Spark makes her entrance." Her eyes twinkle as she sees a flash of concern in Junior's eyes. "Oh, for heaven's sake, Junior," she laughs. "Don't mind me. Unlike you, I'm not cursed with imagination."

And with that, she steps out into the corridor.

Meanwhile, backstage, the feeling is akin to taking off in a jumbo jet filled with white-knuckle fliers. Screaming is beside the point. There's nothing to be done but ride the rush. And what a rush! Judging by the pandemonium, the audience is pumped.

And so are they! Lydia, the Ts, and Bob give each other the thumbs up, followed by a series of high-fives. And another series of high-fives. And another. And it's time. With one minute to go before her entrance, Lydia takes her place on the hydraulic lift under the stage. She is striking in a diaphanous, fire-retardant gown and welder's goggles. The others likewise project bravado in their flourescent chaps, body paint, and rollerblades.

Lydia disappears in a cloud of dry ice as Pigjam launches a heavy metal version of Stravinsky's *Rites of Spring* and begins to rotate offstage. The mirrored curtain descends in front of the *Self-Portrait*, blinding the house with spears of reflected light. The crowd goes wild. It's on its feet as Lydia rises from the depths of the pit on a lift that takes her high above the stage. This is no Grisabella ascending to Kitty Heaven in some tired *Cats* road show—this is LYDIA SPARK, PERFORMANCE ARTIST, CONQUERING THE UNIVERSE!

Lydia rears back her head and emits a primal scream such as surely rent the heavens at the dawn of creation. The fans fall back in their seats and sit mesmerized as she intones an incantation to Isis, Egyptian goddess of fertility, who resurrected her brother Osiris after his unfortunate dismemberment by the evil Set. Lydia is particularly proud of this prayer, delivered in an ancient tongue that came to her whilst channelling the spirit of a dead Saskatchewan farmer. The poor man, driven mad by endless vistas of wheat, had suddenly snapped and ploughed a furrow fifty miles long before dropping dead with his dehydrated oxen in the middle of nowhere. At any rate, there'd been a glitch in the communication and Lydia'd found herself listening to the aforementioned incantation which she subsequently transcribed. As the ancient tongue is unknown, Lydia has thoughtfully provided a translation in the souvenir program.

The ritual complete, the hydraulic lift descends to the stage and the backlights fade out on the oversized spiderweb flats stage left and right. These flats now serve as screens for slides featuring recreations of tribal sacrifices: Aztec priests, unacquainted with the Geneva Convention, hold up still-beating hearts ripped from the breasts of their warrior captives; Mayan youngsters are pitched into the bottomless well at Chichen Itza to satisfy the rain gods; and heretics are burned at the stake by the Spanish Inquisition for the greater glory of God. These and other images bombard the senses as Pigjam turns its musical attention to a heavy-metal version of Mozart's *Requiem* and Lydia performs a free-form dance, imbued with the spirit of Isadora Duncan, seeking guidance and protection from Owl.

And now it's time for the Four Horsemen of the Apocalypse, their body paint and chaps blazing colours designated by The Book Of Revelations: Tibet's in white, Trixie's in red, Trina's in black, and Bob's in green. ("Green makes me look like shit." "Well sorry Bob, but it's in the Bible, so get over it!") They whip around the stage on the raked ramp, circling Lydia who writhes in ecstasy at the promise of a post-Apocalyptic world featuring a culture reborn, baptised with the fires of ancestral atonement.

No! They're circling Lydia who is *supposed* to be writhing in ecstasy at the etcetera. Instead, she's staring into the mid-distance, frozen in horror. "Snap out of it, Lyd!" Tibet screams as she whizzes by. "This is no time for stage fright!"

Lydia can't hear Tibet over Pigjam and the crowd. Even if she could, it wouldn't make a difference, because stage fright has nothing to do with her terror. She is watching a raven the size of a condor, draped in a white sheet with a blue stripe and trailing yards of purple ribbons, extend its wings, flex its talons, and take direct aim for her head. "Putana! Putana! Figlia di putana!" it screeches as its wings flap, sending powerful gusts of warm air through the Dome.

In the moment before impact, Lydia leaps to her left. The raven banks right, ascends with the speed of a kite in a windstorm, and dive-bombs again. Again and again it dives and ascends in a furious series of loop-the-loops as Lydia, dodging desperately for her life, bounces around the stage like a pinball.

"HELP!" she cries. No one does. Not Bob! Not the Ts! Not the audience! What's the matter with them? Don't they care? Don't they know this bird isn't in the show?

"CAN'T YOU SEE IT? CAN'T YOU HEAR IT? CAN'T YOU FEEL IT?" Lydia screams, as Bob and the Ts zip by bewildered.

There's one person in the Dome who knows what's happening. In his private room, face pressed to the window, Junior spots the spectre. But it's not a raven he sees; it's the Pillow Lady. Casting caution to the wind, he flies from the room, races down the corridor, and takes the stairs three at a time. He's got to save Lydia.

There isn't time. She's too exhausted to dodge any longer. "THE BLOWTORCH! THE BLOWTORCH! TOSS ME THE BLOW-TORCH!" she screams into her body mike, as the raven wheels on high.

The audience roars, but Bob and the Ts know she's off script. What the hell, it's her show, they'll do what she says. Bob races to the wings, grabs the blowtorch from the startled stage manager, and throws it to Lydia. She catches it in a rolling dive.

The raven zeroes in for the kill. Lydia fumbles with the knob. The raven smells blood. The valve opens. Out of nowhere, Tibet skates by with a flaring Bic, the gas ignites, the blowtorch shoots a five-foot flame, and the raven screeches a retreat into the ether.

Gasping for breath, happy to be alive, Lydia sees Junior at the lip of the stage. She waves him off, struggling to regain her bearings, no mean feat, as the show is a runaway train. Pigjam, realizing Lydia's lit the blowtorch, takes its cue for the climatic "Thus Spake Zarathustra." The stage manager panics—they've just cut twenty minutes. Frantically, he pages the IATSE crew, who are off on a smoke break, and makes a mental note to fire his agent.

Lydia's brain begins to short-circuit. This isn't how she planned it. But fate is no respecter of persons: it catches us with our pants down more often than in our Sunday best. And so it is that Lydia Spark, surrounded by chaos, prepares to meet her destiny. She stands on the Skydome stage before the overflow crowd, her blowtorch flaming. Bob and the Ts careen around the stage, Pigjam shatters the speakers, and pinwheels whiz sparks as the IATSE boys return, muttering about a job grievance.

"Live in the moment," Lydia thinks, as the mirrored screen shielding the *Self-Portrait* flies up out of sight. She turns.

The moment of truth is now.

But no! The audience gasps as one.

The altar is empty.

The *Self-Portrait* has vanished.

The Mission

W hen Emily Pristable leaves Junior to stretch her legs, it has nothing to do with the musical delights of Pigjam. Rather, she is on a mission: a mission conceived the day prior, as Cardinal Wichita sat on her living-room sofa, smug as a cat with a mouse in its claws.

Wichita had gone to her St. George Street apartment directly after clearing customs. "Varadero. A great many prostitutes. I haven't been for a long time." He stirred his tea. "To Varadero." He smiled. He could see her discomfort, the slight tightening in the muscles around her throat. Good.

"I'm missing church on your account," Emily said. "Now, whatever you came to say, spit it out."

"I've been in contact with your former lover."

"My what?"

Wichita stared her straight in the eye. "Dr. Betts. The Hotel Capri. Five toenails of a rooster."

So it was true. He really *had* been speaking to Edgar.

"My relationship with Mr. Beamish . . ." She took the lace handkerchief from her sleeve, blurted, "Excuse me," and ran to the bathroom. When she returned five minutes later, Wichita was looking out the window. She steadied herself behind her chair. "You mentioned you were speaking to Mr. Beamish," she said carefully.

"Yes." Wichita paused, then in a clear, measured tone: "I can arrange for you to do the same."

Emily gripped the back of the chair.

"But first," and his eyes glittered, "Mr. Beamish requires you to prove your love."

"I beg your pardon?"

"Leave her alone!" Edgar protested, materializing outside the window.

Wichita blew him a kiss. "Mr. Beamish was a lover of art," he continued. "His van Gogh *Self-Portrait* must not be destroyed. You are trusted. You have access to backstage. Tomorrow you will save that painting or he will curse you to your grave."

"He wouldn't!"

"You saw him do business. There's nothing 'your Edgar' wouldn't do to get what he wanted."

Emily faltered.

"No, I'd never hurt you like that," Edgar insisted, horrified at her uncertainty.

"Once the painting is secure," Wichita continued, taunting the ghost with a wink, "I will use the powers vested in me by Mother Church, and the instruction imparted to me at the University of the Sacred Heart, to reunite you with your beloved."

"But Junior . . . The Angel . . ."

"They will be taken care of."

"Why should I believe you?"

"Because you have no choice."

Emily hesitated. And like all who hesitate was lost.

And so, as Emily leaves the Skydome room to stretch her legs, she's torn between her loyalties to father and son. Edgar's spoken to Wichita. That much is certain. And why would he do that if not to save the painting? And saving a painting isn't a sin, is it? It may even be good, and Junior may come to thank me, and we'll all be taken care of, and I'll be with Edgar again, yes? Besides, the time for thinking is past. She's made her decision and, come hell or high water, she'll see it through.

I'll be with you every step of the way, my love. Emily stops and listens. The corridor is empty. Strange.

She makes her way to the north end of the building. She looks through the third-floor windows, over the tent city and out to the corner of Front and Spadina. There she sees the navy van idling. The barricades have done their job; the police have kept the route up Blue Jay Way absolutely clear. Wichita and his bodyguards, two beefy friars, will have no trouble reaching the northwest corner of the Dome, the one corner which never attracts more than a smattering of loiterers.

She takes the cellphone from her purse. "Ladybird to cardinal. I'm flying to the nest. Start the egg-timer."

A quick prayer for forgiveness and she heads downstairs to the heavy metal doors leading backstage. She sees the two crew members responsible for the mirrored curtain having a smoke in the hall. She nods to security. The guard recognizes her from the afternoon's rehearsal and lets her through. "Keep up the good work," Emily nods.

Adjusting to the dim backstage light, Emily can see the *Self-Portrait* on the altar, masked from the audience by the mirrored curtain. To reach it, she will have to go under the raked outside ramp, on which Bob and the Ts are rollerblading, and over the inner revolve, on which Pigjam continues to mount its assault on sanity. She will then take the painting, and before anyone has a chance to react, make her way to the northwest exit, where, on cue, Wichita is to arrive with the van to make the pick-up.

In masterminding the endeavour, Wichita has put his youthful talent for larceny to good use. Nothing has been left to chance. At his insistence Emily had been at rehearsals all day, timed each segment of the show on a stopwatch, and relayed the information to him by cellphone. She is to make the heist early in the program, when the cast won't be thinking about anything but personal survival, and exit backstage as calmly as possible.

"Are you out of your mind?" she said on hearing the plan. "Once I've got it, I've have to run like the dickens!"

"The hell you do," Wichita told her. "People who walk in a clear, direct line don't get asked questions. Especially if they're elderly. I'm surprised more grannies don't take to robbing banks.

They'd have tellers helping them haul the loot to their getaway cars." He'd made Emily laugh despite herself.

In any event, timing is all, and according to her stopwatch, the plan calls for her to wait backstage for the next ten minutes. However, the surprise is on Emily. She has just begun her countdown when she sees Bob in the wings grabbing the blowtorch.

"My God," she thinks, "They've cut twenty minutes! The curtain's going to rise! I've got to go now!"

In a panic, Emily heads for the *Self-Portrait*. She nips under the outside rake, through the bewildered Pigjam—"Excuse me, pardon me, if I could just squeeze through, thank you, dear"— and grabs the painting. Good Lord, the frame is heavy, awkward to boot.

She turns to exit, but Pigjam has massed in front of her.

"I'M GOING TO THROW UP!" she cries. The musicians dive out of her way and she charges through, overturning cymbals and snare drums en route. Now for the getaway. Heart pumping faster than her feet, she reaches the backstage doors. They swing open thanks to the equally panicked IATSE crew racing back to raise the mirrored curtain.

"Thanks, boys," she calls out, scooting between them and flying for the northwest door. She makes it outside. But there's no getaway van. Of course not! Wichita's not expecting her for another ten minutes! Where's the damn cellphone. "Help."

"She's outside!" Wichita screams from his position blocks away. "Boot it!"

The van screeches into action, but it's too late. There may be few loiterers at this corner of the Dome, but it's amazing what a few cries of "Check out the van Gogh!" will do to attract a crowd.

Emily drops the cellphone and turns into a linebacker. She charges back to the Dome, past a slack-jawed guard—"OUT OF MY WAY, SONNY!"—only to be confronted by Bob and the Ts racing her way. They'll be on her in no time. There are stairs going down to her right. She takes them two at a time.

At the landing, a door. She goes through and finds herself in the underground parking garage. Where to now? Oh, to heck with it, there's another door at the opposite side. She runs toward it—it's a wonder she hasn't had a heart attack—with Bob and the Ts, who've somersaulted higgledy-piggledy down the stairs, hot on her tail.

But so is Wichita. He roars down the south-end ramp into the garage. "Seek and ye shall find!"

He blares his horn, but all Emily hears is Tibet screaming: "Say yer prayers, y'old bitch!" Tibet's cry gives Emily the goose she needs to bound through the door opposite and rabbit up the stairs.

As the skaters follow like hounds on a hare, Wichita squeals to a stop. He and the friars leap from the van. "For Santa Maria!" Wichita cries, as they, too, take up the chase.

Exhausted, Emily exits at the first floor. She finds herself returned to the corridor accessing backstage. Only this time she's trapped. A mob outside, the Horsemen behind, and ahead—Lydia with her blowtorch.

Lydia and the Ts converge. Emily's doomed. But a door opens to her left. She runs through like a chicken with its head cut off. It's dark. She sees light. She runs to it—and finds herself onstage in front of sixty-eight thousand disgruntled fans screaming at Junior who's pleading for calm.

Emily's stage debut is more than promising: it's "a revelation" as Rudyard might have said. At the sight of the painting the audience cheers. Junior, surprised by the applause, which he assumes is for him, takes a deep bow. Bent over, he sees Emily running toward him, pursued by Lydia, the Horsemen, and his father overhead.

"Emily, what's got into you? Give me the painting. Please."

"No!" Emily weeps, unable to accept that the game is over, that she has failed Wichita, that she will never see her beloved again. "No!" She runs to the lip of the stage and turns to face her personal Armageddon.

"I want that painting! It's mine!" says Lydia, advancing.

"No!"

"I'm going to burn it. Now."

"Then you'll have to burn me first," Emily confronts her.

Edgar flies to the rescue, invisible to all save Lydia and his son. He raises his arms to block the fire's rage. "You don't exist," the artist laughs in her delirium. "You're just a figment. I'll burn my way right through you!"

The audience is rivetted, staring at the face of the *Self-Portrait* and of the antagonists about to decide its fate. Sixty-eight thousand souls hold their collective breath. The only sound, the harsh roar of the blowtorch facing the old woman.

Lydia opens her mouth again, and from her gut wrench the words of a child. "All my life I've been a failure! All my life I've been a fool! You are not going to take this moment away from me! I will not be laughed at! I will not be destroyed!"

"Lydia! Emily!" Junior cries. He tries to intervene, but is pinned by the Horsemen of the Apocalypse.

Lydia moves forward.

"Security! Security!" Junior screams, but they're out in the corridor wrestling Wichita and the friars to the ground.

He appeals to the crowd. "For the love of God, help me! Do something!" But they drown him out. They're on their feet, cheering. This is what they paid for! The blood lust! The savagery! Their animal passions, so feared by the cardinal, contort mouths, muscles, and eyes.

Emily feels the heat of the flame. Smells it. Shuts her eyes tight and braces.

And then—out of nowhere—impossible, but still—a force sheers through the air with such crisp precision that it appears to materialize as an oversized open razor. It flies to the wings where it hovers, turns, and slices back between Emily and Lydia, twisting in mid-air before the young artist's face.

As it does, a voice reverberates throughout the Dome, shaking the stage and vibrating spectators body and soul. "NO!" it rumbles, "NO! YOU WILL NOT BURN THIS PAINTING! I WILL NOT LET YOU DO THIS TO THEO!"

That, or something very much like it, is what all who witness the event will swear to. Those who do not, will scoff. They will point to hard evidence, the film and videotape recordings, none of which show a razor, nor register so much as a whisper, much less a voice to shake the Dome to its foundations. Talk shows and papers will be filled by professional debunkers, experts on mesmerism, mass hypnosis and other techniques of illusion with which con artists have gulled the credulous since time began.

But the skeptics will never convince the believers. For just as multitudes know in their bones that, against all evidence, the Red Sea once parted and the son of a carpenter was resurrected, so every man, woman, and child who witnessed *Lydia Spark's Inferno!* on stadium Jumbotrons around the world will swear to their graves and on the lives of their children that there *was* a razor that came out of nowhere and rent the air, accompanied by a voice that has haunted their dreams ever after.

They will point to their eyes and their ears as their proof, and to one final element which *is* on film and video. The final overpowering image which now brings them to their knees on this night they will never forget. As the blade twitches inches from Lydia's throat, in the instant before she and Emily also fall to their knees, all present bear witness to a miracle.

The *Self-Portrait* begins to bleed.

First the eyes. Vermilion tears well and spill from green lids, trickling down haggard cheeks, wetting russet beard and soiled shirt. And then the ear. That mangled stump of flesh, raw and exposed, glistens a thick oily red, which slowly begins to ooze and flow, running along the jaw line and tumbling from the chin.

This is no trick of the light.

X

That Night
in
Varadero

Aftermath

Immediately, the *Self-Portrait* is whisked to the BEI vault to await inspection by an independent team of scientific and art experts. This inspection will settle whether the secular stigmata are indeed the "Miracle of the Millennium" as some headlines have it, or merely "Big Burn Bunkum."

In any case, prospects look promising for all. Junior's Lottery has ultimately saved BEI and The Angel. At the same time, the *Self-Portrait* is in one piece and restorable, good news to art lovers, the Vatican, and the Dutch. The evening's miraculous denouement, meantime, has done as much as any burning could to secure Lydia's status as a celebrity and performance artist *extraordinaire*. It has also won Emily the chance to be reunited with the love of her life. Finally—and perhaps most amazingly—all this has been accomplished without a single lawsuit from promoters or spectators, whether because the novelty of the climax offset the absence of destruction, or from their unholy terror of the essence that materialized that razor.

Still, life teaches that no matter how good the weather, there's always one camper who can't see the picnic for the ants. In this case, surprisingly, the grousing comes from none other than Cardinal Giuseppe Agostino Montini Wichita. Maria Carlotta has told him about her airborne activities at the Dome, but instead of praising her exertions, he's launched into a rant about meddling. "Go ahead," she flaps her hands. "Abuse your poor old mother who bore you in love and shame and unbearable agony. We'll just see who helps Mr. Smarty-pants at the next Vatican conclave." With that, she vanishes, taking hurt feelings and the scent of singed feathers with her.

(She takes up residence in Caledon, where she's found a kindred spirit in the dotty Althea Danderville. The two women share a love of gardening, Maria Carlotta from her days at the

convent in Nivoli, Althea from her days with the Royal Horticultural Society. Together they plant acres of invisible flowers.
"Best delphiniums in years," Althea says daily. And Maria Carlotta nods in happy agreement.)

Wichita is hardly downcast at his mother's exit. It means he
can soak in a hot bath without wearing a bathing suit as a precaution against her curiosity. With this in mind, he pours a steaming
tub, adds three capfuls of patchouli oil, uncorks a bottle of wine,
and settles in for an hour or two of prayerful contemplation.

Vincent. Genius of the damned. A man who lived his life in
asylums, misery, and pain. As a young itinerant preacher, he
ministered to miners and whores, and for his troubles was
defrocked by the church. A shame to his family, a scandal to the
faith, he quarrelled with his father and turned to art. Sustained
by his brother, Theo, who played midwife to his work, he failed
again. He heard voices, cut off his ear, and finally took his life.
Nor is that all he took; six months later, Theo died of grief,
leaving a widow and newborn. The brothers were buried beneath
one stone, united in death as in life.

Yet, thinks Wichita, this lottery has been the devil's jest.
For who sought to torch mad Vincent's art? A lunatic genius
who quarrels with his dead father and seeks to save the world's
poor from the power of the mighty. Yes, and an unknown artist,
a scandal to her family, who likewise hears voices and lives a
young life destined for regrets. Two lost souls who seek to
immolate the work of one whose life is a larger mirror of their
own.

And who has served as Vincent's champions? Why, the
father of the lunatic, a businessman of the sort who trod on the
poor to whom Vincent ministered, and of the sort who ignored
Vincent in life, only to make a fortune off him after his death.
Yes, and a prince of the very Church which preaches an
afterlife of hell for suicides like Vincent who cannot bear their
hell on earth.

So here at last is van Gogh's fate: to be attacked by his own
kind and succoured by his tormentors.

Then it strikes Wichita—No!—the final irony belongs to Vincent. The miracle of the weeping painting has redeemed his kindred spirits, the mad genius and young artist. As for those who made his life a misery in this world and the next—Dear God!—Wichita leaps from the tub. He has discovered Satan's trap. The *Self-Portrait*'s salvation is not the godsend it seemed at first blush. Indeed, it holds within it the first step in the destruction of the Church. There is no time to lose.

The pontiff is in bed when Wichita's call is transferred to his room. He is in acute pain. His diverticulitis is acting up, penance for having consumed an entire box of peanut brittle, a gift provided by Cardinal d'Ovidio in celebration of the painting's deliverance. Innocent checks the ornate clock that stands beside his bed, a gift from a Swiss industrialist who'd been granted a papal audience. The numbers have been replaced by carved figurines representing the twelve disciples, with the apostle Paul filling in at twelve for Judas. On the quarter-hour, the figures genuflect; on the hour, they sprout halos and wings; the alarm is the Hallelujah Chorus. According to the clock, it's the middle of the night in Toronto. This means that Wichita is no doubt promoting an enthusiasm.

"Congratulations again," says Innocent into the phone. "You've served us well. Great will be your reward in Heaven and, in the meantime, I'll see what I can do for you on earth."

"With respect, Helmut, celebration is premature."

Oh no. It is going to be one of *those* conversations. Innocent turns the speaker phone on low, flops back on his pillows, and pulls the eiderdown over his head. On the plus side, the incipient migraine will distract him from the pain in his guts.

"Mother Church is in danger," the cardinal begins, launching into his theme without so much as a how-de-do. "Her authority comes from God, revealed through the person and resurrection of Christ the Lord our Saviour. But her power comes through faith."

Innocent pulls the eiderdown off his head. "Please Giuseppe, you're tired. Call me when you've had some rest."

"There's no time for rest! Within days, a team of scientists will be examining the *Self-Portrait*. If we fail to act before then, it will be too late."

Innocent groans. He can't handle both Apocalypse and a migraine. Especially before breakfast.

Wichita, meantime, is a locomotive gathering steam. "Our greatest weapon to convert the heathen and allay doubters has been the power of our miracles. Miracles in the form of stigmata on the brows, hands, and feet of our most fervid believers. Miracles following on prayers to the saints and to their holy bones. And last, but not least, miracles attaching to our sacred objects. The Shroud of Turin. Pieces of the True Cross. Weeping statues of La Vergine and our Lord. Those miracles produce wonder. Awe. And terror of the power of him who sent them. Lose those and we lose the faith. Our Church forebears understood that well, for which alchemists and magicians burned at the stake. If those devil's disciples could turn sand into gold, levitate, and otherwise break the laws of nature established by God, what special power then had Mother Church?"

"Either you're drunk or I'm stupid," Innocent interrupts. "Get to the point."

"This painting is a living miracle. It bleeds. It weeps blood." Wichita pauses. Surely now Innocent will grasp the obvious.

But all the Holy Father can muster is a pitiful, "And?"

"AND?" Wichita bellows. "Once this miracle is certified by science, we can no longer claim God's grace extends to Mother Church alone. Think of it. God working miracles through van Gogh? An apostate Lutheran? A suicide? We can kiss goodbye two thousand years of Church teaching. Kiss goodbye our claim to a monopoly on miracles. Our monopoly on God's truth."

"Calm down, Giuseppe," Innocent pleads. "This 'miracle' will never be certified. The heat of the stage lamps caused condensation, which created odd reflections under the light. Or the blowtorch melted red pigments. Something like that."

"No. This painting is miraculous. I've seen it with my own eyes."

"Well what am I supposed to do about it?" comes the plaintive cry. "I'm only the pope. I'm not God. Miracles are his department."

"What if they aren't? What if the faithful come to believe the miracles which follow their prayers to our saints and sacred objects are luck? The luck of winning a lottery, say."

"Sacrilege, Giuseppe!"

"Our holy relics live by faith; they die by science. The Shroud and fragments of the True Cross will never pass carbon dating, much less common sense. And if our reliquaries are to be believed, Saint Paul had ninety knuckles and Saint Jerome two hundred toes. As for all the self-portraits bestowed by Our Lady during her various visitations—if La Vergine can't draw any better than that, one despairs of culture in the afterlife!"

"Enough, Giuseppe!"

"Wake up, Helmut! What if the only miracle to be proved by science is this painting, its provenance unknown? If it *is* from God, the bad news is he's chosen to reveal himself through secular stigmata, a snub to Mother Church. But if it is *not*—if it is not, the worse news is that the only verifiable miracle on earth is demonic. Then whither the flock? In what power will it believe, if it sees miracles with its eyes instead of its faith?"

"Pray to God, Giuseppe." cries Innocent, alarmed. "The Lord provides."

"And Heaven helps those who help themselves. This painting must never again see the light of day!"

"Giuseppe?"

"We must bury it before it buries us."

Cardinal Wichita isn't the only one burning up the phone lines. Within hours of *Lydia Spark's Inferno!* a call goes through to The Mercy Inlet Diner.

"So, Isaac. It's about your grandmother."

"Is that you, Lydia?"

"Don't change the subject."

"Gramma said I'd be hearing from you. But I thought she meant in a dream or something."

"Isaac. Focus. I did like your grandmother said. I did a dance to Owl. For protection."

"So?"

"So I get attacked by a raven the size of a chesterfield!"

"You weren't hurt, were you?"

"No."

"So you got protected."

"Isaac, I really like you and your grandmother, but right now I am having a bit of a nervous breakdown."

"No kidding. I just saw you on the news. Gramma says to tell you to trust the man in red."

"What? Last month she told me to *beware* the man in red."

"That was last month."

"Are you saying she just makes stuff up?"

"She's pretty old, you know."

"Don't mess with me, Isaac."

"Heck no. Trust the man in red. Hey, if Mom and Dad'll spring for a trip south, would you put me up on your floor? . . . Lydia? . . . Lydia?"

The Deal

The morning after the big show, Emily ushers Wichita into the BEI boardroom. He has come to duel with Junior, Lydia, and their seconds, Ernest Hoyt and Tibet. It is Wichita who has requested the meeting, his agenda unclear but for a mention of a business proposition, the details of which he declined to share over the phone. Presumably this proposition accounts for the small suitcase he's brought with him.

No one present has slept since *Lydia Spark's Inferno!*, least of all Emily, who is eager to conclude her own business arrangements with the cardinal. After rolling in a tea service loaded with sandwiches, beverages, and petits fours, she sits to the left of Ernest and Junior, to whom her disloyalty the other evening has been quite forgiven due to the love between them, not to mention the miracle that followed. Lydia and Tibet are seated to the right of the BEI brigade, while Wichita stands facing the lot of them. Watching unobtrusively, a speck on the Monet by the door, is Edgar Beamish.

Wichita takes his time. He stares deep into each set of baggy eyes. They stare back, pupils bloodshot, irises blazing with various combinations of adrenalin, caffeine, and uppers — the eyes resemble those of demons as rendered by eighteenth-century monks with a taste for Gothic fiction.

"I trust my news will be as happy as it is brief," he begins at last. "I have been in contact with Rome. As a favour, His Holiness would like to acquire the van Gogh *Self-Portrait* for the Vatican collection. Clearly, the painting has done all it can for you. In its present damaged state, its value is in doubt."

"Depending on the scientific evaluation," Junior counters. "As soon as independent experts confirm what we all know, there's no telling how high its price may go. I myself might choose to keep it for display. It'd make a wonderful shrine to

The Angel, don't you think? I understand the gate for such exhibits can be extraordinary."

Wichita shivers, his worst fears realized. What he forgets is that Junior has Beamish in his genes: he's bluffing to raise the ante. With the painting terrifying him half to death, Junior wishes himself well and truly rid of it.

Of this, Tibet is unaware. "Not so fast there, Mister B. Heretofore, inasmuch as, notwithstanding, and as for the afore-mentioned etcetera, my client here has a ticket giving her the right to torch your painting. Last night didn't end that right. It just delayed the execution."

"You want me back on that stage with a blowtorch? No way!" Lydia protests. "I was attacked by a raven! A psycho poltergeist held a razor at my throat. I'd have to be crazy!"

"Shut up, will ya? How can I be your agent if you make me look stupid?"

"I say we listen to the angakoq. Trust the man in red."

"Fine then. Listen to your damn angakoq. I quit."

"Don't be like that, Tibet. Jeez."

Delighted that the opposition is in disarray, Wichita makes an obvious point. "Naturally, if you want to waste your fortunes and lives in complex litigation, far be it for me to intervene. Like-wise, if you wish to tempt a spirit vexed by disrespect, I shall happily sit on the sidelines until called to administer last rites."

His audience is suddenly contrite. "As I thought," Wichita resumes. "In order to acquire the van Gogh from Mr. Beamish, the Holy See is prepared to make a one hundred million dollar charitable donation to The Angel as an ecumenical gesture to honour good works wherever found. This is contingent on Ms. Spark waiving her rights to the painting's future, for which the Holy See is prepared to give her fifty million dollars with which to finance The Lydia Spark Foundation, a private arts organi-zation to underwrite the work of young artists, to be adminis-tered as Ms. Spark sees fit."

While all know contracts require due deliberation, Junior is so keen to get rid of his father's painting, Lydia so terrified of its power, and Ernest and Tibet so boggled by the numbers, they all instantly yell, "AGREED!"

Wichita promptly opens his suitcase and proffers certified cheques drawn on The Vatican Bank, as well as contracts, drafted in Rome and faxed at dawn. Cocky bastard, thinks Junior. While the recipients of the Holy See's largesse review the fine print, Emily retrieves the *Self-Portrait* from the vault, blood newly congealed, and lays it on the glass coffee table in the centre of the room.

"Shall I get some wrapping paper?" she asks Wichita. "I think there's some in the bottom of my desk."

"A fine thought," Wichita replies, oozing goodwill as he finishes overseeing the signing of the documents. "However, with your permission, I should first like to conduct an exorcism."

"What?" from all corners, including a suddenly nervous Edgar.

"This painting is possessed. You hardly think I'm about to step on a plane with it, do you? I've no wish to revisit last evening at sixty thousand feet over the Atlantic."

And so it is that the sleep-deprived company prepare to witness their second unique performance in less than twenty hours: an exorcism conducted by none other than Cardinal Giuseppe Agostino Montini Wichita, Cardinal Deacon, titular Bishop of Tangiers, star of the Curial firmament and future pope and tabloid cover boy.

From his suitcase, Wichita takes nine white candles representing the Holy Trinity thrice, and places them on the floor, evenly, in a circle around the painting. Next, he takes a piece of chalk and connects the points, drawing lines on the carpet so that they form three overlapping triangles. This accomplished, he withdraws incense to cover the almost certain smell of sulphur, a bottle of holy water, a small fire extinguisher to handle conflagrations, and a well-thumbed Bible, charred round the edges from exorcisms past.

"I think that about does it," he says, running over his checklist. He lights the candles. "Now if you could all stand back, we'll open with the Lord's prayer, follow with the ritual of exorcism, and that should be it. It's all rather *pro forma*, really."

"Aren't you forgetting something?" Emily blurts out.

"I beg your pardon?"

"You know perfectly well," Edgar interjects, assuming human size and startling Lydia and his son.

Emily looks expectantly to Wichita. "You said if I saved the painting . . ." She's certain her reminder has nudged his memory. But the cardinal stares right through her. There's no more time for games. She swallows her pride, takes a deep breath and says, "You said if I saved the painting you'd arrange something for me."

"I'm sorry. I have the power to exorcise spirits," Wichita says, "not to manifest them."

"But you promised."

"I needed your help," the cardinal continues evenly. "Look to your soul. It holds the key. Sins hidden breed guilt, the veil separating us from peace, grace, and redemption."

If Wichita has more to say, Emily doesn't hear it. She runs from the room in tears followed by the Beamishes, father and son. At Junior's office she flies to Edgar's chair, collapses into it, and sobs uncontrollably. "Oh, Edgar, Edgar. I tried so hard. Forgive me. Please."

"Emily, what is it?" Junior says, kneeling beside her.

She tousles Junior's hair and looks away. He has Edgar's look. And here in this chair, she feels Edgar's spirit so near. Cradling her. If only she could find the words. If only . . .

"What is it?" Junior asks again. "Please."

"Tell him," Edgar murmurs. "Tell him from the beginning."

And Emily does.

Emily's Tale

I met your father in Havana in 1953. I was eighteen. Cuba was the end of the road for my father and me. He used to be pastor at First Baptist in Goderich. Then came the war. He went overseas as an army chaplain in 1940. Shortly after, I discovered I had an "Uncle" Ron, who showed up to do odd jobs and ended up staying in my mother's room, as she needed comforting, being so afraid of what my poor father must be enduring over in Europe.

Shortly after Uncle Ron moved in, the folks at First Baptist kicked us out of the manse, and we moved into a carriage house on a farm near town where Uncle Ron got work as a labourer. It was a lonely time. Mostly I just stayed around the farm, reading, playing with the cows, and waiting for father to come home.

He did, eventually. There were such tears and a fight that only ended when the police arrived. Father said the folks at First Baptist wouldn't have him anymore, and we'd have to leave town, him and me; mother and her damned whoremonger could go fornicate in hell.

We went from town to town, but the rumours always followed, ever bigger and juicer, and within months it would be time to move on. I swear, if Christians loved the Lord as much as they do gossip, the devil would have to close up shop.

In late spring 1953, my father read an article in *The Mission* about a Baptist teacher, Frank País from Santiago de Cuba. He was putting out a call for missionaries to come spread the gospel on the island. Apparently this fellow Batista had turned it into the devil's own playpen. Well, my father never took much mind of politics. All he knew was that nobody in Cuba would know about our family's shame. So down we went.

Mr. País told father he could do the most good in Havana. He sent a letter of reference for us to some friends, Abel

Santamaría and his sister Haydée, and they got us rooms in their apartment building, 164 Calle 25 by Calle O. Our place was perfectly situated to serve God, right in the heart of the Vedado district, chockablock with hotels, high-rises, casinos, and whorehouses. Why, you couldn't spit without hitting sin, or so it seemed to me, a slip of a girl who'd not had a date nor seen any town grander than Owen Sound.

Abel and Haydée were kind enough to invite us up for suppers twice a week as we didn't know a soul, and generous enough to speak English, which I'm afraid we Canadians and Americans have a habit of taking as our right. They also introduced us to their friends, professional people mostly, including a young lawyer with a beard whose eyes had a habit of making me feel undressed.

They say he's going places, father told me.

No doubt, I replied. I'm afraid to think of the places he's already been. I was such a priss. Like all puritans, it was only because I feared where my own feelings might lead if not kept on a short leash. As father used to say, tell me what a pastor preaches against most often and I'll tell you his private sin.

Over time, our visits with the Santamarías decreased as theirs with the young lawyer grew. By now, I knew his name was Fidel and that he was very bright and an outrageous flirt. I hate tobacco, but I confess my heart skips a beat when I think of how he used to smoke his cigar! Anyhow, Abel and Fidel soon dropped out of sight, off on business, word was, but father and I kept checking in on Haydée. Until July. That's when Abel turned up dead in Santiago de Cuba, my father was murdered, and I found myself trapped.

But I'm getting ahead of myself.

After settling in, Father set up an outdoor soup kitchen in Parque Maceo, and I took to handing out Bible tracts outside the big hotels. I especially loved witnessing at the Capri and the Riviera because that's where the mobsters were. A pretty glamorous locale for missionary work. Now I've never been to missionary school, but if I was a teacher at one of those places, the first lesson I'd give my students would be to get themselves a comfortable pair of shoes, because there's nothing worse than walking around handing out tracts to a bunch of people who look at you like you're crazy, unless it's doing it with sore feet. Trust me. Sore feet were my undoing.

The particular day that changed my life, I was outside the Capri and my feet were hurting so bad I decided to have a sit-down in the hotel lobby. The staff all knew me from the side-walk, and in no way did they want a Baptist missionary pestering their clients. So before I knew it, they were on me like jam on toast. They said if I wanted a seat, I'd have to buy a drink in the bar, sure that I'd rather run like the blazes than to do such a thing. But I surprised them. Fine, I said, and wheeled my shopping cart full of tracts into the lounge, where I plunked myself down and ordered a lemonade.

I caused a bit of a stir. But nothing like what I caused when it came time to pay. I reached for my purse and it was gone! I'd been robbed. I was horrified, sure that I'd be arrested and have my face plastered on the cover of those crime magazines: "Baptist Girl Busted In Mob Bar."

Well I started to cry. Next thing I knew, the handsomest man in the world was sitting right beside me, putting his arm around me, handing me a hankie, saying, that it was okay, that he'd taken care of it.

And that was how I met your father.

Lord but he scared the life out of me. Twenty-seven, don't you know, and full of piss and vinegar; he had me all atingle. Thank you thank you thank you, I babbled, and ran out of that place as fast as my legs would carry me, sure I'd escaped hell by the skin of my teeth.

Haven't you forgotten something? he called after me on the sidewalk. And there he was with my shopping cart.

I thanked him again, and asked him not to think badly of me, I'd never been in a bar before.

Then no wonder we haven't met, he replied, cocky as all get-out, and introduced himself

Out of courtesy, I did the same. He had one devil of a smile and he was giving me that look I got from Fidel. I got so flustered I just mumbled goodbye before skedaddling home, kicking myself for looking the fool.

I saw him every day after that. And every day it'd be the same. He'd ask if he could buy me an ice cream, and I'd say, no, thank you very much. At first I thought it was coincidence, him bumping into me, because I kept changing where I'd witness in order to avoid him. Finally I realized he was searching me out.

I'll thank you to stop following me, I said, the next time I saw him.

How are you supposed to win converts for the Lord if you won't talk to sinners like me? he laughed.

I rather think you've a mind to be converting me, I said, and to something quite ungodly at that.

Well, he said he was sorry, and that I was quite right to look out for the likes of him because he was a scoundrel. And the way he said it, well, he was so charming about how dreadful he was that my heart just melted, even though I'd a good idea he'd stolen the line from a movie. All right, I said, and allowed that he could buy me an ice cream, just this once.

We met daily after that, one o'clock at Coppelia's. He'd have a double scoop of chocolate and I'd have butterscotch ripple. He was a perfect gentleman. Never tried to take advantage. Never made an improper suggestion.

Then one day, out of nowhere, he asked if I could type. I said, a little.

Perfect, he replied. How'd you like to be my secretary?

I didn't know what to think. Father and I were living pretty hand to mouth on a pittance from the church missionary fund, so the money would certainly come in handy. Still, as a Baptist, I knew all about businessmen and their secretaries.

I'd have to talk it over with my father, I said.

And I did, explaining to him how I'd still be living at home and doing church business at night, so there'd be nothing for him to worry about. Also, in my new situation I'd be able to provide a moral example and save souls within the temples of Mammon. And best of all, I pointed out that my new income could be used to serve God. Father was none too happy, but it solved some of our immediate difficulties, so he gave his blessing.

Of course, I knew Edgar was married. Your mother used to always be dropping by the office, checking up on him. I couldn't blame her. He had quite the reputation.

So you're the new girl, she said, the first time she laid eyes on me. Edgar tells me you're a Baptist. Good. His last secretary was a slut.

I went beet red, but Edgar made a motion indicating she was drunk, so I just said I was sure I didn't know what she meant.

Naturally, she said, and waltzed out the door.

Edgar gave a weary shrug and I went back to my typing. But, oh, I was cross. Here she was married to a handsome, wonderful man, and yet she was getting drunk and embarrassing him in front of his colleagues. Well! If I was ever lucky enough to find someone like Edgar I'd treat him properly.

That night when he asked me out for dinner, of course I said yes. He needed someone who'd listen. Who'd care. And didn't God put us on this earth to comfort the afflicted? We ended up in a hotel room the company held on permanent reserve for out-of-town guests. It was so we could be alone and talk without fear of anyone listening in. We'd no thoughts of hanky-panky. Really. Or so I convinced myself.

He talked a bit about his marriage, his betrayals of Kitty, his worthlessness. And I told him how it wasn't true, how he wasn't worthless, how God redeemed lives and had a plan for him even if he couldn't see it.

He laughed. How could I believe in God? he asked me.

How could I not? I replied.

Because God is for dummies, he said, just superstitious crap.

So I asked, if he didn't fancy superstition, why did he carry a lucky rabbit's foot? I had him there. We won't know for sure if there's a God until we're dead, I went on, but in the meantime, it makes me feel good to believe I've a Lord who treasures and cares for me like a loving father.

A loving father? What's that? he snorted. He said his own had tried to kill him.

I wasn't prepared for that. Indeed, I was so shocked at the boldness of it I didn't know whether to laugh or cry. Then think of God as a loving mother, I improvised.

He turned bitter at that. At least she hadn't tried to kill him, he said. As a matter of fact, he'd killed *her*. In childbirth. So where was my loving God?

What was I to say? Or do? All I knew was that all of a sudden my arms were around him, and he was weeping, and, before we knew it, our story was the same as millions of others who end up in one situation after starting out in quite another.

My father was waiting up when I got home. I told him I'd been working late. He didn't say anything. He knew. That silence was more than I could bear. I was awake all night, filled with guilt. Remorse. The next day I phoned the office and asked to speak to Edgar. As soon as he came on the line he started apologizing. I told him there was nothing to be sorry about, that these things happened, just not to me, and that I wouldn't be in to work again. That he musn't try to see me.

I hung up without giving him a chance to get a word in edgewise. I wept uncontrollably for days. That's the end of it, I thought. Of course it wasn't. Life is so unfair: couples everywhere try for children without success, while others get pregnant fresh out of the gate.

When I told my father, he began screaming at me about "Eve's curse," and how his harlot wife had ruined his work for God in Canada; he was damned if he'd let his harlot daughter do the same to him here. Then he kicked me out. It was the last I ever saw him or heard his voice.

I wandered the streets not knowing what to do, carrying an overnight bag, a change of clothes, a toothbrush, and five dollars. Next thing I knew I was on Edgar's doorstep, hysterical. He heard my story in the vestibule.

Kitty lurched into the entryway. Edgar had to remind her who I was. Oh yes, she sniffed, the Baptist creature who can't spell. Edgar told her I was pregnant and that my boyfriend had run off.

Did he now, Kitty growled. She turned on her heel and called the maid. Nita, she said, show our Baptist friend the guest room, would you dear, then pour Edgar and me some Scotch in the den. Leave the bottle out.

I must say, Kitty had style. Edgar, on the other hand, was a blithering idiot. Like a lot of men, he was such a stranger to his emotions that he frequently forgot what they were. In times of personal crisis he could be counted on to say one thing when feeling quite another. The next morning, he offered to leave Kitty and run away with me, if you can imagine.

And end up on the streets? I said. What would become of us and our child then? I know you love me, Edgar. And I love you. But if we ran off together, how long before you'd resent me and the baby for ruining your life?

He swore he'd never resent me, but when all is said and done he was only human.

Anyhow, I said, she'll never give you a divorce.

I was right, but for the wrong reasons. I thought she'd hold on out of spite, but, as I was to learn, Kitty was a pragmatist. Leaving Edgar would mean returning to Caledon, where she'd face a lifelong I-told-you-so from her mother. Besides, the scandal would scotch her social standing.

Naturally, there'll be no divorce, it isn't done, Althea announced first thing when she and your grampa arrived two days later for The Drawing Room Summit. Your grampa, he might as well have stayed home in Caledon. Only opened his mouth once to say hello. Button it, Althea ordered, sailing into the drawing-room. From then on he didn't let out a peep.

Edgar and I had our laughs about that summit later, but it was no joke at the time, because, while divorce wasn't done, other things were, if you knew the right people. Althea informed us there was a Dr. Betts in Miami. Very discreet. He'd see me that Wednesday, and the business would be over with. She gave me his card, a plane ticket, and fifty dollars to cover a hotel for the night and a new dress.

I didn't know what to think, where to look. I'm a Baptist! was all I could say.

Yes, she replied, and I'm a Danderville and you will do as I say.

Edgar told her to leave me alone.

Good advice, she shot back. Too bad you didn't take it.

Junior, if what happened then happened today, I honestly don't know what I'd do. That's why, in my heart, I've never been able to judge these things. All I know is that it was the fifties, and I had my pride. I'll thank you not to make my decisions for me, Mrs. Danderville, I said. I'm having the baby. As I heard the words come out of my mouth, I was sure I'd gone crazy. But, oh, it was worth it to see the look on her face. I don't think any- one had said no to Althea in years.

How much do you want? she said at last.

Good heavens, here we were negotiating and I had no idea what I wanted. I'm not going to let my baby starve, was all I could think to say.

Cute, Althea spat, you've fucked a little blackmailer, Edgar. They always bring up "the baby" to front their schemes. And rest assured, the baby's needs will never stop growing.

As a matter of fact, Mother, Kitty interrupted, Edgar and I are going to adopt the child.

If Edgar and I were floored, Althea was sucker-punched. Her knees buckled, and it took a few gasps before she could splutter, You're doing nothing of the kind!

Why not? asked Kitty. She said she wouldn't be the first wife to raise her husband's indiscretion, just ask Aunt Caroline. Besides, she wanted a family, and her plumbing didn't work.

I've often wondered what made your mother speak up. Did she think it would win your father's love? Or keep him closer to home? Did she want to defy your granny? Or have a family? Was it the liquor talking? She never said and I never asked. All

I know is, it was an act of kindness I have always tried to remember whenever I've been tempted to unkind thoughts.

For a moment after she spoke, time stood still. Althea was speechless. So was your grampa, though that went without saying. I could tell Edgar wanted to keep our child. He looked at me to see if I approved. And I thought, if I say no, my baby will grow up poor and a bastard. If I say yes, it will have a good name and all the advantages money can buy.

So I said yes, but I wanted to see the child as it grew up. I didn't want to be a stranger to it.

Kitty said that was impossible; my presence couldn't be explained.

It wouldn't be a problem if she was my secretary, Edgar volunteered.

Kitty balked. She was not about to let her husband's mistress be a fixture in her home.

I said I wasn't his mistress, how it was only ever the one time, and that I would carry the sin with me all the days of my life.

Althea snatched the moment. Rehire the girl, she said, and put it in her contract that should she ever reveal her identity as the child's mother, she'll be fired, lose all visitation rights, and expose herself to serious litigation.

Kitty and I were sent to Varadero to hole up at Xanadu. It was a bit like being in prison, but of course it was the best way to keep things hidden. Only the servants knew, but they only talked amongst themselves, and in Spanish at that, which meant as far as society was concerned the truth didn't exist. In such close quarters Kitty and I developed a curious relationship. There was always a rivalry, but also an accommodation. We were like a dog and cat who find themselves stuck with the same human. Or like a father and son trapped in the same family.

I must say, Kitty was very kind when word came about my father. I'd missed the funeral by several months, as it turned out; no one at the apartment building knew where to find me. By the time they did, his body had been flown back to Canada for burial in Goderich.

It seems Abel and Fidel had indeed left Havana on business. Very serious business. July 26th they'd led an attack on the Moncado Barracks outside Santiago de Cuba. Abel had held the nearby hospital with a handful of others. Mr. Castro's group had been spotted by a patrol and their assault collapsed in disaster. He and a few others fled. Of those captured, the lucky ones were butchered on the spot. The others, like Abel, were tortured to death.

The next night Batista's thugs showed up at the apartment building at Calle 25 and Calle O. They broke into the Santamaría's flat and trashed the place, looking for documents. Downstairs, my father heard the kerfuffle. Everyone else knew enough to sit tight, but he ran up, sure that they were thieves. When they said they were with the government, he demanded to see their papers. They shot him through the heart. The official report said he was killed by Communists. No one argued.

A few months later you were born.

Exorcism

Junior's been listening to Emily's story as if in a dream. If he pinches himself, surely he'll wake up. But Emily and his father are peering into his face with expressions so intent that he suddenly realizes no amount of pinching will wake him from the reality he used to pray for.

"Emily. Mom."

She throws her arms around him. "I thought I'd take that secret with me to my grave," she weeps. "It never seemed the right time to tell. I was afraid to say anything before you were of age and by then, well, life drifts along, doesn't it? Soon the present was the past and the future the present until here we were, me old and you middle-aged. 'Why risk what we have?' I thought. 'Be content.' And I was, until along came this lottery, our lives turned inside out, you asked, and I thought, 'Tell the truth, Emily. Let the chips fall where they may.'"

"Did you love my father?"

"Oh yes." She laughs. "That made him so unhappy."

"I felt so guilty," Edgar says.

"He did some terrible things, but I refused to let him push me away. 'How can you love me? It's cruel,' he'd cry. 'I can't live up to your expectations.'"

"I don't deserve her, even now," Edgar whispers. "That's why we're apart. It's my punishment."

"Your father . . . your father felt a need to be punished for his sins. Some people find their punishment in God. Others in life. Or with folks like Millie Gingrich. Pain is a lot like love that way. Sad, isn't it? That's why I found him so easy to forgive. Under all the bravado he was a little lost boy."

"A little lost boy who did real damage," says Junior.

"And haven't you in your time?" She watches him shift uneasily. "You've settled his accounts with the world, and more power to you. But if Edgar never played the saint, he some-times acted one. They called him a crook, and worse, when those duPont heirlooms turned up on the Canadian black market. That scandal even made his obituaries. You yourself threw it in his face, yes, you did, I heard you. Well, your father wasn't a thief, nor did he finger the one who was."

"Let it be," says Edgar.

"It may be over and done with, but I won't let it be. Not now," Emily continues, an echo rattling through her brain. "Today we set the record straight. The one who stole those heirlooms was your Granny Danderville."

"You're kidding!"

"Fingers light as popcorn. I saw her lift two items and put them in her suitcase. I told Edgar, he told Kitty, and Kitty put them back in their place without saying a word. She'll fancy something else, I thought. Sure enough, back in Caledon your grampa got a visit from the RCMP. Right off he recognized the items they described as the new additions to Althea's jewellery collection. After they left, he grilled her. She said she couldn't remember where the pieces came from, she must have picked them up at some store in Havana. Well, Henry calls Edgar. He can't have the jewellery in his house, but he can't return it either; the theft is in the papers and Interpol and the RCMP are on the case. So Edgar did him a favour."

"I gave him the name of a reliable fence," Edgar says. "Henry left the items in a locker at Union Station. No prints. No evidence. No case."

"He saved Althea's neck, Henry's too. And he never said a word. Some thanks he got. From his own son, too."

They sit in silence, the three of them. Emily puts her hand on Junior's shoulder.

"Junior," Edgar says, "please tell your mother I . . . I . . ." He stops, unable to say the words.

A pause. And then Junior says them for him. "Emily. Mom . . . Dad says he loves you."

"He's here?"

Junior nods.

Emily closes her eyes, whispering the words back. Edgar kisses her gently on the forehead.

"I love you: the three hardest words in the language," she says at last. "So hard that even two powerful men like you and your father could never say them to each other."

Junior looks at his father, but Edgar's turned away, unwilling to give his son the opportunity to wound once more. And so Junior doesn't see the tears, just the cold back shutting him out. "Why should we say them? It's not what we feel."

"Isn't it?" Emily says, "I see you stare at his picture when you think no one's looking." She shakes her head, cross at the both of them. "You two are so alike. Proud and stubborn. You blame each other for all your problems. And it's such a shame. Of all people, you two should understand each other." Junior's about to retort, but she cuts him off, "No buts, young man. You each fought your fathers to make a place for yourselves, to prove you exist. Even took on the world to do it. Egos big as mountains, fragile as eggs. And you're neither of you perfect, you know, so you can get off your high horse. And that goes for you too, Edgar, wherever you are!"

"That night in Varadero. I can't forget that. Don't ask me to," Junior says.

"That night in Varadero. Horsefeathers," Emily snaps. "He tried so hard to tell you about that night. And you'd never listen."

"Why should I? What could he have said? 'I didn't run out on you'? Of course he did. I saw him."

"You saw what you wanted."

"You don't know," Junior yells. "You weren't there."

"Oh, wasn't I though, Mister-Know-It-All?"

"No! You were downtown with your Baptist friends. If you hadn't come back, he'd have swum to Florida he was so scared shitless, and God only knows what would have happened to me."

Emily is furious with Junior, but mostly with herself for letting guilt lock up her tongue. The guilt that came between her and Edgar, that made her life a secret, that drove her to late night medicine because who in the world can she tell without gossip, scandal, shame.

"I said your father and I made love only the once. That was a lie. Each morning I'd pray God for the strength to keep me free of sin. And I'd be so filled with grace, so strong in the Lord, that I'd march to work happy to tempt the devil. But once there, with Edgar, we'd fall."

"Sara said Dad made a spell to win back my mother's love. She meant you?"

Emily smiles. "So you know about that? 'To return a lost love, hollow a pumpkin, put in marjoram, an egg, pepper, Florida water, some article from the beloved, their name on a piece of paper, and five toenails of a rooster."

"Spit three times in the pumpkin, place before Oshún's image, let stand ten days, and throw in a river," Edgar concludes. He'd done it, too, to bring her back from her friends that night.

"I never stopped loving your father," Emily says, "I only told him so. I needed to leave. It hurt too much being near you both and living a lie. I said I'd be gone that New Year's Eve, once the Dandervilles left for Havana."

"I went to Sara," Edgar says.

"Edgar said he knew how much he loved me the moment I said I didn't love him. Men. They always want what they can't have. Anyhow, that New Year's Eve I tucked you in and drove to my friends. Well, no sooner was I settled than I was possessed by an overwhelming compulsion to return. I knew it was wrong. I knew I should leave forever. But I had to have Edgar. If I didn't, I knew I couldn't, wouldn't be able to breathe, to live. I was obsessed. Like a puppet, I found myself walking to the car, propelled by some power beyond my control. It opened the door and put me inside, started the car and drove me back to Xanadu. I don't know if it was the spell, the devil, or an addiction to your father. I only know we ended up in each other's arms, thrashing about in the shrubbery, if you can imagine. So much for violins and moonlight!" Emily hoots with shock and amusement to hear herself finally say it.

"And then the phone rang," Edgar says, and Emily is suddenly back to earth.

"Oh, and then the phone rang. Did I mention the phone? 'It's Kitty,' I said, 'I know it. We have to get back inside. She'll be calling back!' And sure enough she did, with wild talk about a slaughter in Havana. Edgar's first words were, 'Junior! We've got to save Junior!' He raced to your room and flew back, white as a sheet. You were missing. 'Don't panic,' I said. 'I'll take the car and circle round looking for him. You search the house. He can't have gone far.' As I drove off, I heard celebration drums coming from town. 'Lord, if that doesn't raise the dead, nothing will,' I thought."

"I turned the place upside down," Edgar says.

"He was a madman. He got on that darn fool golf cart and took off looking for you in such a panic he flipped over in a sand trap. By the time he came to, I'd circled round in the car, found you, and had you tucked in bed. Dear God, your father'd have died for you."

Junior covers his face.

"It's okay, " Edgar says gently. "It's all blood under the bridge."

"It's not okay!" Emily retorts. "It's time Junior said he was sorry!"

The hairs on the back of their necks stand on end.

"Emily, you can hear me."

Emily stands frozen, save for her bobbing jaw.

"Say something," Edgar grins.

"Edgar!" she cries, seeing him fully, her secrets and guilt quite washed away. "Oh, Edgar!" They embrace and waltz around the room until Emily runs out of breath.

"You know," Edgar says shyly to Junior, "About you . . . me . . . I . . ."

"I know," Junior smiles. "Me too."

Benediction

By the time Junior, Edgar, and Emily return to the board-room, the exorcism is in full swing. Wichita is in fine voice, invoking God's power in a rich, full-bodied baritone. Such is the sonorous musicality of his performance that even the crassest Philistine would thrill to its sound and run to establish petitions for the return of Latin as a high school requisite.

"*Quod daemon ad multa mala perpetranda inducit. A Deo permittantur; non tamen approbantur ac talia odio habet.* We command you, profligate beast, in the name of the spotless Lamb who has trodden down the asp and the basilisk, the lion and the dragon, quail, cower before thy God who is coming to judge both the living and the dead, cower and depart, depart in flame thou foe of virtue and persecutor of the innocent! *Puta ad blasphemias, ad peccata, ad rixas, ad odia fouenda ad parentes contemnendos, in dies experientia docet!*"

It would be nice to report that the poltergeist at the centre of the exorcism is living up to Hollywood expectations, that the cardinal's head is spinning round while hurling green pea soup, for example, or that Lydia, Tibet, and Ernest are stuck to the ceiling while blisters spelling the number of The Beast sprout on their foreheads, or that spectral hounds sit mid-air spewing fire as the pale horse with the pale rider manifests on the coffee table, tapping out a fiendish flamenco with the insouciance of a Lippizaner.

Alas, no. There's been nothing even remotely apocalyptic about this exorcism. To be sure, there's been a whiff of sulphur and a couple of scorch marks on the carpet. But these manifestations have been quite perfunctory. As Wichita foretold, this exorcism has been strictly pro forma.

Lydia, hoping for material for her next *Spiritual Descents,* is majorly pissed off. "Are you in the union, or what?" she's taunted the painting. "Last night you were this Big Man with a Switchblade. Yeah, terrorize a poor female artist, why don't ya? Whoa, ever brave. But put you up against some schmuck cardinal and you're nothing but a wuss."

Neither taunts from Lydia nor a full moon from Tibet have managed to get a rise out of the *Self-Portrait*. In fact, when Junior, Edgar, and Emily enter the room they see a van Gogh at peace. Asleep, it seems. The blood has vanished, the eyes which once burned in judgment are closed, and there's a smile upon the dreamer's lips, as if its torments have been laid to rest and it dreams instead of still waters, green valleys and gardens everlasting.

Junior puts his arms around his mother and father. He bows his head and says to the painting, "May love bless you and keep you. May love make its face to shine upon you and be gracious unto you. May love lift up the light of its countenance upon you and give you peace."

To which all present find themselves saying, "Amen."

Officially, this is the end of the story.

According to news reports, the van Gogh *Self-Portrait* was immediately sent to Rome. Now restored, it rests in a sealed Vatican collection as safe, sound, and unprepossessing as a painting can be. Tabloid rumours of its possession by an otherworldly spirit have been discredited by scientists appointed by the Holy See.

Other rumours fail to disappear so quietly.

Within five years, Pope Innocent takes early retirement when he inhales a communion wafer during a trip to the Himalayas. At the ensuing Vatican conclave, Cardinal Giuseppe Agostino Montini Wichita is elevated to Supreme Pontiff, adopting the unlikely moniker Pius XIII. Millie Gingrich, a.k.a. Madame de Sade, immediately publishes *Ties That Bind: Confessions of a Rural Dominatrix*. It hits the bestseller lists, and all hell breaks loose.

A lively account of S&M in cottage country, *Ties That Bind* discusses the virtues of flogging (increased blood circulation), and the chiropractic benefits of the rack. However, sales are propelled less by what her book has to say, than about whom it has to say it—to wit, a none-too-cleverly disguised rogues' gallery of judges, doctors, politicians "and a future pope, off for a little activity on the q.t." According to the Bondage Queen, "he registers under the name Benito Benelli, but he can't fool me, I've seen him in *Time*. 'I'm a plumber,' says he. Fine, I think, if that's his trip, and I make a mental note to grease the snake."

The Vatican holds a press conference to deny that Pius XIII has sexual proclivities, "special" or otherwise, but Franklin K. Bender III is tracking down leads. His front-page bombshell in *The Times* authenticates Millie's memoirs and wins him the Pulitzer Prize, the proceeds from which he uses to erase old Minnie's handiwork from his rump.

Benito Benelli Jr. is likewise on the case. The former Riviera Hotel bellhop has been living in semi-retirement in New Jersey, where he's spent his adult life as a highly respected extortionist. Wichita's alias, an inconsequential footnote to the rest of the world, does not go unnoticed by the now geriatric orphan. He sees the name Benito Benelli linked to a man who has the age, look, and the first two names of his pater's long-vanished assassin. Benelli can do the math. Out to avenge his father's murder, he receives absolution in advance from a priest who needs help with some gambling debts, and books a trip to Rome.

The planned assassination, however, is aborted when a maid at the Holiday Inn finds a portable rocket launcher under Benelli's bed. Arrested, Benito spills the beans; if he's going down, he's taking the former Giuseppe Castelli with him. Pope Pius XIII, already reeling from charges that he's frolicked in an S&M brothel, now finds himself linked to a Mafia hit in the Bari basilica and a picnic basket filled with the body parts of a dismembered playboy.

Cardinal d'Ovidio drops dead of delight. The Church has yet to recover.

Others fare better. The Lydia Spark Foundation for the Arts has done much for business at The Rabid Squirrel, as well as bringing attention to the work of artists from Mercy Inlet, including a certain Isaac McBean who's moved south to take up residence with Lydia and the Three Ts on Queen West.

Likewise, The Angel Foundation continues its fine work, expanding its mandate to include programs for youth. These are headed by one-time hustler, Bob "Ryder Knight" Rintoul, assisted by the former Betty Gardenia, now Betty Belltower, new wife of the Anglican Canon. Bob, incidentally, has a new partner himself, an editor at *Xtra!* They live off Church Street where, on occasion, they entertain Bob's mother, who finally left his father to find happiness in the arms of the local florist.

As for Junior and Emily? With the lottery's aftermath ensuring The Angel's long-term success, they retired, their dreams complete. Mother and son prefer to be out of the spotlight, and live in a small picturesque Ontario town. Choosing anonymity, they go by the names Maude and Hershel Smith and are happy as birds in a puddle. They enjoy sunshine, long walks, and picnics. But mostly they enjoy scandalizing local gossips by striking up conversations with a genial unseen friend.

That, at least, is the official version. But, while gentle readers need have no doubt as to the fate of Emily, Edgar, Wichita, Lydia, Isaac, the Ts, Bob, Betty, or even of Kitty and Althea up in Caledon with Maria Carlotta, off-the-record rumours sourced to the Curia and The Rabid Squirrel question the whereabouts of Junior Beamish. These rumours are so outlandish that it is not surprising that those with a rational bent dismiss them out of hand. But they are so persistent that their very repetition leads others to report them as if they were God's own truth.

According to the Gospel of Junior Beamish, the *Self-Portrait* never left for Rome with Cardinal Wichita. In fact, it never left the boardroom. Nor did Junior Beamish. Apparently, the exorcism over, Lydia, Tibet, and Ernest prepared to make their exit, while Cardinal Wichita packed up his suitcase. Not so Junior, Emily, and Edgar. They stood silently in front of the painting, contemplating the private journeys that had brought them all to this place. The painting, which had once held their future, then present, was now to be in their past. Transformed, they were about to start off on new beginnings.

It was then, they say, that the final miracle occurred. Emily and Edgar stood back to give their son a moment alone with his thoughts. And Junior saw the most wondrous thing. The mangled stump of ear on the *Self-Portrait* began to grow, grow until it was whole again. And as it did, the face of the *Self-Portrait* transfigured. It became the face of Junior Beamish. It opened its eyes and it smiled upon him saying, "Friend. In whom I am well pleased. Your destiny is here. Take it. Seek and ye shall find."

Suddenly the colours of the painting began to turn into music. Yellows, greens, blues, and vermilions began to fill the room with notes of woodwinds, brass, and piccolos. The very atmosphere was alive with an orchestra of light and sound, as the painting began to disappear into the very air they breathed, vanishing into eternity.

As the others stood transfixed, Junior turned to his mother and father. "So long," he said, "I'm off on a journey into the unknown. I'm off to recreate myself."

Edgar grasped Emily's hand. He'd always known this painting and his son would be together in the end. He had a nose for things, and his nose was never wrong. "Much luck, son," he smiled.

"Yes," Emily added, uncertain but supportive, "much luck and much, much love."

Junior beamed, gave a cheery wave, then turned to the colours of the painting floating beneath him. "Here's to whatever's out there!" he hollered, and leapt into the air, up to the ceiling it seemed. He turned in slow-motion, performed a graceful somersault, extended his legs, and made a clean dive into the pool of air beneath. As he touched through the surface of the colours, his body scarce made a ripple, swallowed up by the light as it disappeared in a breeze of music.

The painting had left this earth on a journey of adventure. And so had Junior Beamish.

Acknowledgements
and a Note on Fact and Fiction

Throughout the writing process, I've been fortunate to have access not only to my own travel notes and general research materials, but to friends from the wide range of worlds the novel describes. They've been kind enough to vet the material for accuracy, and to suggest alternate possibilities when fiction has pressed too hard upon fact.

I'd like to begin by thanking good friends José Luis and Silvia Pérez Pérez from Coliseo, a town about thirty miles outside Varadero. Visits and correspondence with them over the past ten years have had a profound impact on my thinking and travel. I have also found two books on Cuba particularly helpful. *Cuba*, by David Stanley (Lonely Planet Publications, 1994), provides an encyclopaedic overview of the country's literature, history, geography, agriculture, industry, towns, cities, music, social life, religions, and marine life. Also valuable is the aptly named *Cuba: The Land, the History, the People, the Culture*, by Stephen Williams (General Publishing, 1994), particularly for its period photographs.

Both books mentioned above briefly discuss Santería, the Spanish amalgam of Yoruban ritual magic and Catholicism so pervasive throughout Latin America. For those seeking detailed understanding of the religion, I highly recommend Migene González-Wippler's *Santería: The Religion*, (Llewellyn Publications, 1996), *Santería: African Magic in Latin America* (Julian Press, 1973), and *The Santería Experience* (Prentice-Hall, 1982).

I should add that santeros generally welcome those interested in their ceremonies and are happy to answer questions. Here, too, I must thank friends who've had need of Santerían spells and have shared their experiences with me: Arnon Melo from Saõ Paulo, whose family reversed a particularly nasty spell cast by a mayombero on behalf of the mistress of a politician;

and the family of Ernst Eder, healed of a variety of ailments by a santero while living near the Peruvian jungle in the days of the Shining Path.

Especially, however, I should like to like to thank my friend Isabel Gusman Días, the santera at Yaguajay. Over the years, in addition to a much needed spiritual cleansing, courtesy of her orisha, Santo Lazaro, she has given me several private meetings with the spirit José, an eighteenth-century Yoruban who delights in cigars, rum, and salty discourse.

As this book heads to press, I'm turning into Lydia, heading off to the Arctic Circle with my partner and mother on an eagerly anticipated trip to Baffin Island, Beechey Island, and Greenland. My fascination with the north was fueled by research conducted at the Spadina/Mahsinahhekahnikahmik branch of the Toronto Public Library, which has an excellent collection of books and videos on the north by both First Nations and European authors and filmmakers, plus a knowledgeable staff headed by Gloria Reinbergs, to help kadluna such as myself. *Becoming Half-Hidden*, by D. Merkur, (Garland Publishing, 1992), had much information on shamanic power and ritual. But most valuable have been my conversations and correspondence with ethnographer John S. Matthiasson, a former resident both of Mittimalalik (Pond Inlet) and of one of its nearby winter camps, Aullativik. His book *Living on the Land* (Broadview Press, 1992) is packed with north Baffin Island history, as well as first-hand descriptions of daily life, social, and political structures, and the syncretization of Western and Tununermiut spiritual traditions. I am also hugely indebted to him for his personal correction of details in my text.

For different perspectives on finance, I'd like to thank Gordon Floyd of The Centre for Canadian Philanthropy for his insights on charities and current case law affecting taxes and charitable status; and equally, Jim Nichol, Vice-President of Magna Inc., and his wife, lawyer Christie Milne, for vetting observations on business practice, and providing perspectives on those practices quite different from my own.

Thanks to friends formerly of southern Italy, Sandy d'Ovidio and Mary Camardo, for their help on chapter three's Italian details. (How long did it take to drive from Barí to Rome before the superhighway cut through the mountains?) Their translations were also valuable, as were their discussions of local foods, wines, produce, and liqueurs.

For checking psychiatric references, special gratitude to old friend Dr. Peter Moore. I'd also like to thank Dr. Murray Wilson and Dr. Alan Bannack.

Friends, Rev. Don and Mimi Gillies and Rev. Gene Bolin were of great help on matters religious. Aside from their input, the best layman's book I found while researching the Roman Curia was *Inside the Vatican*, by Peter Hebblethwaite (Oxford University Press, 1987) which includes a detailed breakdown of the evolution and operation of the Vatican's political structures. I also checked out the Internet's Catholic Supersite, in which "Popes through the Ages," by Joseph Brusher, (S.J. Electronic version © 1996 New Advent Inc.) gave me valuable information about the last Pope Innocent (XIII).

I had no personal contact with van Gogh experts, but I made use of a wide range of research texts. I found Jan Hulsker and James Miller's *Vincent and Theo van Gogh: A Dual Biography* (Fuller Publications, 1990) to be the most satisfying overview, especially for the light it cast on Vincent's conflicted relationship with his brother. Those interested in the social concerns animating the novel will find Andre Krauss' *Vincent van Gogh: Studies in the Social Aspects of His Work* (Goteborg: Acta Universitatis Gothoburgensis, 1983) interesting reading. And anyone will be moved by the artist's own words found in an edition of *The Letters of Vincent van Gogh*, edited by Ronald Leeuw (Allen Lane, 1996). But more than studying texts and letters, my most satisfying hours on van Gogh were those I spent with his paintings.

A tip of the hat to hockey fiend Dan Diamond who gave me the play-by-play of the Stanley Cup game referred to in chapter six, and to Mike Flint for a backstage tour of Skydome.

Finally, thanks to my partner Daniel Legault, my Mom and stepfather, Dorothy and Alex McPhedran, Attila Berki and John Terauds at Riverbank, my agent Dean Cooke, The Toronto Arts Council, and friends Victoria Stewart, Rob McCay, Peter Hawkins, Louise Baldaccino, Craig Shipler, Portia Boch, Jon Pearce, David Walker, and Bill and Jane Love who read the book and provided comments over the past few years. Their feedback and encouragement mattered more to me than they will ever know.

A Brief Note on Fact and Fiction

With respect to the Cuban Revolution, the attack on the Moncado Barracks in Santiago de Cuba took place, as stated, on July 26, 1953, and was a significant event in the history of the Cuban Revolution. As in the novel, Fidel Castro planned the attack from the Havana home of Abel and Haydée Santamaria, apartment # 603, 164 Calle 25 by Calle 0. Other leading members of the underground included Baptist teacher Frank País and his brother Josue from Santiago de Cuba. History, however, is silent on the role of itinerant missionaries from Goderich.

Early morning, New Year's Day, 1959, the crowd really did decapitate the hated parking meters along the Malecón, which had been used to feed Batista's family fortunes rather than the poor. George Raft stood at the door of his casino and dared the mob to a fist fight, and apocryphal stories have the lobby of Meyer Lansky's Riviera Hotel full of pigs and goats. (As far as I know, Lansky's words that night to the revellers at his hotel are unrecorded, but in a humanizing touch, when the mob boss found himself without a chef the next day, he took to the Riviera's kitchen and personally prepared brunch for shaken guests while his wife scrubbed the lobby.)

Further on the revolution: a dove did indeed light on Castro's shoulder during his victory speech in Santiago de Cuba. This signalled God's approval to many Catholics, who recognized in it a New Testament parallel; while to followers of Santería, it spoke to the blessing of the orisha Oblatá. Despite the passage of time, this image must rank high in the pantheon of political optics, even when one acknowledges that the flock of doves from which it descended had been released by Castro's own supporters moments earlier. Let's face it, no matter where one stands on the revolution, releasing a flock of doves at a political event has a lot more pizzazz than releasing a flood of balloons.

The history of Varadero and Xanadu are as described; dish on Irenée duPont's drinking habits, sleeping arrangements, and final words came from my guide at the duPont mansion; and the Santerían spells and herbal remedies are as reported by Migene González-Wippler. Interestingly, I've recently discovered that yerbabuena, which Sara has Edgar put in Mrs. Resguardo, is a major ingredient in at least one popular aromatherapy bath oil.

Moving from the Caribbean to the Arctic, Mercy Inlet (Mattimitalik) and its residents are complete inventions. While sharing some geographical, historical, architectural, and social features, Mercy Inlet and Pond Inlet (Mittimalalik) are different in several major respects. For instance, in Mittimalalik, the Catholic community is almost extinct and is certainly outnumbered by the ever-growing number of Anglicans.

As the novel indicates, the Tununermiut are the oldest and possibly also the most northerly community in the Canadian Arctic, the latter assertion depending on whether or not one includes the recently created settlement of Grise Fiord further north. Within shamanic and Santerían traditions, female leaders are not uncommon; powers used by our angakoq are among those claimed by shamans, with certain powers being specific to shamans on Baffin. The description of the angakoq's clothes is also true to shamanic dress.

Finally, a few fun facts about van Gogh, Bari, and the last Pope Innocent.

The surname of the unfortunate guard attacked by van Gogh at the Asylum at St. Rémy really was Poulet; he died two years later at age twenty-eight. As well, it's true that van Gogh gave away his paintings to a host of unappreciative friends: the postman Roulin lost every one he was given; the hospital bursar, Neuvière, refused to accept his; and Dr. Félix Rey used his to patch up a chicken coop. Whether any were given to the young attendant Poulet is unknown.

The San Nicola buried in the Bari basilica is the saint we know as Santa Claus. His statue enjoys its tour of the harbour during the annual Bari festival, while his bones, brought from Turkey to Bari by medieval pirates, continue to produce a white mould with apparently miraculous properties.

The Grotte di Castellana, where Maria Carlotta was first visited by La Vergine and where she later martyred herself, features a stalagmite that resembles the Virgin Mary in certain lights, and which has been claimed as the source of several visitations by Our Lady.

The last Pope Innocent, Innocent XIII (1721–1724), was born Michelangelo de' Conti. Save for his strong sense of dignity, he was much like his fictional successor, Innocent XIV. Overweight and in ill health, he was a compromise candidate elected for the short-term when the favourite, Cardinal Paolucci, was blocked by Emperor Charles VI. As so often happens with the decent and well-intentioned, he was badgered from all sides. His short and miserable pontificate ended when he dropped dead of the dropsy, a nasty condition in which body tissues and cavities swell with fluid.

The moral of the above is that the more history one reads, the more hesitant one becomes to dismiss any tale, no matter how wild, as fiction.